ABANDONED

C.J. PETIT

ABANDONED

TABLE OF CONTENTS

ABANDONED 1
PROLOGUE 2
CHAPTER 1 7
CHAPTER 2 42
CHAPTER 3 88
CHAPTER 4 109
CHAPTER 5 158
CHAPTER 6 191
CHAPTER 7 209
CHAPTER 8 251
CHAPTER 9 282
CHAPTER 10 342
EPILOGUE 408

PROLOGUE

1710 Chicago Street
Omaha, Nebraska
April 11, 1879

Luke Casey, the Brennan family attorney, stood beside the shorter, well-dressed man as they stood before a seven-year-old boy who was sitting on a dark red, embroidered couch in a lavishly appointed parlor. He was sitting closely beside a tall, dark red-haired woman, who sat with her hands folded over her lap.

"Master Joseph, I'd like to introduce you to your new guardian, Mister Noah Gallagher. He is your mother's brother, your uncle, and just like a guardian angel, will watch over you until you are eighteen."

The boy's eyes shifted from the lawyer to the woman then asked, "Why can't Mrs. Doyle be my guardian?"

"She's just your nanny, Master Joseph. She's paid to keep you well-fed and safe. Mister Gallagher is your family and has been appointed by me and the board of directors at your father's company to be your guardian. Mrs. Doyle will still be here to care for you."

Joseph glanced at his uncle and now guardian and said, "Alright."

Luke Casey smiled and said, "Then, I'll leave so you and your uncle can get better acquainted."

The attorney shook hands with Noah Gallagher, turned and walked out of the parlor as Joseph's uncle smiled at the boy and said, "Hello, Joseph."

———

ABANDONED

August 3, 1880

Noah looked down at his nephew and asked, "Well, Joseph, what do you think?"

The boy's excitement was overflowing as he rushed his reply, "Really, Uncle Noah? You'll take me with you?"

"You're growing up very quickly, Joseph, and I believe you need to see something of the real world before you return to the classroom at St. Ignatius next month."

"Will I be able to shoot a gun, too?" he asked with wide eyes.

"I believe that's the reason it's called a hunting party, Joseph," his uncle answered with a smile.

Joseph turned to look at his silent nanny to his left, and asked, "Isn't it going to be exciting, Mrs. Doyle?"

Emily Doyle smiled at her charge, then looked back at his uncle and said, "Mister Gallagher, don't you feel that a hunting trip hundreds of miles away in the middle of the wilderness is too reckless of an enterprise for an eight-year-old boy?"

Before his uncle could respond, Joseph exclaimed, "But Mrs. Doyle, I'll be nine in December!"

Noah Gallagher answered, "Now, Mrs. Doyle, he'll be perfectly safe. We'll have our guide with us, and we'll be close to the train and telegraph. There's nothing to be concerned about whatsoever."

Emily Doyle knew she was pushing her luck by disagreeing with the man who could terminate her employment with the snap of his fingers but felt an overwhelming sense of danger in the endeavor and needed to protect Joseph.

"Nonetheless, Mister Gallagher, as Joseph's nanny, I feel a responsibility to ensure his safety both here in Omaha or wherever he may be. I simply believe that this risky adventure is both unnecessary and without merit. Perhaps an outing someplace closer like Headland Forest would be a wiser choice."

"There are no elk or bears in the Headland Forest, Mrs. Doyle. And may I remind you that as Joseph's guardian, if I wish to take him with me on our hunting trip, then you have no say in the decision. If Joseph wishes to join me, then he's going and that's the end of this discussion."

Emily knew she had no choice but to acquiesce. Her only hope was Joseph's devotion to her.

"As you wish, Mister Gallagher."

"Look on the positive side for you, Mrs. Doyle. You'll have two weeks off with pay. You'll be able to do anything you wish while Joseph is with me."

Emily Doyle just smiled at Noah Gallagher as all hired help seem able to do, even if they'd prefer to plunge an eight-inch dagger into the man's chest.

Noah then turned to Joseph, expecting to see a smiling face, but his nephew looked confused.

"Joseph, what's wrong?"

"I thought Mrs. Doyle was coming."

"I'm afraid not, Joseph. This trip is for men only. Women aren't meant to live in the savage wilderness. You wouldn't want to see Mrs. Doyle attacked by an angry grizzly bear, would you?"

Joseph looked at his nanny and said, "No, I wouldn't. But I don't want to go if Mrs. Doyle is staying here. I'm sorry, Uncle Noah."

ABANDONED

Emily maintained a composed demeanor, despite a desire to gloat as she watched Noah squirm.

"But, Joseph, don't you want to shoot a bear? I'd let you use my new Winchester, too," Noah pleaded.

Throwing the Winchester onto the scales almost tipped the balance, and it probably would have if Joseph was nine going on ten, but not now.

"I do, but I don't want to leave Mrs. Doyle, Uncle Noah."

Emily thought she had won the battle when Noah threw his trump card, something she simply hadn't expected.

"Alright, she can come along, but she can't bring a lot of clothes because we won't have a wagon. We'll be going places that only horses can reach."

Joseph whipped his eyes back to Emily and grinned as he said, "Isn't it going to be wonderful, Mrs. Doyle? We'll camp out and hunt bears!"

Emily may have managed a smile for Joseph, but she was terrified inside. She had only two unwelcome choices, and she knew that Noah understood the dilemma she was facing. Either she went along on the hunting trip, or she would have to quit the job she'd held for six years and lose much more. She would lose Joseph, who was the center of her life.

She looked at Noah's smirking, but handsome face with its meticulously trimmed beard and moustache, and said, "Well, Mister Gallagher, it appears that I'll be joining your hunting party in two weeks."

Joseph leapt from his chair, ran to Mrs. Doyle and hugged her, saying, "Thank you, Mrs. Doyle!"

She kissed him on the cheek, gave him a genuine smile and replied, "You're welcome, Joseph."

Noah maintained his smile, even though he'd hoped Mrs. Doyle would have quit. But it wouldn't be that much more difficult, and he doubted if she'd last a day on the trail before she was begging to return to someplace with a warm bath. Women just couldn't tolerate the discomfort of living in the wild.

"Mrs. Doyle, I'll notify my guide, Claude Boucher, to prepare for your addition to our party. We'll still be departing Omaha on the 16th and arriving in Laramie the following day. Our adventure will begin on the eighteenth of the month. When you prepare for the trip, you'll need to pack judiciously."

Noah then smiled at Joseph, stood, picked up his beaver hat from the side table, turned and left the parlor, then the house.

As soon as he'd gone, Joseph turned to Emily with an animated face and said, "Isn't it wonderful, Mrs. Doyle? We'll be going on an adventure together!"

Emily smiled at him and replied, "Yes, Joseph, I'm sure it will be an exciting adventure."

ABANDONED

CHAPTER 1

August 18, 1880
Laramie, Wyoming Territory

Emily was already tired, and they hadn't even left Laramie yet. The train had pulled into the station just after ten o'clock the previous night and she hadn't reached her room at the Intercontinental Hotel until after midnight. She hadn't slept much on the thirty-four hour train ride, and just five hours after she'd fallen asleep, Noah was pounding on her door.

Now, not even given enough time to have a bath, Emily was astride a mule following a train of horses as they wound their way through the last vestiges of civilization that she would see for another ten days. *A mule, for God's sake!* Each of the men was riding a horse, and they were even using a horse to carry the heavily loaded packs, but she was given a mule. And the saddle she was sitting on smelled as badly as the beast that wore it. The foul animal had a jarring gait that made her lack of riding skills worse, too.

The guide was an unkempt man named Claude Boucher and Emily hadn't liked him at all when she had been hastily introduced to him just an hour earlier. Noah had told her that Mister Boucher had led his prior hunting expedition last June and was the best guide in Laramie. That may be, but he certainly wasn't the cleanest.

She watched Joseph just ahead as he rode the small black horse and that sight did offset her own discomfort. He'd been in an almost euphoric state since they'd stepped onto the first-class passenger coach in Omaha. He'd slept well as he was able to lay down on the leather-cushioned seats and because he was eight-going-on-nine years old. Children seemed to be able to sleep anywhere.

Noah had bought some appropriate hunting attire for him in Omaha: denim pants, a heavy wool shirt, a jacket, boots and even a cowboy hat. She, of course, was limited to the wardrobe she had with her and suspected she may have selected poorly. She had failed to perceive the lack of consideration that would be given to her when she arrived and chastised herself for failing to do so. She believed she would have had the opportunity to purchase some more appropriate footwear and clothes but had been rushed everywhere right up to the moment she boarded the mule. Emily should have expected that Noah would add nothing to the packs that would make the trip any more comfortable for her. If she didn't bring it with her, it wasn't there. But, discomfort aside, Emily still believed she was doing the right thing by accompanying Joseph on his first hunting trip. She hoped it would be his last.

At the head of the column, Claude Boucher still wasn't pleased with the addition of the woman, even though she was an impressive sight. In town, he'd be more than just slightly interested, but not on the trail. Women didn't belong here. When he'd received Noah's wire two weeks earlier, he couldn't understand why she would be accompanying them, until he received a letter from Noah explaining in greater detail who Emily Doyle was and why Joseph had insisted that she come along. Noah had also instructed Claude to make no changes to the supplies they would take on the trip, and even specified that he obtain a mule for her conveyance, and the ornerier, the better. He had even instructed Claude to adjust the stirrups excessively long which would make her even more uncomfortable.

The last hunting trip that Claude had guided for Noah Gallagher with his companion, Luke Casey, had been to the southeast of Laramie, but this time, they'd be heading to the southwest, into the Medicine Bow Mountains. They were also going much further into the wilds, almost fifty miles as the crow flies, but closer to seventy or eighty by horseback. It would be three long, meandering days in the saddle before they finally set up their camp. Claude had never even been to that part of the territory. Few white men had, and only the Utes and Arapaho populated it now, and even they only ventured into the area when hunting. It was rugged territory, even for him.

ABANDONED

An hour later, as they left Laramie behind and the buildings were no longer in sight, the caravan of four horses and a mule turned off the wagon ruts that they called a road and turned west, entering the trackless terrain of southern Wyoming Territory.

Claude was familiar with the area, at least for the first ten to fifteen miles, so they made reasonably good time that first day, covering almost thirty miles as they wound their way around rocks, trees and crossed the seemingly endless number of creeks and streams.

They'd stopped twice to rest the horses and their lunch consisted of nothing more than beef jerky and crackers washed down with water from one of the streams, which Joseph thought was a real treat. Emily didn't complain because she knew that it would provide Noah with satisfaction, but she was far from happy. Her behind and back were already sore after the first five miles on the back of the bouncing mule. She hadn't ridden for almost twenty years and this wasn't a good reintroduction.

By the time they stopped to set up camp for the first night, Emily could barely walk, and even Joseph seemed uncomfortable. Claude and Noah set up two tents before the guide built a firepit and had a healthy fire going just as the sun disappeared over the mountains.

Emily was sitting on a log with Joseph as Claude cooked dinner. She had no idea what was in the frypan and wasn't about to ask.

Noah approached, then stopped and asked, "Well, Joseph, how do you feel after your first day on the trail?"

"It's really exciting, but my butt's sore."

"It'll get worse before we get there, but you'll get used to it."

"Can I shoot your rifle now?"

"Oh, no! We don't want the Indians to know we're here," Noah replied as he scanned the darkness.

"*Indians? There are Indians here?*" Joseph exclaimed as his head whipped around as if on a swivel.

"Sure, there are. I'll bet there are a thousand warriors within ten miles of us right now. But don't worry, Claude and I have enough guns to keep them away."

Joseph slid closer to Emily, who put her arm around his shoulder and glared at Noah.

"I believe you're exaggerating, Mister Gallagher, and I'd ask you to refrain from saying such things just to alarm Joseph."

Noah grinned and said, "Sorry, Joseph. I was just joking. There probably aren't more than a few dozen Indians nearby."

Then he turned and walked back to the fire to see if the coffee was ready.

Joseph looked at Emily and asked, "Mrs. Doyle, do you think there are lots of Indians out there?"

"Honestly, Joseph, I simply don't know, but I do believe your Uncle Noah was just telling tales. Men like to tell scary stories around campfires for some reason, and I'm sure that's all it was."

Joseph nodded but slid closer to Mrs. Doyle as he peered out into the unlit forests that surrounded them, suddenly wishing he was back in his bedroom in 1710 Chicago Street in Omaha.

Emily wondered why Noah had obviously been trying to terrorize Joseph. If anything, she would have thought he would be attempting to soothe his nephew's worries on his first night in the wilderness.

After a surprisingly tasty supper, Mrs. Doyle arranged her and Joseph's sleeping arrangements in one of the tents. She and Joseph had been given the smaller of the two tents, and she understood the reason for the assignment, but it was still going to be a tight fit. It meant she would have to leave her large travel bag outside and sleep in the split riding dress she'd worn all day. She hadn't slept with Joseph since he was three and wondered if he was reaching an age where he began to notice the differences between men and women.

She'd already been embarrassed when having to find some privacy for simple bodily functions earlier in the day, knowing Noah, and even worse, Claude Boucher, were watching as she went behind rocks or bushes. Now, after she'd set up their tent, she had to go into the dark trees to empty her bladder and as she stepped into the pines, that damned story Noah had thrown at Joseph about hundreds of Indians close by suddenly haunted her imagination and made it difficult for her to do what she desperately needed to do. She swore that each muffled sound that she heard while she was there with her riding skirts pulled down was a hostile Indian with his face painted and his tomahawk ready to strike.

Eventually, she finished and raced quickly back to the campsite, her heart pounding as she ducked into the tent where Joseph had already slid into his bedroll.

Noah had watched Emily scurry back from the trees and disappear into the tent with a measure of satisfaction. She hadn't complained at all, which had been a disappointment, but now, he knew she was terrified, and the trip had just begun. He snickered when he thought about the Indian warning he'd mentioned. Claude had told him that the likelihood of meeting any was very low, and that if they were there, they would usually ignore a hunting party.

As she lay in her bedroll, her muscles and joints aching, Emily was almost back in control of herself when the night calm was shattered by the chilling howl of a nearby animal. She felt a cold streak of terror rip up her spine as the tiny hairs on the back of her neck stood on end. *It sounded so close!*

Then, a second howl answered the first. Then different animals replied or argued with yips, barks and finally a deep roar that momentarily silenced them all. Emily had her eyes closed after the first howl, but after the roar, she opened them and looked over at Joseph in the sliver of moonlight that filtered through the tent's flap. He was looking at her with wide, frightened eyes.

"It's all right, Joseph. They're just singing to each other."

"Mrs. Doyle," he asked softly, "Can you sing to me?"

Emily rolled onto her side and as she looked into those fear-filled blue eyes, began to sing in a sweet, melodious voice.

"Beautiful dreamer, wake unto me, starlight and dewdrops are waiting for thee…"

After the first lilting words floated across the small tent, Joseph closed his eyes and despite the renewed animal sounds outside, began to breathe more easily, and before Emily finished the first verse, was drifting off to sleep. Emily continued softly singing even after she thought he was asleep because the music was soothing her worried mind as well.

After she finished the short song, she just hummed the tune for a while with her eyes closed and soon fell asleep herself.

―――

Emily was startled awake while it was still dark by Noah's shout of "Get up! We need to move!"

She bolted to a sitting position in the bedroll, then quickly slid out, pulled on her shoes, then turned to see if Joseph was awake. He was, so she straightened out her dress, felt her voluminous hair, knowing it needed to be put back in place soon, then lifted the flap to the tent and noticed the lightening sky. It was the predawn and must have been about five o'clock in the morning. She was incredibly stiff but managed to ignore the discomfort as she walked quickly into the trees, knowing that Noah was watching with amusement, but unsure of Claude Boucher's intent as he watched her leave.

When she reappeared, Claude was already at the fire, cooking with Noah sitting on his heels next to him talking about something. She didn't care what they were doing as she hurried back into the tent and was startled to find it empty. *Where was Joseph?* For just a moment, she panicked, then quickly turned around and scanned the camp, just as Joseph appeared from the other side of the big tent carrying more firewood.

Emily exhaled in relief, then entered the tent, spent a few minutes putting her hair back into its usual thick bun, then began rolling the two sleeping bags back into their tightly bound state and tied their binding straps. She picked up each bedroll and keeping her recently repaired hair down, exited the tent with the bedrolls. She looked for her travel bag, thinking she might be able to change, but found that it had already been loaded and strapped down on the pack horse. All of the horses and her mule had already been saddled as well. So much for her morning toilet, too. She ran her tongue over her teeth and decided to at least keep her tooth brush with her after they stopped for the night.

She walked to the fire, dropped the bedrolls and Joseph stepped to her side, saying proudly, "I helped with the fire, Mrs. Doyle."

She smiled down at him and said, "I saw that, Joseph. You are becoming a young man already."

He grinned at her, but before their conversation could continue, Noah thrust a tin plate with some scrambled eggs and a chunk of ham in front of her and said, "Eat quickly, Mrs. Doyle. We'll be riding in twenty minutes."

Emily took the plate, then sat on the ground with Joseph and they both began cramming the food into their mouths, washing them down with bitter, unsweetened coffee.

True to his word, in twenty minutes, the tents had been collapsed and rolled into tight balls, stored on the packhorse, the fire covered in dirt, and they were all mounted and moving again, going deeper into the forests and valleys of Wyoming.

―――

The hunting party continued its southwestern course as Claude found new paths up into the Medicine Bow Mountains. He knew that he'd be able to find his way out by following the hoofprints, but still marked the path with landmarks. He wasn't using a compass but using the sun as a basic tool for maintaining the southwesterly heading. But even then, as they had to veer one way or the other, finding passes and gaps, he wasn't sure of their direction or location. But it didn't matter much. They weren't going to anyplace in particular. They were riding to the middle of nowhere.

The terrain was growing even more rugged as the sun continued its path across the sky, and soon, they were on a downslope, having crossed the foothills of the Medicine Bow Mountains.

They set up their second night's camp earlier than the first because they'd found what Claude believed to be an ideal campsite.

After the tents were up and the firepit dug, Claude began to cook their evening meal. Emily was in even worse physical condition than she was the night before and wasn't sure how she could handle any more riding for a while, but knew she had to stay with Joseph. She just couldn't imagine going any further into the wilderness. They'd already spotted deer, elk, some bears and even a cougar. *Why didn't they just stop here and do their hunting?* She really should have asked Noah but wasn't going to give him the satisfaction.

But at least the earlier stop gave her a chance to take care of her personal grooming. So, while the dinner was being cooked, she opened her travel bag, found her hairbrush, entered the tent and sat on the bedroll. She would have preferred to brush her hair outside but didn't want to let Claude watch her. He just made her uncomfortable.

She pulled the pins from her hair and let her deep red locks fall around her shoulders. She first ran her fingers through her hair to get out the twigs and leaves she knew were in there, then began to stroke the brush through the long strands. As she did, she contemplated cutting it a couple of inches before she pinned it again but decided to wait until they returned to Laramie when she would have the opportunity to have it done properly.

ABANDONED

Once it was free of debris and reasonably workable, she expertly wound it and pinned it until it was back where it belonged. She sighed, bent at the waist, flipped up the flap, exited the tent and returned the hairbrush to the travel bag. When she did, she saw the bar of lilac soap inside and wondered when and where she would be able to bathe. Then, she glanced at the fire, saw Claude Boucher and knew she wouldn't dare until she returned to Laramie. She would smell as foul as the mule by the time she returned, but she did remember to take her toothbrush and slipped it into her riding skirt.

The night was almost a mirror image of the first, only Joseph seemed less afraid this time, but still requested that Emily sing him to sleep as the coyotes and wolves argued in the darkness. This time, she sang a song that her mother had sung to her, knowing that Joseph wouldn't understand the words. But it wasn't the soothing lyrics he needed, he just needed to hear her sing.

As the coyotes yipped in the background Emily sang, "Seoithín, seo hó, mo stór é, mo leanbh…"

Joseph closed his eyes, a slight smile curled the corners of his mouth and sighed. He was happy that Mrs. Doyle had come with him.

Noah's waking shout still startled Emily, making her snap into a sitting position, which caused a stab of pain in her lower back. She grunted and put her hand on her back as she breathed deeply. Joseph awakened more normally but saw her in pain.

"Are you all right, Mrs. Doyle?" he asked.

"Yes, Joseph. I'm fine. It's just that these old bones aren't happy with riding for two days."

"Do you want me to ask Uncle Noah to stay here until you're better?"

"No, Joseph. I'll be fine. I just need to stretch my back. It will be all right."

To prove her point, she managed a smile, slid from the bedroll, then had to bend over to leave, before she could straighten up outside the tent, testing her back. As soon as she'd left the tent, she saw both Noah and Claude watching her. She ignored them both, made a show of standing straight as if her back wasn't aching, then walked quickly for the nearest trees, which were further away this time.

When she left the trees five minutes later, both men were huddled near the campfire again and Claude was already cooking. Neither turned to look at her as she hastened to the tent, grabbed her travel bag, then went inside. Joseph was still inside this time, apparently already returned from answering nature's call much closer to the tent than she could.

"Joseph, I'm going to change my clothes. Could you wait for me near the campfire?"

"Okay, Mrs. Doyle," he replied before he stood, walked past and exited the tent without having to stoop at all.

She closed the flap, then went inside and turned to face the flap in case one of the two men decided to surprise her in the state of undress, and if one did, she knew which of the two it would be.

Emily first laid out her change in clothes on the bedroll to speed the process. Then, she quickly disrobed and before she put on her new wardrobe, she quickly raced the bar of lilac soap across her skin. It may not have been a bath, but it helped. She tossed the soap into the travel bag, then rapidly dressed, cursing the length of time it took for a woman to put on all of the layers of almost protective undergarments that fashion dictated.

But, once in her clean clothes, she felt better and rolled her dirty laundry into the riding dress and laid it on top of her one remaining change of clothes. She'd need to get them washed when she could. If she could.

ABANDONED

After their hasty breakfast, she completed her modified toilet by brushing her teeth at the nearby stream using salt rather than tooth powder, another unpacked item.

Forty minutes later, they were on the animals again and headed west, entering a long, wide valley that ran east and west between two tall mountains.

After a brief lunch break, they mounted again and entered a thick forest of tall pines. Joseph dropped back on his short horse until he rode beside Emily on her mule. She could tell he was worried being among the trees and not being able to see more than twenty yards in any direction. That Indian story must have still bothered him.

As she looked at his frightened eyes, she ignored her own concerns, aches and pains, and began to sing again, only this time, her voice was vibrant and full as she began:

"What shall we do with a drunken sailor…"

Joseph looked at her, began to smile and then laugh as the mischievous lyrics rolled from her mouth and filled the forest.

Noah glanced back at her but didn't say anything before he turned to look ahead. Claude never looked back at all.

Emily finished her rousing song, then just smiled at Joseph, who was still giggling as her mule took her deeper into the seemingly never-ending forest.

But it did end ten minutes later when they popped out into a wide clearing. As soon as they left the trees, they spotted a large herd of elk grazing in the grass just a hundred yards away who didn't seem to care about the intruders. At least they didn't for the first three seconds until suddenly their heads popped up, their eyes all turned toward them and without any apparent coordination, they all sprang away down the clearing and soon disappeared into a smaller forest a half a mile away.

The mountains seemed to rise in all directions around them, but still, Claude led them further along the valley. The mountains were probably a mile or more away, but their size made them seem so much closer.

The mountains disappeared again when they entered the second forest the elk had used as their sanctuary.

Emily wondered again why Claude was taking them so deep into the wilds when there was already game in abundance. In addition to the herd of elk, some of them enormously large, they'd seen all sorts and sizes of bears, wolves, coyotes and now three cougars. She didn't know if it was the same cougar and it was just following them, but still, it made no sense to her. Joseph, on the other hand, seemed to be getting more comfortable with the journey, not less.

Four hours and two forests later, they reached a jagged, rock-filled clearing with a large brook running down the side of a not-so-distant mountain and Noah said something to Claude who nodded and pulled his horse to a halt and dismounted. When Noah stepped down, Emily slowly and painfully swung her leg around the mule's saddle then set her feet down on solid ground again while Joseph practically bounced from his saddle.

Noah walked back to Joseph, smiled and said, "Well, Joseph, we're here at last. What do you think of it?"

Joseph scanned the rugged landscape and replied, "It's really pretty here!"

"And tomorrow morning, we'll go out hunting. What do you think about that?"

"And I'll get to shoot your Winchester?"

"You sure will. Now, let's set up camp."

Emily did her own survey of the campsite and its surroundings and had to agree with Joseph. It was beautiful, but it was also frightening in its isolation. The biggest positive was at least she wouldn't have to ride that damned mule tomorrow. While they were out hunting, she assumed she'd be given a gun for protection and allowed to remain in camp. The only gun she had ever fired was her father's shotgun, and that was eighteen years ago. She knew they had four long guns because she had seen the stocks but didn't know what kind they were. She assumed one was a shotgun, though.

As they set up the tents and dug the firepit, Joseph was rushing around the campsite helping wherever he could, excited with the idea of tomorrow's hunt. She had to seek privacy behind some tall boulders as the nearest trees were about a hundred yards away, and after returning, she walked to the tent, went inside and set up the two bedrolls.

It was getting to be almost routine for Emily now, but it didn't mean she was any more comfortable in the presence of Claude Boucher. She should have bought a derringer before she left Omaha, but that was before she met the man and never believed she was in any danger. She wished she had the shotgun now rather than tomorrow, assuming Noah was going to give her one. Surely, he wasn't going to go off with Joseph and leave her in the camp with the guide. The thought sent a chill down her back that was unrelated to the poor condition of her spine.

After eating, she and Joseph returned to their tent, and when darkness dropped like a sudden curtain, she sang another song to Joseph and she finally succumbed to sleep herself, exhausted, but more content knowing she would have a few days to recover before the three-day ride back to Laramie.

The full moon rose over the camp just before eleven o'clock and Claude and Noah shared coffee by the dying fire.

"You think they are sleeping?" Claude asked quietly.

Noah glanced back at the small tent and replied just as quietly, "Give them another hour. But we can do some things now."

Claude nodded, tossed the last of his coffee onto the fire, then stood, walked to the big tent and pulled one of the pegs while Noah walked to the horses and began to saddle his gelding.

As the moon continued its silent march past the stars, their progress continued, and assured that Edith and Joseph were sound asleep by now, picked up the pace, but still kept as quiet as possible.

The four horses and the mule were all saddled when they began to hang the heavy panniers on the pack horse, which they both knew was the loudest noise that they'd be making. It was, but the frequent yelps and howls from the wolves and coyotes disguised much of it.

Once the animals were ready, the tent dismantled and stowed, the campfire extinguished, there was one thing left to do, and that job fell to Noah.

He reached into his left saddlebag and pulled out a large Mason jar. In the bright moonlight, it appeared to be filled with black liquid. He unscrewed the cap, walked slowly toward the small tent, then, after reaching it, bent over and slowly began stepping backwards, pouring the contents on the ground across the side with the flap. When there was only an inch left in the jar, he splashed it onto the tent's roof, before gently lowering the empty jar and its cap to the ground near the back side of the tent.

He walked quickly back to his gelding, then he and Claude slowly led their two horses and the trailing pack horse, Joseph's small horse, and Emily's mule out of the camp and then quietly eastward in the moonlight until they disappeared into the forest.

Once in the trees, they mounted and set their horses to a walk, letting the horses choose the path through the trees. The forest was thin enough to allow some moonlight to filter through, but not a lot. Once they left the forest, they could pick up the pace until they met the next one. But Noah knew that once they had reached the forest, the job was done, and he was on his way back to Omaha and would soon be a wealthy man.

ABANDONED

Back at the campsite, now occupied by a single, small tent, Emily and Joseph slept while the enticing scent of the oxen blood that Noah had spread near the tent wafted into the breeze to attract the attention of hungry predators.

Once they had exited the first forest, Noah and Claude set their horses to a medium trot and now could speak freely.

Claude finally was able to ask, "Why didn't you just shoot them both? It would have been faster, and we wouldn't have to ride so far to get way out here."

"Because, Claude, I'm not as bloodthirsty as you are. Besides, that brat was family. This way, my conscience is clear. I didn't kill anyone and if I'm asked about it later, I can answer any questions honestly. Well, at least I can say that I didn't kill him. No one will care about his nanny."

"If you don't care about the nanny, why didn't you let me have her?"

Noah turned to him and laughed, "You've got to be kidding, Claude! Mrs. Doyle is over thirty and a nanny! You can get better in Laramie for a dollar and a half."

"She was a redhead and looked like a lot of woman to me. I've never had a redhead."

"Well, Claude, I'll tell you what. I'll treat you to be best redheaded whore in Laramie. How's that?"

"Okay, but she'd better be a real redhead."

Noah laughed again as they left the clearing and entered a second forest.

The first visitor to the one-tent camp was a lone coyote, who arrived just around four o'clock. He walked slowly into the clearing, his eyes scanning for competition as his nose localized the source of the blood scent.

He approached warily. Even though his only contact with humans was with a Ute hunting party a year earlier, these odors were new and different to him and made him even more cautious. He was still fifty yards from the tent when his first challenger arrived in the form of a black bear, who was coming from the other side of the campsite.

The coyote knew he was no match for the bigger bear and those sharp claws, but the strong scent of nearby carrion emboldened him to keep walking toward the tent's powerful odor.

The bear spotted the coyote, now just thirty yards on the other side of the tent and stopped her approach. It was late summer, and she needed to eat as much as possible to last the cold winter and still provide for the cubs she would be feeding soon.

She stared at the coyote and waited for him to run, but after a few seconds, realized that he was still warily approaching. She was surprised, but not in the least afraid of the smaller animal. She made a short, aggressive run toward the coyote to let him know that this was her kill, not his.

The coyote leapt backwards and yelped at the bear three times before standing his ground.

The bear immediately rose to her hind paws, spread her arms wide and let out a roar to frighten him away.

Emily and Joseph both awakened with a start at the loud roar that sounded as if it were just outside their tent.

"Emily!" Joseph shouted, calling her by her Christian name in his terror.

ABANDONED

Emily quickly pulled herself out of the sleeping bag and helped Joseph out of his as the bear roared a second time.

She knew that the animal was nearby, *but why hadn't Noah or Claude shot him?* She hurriedly yanked on her shoes and told Joseph to pull on his boots in case they had to run.

Then Emily turned, threw back the tent flap and was horrified by what she saw in the bright moonlight. The bear was just thirty feet in front of her and the camp was empty.

She had nothing she could use to defend herself and Joseph, and the bear was blocking the only way out, so Emily turned and grabbed Joseph in her arms and closed her eyes, expecting the bear to charge into the tent and kill them both.

The bear had seen the flap fly open and had been startled by the unexpected sight. She dropped back to all fours and studied the tent. The scent of blood was strong, but like the coyote, there were other, unknown smells that bothered her. The opened tent and the strange odors created a confused hesitation, so she stayed in position as she decided what to do.

The coyote hadn't moved back any further, and, like the bear, was uncertain of what he should do next. It was a brief, confused lull for all of the living creatures in that small, moonlit location in the middle of the wilderness of the Medicine Bow Mountains.

The entire time from the first roar to the current static situation had lasted less than a minute, and Emily suddenly released Joseph and said, "Stay here, Joseph. I think the bear might have gone."

Joseph nodded as Emily turned, opened the flap slowly and stuck her head out again, then discovered she was wrong. The bear was still there, just looking at the tent. Then, she saw the blood on the ground and thought some animal had been killed by the bear and had run past the tent, which was why it had come to the campsite.

She lowered the flap slowly, then backed into the tent and said quietly, "The bear is still there, Joseph. But it's just staring at us. There's blood on the ground, so I think it must have wounded a deer or something and it ran past the tent. What we're going to do is sneak out under the tent in the other direction, then go up into the rocks on the hill and climb on a boulder. I don't think the bear can get up there."

Joseph asked, "Why doesn't Uncle Noah or Mister Boucher shoot him?"

She sighed and answered, "They're gone, Joseph. We can't talk about that right now. We need to get out of here before the bear changes its mind. Okay?"

"Okay."

Emily hugged him quickly, then slowly lifted the back edge of the tent and said quietly, "Okay, Joseph, you go through first and I'll be right behind you."

Joseph dropped to his hands and knees and crawled through the lifted opening before Emily did the same. She barely had her feet free of the tent when she spotted the coyote staring at them fifty feet away.

She grabbed Joseph's hand, then, keeping her eyes focused on the coyote she began walking up the rocky incline, only glancing forward long enough to make sure she didn't walk into a large stone.

The coyote watched the pair as they began walking away. He was still confused because they appeared healthy and human blood wasn't the scent he'd processed. He shifted his eyes back to the tent and the bear. Whatever had died was there.

The bear also saw Emily and Joseph leave from behind the tent and had reached the same conclusion as the coyote. The source of the strong smell was still there, in that tent, so she ignored the two humans and began slowly walking closer to the tent, swaying as she approached the bloody ground.

ABANDONED

The coyote also began to close the gap to the tent but swung wide to his left, so he could keep the bear in view. He wasn't stupid.

Emily and Joseph continued to climb, shifting their eyes between the coyote and the bear, neither understanding why both wild animals were concentrating on the tent when two defenseless human beings were just a hundred feet away.

When Emily thought it was safe enough to change her focus, she turned to look ahead, and still gripping Joseph's hand, she picked up the pace and they made faster progress up the rocky terrain until she spotted a boulder that could serve as a temporary respite from attack. *But how could they get on top?*

When they reached the eight-foot tall boulder, Emily spotted a smaller boulder nearby, and said, "Joseph, we need to roll that other boulder closer to the big one, so we can step up on it. I'll need you to help me."

"Okay."

Emily and Joseph walked to the higher ground behind the big boulder and Emily thought that because the smaller boulder was reasonably round, it would be easy enough to roll it down the hill to the tall boulder just four feet away.

She stood behind the boulder, bent at the knees and waited for Joseph to do the same. When all four of their hands were just below the belt of the round boulder, Emily said, "Push!"

She strained to get it to move, but it didn't budge. She stood up, exhaled sharply, then looked at Joseph.

"Let's try once more and give it everything we have."

Joseph nodded but didn't say he had just pushed as hard as he could the first time.

Emily squatted a little lower this time and once in position, said, "Now!"

She shoved with her legs bulged and her arms tight, then suddenly felt a stab of pain in her back that made her scream as she collapsed forward onto the small boulder.

Joseph was startled as Emily sobbed in pain, her arms stretched out across the round rock.

"*Mrs. Doyle! What's wrong?*" he shouted.

Emily replied through gritted teeth, "It's my back! Joseph, I'm so sorry!"

"Can I help you?"

She gasped her reply, "No, dear, I just have to stay here. What is the bear doing?"

Joseph looked down to the tent and saw the bear sniffing around the front of the tent and the coyote just watching about fifty feet further away.

"He's just smelling the tent and the dog is just sitting there."

"Good, keep watching." Emily said as she hugged the rock waiting for her back's pain to lessen enough for her to stand.

She could feel the pain's intensity diminishing when Joseph asked, "Where did Uncle Noah and Mister Boucher go, Mrs. Doyle? They even took my horse. Did they go hunting without me?"

Emily briefly considered lying so she could break the news to him slowly, but expected he'd guess soon enough.

"No, Joseph. Your uncle has abandoned us out here in the wilderness."

Joseph surprised her when he didn't sound panicked or even surprised as he asked, "Why would he do it, Mrs. Doyle?"

ABANDONED

Her back had almost returned to its previous level of pain from riding when she replied, "Joseph, do you know who you are, and why you live in the nice house in Omaha?"

"Yes, ma'am. I'm Joseph Charles Brennan the third, and I live there because my father bought the house."

"Yes, that's all true, but do you know what your father did before he died?"

"No. It was something to do with coal, though."

"Yes, it was something to do with coal. Your father owned a company that made coal furnaces for homes and factories, then distributed coal from the railroad to the houses and factories that bought those furnaces. Your grandfather made a lot of money doing that."

"Oh. Is that why I have nice things?"

"Yes, dear. It's why I was hired six years ago to be your nanny when your mother died, and we have Mrs. Thornton to do the cooking and Miss Flaherty who keeps the house clean and Mister Moore who is in charge of the household. Well, your Uncle Noah is supposed to watch out for you until you are a man and can take over your father's business."

"But that won't be for a long time, will it?"

Emily slowly began to stand as she answered, "Yes, dear. Almost ten years."

As she finally stood upright, he asked again, "But why would he leave us here?"

Emily had hoped that he'd make the obvious conclusion, but when he hadn't, she was suddenly reticent to give him the answer, because she almost didn't want to believe it herself. Noah had abandoned them, so they would die out in the wilderness and had spread the blood to make certain of it. Just as Claude had asked Noah, she wondered why he hadn't just shot them both.

"I don't know, Joseph," she finally replied.

Then, as she studied the two carnivores down near the tent, she made a mistake and twisted her back, believing it could just pop back in place, and the jolt of pain dropped her to her knees, smacking them into the hard granite boulder and adding more excruciating pain in the process. She screamed again and lay writhing on the ground, sobbing from the intense pain from her back and now her knees.

Joseph was close to panic as he watched his beloved nanny crying in pain. He forgot about the bear and the coyote just a few hundred yards away as he bent over Emily and put his small hand on her shoulder.

He couldn't speak as tears began to fall from his eyes.

The bear and the coyote had heard the first and second screams from the rocks and were even more confused as neither had heard the sounds before. The strange smells and even stranger sounds finally made each of them decide that whatever had died here wasn't there any longer and the bear then looked at the coyote as replacement for the missing carrion. She had never attacked an adult coyote before because they were too quick, but maybe…

The coyote had seen the bear turn her attention towards him and knew it was time to leave. Just as the bear suddenly made a dash in his direction, he whipped around to his right and raced away. The bear kept running in her loping, almost bouncing pace, but the coyote was simply too agile and didn't keep a straight path until it entered the trees and the black bear slowed down then just walked into the forest, frustrated by the lack of a kill. She didn't even think of returning to the humans on the hill.

Neither of the humans had noticed the departure of the two animals as Emily continued to lay on the ground in pain. Her knees were growing numb from the shock of striking the boulder and she wondered if she had broken her kneecaps on the rock when she fell. But it was her back that truly frightened her. If she couldn't even stand, there was absolutely no chance of them staying alive.

As afraid as she was for herself, she was much more worried about Joseph. He was only eight and knew nothing about the wilderness except what he read in his adventure stories. *How could she protect him if she couldn't move?*

"Joseph," she said as she took his hand from her shoulder, "you must be strong now. You can't be a little boy anymore. You have to grow up. Can you do that for me?"

Joseph looked at the face of the woman he loved more than anyone else and said, "Yes, Mrs. Doyle. I'll do whatever you need me to do."

"Good," she said as she managed a smile and touched his young, smooth face with her fingertips.

The predawn was beginning to lighten the sky as Emily managed to lay out straight on the rocks and felt some relief in her back, but her right knee still throbbed painfully while her left knee's pain eased.

Joseph finally stood and looked down to the tent and said, "Mrs. Doyle, the bear and the dog are gone!"

Emily replied, "He was a coyote, Joseph. Now, we'll stay here for a little while. If you want to get something to drink, just go to the brook. Okay?"

Joseph wanted to ask about breakfast, but just nodded and walked to the small, fast-flowing brook fifty feet from Emily's head and scooped some water in his hands and began to drink.

Emily lay relatively pain-free and thought about their predicament. It was much more than just a predicament, it was nothing less than a death sentence. The only question would be how they would die. They wouldn't die of thirst, but hunger would start soon and would worsen with each hour that their stomachs remained empty. She'd seen berries of a type she hadn't recognized before but wasn't sure if they were safe to eat. If they found them again, she'd try some and if she didn't get sick, she'd let Joseph eat most of them. But that would mean she'd have to be able to walk, and right now, that was impossible.

She knew that Noah and the guide had headed back to Laramie, so she and Joseph could just follow their trail back, but even if they could maintain their strength, it would take at least a week, but probably closer to ten or twelve days. Then, there were the animals. They'd been lucky with the bear and the coyote, but she'd seen so many bears, most of them larger than the one they'd seen this morning. Then there were the wolves and cougars, too. Then there was one more major obstacle to their safe return – the large creeks that were almost rivers. She couldn't swim, and neither could Joseph, not that the ability to swim would have helped them cross the fast-moving water safely anyway.

Somehow, Emily had to fix her back and then find some way to protect her and Joseph for the walk back to Laramie with no weapons, no food and with no idea of how to survive.

Noah and Claude were already nine miles away from the campsite as the sun rose in their eyes when they decided to stop, have breakfast and maybe get some sleep.

They didn't unsaddle any of the horses, but Noah took enough food and some all-important coffee from the panniers while Claude built the fire.

As he cooked some eggs, Claude said, "You know, Noah, I still think you were wasting that woman."

"Will you please stop talking about Mrs. Doyle? I already told you I'd fix you up when we got back to Laramie."

ABANDONED

Claude was scraping the scrambled eggs as he said, "It's not the same. Those whores are being paid to satisfy a man, but a woman who doesn't want you to take her, now that's exciting."

Noah laughed as Claude dumped the eggs onto plates and asked, "You're a real hard case, aren't you, Claude?"

Claude shoved a large forkful of eggs into his mouth, barely chewed and swallowed before replying, "Maybe, but I didn't leave my nephew to get eaten by a grizzly."

Noah laughed again and said, "Yeah, but you don't get a lot of money for raping a redheaded woman, either."

Claude just shrugged and continued eating.

Thirty minutes later, they were both just lying on their bedrolls and snoring in the bright morning sun.

Emily had barely managed to get to her feet and asked Joseph to go to the other side of the big boulder for a few minutes. Once he was out of sight, she finally was able to relieve herself, and then carefully walk to the brook and get something to drink.

Her back was still too painful for her to continue, so she sought a space relatively clear of rocks and gingerly laid back down on her back, then sighed in relief. She hadn't seen her right knee but was sure that it was swollen. She was now convinced she had broken her kneecap but thought she could get past that if her back ever stopped hurting.

Emily could see the tent from where she was lying, and said loudly, "Joseph, can you come here, please?"

Joseph walked around the boulder, saw Emily stretched out on the ground again and thought she had fallen, and scrambled closer up the hillside.

"Are you all right, Mrs. Doyle?"

"My back and right knee are still hurt, Joseph. Now, I'm going to ask you to do something brave, but you have to be quick and if you see any animals, you come right back here. Do you understand?"

"Yes, ma'am."

"I want you to go down into the tent and get our bedrolls and come back here so we can talk about what we're going to do. Okay?"

Joseph glanced at the tent fifty yards down the hill and nodded.

"I'll be careful, Mrs. Doyle," he said before he turned, then began to slide and stumble his way across and down the rocky slope.

When he reached level ground, Joseph walked to the front of the tent and he saw the blood that had been splashed on the tent's canvas roof and felt creepy, but quickly dashed through the flap, then was smart enough to roll both sleeping bags quickly so they didn't collect any of the still damp blood onto their cloth. He didn't tie them, though, as he pulled one under each arm, then left the tent and headed back up the slope to Emily. It was much slower going on the return as he watched his footing, but soon reached his stricken nanny, dropped the bedrolls, then sat next to Emily.

"Thank you, Joseph. Now, it will be difficult for me to move, but we need to get further away from that tent. Can you find a place for us further up the hill that's a good hiding place? It has to be big enough for the bedrolls, too."

Joseph looked up the hill, then looked further to his right and said, "I think I see one, Mrs. Doyle. I'll go there and look closer."

Without waiting for her approval, Joseph stood, then began a scrambling climb diagonally in front of the big boulder they'd tried to use as protection from the bear and kept going until he reached another large boulder that wasn't as round as the first one. When he reached the rock, he found that it wasn't a boulder at all, but a piece of the mountain itself that thrust out of the stone like a jagged, jutting shelf. It was barely large enough for the two bedrolls, but it was reasonably flat, and he thought it would help Mrs. Doyle. When he reached the shelf, he stood atop the surface and looked down at the tent now about eighty yards away. Then, he dropped down to his knees and most of the tent disappeared, which meant they'd be invisible to the bears and wolves. He was sure that this was exactly what Mrs. Doyle had asked him to find and stepped back off of the shelf and began his crabbing, slipping return to his nanny.

Emily had lost sight of Joseph when he'd passed the boulder and tried to think of what she could do to be useful. She learned her lesson earlier about trying to twist her back to make it hurt less, and it had cost her a broken knee. *But how long would it take to get better?* If it didn't heal at least marginally soon, she would be dead up here on the side of a mountain and sentence Joseph to a similar fate.

Emily Ann Doyle then began a string of Irish Gaelic curses focused on Noah Gallagher for what he had done. She knew that she was just an unintended victim in his plan to gain control of what wasn't his, but the fact that he'd even considered hurting Joseph set her well-disguised Irish temper aflame.

Joseph heard Emily's normally sweet voice spitting out words he didn't understand but the anger behind them made him glad that he didn't know what they meant as he passed the boulder and soon slid next to Emily, who'd stopped her cursing when she spotted him.

"I found a good spot, Mrs. Doyle," he said as he sat down.

"Thank you, Joseph. Now, I'm going to try and stand again, and I might need your help."

"Okay."

"I need you to stand right here by the bedrolls."

Joseph got to his feet and stood near Emily's left elbow, with the bedrolls on his other side.

Emily then squirmed until her painful knees were on the downslope, then put out her hand.

Joseph took her hand, Emily gritted her teeth, and pulled herself into a sitting position with a loud grunt.

"Okay, Joseph, I think I can get up now," she said as she let his hand go.

She placed both hands on the rocky ground, bent her knees and slowly stood, and was breathing heavily when she finally managed to stand upright.

"Can you give me my bedroll, Joseph?" she asked, not wanting to bend over to pick it up.

Joseph picked up her bedroll and rather than just hand it to her, unraveled it, then folded it once and then gave the end to her.

Emily smiled and hung it over her shoulder, before saying, "That was very thoughtful. Thank you, Joseph. Now, show me what you discovered."

Joseph smiled back, then picked up his own bedroll and began to slowly walk back to the shelf. He took the first six steps then glanced back at Emily who was struggling to follow but was still behind him.

He continued his angled, climbing walk, checking Emily every few steps. He could see the pain in her face, and hear her wincing gasps when she stepped, but she was still following.

He reached the shelf and tossed his bedroll onto the back end, then turned back to his nanny to help her if she needed it for the last few yards.

Emily saw the shelf and was proud of Joseph. It was as good as she could have hoped to find. She took his hand at the edge of the shelf and had to lift her right knee to step onto the flat rock. When she did, her left foot slipped, just a couple of inches, but it torqued her back just enough to send another lightning stab of pain up her spine.

She had to ignore it as she pushed off with her swollen, horribly painful right knee and lifted her left leg onto the shelf, then just dropped her bedroll onto the flat rock.

"Could you lay out the bedroll for me, Joseph? Leave enough room for yours, too."

"Okay," he said as he unfolded her bedroll and then spread his just to the right on the edge of the rock shelf.

Emily then turned, and as she prepared to lower herself to the bedroll, caught sight of a rock jutting out of the hill just below her left elbow. She stepped back a bit more, then put her hand on the rock and used it as support as she slowly settled onto the sleeping bag.

Once she was down, she quickly laid flat again and emitted a shuddering sigh in relief.

Joseph sat on his bedroll and asked, "What do we do now, Mrs. Doyle?"

"I need to rest, Joseph. But, when you feel up to it, could you return to the tent and take one of the support poles and bring it to me? I can use it as a staff when I think the pain has subsided sufficiently for me to walk again."

"I can do it right now, Mrs. Doyle. I'm okay."

Emily looked at Joseph, smiled, and said, "You're a lot better than just okay, Joseph. You're an amazing young man."

Joseph smiled at her, then stood, walked off the ledge, and quickly began his sliding, stepping trip down the face of the hill.

When he reached the tent, he was about to enter the flap when he spotted the Mason jar that Noah had used to spread the oxen blood. He stepped over, picked up the jar with the dried blood caked in the bottom, then found the lid a few feet away. He picked up the lid, screwed it in place, then set it down and entered the tent. He looked at one of the two six-foot long hickory shafts that served as supports for the tent and knew when he pulled it free the tent would collapse on top of him, so he turned and left the tent, then headed for the nearest stake. He untied the binding cord, then let that corner of the tent slide away. He walked all the way around to the opposite stake, released that cord, and the tent was then only held in place by the two opposite corners.

When he untied the third, the tent leaned precariously toward the lone attached stake, then when Joseph reached the last one, instead of untying it, just pulled on the tent and the canvas structure collapsed.

Pleased with himself, Joseph untied the last cord, then slipped it free and stuck it in his pocket before walking around and taking each of the other cords. Each cord was only a foot and a half long, but when you have nothing, anything was valuable.

With the tent down, Joseph pulled aside the canvas, then extracted the two long, thick hickory poles. Each was an inch and a half in diameter and should serve as excellent walking sticks.

With the cords in his pocket, and the two poles balanced over his shoulder, Joseph picked up the Mason jar and began to climb the hill and soon found that with both of the poles, it would be impossible. So, he dropped one, then just dragged the second as he restarted his ascent.

Emily wasn't able to see him at all from the shelf as she lay there looking at the bright morning sky. She had gotten past the concerns about her back and knee because she knew that even with the walking stick, she wouldn't be able to make it. She was going to die on this shelf, and now, all her thoughts were about trying to save Joseph, but she hadn't even the slightest idea on how to go about doing it.

Joseph set the Mason jar down near the shelf before climbing over the edge and leaning the tent pole against the side of the mountain.

"I have one of the poles with me, Mrs. Doyle. I had to leave the other one near the bottom of the hill because it was too hard to bring them both. I'll go and get it later."

Emily looked at him and said, "Thank you, Joseph. I'll try using the pole when my back is better."

"I took the cords from the stakes, too, but they're not very long."

"We might have a use for them. Did you find anything else?"

Joseph hesitated telling her about the jar because of the blood, but said, "I found a jar and a lid, too. I have to wash it out first, though."

"Did it have dried out blood in it?" she asked.

"Yes, ma'am."

"I thought it might. I think your Uncle Noah used it to splash that blood everywhere. I wondered where he had gotten it."

Joseph sat down and asked, "What can we eat, Mrs. Doyle? He didn't leave us anything to eat, did he?"

"No, dear. We'll worry about that later. Right now, I need to rest and let my back get better. Okay?"

"Alright. I'll go and wash the jar in the brook and then when it's clean, I'll fill it with water."

Emily was about to protest, but knew she needed the water soon, so she just nodded before she closed her eyes, hoping she could nap and let her back and knee heal.

Joseph watched as she closed her eyes, then slid from the shelf, picked up the Mason jar and crabbed to the brook to wash it, then fill it with clean water for his nanny. He drank from the brook while he was there, so she could have all the water.

He didn't say anything to Mrs. Doyle, but he was terrified about what would happen to them. He knew she was hurting much more than she showed, and he wasn't about to leave her here alone. If Uncle Noah returned, he'd throw a big rock at his head. He had realized why his uncle had abandoned them there, and surprisingly, had the same questions that Claude and Mrs. Doyle had. *Why do it this way? Why hadn't he just pulled his pistol and shot them both?*

He returned to the ledge, found Mrs. Doyle napping, then set the jar in the shade of the hill, stretched out on his bedroll and soon fell asleep himself.

Joseph had been lucky and never knew it, when just twenty minutes after returning to the rocky shelf, a pack of gray wolves exited the forest looking for the source of the blood. There were five animals in the pack as they cautiously entered the campsite. After ten minutes of sniffing and listening, they left the campsite and reentered the trees.

In the next few hours, the campsite was visited by another black bear, a pair of coyotes, and one mammoth male brown bear. None stayed for very long in the absence of carrion and the nearby unpleasant smell of humans, and none detected the scent of the living humans just fifty yards up the rocky hill, not that they would have cared. Humans would only be on the menu if nothing else was available, and right now, there was food aplenty.

Emily awakened three hours later and all she could see was Joseph asleep beside her. She looked at his peaceful face, smiled, then thought she'd see if the rest had done her back any good.

ABANDONED

She bent her left knee and didn't feel any pain, which is what she expected. But when she bent her right knee, she received the jab of pain that she knew would be coming, but it wasn't quite as intense.

She took in a deep breath, and supporting herself with her elbows, tried to sit, but the pain in her lower back made her drop back to the bedroll immediately. She was angry and frustrated with her inability to do anything more than lay here like a dead log and didn't know whether to swear or cry.

Joseph's eyes slowly opened just after she'd returned to her supine position.

"Mrs. Doyle, is your back still hurt?"

"Yes, Joseph. I'm afraid I'm going to have to stay here until I can sit up."

"I'll help you to sit up if you want me to, Mrs. Doyle," he said.

"Not right now, Joseph. I just tried, and it wouldn't let me. But soon. Okay?"

"Alright."

The sun was setting as they lay on the ledge and Emily realized that she would have to use the Mason jar for more than one purpose and it was that thought that sent her into a deep sense of despair. It was the first tangible indicator of the absolute hopelessness of their situation.

Nineteen miles east, Noah and Claude had set up camp near a wide creek, unsaddled all the horses and had a big fire going. Neither had spoken much after their last interchange, as Noah was trying to choose a location for ridding himself of Claude. It had to be close enough to Laramie, so he would be able to find his way back on his own. They'd been following their own outbound trail, but he couldn't count on it. But he didn't want to do it too close to Laramie, either. There was the possibility that another hunting party might be close. He thought that tomorrow, just about this time would be perfect.

Claude, meanwhile, was growing more obsessive about Emily Doyle. Granted, she wasn't that young anymore, but Claude always preferred more mature women and Emily had attracted his eye from the moment he'd seen her step off the train. And she was a redhead, too. Not a bright red, but a darker red, which was even better. The thought of her just wandering around back at their old campsite led his mind to all sorts of fantasy images of her in various stages of undress.

As they ate, they did pass meaningless conversation about tomorrow's leg of their return journey during which Noah asked about landmarks and the likelihood of their trail still being visible. He hoped that Claude wouldn't notice the intent behind the questions, and amazingly, he didn't. His mind was too full of Emily, and when he talked to Noah, he asked about her background. He wasn't surprised to find that Noah knew nothing at all about her. She was only hired help, after all. Just like Claude was.

They didn't bother erecting the tent but slipped into their bedrolls just as the full moon arose between two of the nearby peaks.

―――

Emily had to embarrassingly have Joseph help her use the Mason jar, and to his credit, he just talked to her about how big the moon was or how many stars he could see rather than what he had to do. The moon was bright enough for him to take the jar to the brook, empty it and wash it as best he could before refilling it with water. After drinking at the brook, he returned to the ledge and gave her the Mason jar, so she could drink.

Then they both watched as the moon seemed to grow even larger, and both had the same thoughts, but didn't express them. *Would this be the last time they would see moonrise? Would they even be alive when the sun rose in the morning? Would some of those beasts of the night find them in their sleep?*

ABANDONED

As they tried to sleep, they were reminded of the dangers that lay all about them when the wolves began to howl, and the coyotes yipped and barked. There was an occasional bellow from a bear that would silence the others for a few minutes, and twice, they heard the distinctive cry of a cougar.

The naps and the terrifying noises kept them awake, and Emily had to try and sleep atop her bedroll, which made it more difficult when the late summer chill took command of the night. But eventually, her utter exhaustion allowed her to escape the fears and worries and drift into a troubled sleep.

Eight miles west, even deeper in the wilderness, Jack Tyler sat in front of his small campfire with his two friends, Abby and Billy standing ten feet away.

"Well, Abby," he said before he took a bite of his roasted rabbit thigh, "we'll be heading home tomorrow. Once we get back, you and Billy will have a few days off and get all the oats you want. Maybe I'll treat you both to some apples, too."

Abby didn't reply but just stared at him with her big brown eyes. Billy was already half asleep.

Jack didn't expect an answer. He knew that once he did, it was time to stop making the journey.

He tossed away the clean bone, licked his fingers, then took a big drink of water. It had been a good haul this time, maybe the biggest yet, but he knew that there was even more to be found further downstream.

He stretched out on his bedroll and marveled at the Milky Way as it stretched across the sky. It always had the ability to make him feel so insignificant, and he was pleased that it did. Every man needed to be put in his place from time to time, but some never seemed to risk the possibility, content to revel in their own self-importance.

In three days, he'd be back in his cabin, and doing some serious reading about the stars, but right now he just admired them and let their majesty fill him with awe.

CHAPTER 2

Joseph was the first to awaken the next morning when his stomach growled in protest of a new day without any food. He slipped out of his bedroll, noticed Mrs. Doyle was still sleeping, then quietly left the shelf, relieved himself, then when he returned, he took his bedroll and was about to lay it on top of her when her eyes opened.

"Good morning, Mrs. Doyle. Did you want my bedroll to get warm?" he asked.

It was still chilly, but Emily needed to use the Mason jar again, so she replied, "No, Joseph, but I hate to ask if you could get the jar for me to use."

"Yes, ma'am," he replied as he found the jar, emptied the water, and then helped Emily again.

Emily was beyond being embarrassed any longer as her stomach joined Joseph's in loud rebellion.

After he'd gone to empty the jar, then rinse and refill it, Emily tried her knees and back again. The back was painful, but not as bad as it had been yesterday but was now stiff, too. She held out hope that she might be able to stand soon.

When Joseph returned, he asked her if she could sit up yet, and she told him that she might be able to do it later but didn't want to risk damaging it again right now. He gave her some water, then sat on the edge of the ledge and looked down at the collapsed tent and was surprised that there weren't any more wild visitors nearby.

———

Noah and Claude had finished a big breakfast, packed the horses, and were on the trail back to Laramie just an hour after sunrise.

Noah was looking for his opportunity to rid himself of the guide, and Claude was still thinking about the redhead they'd left behind.

In the absence of food, and her inability to move, Emily began to recite poems she'd loved when she was younger as Joseph listened from his perch on the edge of the rocky shelf. He was still watching the campsite wondering where the sharp-toothed beasts were.

When Emily paused between poems, she noticed that Joseph was probably as depressed as she was and that she should try and boost his spirits.

"Joseph," she began, "since we were left alone here, you've been nothing but smart and brave. I'm very proud of you."

Then, instead of smiling at her praise, he dropped his eyes and said, "I'm sorry, Mrs. Doyle. This is all my fault. If I'd listened to you, we'd be back in Omaha having one of Mrs. Thornton's chicken dinners with some apple pie for dessert. I'm not very smart at all."

Emily said, "No, you are very smart, Joseph. It's just that your uncle took advantage of your desire to be a man, but I'll tell you something. You're already more of a real man than your Uncle Noah. You'll be a good man someday."

Joseph knew that the someday would never have a chance to arrive because they were trapped here on this rock. Mrs. Doyle couldn't walk, and he wasn't going to leave her, even if he could. But he knew that sitting here being sad wasn't a good thing to do, either.

"Mrs. Doyle, could you sing something funny?"

ABANDONED

Emily thought about it for a few seconds and then began to sing, "I've got the gift of prophecy, as I will quickly show…"

Joseph felt better and when she reached the chorus, "When the pigs begin to fly, oh! won't the pork be high," he began to laugh.

It was a long, silly song and it was just what she needed as well. When she finished, she looked at his happy face and wished she could do more for him than just sing.

Forty minutes after Emily had finished her song, Joseph sat on the edge of the shelf, his feet dangling above the sloping ground. Emily had fallen asleep again and Joseph was thinking about what he could do to help her, when he caught sight of something moving on his left. He turned, then his eyes grew wide as he saw an enormous bear walk out of the trees. His nose was in the air as he turned his massive head back and forth.

Joseph was terrified as he stared at the bear but kept quiet hoping that the bear hadn't seen him. But the bear kept getting closer and when his head stopped and seemed to look right at him, Joseph thought he was going to climb the hill and eat him and Mrs. Doyle, but he didn't think the big bear knew she was there yet, so he just slipped from the protective shelf and then began to scramble to his left away from Mrs. Doyle, so the bear wouldn't find her. He had to save Mrs. Doyle.

The bear hadn't seen Joseph yet, but the sudden movement attracted his attention, so he changed his direction and began to move toward the side of the hill. It wasn't a very favorable place for him to mount an attack, but when he noticed the animal scrambling across the face of the hill and not up, he just began to trot, paralleling Joseph's slipping, tilted scramble across the face of the rocky hill, sending rocks and dirt sliding down as his feet broke the ground.

The bear just followed him on the level ground, trying to pick up the scent of the unknown animal on the hill. The potential dinner was downwind of him, so all he had was visual cues. The possible victim wasn't large and was moving strangely, but because Joseph was scrambling rather than walking upright, the bear wasn't sure what he was.

Joseph kept glancing at the bear, and one of those glances cost him a misstep when his right foot slipped over a small rock, sending him into a sliding roll as he frantically tried to regain his balance and climb back up the hill.

The big bear saw the tumble, found his chance and began to run to the base of the hill as Joseph finally stopped his roll just thirty yards from the bear who thought the creature was close enough for him to attack now, so he started his clawing ascent.

Joseph saw the giant head and massive teeth, then screamed as he began to dig his fingers into the rocky soil and clamber up the side of the hill.

Less than a mile away, Jack Tyler was leading his pack mule when he heard Joseph's scream and was startled. He immediately thought he'd heard an Arapaho boy or girl, then quickly turned, released his pack mule, Billy, and sent his jenny, Abby, at a dead run heading for the distant sound, soon spotting the bear trying to climb the hill. He snatched his Winchester from his scabbard and was surprised again when he was close enough to identify the potential victim as a white boy.

He set aside his shock at seeing a lone white boy out here in the middle of nowhere and raced toward the bear. If the boy kept going up the hill the bear would reach him in less than a minute. Abby was running as fast as she ever had, and Jack knew it would be close.

Emily was awakened by the scream but confused when she didn't hear it repeated and wasn't sure if it was a nightmare or real. When she thought she heard the sound of hooves she was confused, but she couldn't move to verify the sounds.

ABANDONED

Then, she suddenly realized Joseph was gone and shouted, "Joseph!" before she tried to sit up too quickly and the stab of pain in her back sent her right back down. She felt so damned useless!

Joseph's wide eyes were focused on the enormous jaws that were getting closer despite his desperate attempt to escape. His hands were raw from digging into the rough dirt to try and pull himself away, but the bear was gaining. He knew he would soon die, but at least it would be away from Mrs. Doyle.

Jack hadn't heard Emily's shout over the pounding of Abby's hooves, but when he was close enough to the hill, he pulled Abby to a quick stop, slid from the saddle and raced to the bottom of the hill, just sixty yards from the bear, cocking his rifle's hammer as he ran.

Joseph collapsed onto the rocky dirt, throwing his arms over his head, knowing that he was about to be mauled when he heard a man's voice scream, "Bear!"

The bear was startled by the human voice, having had experience with Arapaho hunters, and turned his mammoth head to see where the human was.

Joseph was equally surprised but used the brief respite to rise and continue his climb.

Emily had her eyes closed and thought she was imagining things because the sound of a man's shout was impossible.

The bear looked at the man as Jack continued to get closer and then began to slide back down the hill to defend himself against the new threat. He had finally recognized Joseph as a human and had set his normal fear aside until he heard the man's voice. Now, he had a problem and wasn't sure how to avoid the much larger human.

Once he saw the bear's attention shift, Jack had slowed to a walk and then as he passed the collapsed tent, he veered to his left to give the brown bear a chance to escape.

Why the big human had changed his course didn't matter as the bear quickly slid the rest of the way down the hill and after it reached the flat ground, gave one long look at the human before he loped quickly into the protection of the trees.

Jack then looked up at the boy, who'd stopped and was watching him, and shouted, "It's safe to come down now, son."

Emily heard the second shout and knew she hadn't imagined it. It was a man's voice and he spoke English. It wasn't Noah or Boucher, *so what was he doing way out here?* It didn't matter, as she suddenly realized that she and Joseph weren't going to die and let a giddy feeling of relief flow through her.

Joseph began to slide back down at an angle as Jack set his Winchester against a rock, then walked carefully up the slope, not realizing that Emily was lying on the shelf just sixty yards above his head.

When he was close enough, Joseph said loudly, "We have to get Mrs. Doyle."

Jack may have been surprised to find Joseph out here, but he was flabbergasted when the boy said they had to get Mrs. Doyle. He turned back toward the collapsed tent and couldn't see how anyone could be inside. It was just stretched out flat across the ground.

"Who's Mrs. Doyle?" Jack asked as Joseph slid closer.

"My nanny. She's up there," he said as he pointed at the ledge.

"Okay, son, let's go get Mrs. Doyle," Jack said as he wondered why the woman had allowed the boy to confront the bear by himself. She may be seventy years old, but that's no excuse for her cowardly behavior.

Jack and Joseph both began to climb, but Jack's longer, stronger legs made shorter work of the hill, and soon had taken hold of Joseph's left hand to help him the rest of the way to the shelf. When his hand closed over Joseph's he felt the blood from the boy's fingers as they had been sliced open by the rocks as he'd tried to claw to safety.

Jack's eyes reached the flat of the shelf first and he was surprised again that Mrs. Doyle wasn't seventy, but apparently less than half that, which made his opinion of her drop even further. A frail old woman was bad enough, but an obviously healthy younger woman was worse. She had stayed, shivering in fear while the boy was luring the bear away from her. Jack Tyler was disgusted.

Emily saw his head appear and wasn't that surprised as his voice closely matched his appearance. He was older than she was, grizzled with a dark beard and his skin was almost leathery from living outside. Yet, despite that, she thought he was handsome and exuded masculinity. What did surprise her was when she saw the obvious distaste in his blue eyes.

"Mrs. Doyle?", he asked as he reached the ledge and hoisted Joseph onto the rock.

"Yes. And who are you?"

"My name is Jack Tyler. This young man tells me that you're his nanny. Is that right?"

"Yes, I am. His name is Joseph Brennan."

"Isn't a nanny supposed to protect the children in her charge, ma'am?" he asked sharply.

"Yes, and I failed terribly when I was needed the most."

Joseph interrupted when he quickly said, "Mister Tyler, Mrs. Doyle is hurt, or she would have helped me. She can't walk."

Emily watched Jack's eyes soften instantly and understood his initial hostility.

Jack said, "I'm sorry, ma'am. It's just that I found the boy fighting off that bear by himself and when he said you were with him, well, I made a poor assumption."

"I understand, Mister Tyler, and there's no need to apologize," then she asked, "Can you take us back to Laramie?"

"Yes, ma'am. I'll have to go back and get my pack mule in a few minutes, but before I go, can you tell me how you and Joseph managed to be stranded out here? Ma'am, I don't mean to sound as if I'm shortchanging the female sex, but this isn't a place for women or boys."

"No, you're not shortchanging anyone. I totally agree with you. Joseph's uncle convinced him to come here on a hunting trip and I refused to let him go without me. I was hoping that his uncle would change his mind, but he didn't. He told Joseph that I could go along. I hated the idea, but I could either quit my job or stay with Joseph. We arrived here last night, and then when we were awakened by a bear roaring outside our tent, I discovered that his uncle and the guide had taken everything and disappeared. We escaped out the back of the tent and came up here. My back was already bad from riding and then when we tried to move a boulder, I wrenched it and then smashed my knees against it. I think I may have broken my right kneecap. It seems to be getting better, but I'm not sure if I can move."

Jack put his hand against the wall of rock to his left and processed all she had just told him, finding it hard to fathom.

"They abandoned you and Joseph out here to die?" he finally asked as he stared down at her.

Emily looked up at his upside down image and replied, "He's Joseph's legal guardian, and if Joseph was dead, then he would inherit the family estate. It was even worse than simply abandoning us. He soaked the ground in front of our tent's opening with blood."

Jack understood the motive but at the same time, didn't. Just as Claude and Emily had wondered, he couldn't comprehend why his uncle hadn't just shot them both. But, it didn't matter. Now, he'd help them return to Laramie and after that it was the law's problem.

"I have to tell you, ma'am, I've met some greedy bas…, men in my life, but this takes the cake. Can I guess that the guide's name was Claude Boucher?"

"How did you know?" Emily asked.

"I was a guide in Laramie for a few years, and still take on one or two parties each year, and of the half dozen that are operating out of there now, five would have told that uncle of his that this was no place for a woman and a young boy and would have turned down the job and then tried to talk him out of it. Claude is the only one without any scruples when it comes to the jobs he accepts."

"Will you help us, Mister Tyler?" she asked.

"Well, ma'am, I'm not about to walk away and leave you here. Right now, I'll go and get my mule and when I return, we'll see about bringing you down from here."

Joseph then asked, "Mister Tyler, how come you didn't shoot the bear? You had your rifle."

Jack looked at the boy, smiled and replied, "Well, son, you have to understand bears. Most of them don't want to have anything to do with people. That big brown bear that was chasing you probably thought you were an injured deer or something else that would be an easy kill because he couldn't smell you yet because of the wind direction. When I was close enough, I yelled at him to let him know that humans were here. Now, if I'd shot him at that range, I probably wouldn't have killed him and if I didn't kill him, he'd be pretty mad and might come after you in his anger. But even if he didn't, he'd be injured and would probably die later. There was no point in killing him yet, so I shouted at him, then watched what he was going to do and gave him enough room to escape while I got closer and might have to take the shot. Once I saw him turn, I knew he was leaving."

"Are all bears like that?"

"No, sir. Some are hungry enough it doesn't matter, and other times, you catch them by surprise or if it's a mama bear with her cubs, she'll protect them if you get too close. You have to read the bear's intention just like you read people. That bear was pretty fat already, so he didn't have to eat. He was probably more curious than anything else."

"You know a lot about bears."

Jack smiled and said, "If you come up here often enough, you'd better know a lot about the bears, wolves, coyotes and the pumas if you want to stay alive. Now, you stay here with Mrs. Doyle and I'll go get my supplies. I imagine you're both hungry by now."

"Yes, sir, we are," Joseph said.

He noticed the two long tent poles leaning against the rock and thought they'd be a good way to get Mrs. Doyle down to level ground if she couldn't walk.

Jack then stepped off the ledge and quickly slid and walked down the hill, retrieved his Winchester and slid it into his scabbard before mounting Abby, and turning her back to the west to get Billy.

After he'd gone, Joseph said, "Mrs. Doyle, I think Mister Tyler is a good man."

"So, do I, Joseph," she replied.

Jack reached his pack mule, Billy, who hadn't budged from where he'd been cut loose, and staying in the saddle, just grabbed hold of the trail rope, turned Abby around and headed back to the campsite. He was finding it hard to believe that anyone could be so cold-hearted as to leave a woman and a boy out in the wilderness to die. He knew that Claude would have done it for a couple of hundred dollars but wondered if the boy's uncle was so naïve to believe that Claude would let it go at that. Claude would milk the uncle for years.

ABANDONED

Joseph's behavior had surprised Jack after Mrs. Doyle mentioned that he was the son of a wealthy man and would inherit his father's fortune. He seemed like a smart, resourceful boy with none of the snootiness he would have expected from an upper class child. He was polite and deferential, despite Jack's somewhat crude appearance. He rubbed the heavy stubble on his chin, having failed to shave for almost two weeks. Then, he hadn't expected to see another human being for another week or so, either. Yet despite his unkempt exterior, Joseph had treated him respectfully. He suspected it had more to do with Mrs. Doyle than anyone else, doubting if his uncle taught him anything of value.

Joseph was sitting on the ledge again and was able to watch Jack as he recovered Billy and as soon as he saw him turn back, said, "Mister Tyler is coming back, Mrs. Doyle."

"You didn't think he'd leave us, do you, Joseph?" she asked.

"No, ma'am. I just wanted to let you know."

Jack dismounted and just let Abby's reins drop, then attached Billy to the jenny again. She was well-behaved and wouldn't let Billy wander off. She might take them both to the brook, though.

He began his climb to the ledge and waved at Joseph who was perched on the edge. Joseph happily returned his wave as he watched Jack quickly step up the rocky grade.

Once he arrived at the ledge, Jack sat down near Emily's head, so he could talk to her without appearing upside down.

"Mrs. Doyle, how bad is your back? Do you think you could manage to sit up?"

"I'm not sure. I haven't moved in couple of hours now."

"How about your knees?"

"I think I might have broken the right kneecap. The left one is okay now, though."

"Now, I'm not trying to be familiar, ma'am, but I'm going to see how badly hurt you are before we try and get you off of this ledge. I don't want to exacerbate your injuries. Okay?"

"No, I understand, Mister Tyler. I won't be embarrassed," she replied.

After the Mason jar, nothing Mister Tyler could do would cause her any more mortification. Besides, it wasn't as if she was some innocent schoolgirl.

Jack nodded, pulled her skirts above her knees, noted the swelling on the right, and the bruising and healing abrasions on both. He then began with the left side and started working his fingers gently up the long bones of her lower leg beginning at her ankle, pressing the bones and watching her face for any reaction until he reached the knee. Then, he slid his hand under the knee and slowly lifted it until it was almost ninety degrees. When she didn't flinch, he lowered the left knee and knew wasn't damaged. Now for the right, which he could already tell had suffered significantly more injury.

He started just above her shoe, which annoyed him because they hadn't even outfitted her with good footwear for the trip. He watched her blue eyes as his fingers began their diagnostic walk up her leg and when he touched just below her knee she flinched.

"Now, this might hurt, ma'am, but I'm going to be pressing on that kneecap to assess the damage."

"Okay."

He slipped his left hand under the right knee, lifted it slightly, noting just a slight flinch, then spread his thumb and forefinger apart and began to press on the sides of the patella. He kept pressing until he reached the top, not seeing any more distress in her eyes. Then he pressed the front of the kneecap, and she jerked.

He gently lowered her knee and said, "Mrs. Doyle, I have good news for you. I don't think you broke your kneecap, but your surely bruised the front of the bone. It's still swollen, but we can do something about that when we get you down on the flat ground. Now, I don't know about the joint yet, but when I lifted the knee to test the kneecap, you didn't seem to have any pain, so that's a good sign, too."

Emily looked at him and asked, "Mister Tyler, if I may ask, your manner of speaking and knowledge of medicine seem oddly out of place with your appearance. Have you had advanced education or training?"

"No, ma'am. I stopped going to school after my ninth year and haven't been back since. As to the medicine part, well, over the years, I've seen a lot of injuries from falls and other trauma, so I've learned from experience."

"But how…" she began.

"I read a lot, Mrs. Doyle," he answered before she asked.

"I apologize if that seemed like an inappropriate question."

"That's all right, ma'am. It was not only appropriate, it was understandable. Now, comes the hard part. I need to check your back. Again, I apologize for any seemingly unwarranted touching."

"What do you need me to do?"

"First, I'm going to have you lie on your stomach. Can you do that on your own, or do you need help?"

"I might need help. I'll try, but all I might be able to do is roll and I don't have enough room."

Jack turned to Joseph and said, "Joseph, I'm going to slide Mrs. Doyle away from the wall and I need you to put the other bedroll where she is now. Okay?"

Joseph nodded and said, "Yes, sir."

Jack could have done it himself, but he felt it was important to keep Joseph involved.

Jack then stood, bent at the knees and grabbed the sides of Emily's bedroll and slid it and her three feet away from the side of the hill.

Joseph quickly dropped his bedroll into the gap and pulled it flat to match hers.

Jack looked at Emily and said, "Okay, ma'am, you can roll anytime."

Emily took a deep breath, then tried to roll, but when she pushed off with her right knee, the pain made her drop back.

"I think I'll need some help."

"Yes, ma'am," Jack said as he dropped back down on his heels, slid one hand under Emily's right shoulder, and the other under her right thigh and asked, "Ready?"

"Ready."

Jack lifted her right side and Emily rolled onto the second bedroll.

Once on her stomach, Emily turned her head, so she could see Jack, not that she expected him to take advantage of her, but because she knew he'd want to see her expression for any signs of pain.

"Okay, Mrs. Doyle, keep looking at me while I check your back."

"Okay."

Jack bent his right index finger and pressed the knuckle firmly on the base of her spine where it meets the pelvis and looked at her blue eyes and didn't observe any reaction.

He then worked his way up a few vertebra, his knuckle rolling over each spinous process. After she hadn't shown any pain, Jack was somewhat relieved.

Then, he pressed on the right side of the lower back and she grunted and closed her eyes for a moment. After she opened her eyes, he tried it on the left and she winced slightly, but nowhere as much as the right.

"Well, Mrs. Doyle, I think you must have pulled a muscle back there. Your spine seems okay, and we won't know about your sacroiliac joints until that muscle is better. But I think we'll be able to get you down the hill. Okay?"

"Thank you very much, Mister Tyler. How can I do that?"

"We'll talk about it after we get you on your back again. Are you ready?"

"Yes."

Jack put his left hand on her right shoulder and his right hand on her right hip then said, "Here we go."

He pulled, and Emily slowly rolled onto her bedroll. She was surprised that her back didn't seem to hurt as much. Maybe his pushing on her back had acted as a massage of sorts.

Once she was flat on her back, Jack sat on his heels and said, "Ma'am, I don't think we can hurt anything by getting you on your feet or by walking you carefully down the slope. Do you want to try?"

Emily smiled and replied, "More than you can imagine."

"Okay, let's do this slowly, then," he said, then stood and straddled her at her knees.

He reached down, took her hands in his and said, "Now, Mrs. Doyle, let me do all the work. Just stay stiff and I'll lift you. Are you ready?"

"Yes."

Joseph watched anxiously as Jack's arms tightened and Emily began to rise from the bedroll.

Jack then backstepped slowly keeping her moving until she was upright.

Emily exhaled and although her right knee was throbbing, her back, surprisingly, wasn't complaining very much at all.

"Okay, ma'am," Jack said as he reached over and took one of the two tent poles and put it in her left hand, "this will be your walking stick on the way down the hill. I'll be on your right side and will provide most of the support. Okay?"

"Yes. I'm ready."

Jack looked at Joseph and said, "Joseph, can you drag the bedrolls down behind you? Just toss the other pole down the hill. You can't hurt it."

"What about the Mason jar? It will break if I throw it down the hill."

Jack hadn't noticed the jar, but said, "Just put it in your bedroll first. Okay?"

"Okay," Joseph replied as he stepped to the jar, picked it up then slipped it into his own bedroll.

"Okay, Mrs. Doyle, let's get you down to the flat earth."

He knew the hardest part would be getting her off the ledge, so after he put his left arm around her back and she had her right arm around his back and holding onto the curve between his right shoulder and his neck, he sidestepped slowly to his right, looking down as his boots left the shelf and reached the loose, rocky dirt of the hill.

ABANDONED

Emily almost floated off the ledge when Jack lifted her with his left arm, then set her gently down on the rocky slope.

"Let's take this slow, ma'am," Jack said as he began to take small, careful steps down the rocky, sandy hill and Emily used her walking stick to give her added balance.

Joseph tossed the other tent pole down the hill on the other side of the shelf, then followed off to the side, dragging the two bedrolls.

Emily only experienced pain when her right knee had to bend to seek a lower foothold as they continued down the hill. She kept the tent pole tightly in her left hand but was depending on Jack's strength for most of her support. She felt as if she weighed twenty pounds, not a hundred and twenty.

Jack, on the other hand, thought he wasn't providing as much support as he believed he would have to as Mrs. Doyle was holding her own better than he anticipated. It bode well for an earlier departure from this place then he'd hoped.

After less than two minutes, they reached the ground near the collapsed tent and he waited for Joseph to arrive with the two bedrolls.

"Mrs. Doyle, you did very well. How is your back?"

"It wasn't as bad as I expected it to be. Only my right knee really hurt."

"That's a good sign. Now, do you want to lie down again, or do you want to try and walk on your own for a few yards?"

"I'd like to try and walk by myself," she said as she removed her arm from around Jack's back.

"Okay. Go ahead and walk closer to the brook," Jack replied as he slowly removed his grip from Emily and stepped back to make sure she didn't fall.

Emily shifted her walking pole to her right hand and began to carefully hobble forward as Joseph finished his sliding return with the bedrolls dragging behind him.

Jack watched her gait and wasn't sure she'd be able to ride for another two or three days. If it was just her knee, it wouldn't be a problem, but her back could keep them here for a while.

Joseph smiled as he watched his nanny walking and thought she was almost healed.

When she was close to the brook, she turned to Jack and said, "It's harder than I thought."

"Is most of the pain in your knee is your back still hurting?"

"Mostly the knee but my back let's me know it's there, too."

"All right. Let's get you reasonably comfortable, and I'll get you and Joseph something to eat."

Emily smiled and said, "I thought you'd never offer. We haven't eaten since for almost two days now."

"I am sorry, ma'am," he said, then turned to Joseph and said, "Joseph, can you bring one of the bedrolls over here for Mrs. Doyle, please? Just lay it right near the brook on the side of the hill."

"Yes, sir," he replied as he grabbed the non-jar bedroll and dragged it behind Emily, then dropped it onto the hill, parallel to the brook, just two feet away.

"Okay, ma'am, we'll do this in the opposite way from how I lifted you. Go ahead and drop the staff and take hold of my hands."

Emily nodded, let the tent pole drop, then took his leathery hands.

"Now, just stay straight, and I'll lower you to the bedroll."

ABANDONED

"Okay," she said, then watched his eyes as he stepped close, then once she felt the strength of his arms, let him slowly lower her to the bedroll.

Emily was surprised how little pain she experienced as she settled softly onto the padded cloth that was now angled so her head wasn't flat.

Once she was down, Jack stepped to the side, then strode quickly to Billy, flipped open the left pack, pulled out a large sack and his jacket, then quickly returned.

Joseph walked over as Jack set the sack near Emily's feet, then folded his jacket and slipped it under her head for a pillow so she could eat and drink more easily.

He picked up the big sack, scooped out some of the dark mash from inside, and said, "This is pemmican. I don't know if you're familiar with it, but each of the tribes seems to have its own recipe. This is my own version. I make it with venison, bear fat, chokeberries, some dried corn and I add some molasses for a little sweetness. Now, it's very greasy, and it's meant to be eaten with your hands. So, go ahead and try it, and I'll get you some water."

Jack then ate the pemmican in his hands and set the sack down on the ground beside Emily as Joseph stood at her left side.

Joseph peered into the sack and gave it a good sniff before sticking his fingers into the pemmican and taking a big bite. Emily watched his eyes grow wide, so she did the same, and was surprised how rich and flavorful it was. It might be greasy, but it was food and she closed her eyes just letting the different tastes fill her mouth. When she opened her eyes, Joseph was reaching for his third handful and as she reached for her second, Jack returned with two canteens.

"Slow down a bit. If you haven't eaten in two days, it could give you stomach cramps if you put too much food in your stomach too quickly."

Emily finished her second scoop, then began licking her fingers, which would have horrified any visitors to Chicago Street in Omaha, but this wasn't Omaha.

She accepted the canteen from Jack and took a long swallow of water, then embarrassed herself when she belched loudly.

Joseph started to giggle, and she had no choice but to laugh as she lay on the ground with a canteen in one hand and a greasy set of fingers on the other.

Jack walked to the collapsed tent and examined the bloody panel. The blood had soaked into the canvas and would attract attention for a while, so he pulled his Bowie knife from his sheath and began slicing the fabric. Once the bloody section was free, he tossed it aside and folded the remaining canvas. It could be repaired.

After sheathing his knife, he returned to the campsite and set the canvas on the ground.

"Mister Tyler," Emily asked, "how did you come to be here? I didn't believe there was another white person for fifty miles except for Noah Gallagher and Claude Boucher."

"I come up here a few times a year to do some prospecting. I was just returning when I heard Joseph's scream."

"Well, we are very fortunate that you do because I believe that Noah was going to get his wish."

Jack looked down at Emily and wanted to ask why they were still alive at all instead of lying dead with bullet holes in their backs, or why she hadn't been molested by Claude, which surprised him even more, but didn't know her well enough to ask such things. He probably would never know her that well. In four days at the most, she and Joseph would return to their lives in Omaha and he'd return to his. But that begged another question that he could ask.

ABANDONED

"Mrs. Doyle, when you and Joseph return, what will Mister Gallagher do?"

Emily, who had only recently assumed she and Joseph would die soon, hadn't given Noah's actions much thought.

"I'm not sure. I assume that the sheriff in Omaha will arrest him for attempted murder."

Jack replied, "Let me unsaddle my mules and I'll be back shortly."

Jack turned and walked back to Abby and Billy, leaving a thoughtful Emily who absent-mindedly licked her fingers as she thought about his question.

Joseph looked at Emily and asked, "Mrs. Doyle, Uncle Noah can't be my guardian anymore, can he?"

Emily was staring into the distant mountains as she replied, "Oh, no, dear. I'm sure that he cannot."

"Can you be my guardian?"

She turned to look at him and said, "I don't believe they would let me be your guardian, Joseph. I'm just a nanny. They pay me to look after you and they'd probably have Mister Casey find another relative or someone else that was a friend of your father's to be your new guardian."

"But I don't like Mister Casey! He's friends with Uncle Noah and went hunting with him, too."

"He's just the family lawyer, Joseph. If your uncle asked him to go, he'd have to go."

Joseph sat down near Emily and fumed. He wanted her to be his guardian and no one else.

After unsaddling Abby, Jack unattached the two large packs from Billy, then took off his saddle. It wasn't a true pack saddle, but a modified army cavalry saddle. At the time he'd made it, it was because he wanted one that met his needs exactly rather than buying a pack saddle in Laramie. Now, having that second seat would be useful. In fact, when he looked at it, he realized that with some minor modifications, it would be an ideal way to transport Mrs. Doyle if she couldn't sit in the saddle seat. But that would have to wait until she was well enough to ride.

When the mules were free of their encumbrances, he pulled his sack of trail mix and a towel from the pack and returned to Emily and Joseph.

When he reached them, he moved the pemmican sack from the hill to the flat ground near her feet, sat down beside Emily, and laid the towel on her dress before opening the sack.

"Now, this is a dry trail mix that I make. It's pretty simple, really. I cook some oatmeal with molasses, bake it until it's dry and crunchy, then break it up, add some nuts, dried apples and cherries."

He held it out to Joseph first, who grabbed a handful, and began to eat it like candy. He offered the bag to Emily to scooped a big batch and began to put some into her mouth.

After she'd chewed some of the mix, she asked, "Why do you have so much of the mix and the pemmican? How long have you been here?"

"Almost two weeks now," he replied as he tugged on his beard, "Normally, I'm clean shaven, but I don't bother when I'm up here. I keep the pemmican and the trail mix for my return trip. When I've exhausted most of my other food, that's the clue for me to head back."

She paused and asked, "So, this is all you have?"

"No, it's most of the food I'm carrying, but there's plenty of food around. I could stay up here another month or so, but I usually follow my schedule."

"So, you won't mind sharing your food?"

Jack smiled, shook his head and said, "No, ma'am."

Emily smiled back and then continued eating some of the trail mix.

Jack then said, "When we begin our return trip is dependent on you, Mrs. Doyle. I'm not going to start back until I'm satisfied that you can ride without further injury or pain. I don't want any noble denials of pain, either. I'll be able to tell. If it takes you a week before you're healthy, we stay."

"But that means that Noah will be able to get all the way back to Omaha and do whatever he's planning on doing," she argued.

"Yes, ma'am. Maybe it will. But whatever he does can be undone. What happens back in Omaha isn't my concern, Mrs. Doyle. Keeping you and Joseph safe is."

Emily nodded and said, "Thank you, Mister Tyler."

He smiled, said, "You're welcome, ma'am," then turned to Joseph and asked, "What about you, Joseph, do you mind staying here until Mrs. Doyle is feeling better?"

"No, sir. But, can I go with you if you have to go hunting?" he asked.

"No, Joseph. You're still to young to be out hunting," then he turned to Emily and asked, "Was there no one else who could have told his uncle how dangerous it would be to have you both along?"

"No. He must not have confided in anyone outside of the household help that he was taking Joseph and me with him."

"I'm sorry, but I find it difficult to understand how that could have happened. Are you in charge of the household?"

"No, that is Mister Wilbur Moore, and he wasn't about to confront the man who had the authority to fire him. None of us would."

"Yet, it appears that you at least tried, to no avail."

"Yes, I tried, but even I knew that he had the final say. If he could convince Joseph to go, I would have to accompany him."

Jack nodded, glanced back at a guilty Joseph, smiled, then turned his gaze back to Emily and asked, "And what young boy doesn't dream about going hunting in the wild country?"

"Do you have a son, Mister Tyler?" she asked.

"No, ma'am, but I still remember being a boy, and I've had a couple of large hunting parties with boys as young as ten, and I wasn't even sure that was a good idea."

He then turned back to Joseph and asked, "How old are you, Joseph?"

"I'll be nine in December, the day after Christmas."

Jack grinned and asked, "I don't suppose you get cheated by only getting one present, do you?"

"No, sir," Joseph smiled back, "I always get lots of presents."

"Well, I'll make sure that you get back to Omaha and enjoy your ninth birthday."

"Mrs. Thornton always bakes me a chocolate cake, too."

"I can't bake a cake, but I can make a good supper for you and Mrs. Doyle. I have some rabbits left and I'll cook them and some other things. I'm pretty good at cooking, if I do say so myself."

"Do you cook at home, Mister Tyler?" Emily asked after swallowing some more trail mix.

ABANDONED

"Yes, ma'am. I don't cook anything fancy, but I keep my pantry well-stocked. I have a large vegetable garden in back that I preserve for the winter months. I eat quite well."

"Do you live by yourself, then?" she asked.

"Yes, ma'am. Well, at least as far as folks go. I do have my canine friend Loopy, but he comes and goes when it suits him. He keeps an eye on my place when I'm gone."

Emily smiled as she asked, "What kind of a dog would you name Loopy? Is he goofy-looking?"

"No, ma'am. He's a bit scary-looking to most folks. I guess technically, he's a dog, but he's really a gray wolf."

Emily's smile disappeared, and Joseph stopped eating as his mouth dropped open, revealing the half-chewed mix.

"*You have a wolf in your house?*" she asked incredulously.

"Some of the time, he mostly stays outside. He only comes in when he wants to, so he can sleep by the fireplace."

"How on earth did you wind up with a wolf?" she asked.

"I was returning from one of my prospecting trips two years ago and found four wolf pups chasing each other near a stream. I watched them for a while and then walked close to them, waiting for their mother to arrive at any moment. The closer I got, the more I noticed how thin they were. They were about three months old, so they were weaned, but they hadn't been fed and they hadn't learned to hunt by their parents yet. They watched me, but didn't seem afraid, mainly because I was approaching them slowly and they were watching my eyes. After twenty minutes and no mother, I walked back to Billy, that's my pack mule back there, pulled out some venison that I'd harvested two days earlier, and then cut up the meat and gave them each a big chunk. I didn't touch them, but mounted Abby, my jenny, and began walking the mules back to my cabin about another ten miles away."

They followed, and I'd toss them some meat every now and then. When I got to the cabin, I gave them all the meat I had left, and they stayed. Over the next few months, they grew quickly and one by one they left. The two females left first, then Loopy's brother left in October. Loopy was the only one who stayed. I've never seen the others, so they've probably joined other packs. He's a big boy now and we have a kind of friendship. He's pretty smart, and he knows when I leave, I'll be back and give him some meat. He still hunts, though, and brings back his rabbits and sometimes small deer. I let him keep them and share them with whichever critters he allows to come near it."

"Does he bite other people?" Joseph asked with wide eyes.

"Not that I know of. I don't have a lot of visitors, and he's been out on his hunting trips when they showed up."

"How long have you lived there?" Joseph asked before starting to chew his trail mix again.

"I arrived with the Union Pacific in May of '68 and stayed in town until it got too ugly, so I bought the mules and headed southeast of town, found a place I thought would suit my needs, then began working on my cabin. I had some of the boys who'd arrived with me to build it, but they wanted to live in town and enjoy the wild side of life. So, I've been there for almost twelve years now."

Emily asked, "You've been living alone for all that time?"

"Yes, ma'am. It suits me fine. When the hunting parties began arriving over the next couple of years, I hired on as a guide and that was what I did for a living, but the trips kept moving further away from town in search of bigger game. Eventually, we reached the Medicine Bow Mountains and I took them further than the other guides, so I was paid more. I guess most of the others were still too attached to town life."

"But you said you were doing prospecting. Why did you give up being a guide?" Emily asked.

ABANDONED

"I didn't give it up, I just stopped taking so many parties. For a few years, I was taking two parties a month, but now, I only take a couple a year. About four years ago, when I took a party to a location about six miles east of here near a big creek, I was washing my frypan and spotted a gold nugget among the gravel just below the water. It was a good-sized chunk of gold, and I just counted my good fortune and put it in my pocket."

"*You found gold?*" exclaimed Joseph.

"If you take the time to look in most of the creeks and streams around the Continental Divide, you can find gold. It washes down from the mountains. It's just not usually in abundance, which was why I thought how fortunate I was in finding the nugget. Well, after I returned the party to Laramie, I stayed at my cabin for a few days then returned to where I'd discovered the nugget. I found some more placer gold and then returned a few weeks later with some basic prospecting gear and began looking in earnest. I didn't find a lot that first year, less than three pounds and I stored it in my cabin. When I returned the following year, I pushed further west into the big valley, searching the other streams. It seemed that the further west I went, the more I found. After the second year, I took the train to Cheyenne, had the gold assayed and then converted to cash and opened a bank account there rather than in Laramie. I didn't want the kind of crazy gold rush like I'd read about everywhere else. It gave me the freedom to indulge in a few things for my cabin, too."

"And you're still finding gold?" asked Emily.

"Yes, ma'am. I have almost six pounds of nuggets and twelve pounds of dust in the taller of the two packs. There's a stream about eight miles west of here that I've been following from the angle of the mountain as it crosses the valley, and after it made a drop into some rapids, I found a lagoon that seemed to have collected a large amount. I could have stayed for another month or so and added a lot more, but it was time to go."

Emily glanced at the pack then asked, "Mister Tyler, you have over six thousand dollars in gold just a few feet away, yet don't seem to be reluctant to talk about it. Why are you even telling us?"

"Well, ma'am, that's a good question because I've never told anyone except the bank in Cheyenne about the gold. I figure you and Joseph will be in Omaha anyway, but I believe I can trust you not to tell anyone. Besides, I didn't want you to think that I was only offering to help you because I was expecting to be well rewarded for the effort. I'm helping you because it's the right thing to do."

"I wouldn't have thought that, Mister Tyler. Besides, we don't have any money or much else."

"I know that, ma'am. But you told me about Joseph's situation right away and after you told me how his uncle had left you both here to die, I didn't want to be associated with that kind of man."

"I knew you weren't when I first saw you, Mister Tyler. You were angry with me when you believed that I had abandoned Joseph to the bear, which told me a lot about your scruples. Now, as much as I'd like to talk, I need to stand and find some privacy."

"Yes, ma'am," Jack said as he stood, then removed the towel from Emily's skirts and slipped it under his gunbelt.

"Now, I'm going to ask you to do something a bit unseemly, Mrs. Doyle."

"And what might that be?"

"After I help you to your feet, we'll walk to where the tent had been. You can see the dark stain of the dried blood. I want you to use that location, as I will and so will Joseph when he feels the need. I don't want that scent to inspire any more visitors. Our scent will let them know that humans are here, and they should leave us alone."

Emily nodded, then said, "Help me up, then, if you will, Mister Tyler."

Jack stood at her feet, took her hands and lifted her from the angled bedroll. Because it wasn't flat, he was able to pull her to her feet much more easily.

ABANDONED

He then stood on her right side and said, "I'll do a better job than the staff for keeping the weight off your knee."

"Thank you," she said as she put her right arm around his back and neck while he put his hand around the left side of her chest and lifted her slightly.

She began hobbling toward the dark red blood stain and appreciated his support and wanted to try to bend her back because it wasn't hurting so badly but recalled the previous attempt and held off.

When they reached the bloody ground, Jack said, "Now, I'll walk about twenty feet away, then Joseph and I will turn around. When you're done, let us know."

"Alright."

Jack took ten long strides then watched Joseph as he turned around without being told. Jack smiled and stood with his arms folded. He was still very surprised by what a good boy Joseph was. The only boys from good families that he'd met were the ten to twelve-year-olds that had accompanied their fathers on the large hunting parties, and they'd been spoiled brats. They'd acted as if he was just an illiterate bumpkin who was nothing more than an unkempt servant and treated him that way, not knowing their lives were in his hands. Joseph was at the opposite end of the spectrum.

He was still thinking about the boy when Emily said loudly, "I've finished Mister Tyler."

Jack turned and walked back to her, keeping his blue eyes locked on hers, so he didn't appear to be looking down at what she had left on the ground.

He walked to her right side, put his arm around her back and when he felt her hand on the right side of his neck, they stepped off.

"You seem to be walking better, Mrs. Doyle," he said as she tried to walk normally.

"It does feel better, but I don't believe I should try and bend my back yet."

"That's a wise decision," he agreed as they reached the bedroll and he lowered her onto the sleeping bag.

Joseph then said, "I'll go next!", before trotting away toward the blood.

Jack snickered, then pulled the towel from under his gunbelt, folded it then walked to the brook near Emily's right side, dunked the towel in the icy cold water, then before he pulled it free, looked at Emily who'd been watching.

"When I give you the towel, go ahead and put it on your knee. It'll reduce the swelling."

"I know. Thank you for being so considerate."

"You're welcome, ma'am," he replied as he handed her the dripping towel.

Emily pulled up her skirt with her left hand then carefully laid the cold towel on the knee.

"That feels better already," she said as she smiled at him.

"If you continue to improve, Mrs. Doyle, we can leave the day after tomorrow. I don't trust your back enough to sit you on a mule for a long period."

"I agree, Mister Tyler. As anxious as I am to return to Laramie, I don't want to risk the return trip if it makes my back worse."

"Good. When we get to Laramie, I'll put you and Joseph in a hotel, then buy you both some new clothes and get you tickets for your return to Omaha."

"I'll make sure that you're reimbursed for your costs, Mister Tyler."

"There's no need, ma'am. I don't have any idea what to spend the money I've already accumulated, not including the gold in the packs."

She tilted her head slightly and asked, "Then why are you still prospecting?"

He shrugged and replied, "I don't really know. I think that it might be necessary someday, but I just can't see it."

"If you don't mind my asking, just how much have you accumulated over the years?"

"Well, I do have a bank account in Laramie from guiding the hunting parties, but that's only around a thousand dollars and my account in Cheyenne has over thirty thousand dollars."

Emily blinked and said slowly, "And you have eighteen pounds of gold in your pack."

"And about that much in my cabin along with some loose cash. So, don't worry about the money at all, ma'am."

"I can't believe you have all that money and don't seem to care about it."

"I just never give it much thought. I'm content with what I do and where I live. The money is just there. I hate to say that it's only money, but that's all it is. Right now, for example, would you rather that I had eighteen pounds of gold in that pack or eighteen pounds of roast beef?"

Emily laughed and asked, "You don't have eighteen pounds of roast beef, do you?"

"No, ma'am. I have about three pounds of dressed rabbit and some half-full jars of onions, peppers and tomatoes and a few more potatoes, but no roast beef."

"You carry that much food with you?"

"I admit that it's more than most men take when they leave civilization behind, but I do enjoy to cook and eat something other than mushrooms, which I never did care for anyway."

Emily then asked, "You don't have any coffee left, do you?"

"No, ma'am. Sorry. I don't even like coffee."

"You don't? I've never met a man who didn't like coffee."

"Well, you've met one now. But I do have some tea if you'd like something hot to drink later."

Here eyebrows peaked, as she asked almost in a whisper, "You have tea?"

"Yes, ma'am. I have more than half a tin left. I usually only drink water when I eat, but I like to have some tea on occasion. Can I assume that you'd like some later?"

She sighed then replied, "Oh, yes, please. You don't have any sugar, though. Do you?"

"Yes, ma'am, but I'm going to have to disappoint you if you ask about cream."

"No, I'm quite happy with just the sugar."

"I'll start a fire in a little while and cook supper for you and Joseph."

Joseph was close enough to ask, "What are we going to have for supper?"

Before Emily could reply, Jack turned to Joseph and answered, "Mrs. Doyle and I are having roasted rabbit, baked potatoes, and vegetables, but you're going to have mush."

ABANDONED

Joseph gaped at Jack for a few seconds before he saw his blue eyes begin to smile, then he started laughing as he said, "You're just kidding me!"

"Any boy who would believe it was a good idea to go on a hunting trip when he was eight sounded like an easy target, but I guess I was wrong."

Joseph immediately stopped laughing and said, "I almost got Mrs. Doyle killed."

Jack noted that he hadn't even mentioned himself and thought for a moment before saying, "Joseph, let me tell you something. If I was your age, and someone offered me the chance to go on a hunting trip for rattlesnakes and only gave me a stick, I would have grabbed the stick and gone looking for the biggest, fiercest rattler I could find."

"Really?"

"Really. Boys do things like that, and I'm not sure we ever stop doing it either. I'll bet if you ask Mrs. Doyle, she'd have stories about boys and grown men who do things that sound really stupid after it was done and never understood why they even thought about doing it in the first place."

Joseph turned to Emily and asked, "Is that true, Mrs. Doyle?"

She smiled at him, then replied, "Yes, I'm afraid it is."

"Do ladies do it, too?"

"Sometimes, but just not as much."

"Have you ever done anything like that?" he asked.

Emily knew that she had but didn't want to admit it because it was something that brought shame rather than pride.

"No, Joseph, I'm afraid that I haven't."

After a short pause, Jack said, "Mrs. Doyle, I'm going to use their old fire pit and set that up, then I'll reassemble the tent over here. I cut out the bloody part and I'll put it in the brook under a big rock, but I'll be able to repair the missing piece of canvas with one of my tarps, so you and Joseph can sleep inside tonight."

"Thank you, Mister Tyler."

Jack smiled, nodded, then went to work. The easiest part was hiding the bloody piece of canvas, when he walked to the brook, found a good-sized rock, wrapped the rock in the canvas and then returned it to the brook's bed.

Next, he found one of his small tarps in his pack, then took his sewing kit from his saddlebags and walked to the stack of canvas. Joseph sat on the ground nearby and watched as Mister Tyler stretched the tent's cut out section on the ground, then laid the tarp over the missing piece. He cut the tarp to a closer match, then handed the leftover tarp to Joseph. He threaded the needle with some coarse threat, then began stitching the cloth with the heavy thread. It was the same needle and thread he would use for any tears in his heavy shirts, britches or his coat. He had a smaller needle and some silk thread for the cuts and gouges that were inevitable when he was out in the wilderness.

It took him over an hour and it was well into mid-afternoon when he finished the sewing job and had Joseph bring him the two tent poles while he walked to the original location and pulled out the four stakes.

After he returned, he removed his hatchet from the heavier pack, then was about to take out his cord when Joseph said, "I have the cords, Mister Tyler."

Jack turned, smiled and said, "Why am I not surprised, Joseph."

Joseph smiled, pulled the cords from his pockets and held them out for Jack.

ABANDONED

"Let's go and set up the tent, sir," Jack said before walking to the new tent location.

Twenty minutes later, the repaired tent was in position and Jack took a few minutes to add his scent to the dried bloody rocks. He was confident that it would keep most critters away from the campsite. He'd purposely assembled the tent to block Mrs. Doyle's view.

Once he was on the other side, he began to set up the firepit by gathering some rocks to set around the base for his cooking grille. He'd need to gather some new branches to use to roast the rabbits, but he'd do that later.

As he did the mundane tasks of setting up camp, he began to think about how Joseph's uncle would react when he found out that his nephew was alive. Would he then send someone to silence him and Mrs. Doyle? He'd have much more to lose than just his inheritance. He'd hang for attempted murder. He knew that it wasn't his business and he surely didn't want to get involved, but he was already developing a sense of responsibility for the nanny and Joseph. He was sympathetic to their plight and despite having never met the uncle, already despised the man. Anyone who did something as despicable as leaving two helpless people out in the wilderness to die deserved to die just as hideously.

Emily, now that she had food in her stomach, her back wasn't hurting much, and even her right knee seemed to be improving, had finally let her thoughts drift to the same questions that Jack was asking himself. *When they arrived in Laramie, did she send a telegram to Omaha? If she did, was there anyone she could trust to let know that Joseph was alive?* She knew her own continued existence didn't matter to anyone, except maybe Mister Moore, and his interest wasn't something she wanted.

She had thought of Mister Casey, the family attorney, but after Joseph had reminded her that he'd gone with Noah Gallagher on the first hunting trip, she realized that maybe there was more the trip than just having to go as someone who was beholden to the family fortune.

Mister Thomas White, the company president was a weak, easily manipulated man who had been put into that position by Noah as the chairman of the board. She felt almost sick when she finally realized that in her six years working in the Brennan household, she knew no one that she could count as a trusted friend. Then she looked over at Jack Tyler as he was setting up the firepit. She'd known him for just a few hours and already trusted him more than anyone she'd ever known before, *but what could he do? He lived in a cabin outside of Laramie with a wolf, for God's sake!*

Surprisingly, even Joseph had come to the same conclusion as his nanny. He knew other boys in his class at Saint Ignatius School for Boys, but he never spent any time with any of them. He spent his spare time with Mrs. Doyle or some of the men from his father's company, including his Uncle Noah. His father had died almost two years ago, and it had seemed so distant and unclear in his mind. It was then that his Uncle Noah had appeared in his life. Now, the fear that had evaporated when Mister Tyler had arrived emerged again, only in a much different form. Before, he'd been afraid for Mrs. Doyle and of being left alone. Then, he'd been terrified by the bear. But now, the fear was for what awaited him in Omaha when his Uncle Noah found out he was alive. Like Emily, he looked at Mister Tyler as his hero, but unlike his nanny, Joseph would ask him if he would come with him to Omaha and bring his Winchester, pistol, and that giant knife. Maybe, he'd even bring Loopy to deal with his uncle.

As their old camp was being reassembled by Jack Tyler, Claude and Noah were putting up their tent near a large stream. Noah could tell by the recognizable landscape they were close enough to Laramie he'd be able to reach the town by late tomorrow. He'd have to get rid of Claude before they left in the morning. He knew that after he'd returned to Omaha and inherited the Brennan estate, it wouldn't be long before he was visited by Boucher with his hand out, and he had no intention of spending another dime on satisfying the guide's greed.

ABANDONED

Claude still had no concerns about any threats from Noah, and what was surprising, wasn't even considering blackmail. He planned on asking for a bonus for doing such a good job, but nothing afterward. Noah wouldn't have believed him even if he'd told him anyway.

After the campsite was set up and the sun was scraping the mountains in the west, Claude had the fire going and was cooking their supper in a large skillet.

He looked over at Noah and asked, "When are you going to leave Laramie? We should return late tomorrow."

"I believe I'll stay in town for another day. I'll wire Luke Casey, so he can prepare the board for the bad news."

"You think he'll believe it?"

"He doesn't have any choice. I own him. Didn't you notice how he always called me 'sir' while we were here the last time?"

"I noticed. I thought it was because you could fire him."

"I couldn't, but that's not it. I found out that he'd been overbilling my sister's brother for years. I have the registers and he knows he'd lose more than his license if I pushed it. It would ruin him."

Claude didn't know anything about lawyers, but just grunted and continued to cook.

Noah felt the growing satisfaction of his long-anticipated plan finally coming to fruition. For more than a year, he'd been building up the boy's desire to come by telling him tales of his hunting trip and buying him adventure stories. He bought him a toy Winchester last Christmas, too.

He had Casey under his thumb and knew that having the boy declared dead and being named as the legitimate heir to the estate would take less than a week.

Noah took the plate of food from Claude and happily ate as he looked at the guide, knowing he'd never see Laramie tomorrow.

Jack only had his large prospector pan, his frypan, a small steel pot, and one tin plate, so he had to make do. He had three sharp knives with eight inch blades, a fork and a spoon, so that would work. He also had a wooden spoon he would use for cooking. He only had one tin cup, but that would be for Mrs. Doyle's tea.

So, he first built his rotisserie for the rabbits, and once the two forked branches were standing with the two dressed rabbits overhead, he lit the fire and began to cook supper. Joseph was sitting on the ground nearby while Emily watched from the bedroll.

He first cooked the rabbits, and when they were done, he set them on the prospector pan and set the frypan on the fire and spooned in some pemmican for the fat and flavor. He added some of the onions, peppers and tomatoes from his jars, sprinkled some salt and pepper on the mix then began to stir it. He sliced the rabbit and left the four thighs aside and stripped off the rest of the cooked meat and dropped it into the simmering mix.

Emily thought her stomach was going to crawl out of her mouth and run to the skillet as the flavorful scent reached her.

Once he thought it was done, Jack pulled the rabbit skillet free, then put the pot of water on the grate.

He scooped out almost half the mix onto a plate, then placed on two of the rabbit thighs on top and handed it to Emily with the fork.

"Thank you, Mister Tyler," she said as she accepted the food with big eyes.

"You're welcome, ma'am," he said before pouring most of the rest and the other two rabbit thighs into the prospector pan and handed it to Joseph with the spoon.

"You can drink from the canteen, Joseph. I'll make Mrs. Doyle some tea."

"Thank you, Mister Tyler," he said as he took the big pan and sat it on his lap before greedily thrusting the rabbit thigh between his teeth.

"You're entirely welcome, sir," Jack said before using the wooden spoon to eat the remaining rabbit stew.

He wasn't trying to be noble by giving them each more than he had taken but knew each of them would need the strength. He'd been eating regularly.

He made Emily's tea and poured in a measure of sugar before handing the cup to her.

She smiled as she took the cup and said, "You're spoiling me, Mister Tyler."

"Just being a gracious host, ma'am."

Thirty minutes later, after cleaning up, Jack asked, "Ma'am, do you and Joseph want me to set up your bedrolls now?"

"I've had several naps during the day, Mister Tyler, and I'd rather stay up for a while, if that's all right."

"That's fine, ma'am," then he turned to Joseph and asked, "How about you, sir? Do you want to stay up for a while?"

Joseph surprised Jack when he said, "Can I take my bedroll into the tent? I'm kind of tired."

"Sure. Do you need any help?" asked Jack.

"No, sir. Thank you for the rabbit. It was really good."

"You're welcome."

Emily had just soaked the towel and put it on her knee when Joseph looked at her and said, "Good night, Mrs. Doyle."

"Good night, Joseph."

He smiled, then said goodnight to Jack, turned and disappeared into the tent twenty feet away.

After he'd gone, Jack looked at Emily and said, "You know, ma'am, I'll admit that I was very surprised by that boy. When you told me that his father was wealthy, I expected him to be another of those spoiled boys like the ones I'd seen arrive with their rich fathers with big hunting parties. He's nothing like that at all. I can only surmise his polite demeanor is thanks to you more than anything else."

"Thank you, Mister Tyler. I've tried to raise him as if he were my son and not like some of the other boys that would sometimes visit the home. I'm not sure that I'm preparing him properly for the world that he may be entering as a man though, but I try to provide the values that I admire."

"You have a right to be proud, ma'am. I'm sure that Joseph will be a good man. If that doesn't serve him in the business world, then it's the fault of that world and not him."

"Were you raised that way by your father, Mister Tyler?"

"I never knew my father, ma'am. I didn't know my mother, either. I was just a few months old when I was left on the steps of the Sisters of Mercy Orphanage in Chicago."

Emily looked at his face in the glow of the nearby fire and asked, "And your name?"

Jack smiled as he poked at the fire with the skewer used for the rabbits.

"When I was left at the orphanage in '46, the director of the orphanage, Mister Richard Greaves, gave me the name because he was a Whig and an admirer of President Tyler. He didn't name me John, though. He wrote 'Jack Tyler' on the registration card."

"You said that you stopped going to school after your ninth year. Why was that? I thought school was mandatory at an orphanage."

"It is, ma'am. I wasn't pleased with my life in the orphanage, especially with our new director, Mister Ian Collins. He was a small man and abused his authority. None of the other kids would do anything to stop him, so, one day, when he was, shall we say, 'bothering' an eight-year-old named Isaac Lincoln, I grabbed him, dragged him into an empty classroom and almost beat him to death. Once I was sure he wouldn't be bothering any of the other children, I just took my clothes, walked away and joined the army."

"But how old were you?"

"Fifteen, but I was always big for my age and had been shaving for two years already. I always looked older, too. Even now, most folks think I'm over forty, if not close to fifty. Besides, they weren't too particular about who signed up in those early days of the war."

"What happened when you went into the army? Surely, someone would have guessed your age, sooner or later."

"No, ma'am. None ever did. On my enlistment papers, I claimed a birthdate of February 8, 1843, so when I enlisted, I was eighteen. When I mustered out in July of '65, they thought I was twenty-two, but I was just nineteen, but by then, I probably looked closer to twenty-six or seven."

"Did you have to fight in many battles?"

"I joined the 23rd Illinois Infantry Regiment that was forming in Chicago. You should appreciate this, ma'am, unless I'm mistaken by your red hair and blue eyes but were called 'The First Irish'."

Emily smiled and said, "No, you're not incorrect. I'm very Irish."

"Well, we were sent down to the town of Lexington, Missouri and in September we surrendered en masse to General Sterling Price of the Missouri State Guard. We were all paroled, because it was early in the war and they exchanged prisoners before General Grant realized that it was helping the Confederates who didn't have nearly the manpower. Anyway, I guess we embarrassed General Fremont when we surrendered, because he had us all mustered out of the army after we returned to Illinois. I wasn't happy about it and was going to enlist again when General Phil Sheridan asked that we be reconstituted and sent east. That spring, we went to eastern Virginia to help Grant chase Bobby Lee all over Virginia. We were there at Appomattox when Lee surrendered and then, finally, we were mustered out. I was a sergeant by then."

"Did you get shot?"

"No, ma'am. I got sick a few times, and had men shot on both sides of me and was nicked by a nearby shell once, but I never took a Minie ball hit."

"How on earth did you find yourself here after being born in Chicago and serving in the army in Virginia?"

"Once we mustered out, I didn't know where to go or what to do, but some of the boys said that they were paying three dollars a day for laborers with the Union Pacific as they were laying track across the country. So, eight of us took a train to Omaha, and I took a job helping to build the railroad. After a few months, the others had all gone, although one didn't go voluntarily. He caught the bad end of a rail that was being carried into place in western Nebraska."

It was like organized chaos as we laid the tracks across the Great Plains. I did everything that needed to be done, including cooking and even some surveying. I guess I had a better education than most of the boys. Anyway, I thought about staying at some of the stops, but they were pretty boring. When we reached Laramie, it was a hard town, but I liked the land, so I just took my pay and stayed. I had quite a bit of money and was able to buy a full section about ten miles south of Laramie that had everything I wanted. I built my cabin and that's where I live. If I need anything I ride into town and I'm back home in a few hours."

"But aren't you lonely out there?"

"No, ma'am. I have my books and it's peaceful. I work when I need to and come out here whenever the mood strikes me. No one bothers me, and I don't bother them."

"That's a somewhat sad way to spend your life, don't you think?"

His answer was interrupted by a loud snarl, and he turned toward the noise.

"What was that?" Emily asked anxiously.

"A puma. He must be unhappy with a bear or a pack of wolves who either have something he wants or they're attempting to take what he has."

"Will he come here?"

"No, I don't believe so. If he does, I'll convince him that he doesn't want to stay here."

"How many guns do you have?"

"I've got my Remington pistol and my Winchester. Then I've got a single barrel twelve-gauge shotgun."

"I heard Mister Boucher say that a Winchester won't stop a bear."

"He's almost right, if he wasn't so ignorant. I used to carry a Sharps for the big animals like bears or large elk, but it stays in my cabin most of the time since I bought this Winchester. See, Winchester didn't like being shut out of the big game market and developed the Winchester '76. It's a much more powerful gun than the '73. Then, they made some newer, more powerful versions, including the one I found on one of my trips to Cheyenne to deposit the gold."

He reached across the saddle and pulled his Winchester from its scabbard.

"This model is chambered to use the .50-95 Winchester Express cartridge. It's almost as powerful as the Sharps and can stop a big brown bear with one shot. It also gives you the advantage of firing multiple shots much more quickly than the Sharps in case that first one didn't stop him. This one has the thirty-six inch barrel, too. It's not ideal for use from horseback, but then again, neither was the Sharps. This long barrel gives me great accuracy and more range, too."

"Why only a single barreled shotgun?"

"I've got a two barrel back at the cabin, but the single barrel is lighter, and it has a shorter barrel. I usually use it for turkeys, quail and other gamebirds. If I have to go hunting for any reason, I'll leave it with you for protection. Do you think you'd be able to use it?"

"Yes. I've fired my father's shotgun before."

"Good," Jack said before glancing at the tent then asking, "Mrs. Doyle, I didn't want to ask you this before, but I'm just more curious than anything else. Why did Joseph's uncle decide to take you both way out here and abandon you rather than just take you about twenty miles outside of Laramie, or Omaha for that matter, and shoot you both?"

"I asked myself that question, too. It doesn't make much sense, does it?"

"No, ma'am. Even if he couldn't do it himself, he could have hired someone to do it. I'm sure that Claude would have pulled the trigger without hesitation."

Emily shivered and said, "That man scared me. He kept looking at me when he thought I hadn't noticed."

"I wasn't going to bring up that subject, but you had a good reason to be concerned, ma'am. Claude Boucher lived up to his name. I'm not even sure he didn't pick his name himself."

Emily blinked and said, "I hadn't even noticed. His name, it means 'butcher' in French, doesn't it?"

"Yes, ma'am, but he was worse than just a butcher. There were rumors about what he did to women, and not just the women in one of the three bordellos in Laramie."

Emily wrapped her arms around her at the thought but wondered why he hadn't even touched her. She knew it couldn't have been because Noah had told him to keep his hands to himself.

"Why do you think he didn't bother me?" she asked.

"I'm certain it was because the uncle didn't want to frighten Joseph. It's the same reason he probably didn't leave you both bound when they stole away. He wanted to be sure that if anyone happened to find your bodies, it would look accidental. That still doesn't answer the basic question of why he believed he had to use such a complex method to eliminate Joseph."

"We may never know why he did it this way, I suppose. But I'm glad that you found us before anything with sharp teeth and claws did."

"So, am I, ma'am."

"I think I'll turn in now. Can you help me move to the tent?"

"Yes, ma'am," he said as he tossed the rotisserie stick away, stood and after taking the damp towel from her hand then setting it on a nearby rock, helped her stand.

It took about fifteen minutes to get her situated in the tent, but once she was in place, she whispered, "Thank you for everything, Mister Tyler. You are a gift from God."

Jack just nodded and whispered, "You're welcome, ma'am," then backed away, let the tent's flap drop and returned to his saddles.

The moon was lighting the campsite with as much of the sun's light as it could reflect, and Jack recalled some daytimes that weren't as well lit.

He picked up his Winchester, slid it back into its scabbard and finally removed his gunbelt and set it on the shorter pack. He had his bedroll nearby but left it in place. He estimated it was around ten o'clock by now. He wasn't tired yet and decided he'd stay up for a while longer.

Jack leaned back against his saddle and scanned the forest to his left, then swung his vision across the front of the landscape. There was a downslope that started four hundred yards away and he imagined that a pack of coyotes could be on the other side, but it was highly unlikely. They were a sociable animal and liked to talk to each other. Wolves, on the other hand, could move much more quietly. He'd been stalked by Loopy a few times, hopefully just in play, and had been surprised to find him. He knew that pumas were even stealthier.

But nothing on four feet approached the camp. There were two barn owls that were carrying on a long conversation, probably arranging a romantic liaison later, but nothing else attracted his attention.

He thought it was funny that he was paying so much attention to his surroundings just because he had a woman and a boy in the camp. When he was alone, he just fell asleep. He knew that Abby, and sometimes Billy, would alert him if they had any visitors, and they were both asleep already.

After another hour, he laid out his sleeping bag, pulled out his sleeping tarp, laid down near his pistol, then pulled the tarp over him. He rarely slept inside the bedroll because he wanted to be ready for instant access to his pistol. During the snowy months, he traveled with a small tent, but that wouldn't be for another month. Then, the snows would come.

CHAPTER 3

Claude was up first the next morning, as he usually was. He'd had a hard time falling asleep as he kept thinking about that redheaded woman just a day or two west of where they were. If he rode back there, she'd do anything for him just for a piece of jerky, assuming she was still alive. *What difference would it make to Noah?* He hated the woman, and if he killed her with the knife after he'd finished with her, it wouldn't spoil his plans.

He had the fire blazing when Noah exited the tent, walked five feet away and relieved himself.

"Breakfast ready yet, Claude?" he asked as he sauntered over to the fire.

"Almost," he replied, then said, "Hey, Noah, now that we're almost back, how about if you let me go back and have a good time with that redhead?"

"Are you still thinking about her? Good God, Claude!" he exclaimed with a laugh, then said, "Well, I'll tell you what. I'm in a good mood, and I think I can find my way back now. After breakfast, I'll take enough food and you can have the other horses and the mule and go back and do whatever you want with her, but no bullet holes. Okay?"

Claude grinned and replied, "Alright!"

Noah took out the two plates and tin cups for their breakfast while Claude prepared the last food he would ever eat.

Jack threw off his tarp, sat up and quickly scanned the campsite, his right hand already on his Remington's grip. It was an unusual way for him to awaken, and assumed it was because he was being protective of Mrs. Doyle and Joseph sleeping in their tent twenty feet away.

He didn't find any intruders, so he stood, walked to the still-bloodstained ground, answered nature's call, then returned to the brook to wash up. He took his bar of white soap from his saddlebags and another towel, walked to the brook and removed his shirt. He thought it was quite chilly, but not that bad. When he soaked the towel he'd given to Emily, the cold water changed his opinion, but he quickly ran the wet towel over his torso, turned to look at the tent, dropped his drawers quickly and ran the towel as low as he could reach before lathering the towel in soap and starting with the lower part, quickly soaped up the rest of his exposed skin. He rapidly rinsed the towel, then used it to remove the soap, then tossed it onto the rock, dried himself quickly, and pulled up his underpants and britches then put on his heavy flannel shirt. Relieved that he was able to wash without offending Mrs. Doyle, he then took time to rinse and wring out the wet towels and lay them on two boulders to dry before brushing his teeth. Shaving was still off the agenda.

He had the fire going and was rummaging through his packs for breakfast when Joseph popped out of the tent, waved, then trotted around the tent to head for the blooded ground.

When he returned just a few seconds later, he saw the soap and towels and asked, "May I use the soap, Mister Tyler?"

"Of course, you may, Joseph. The water is a bit brisk, so be ready for it."

"I will, sir," Joseph said as he took the soap and one of the towels.

As he washed his face, he asked, "When will I be old enough to shoot a gun?"

"It's not an exact age, Joseph. It's when a boy shows he's responsible enough to treat them with respect. Now, you've already done that, but I don't believe you're big enough to fire a man's gun.

ABANDONED

You have to have enough strength in your hands, too. But in your case, I think you'd be able to fire a gun in another year or so."

"Okay," he said as he dried his face.

Jack looked at him, then reached into his right pocket and pulled out his ivory-handled pocket knife. He'd found it in the same gun store in Cheyenne where he'd bought his '76. It wasn't a typical boy's pocket knife, but Joseph wasn't a typical boy.

He held it out to the boy and said, "Joseph, I want you to have this. It's not a boy's knife, either. That's a sharp, strong blade inside that is useful for almost anything. I've used it for a lot of things and once, I had to use it to kill a coyote that had gone mad."

Joseph's eyes were saucer-like as he took the knife in his hands and gazed at the almost luminous ivory handle. Carved in the handle was the head of a wolf.

"Thank you, Mister Tyler. This is the best gift anyone ever gave me. Why did you have to use it to kill the coyote?"

Jack had the big skillet on the fire and poured in some water from a canteen as he replied, "I was gathering firewood, so my arms were full when I heard a growl, saw this lone coyote about thirty feet away, then dropped the firewood and pulled my pistol. Just then, he sprang at me and knocked my Remington out of my hand. I knew I was in trouble, but my pistol was too far away as he leapt at me a second time and I was able to kick his gut and send him flying past me. I knew I couldn't let him bite me with those foamy teeth, so while he was recovering, I pulled out that knife and surprised him when I jumped on him and rammed the blade into his chest. He was snapping at me despite having the knife still in him, but he didn't last long. After he died, I burned his carcass so none of the other animals would get sick. Then, when I got back to camp, I washed the blade and let the flames lick it from my fire."

"Have you ever seen another mad animal?"

"No, just that one and it was enough. So, when you return to school, you can tell the other boys about your knife, and be sure to tell them about the wolf that's carved on the side."

"It wasn't there when you bought it?"

"No, sir. That carving was done by an Arapaho warrior. His fighting days were behind him, but he could carve. I was in their village doing some trading, mostly for information, and the warrior, his name was Standing Elk, saw the knife and offered to carve whatever I wanted in the knife handle. I gave him the knife and when he finished in just an hour, I gave him another knife that I had in my pack as payment."

Joseph opened the blade as a look of awe spread across his face.

Inside the tent, Emily had heard parts of the conversation as she contemplated sitting up on her own. Her right knee was still painful, but not as bad as it had been yesterday. It was her back that she knew could threaten their return to Laramie.

After laying unmoving for almost ten minutes, she decided to risk it. She couldn't stay in the bedroll all day. So, she placed her elbows on the ground and slowly pushed herself up. She shifted to her hands and soon was sitting upright. She slowly slid her legs out from the bedroll, leaned forward, then slowly rose. She was ecstatic at her pain-free success until she looked down and saw her shoes on the floor of the tent near her bedroll. *Did she dare to bend over and pick them up?*

She exhaled slowly, then decided she'd just endure the pain in her right knee rather than tempt fate and bend at the waist. She bent her knees, snatched up her shoes, then stood again before she walked slowly in her bare feet out of the tent but holding her shoes.

"Good morning!" she said brightly as she spotted Jack and Joseph at the fire.

Both turned to her and smiled.

ABANDONED

Joseph hopped up and trotted to her exclaiming, "Mrs. Doyle, you're walking!"

"Isn't it amazing?" she asked with a big smile as she continued to step carefully toward the fire.

"Do you need some privacy, Mrs. Doyle?" Jack asked.

"Um…let me go behind the tent for a little while and I'll return shortly," she replied.

Jack returned to cooking as she turned and began walking back toward the tent. This would be another test of her back, she thought.

———

In the other camp, Claude was happily saddling the animals. He had been surprised by Noah's offer and knew that the mule, horses and all the tack and supplies was a tidy little bonus. But it was the redhead that put him into the good mood.

He was hoisting the pack saddle on the mule when he heard the click of a Colt's hammer being pulled back behind him. Claude didn't even bother turning around because he knew what was coming next. *He was such a fool!*

That was the last thought he ever had when Noah pulled his trigger just four feet away. The .44 slug blew through Claude's chest, splintering ribs, exploding his heart, then breaking more ribs before punching through the pack saddle and slamming into the mule's chest.

The animal screamed in pain as it began to buck around the campsite, smashing Claude's body, then the nearby packs and panicking the horses.

Noah hadn't anticipated the chaos that resulted from the shot. He hadn't expected the pistol's bullet to pass through Claude, and as he backed away with the smoking pistol in his hand, he had to recover from what was turning into a disaster. He finally chased after the mule and began emptying his pistol into the animal as he tried to avoid the slashing hooves.

His pistol's hammer was falling on useless cylinders and he was thinking of getting one of the Winchesters when the mule suddenly collapsed to the ground in mid-kick and writhed for a few seconds, then huffed and died.

Noah was breathing hard as he slid his Colt back into his holster and surveyed the shambles of the camp. He didn't need much for the remainder of the ride, but his biggest concern was the relative proximity of the calamity to Laramie. There might be a hunting party on its way even now. He had to think fast and get on the way back.

First, he needed to get rid of Claude's body. He had already planned for that, so he walked over to the corpse, stripped off his gunbelt, then dragged the body across the dirt until he reached the edge of the stream.

He pulled Claude's body to the water's edge, then left it, picked up a long, dead branch he'd noted yesterday, and headed back to the stream. He rolled Claude's body into the water, then used the branch to shove the floating corpse into the middle of the stream where the rushing current quickly took it downstream. He watched the body float away until it was no longer visible.

Satisfied that Claude's body was no longer a concern, he walked back to the camp, saddled his horse and then Claude's animal, knowing one wasn't enough to move the mule's carcass.

He tied two ropes around the mule's neck, then walked them to the horses, tied them around the saddle horns, then led them toward the trees a hundred yards west of the camp. They both strained when the ropes pulled taut, but after a few seconds, the heavy body began to slide. It took a lot of effort by the two animals to get the mule's body deep into the trees, but once it was among the pines, Noah just cut the ropes, mounted his horse and rode back to the campsite, leading Claude's horse.

ABANDONED

Once there, he dismounted and began to move all of the gear into a small space behind some boulders to the north that was at best a decent hiding place, but he wasn't that concerned. If someone found them in a few days, he'd already be back in Omaha.

Now came the painful part. Noah took off his shirt, then cut off the sleeves and ripped the shirt into strips. After setting them down on the ground, he took out one of his spare shirts, sliced parts of the shirt's torso with his knife, rubbed it roughly in the dirt, then, after setting it on the ground with the torn cloth, stood and stared at his knife.

He exhaled, pointed the blade's tip at his ribs, closed his eyes and with his fingers near the tip to ensure that it didn't penetrate too deeply, sliced his skin. He only went two inches, but there was enough blood to meet his needs. He took the strips of the shirt he'd cut apart and quickly fashioned a bandage around the wound before putting on his other, sliced shirt. He wasn't sure if it was enough to fool anyone who suspected he might be lying about what had happened back in the mountains, but he also knew that no one should question him because he was an important man now.

An hour and a half after shooting Claude, Noah was riding out of the cleared campsite on his horse, having unsaddled the others and let them go free, hiding all of their tack with the packs behind the boulders. He didn't want to arrive in Laramie with the other horses. After all, he'd just heroically fought off a pack of wolves that had killed everyone else in the hunting party.

"Oatmeal?" asked Emily as she sat near the campfire.

"Yes, ma'am," Jack replied, "I add some dried apples and molasses, so it's pretty good."

He'd cooked the oatmeal in the frypan to free the small pot to boil water for Mrs. Doyle's tea.

After pulling the cooked oatmeal from the grate, he put on the small pot of water, then began spooning the oatmeal onto a plate, then handed it to Joseph with a spoon.

He added a large helping to the prospecting pan for Mrs. Doyle, gave it to her and asked, "Would you prefer the wooden spoon or the fork, ma'am?"

"I'll use the fork, if you don't mind."

"No, ma'am," he replied as he handed her the fork.

He began eating his oatmeal with the large wooden spoon as the water heated for Emily's tea.

"Your back seems to be doing better this morning, Mrs. Doyle," he said after blowing across the hot oatmeal in his spoon.

Emily swallowed and said, "Yes, it is. I've only felt a few warning tinges but no real pain. Do you think we can leave today?"

Jack had just put the oatmeal into his mouth, so he put up a finger while he chewed, and after he swallowed, he replied, "Let's play this by ear, ma'am. If you feel up to it, I'll saddle Abby and Billy and we'll try to put a few miles behind us after lunch. We'll take it slow and you have to tell me if you feel any pain at all. Okay?"

Emily smiled and nodded as she answered, "I won't hide anything. I promise."

Joseph then held out his new ivory-handled pocket knife and showed it to his nanny.

"Mrs. Doyle, look what Mister Tyler gave me! He had to use it to kill a coyote that attacked him and the wolf on the side was carved by an Indian!"

Emily smiled at him and said, "That's a very good knife, Joseph. You must take care of it properly. And I assume that you thanked Mister Tyler?"

ABANDONED

Joseph nodded vigorously, before answering, "Yes, ma'am. And I'll take care of it, too. This is the best gift anyone has ever given me."

"I'm sure it is," she said before taking another bite of her oatmeal.

Jack handed her a cup of tea, which she accepted and then set down to add some sugar.

"Do you think that they've made it back to Laramie by now, Mister Tyler?" she asked after taking a sip.

"They'll probably arrive in Laramie sometime today, but I'd be surprised if both of them made it."

Emily was startled then asked, "What do you mean?"

Jack had finished his oatmeal, so he set the frypan on the ground, and replied, "Well, Mrs. Doyle, I expect there's a good likelihood that either Claude will kill Mister Gallagher, or he'll kill Claude before they get back. That may even have happened yesterday. Claude Boucher is a greedy, unscrupulous man with no real concern for anyone, which is one of the reasons I was surprised that you were still unharmed. Now, Mister Gallagher, on the other hand, sounds like a cold-hearted excuse for a man, and wouldn't want anyone to know what he'd done. Claude would know that and might kill him first to avoid giving Gallagher the opportunity to shoot him. He'd be able to get the horses, mule, supplies and weapons in addition to whatever Mister Gallagher had of value by doing it, too. He returned four years ago without his hunting party and said they'd been stampeded by a herd of elk. None of us believed it, of course, but nothing could be proven."

In the case of these two, it would be just a question of whether or not Mister Gallagher had the sand to shoot Claude. He didn't shoot you and Joseph, so maybe he can't do it. He might try and shove Claude into a big creek while they were crossing or push him off of a rock cliff, but it would be difficult because Clause would be expecting it. Either way, I still think it's more likely than not that only one of them will arrive in Laramie."

"So, if only Mister Boucher reaches Laramie, what happens if we show up alive and well?" she asked.

"I've been thinking about that, and not if just Claude is in Laramie. There is another way to get you to return to Omaha without even going to Laramie. Saunders is a water stop for the trains about fifteen miles south of Laramie. I can take you there and get you on a train back to Omaha without anyone in Laramie knowing you're safe."

"But…" she began, then stopped.

She couldn't ask him to accompany them to Omaha. It wasn't fair. He'd already done so much for them and as much as she dreaded taking Joseph into the mess that would surely await them when they reached Omaha, she couldn't bring herself to ask any more of him.

Jack saw her troubled face and simply asked, "Mrs. Doyle?"

She shook her head and said, "It's nothing."

Jack knew that it was far from nothing, but let it go for now. There were at least three more days of riding before them and there would be time to talk on the way.

Noah was in a good mood, as he walked his horse along the trail back to Laramie. He was sure of his path, surprised to find their own hoofprints as the ill-fated hunting party left Laramie for the Medicine Bow Mountains. He was sure that Joseph and that annoying nanny of his were both dead already, and even if someone miraculously found what remained of their bodies, it would only substantiate his own story. He'd decided that rube or no rube, he'd have to tell his story to the sheriff in Laramie. He'd need to get his wound stitched as well. He'd send the telegram to Luke Casey to have him spread the horrific story so when he arrived, he'd be met with sympathy and praise before he sadly had to declare his nephew legally dead. He'd promise the board of directors that he'd run his company just as its founder, Joseph's grandfather, Joseph Charles Brennan had wished. Joseph's father, Joseph Charles Brennan, Junior, had been merely a caretaker of the company and had enjoyed the wealth and privilege that his father had created. Noah intended to follow the tradition of the founder's son but take it one step further. Before the end of the year, he'd sell the company, take his fortune and move back to St. Louis where Luke Casey had found him. No more hunting trips for him, unless it was hunting the affections of some wealthy man's daughter.

It was just after two o'clock when he picked up the poor road leading south out of Laramie. He had less than six miles left in his journey.

Back in the valley in the Medicine Bow Mountains, Jack had saddled Abby, adjusted the stirrups for Mrs. Doyle, then waited for Emily to approach the jenny.

Emily was anxious. Her back hadn't misbehaved all morning, and she'd been taking ever more risky twists and bends with only slight reminders of its precarious condition. This was going to be a big step, literally, when she put her left foot into the stirrup.

Jack thought she might be rushing the process somewhat but could understand her anxiety to return to Omaha. This was no life for a woman. She and Joseph belonged in the comfort of a nice house with a maid and a cook.

After breakfast, he and Joseph had walked to the other side of the tent, sat down and talked while Emily had followed a similar bathing process to the one that Jack had used earlier. She had been shocked by the cold water, just as he had been, but was desperate to feel clean again. She knew her long, deep red hair had to be shampooed, but left it in its bun for now.

As they sat behind the tent, Joseph asked and was told stories about Jack's life as a guide. He didn't embellish any of them, and actually glossed over the bloodier aspects, but they kept Joseph enthralled, so when Emily announced she was finished, he and Jack stayed put until he finished the last tale.

Now, it was time to see if she could ride. Jack had assured her that Abby was a very pleasant animal with a smooth gait, but after her experience with that other mule, she found it hard to believe.

She stood by the jenny, took a firm grip on the saddle horn, carefully placed her left foot in the stirrup, then took a deep breath and pulled herself up, swung her still painful right leg around the back of the mule and slid into the seat.

Emily grinned at the lack of pain from her back and said, "So far, so good."

Jack handed her the reins and stepped back as she started Abby walking through the camp. The mule made a wide loop and Emily was pleasantly surprised that she felt no ill effects at all. After she made the last turn toward the camp, she nudged Abby into a slow trot to see how her back reacted. When she felt no more pain, Emily broke into a big smile as the jenny approached Jack and Joseph.

She pulled Abby to a stop, and exclaimed, "It doesn't hurt at all!"

Jack smiled and said, "Then you just stay aboard Abby, I'll get Joseph on Billy and we'll head east."

"Okay," she replied happily.

They were on their way home.

Jack helped Billy into the modified pack saddle, settling him into the old army saddle seat, then tied a trail rope to Abby.

"Okay, folks, let's go," he said as he began walking east.

When he passed Emily, she asked, "Aren't you going to ride?"

"Not today, ma'am. I think we'll only get four or five miles behind us if we're lucky and I need to stretch my legs anyway."

ABANDONED

Emily wasn't sure, but nudged Abby to a walk as Joseph sat on Billy behind her, happy to be leaving this place.

In the forest near Claude and Noah's last campsite, a pack of wolves waited as a black bear began ripping the dead mule apart with its sharp claws. The pack leader, a massive eighty-six pound male, watched anxiously. He knew that his family could probably scare the bear away, but there was so much meat available that the risk wasn't worth it. Their biggest job was to keep the other predators away, so they could be the next in line to feast.

Further south, Claude's body had been pulled to the creek's edge by a big eddy and had been found by a pack of coyotes who dragged it onto the shore and begun a snapping, snarling race to eat as much as they could before any larger carnivores arrived. They hadn't really started to seriously eat when a big cat snarled nearby. They universally turned, saw the cougar as it walked and snarled to send them away from their kill, but the coyotes ignored her. There were eight of them and only one puma, and she was just bluffing. She could wait and if there was anything left when they finished, they might let her eat.

Jack glanced back at Mrs. Doyle and Joseph every few minutes as he strode quickly across the pine needle-strewn ground in the forest. She still wasn't showing any signs of distress, which didn't mean much while they were still moving. It was when she had to dismount that any problems would arrive.

Emily was convinced that her back was healed but was still wary as she rode Abby. She felt clean, well-nourished and safe, which made her almost laugh when she considered where she was. She was riding a mule in the middle of a wilderness forest behind a man who lived a solitary life with a wolf as his only companion. What had surprised her was how personable he seemed. Despite his stated preference for solitude, he'd surprised her even more when he had narrated virtually his entire life story, including his discovery of gold.

Why would he do that? He hadn't asked a single question about her life at all, but she believed it was out of courtesy, not lack of curiosity. She watched him as he walked confidently in front of them, wondering what tonight's conversations would reveal.

Jack wasn't at all surprised when he had been almost garrulous when he was with Mrs. Doyle and Joseph. Since he'd left the orphanage in Chicago almost twenty years ago, he'd lived his life almost exclusively in the company of men. The only women at the orphanage were the nuns who taught the girls and the girls were kept in a different dormitory and no contact was allowed, even in classes. The boys were taught by a combination of Franciscan brothers and lay teachers. After leaving the orphanage, there were the camp followers in the army, and similar women that followed the railroad as it pushed west, but they were businesswomen. The hunting parties he guided through the wilds of Wyoming Territory were all male, and the only boys were the incredibly thoughtless, impolite rich sons of those that hired him. Jack Tyler had rarely even talked to what he considered a normal woman or child. Mrs. Doyle and Joseph were both well beyond normal. They were both handsome, well-mannered and just enjoyable people to be around. So, when Mrs. Doyle asked questions, he answered them completely and without hesitation.

He realized suddenly that he knew Joseph's full name, including his middle name and the number at the end, but he didn't even know Mrs. Doyle's Christian name. He took a quick glance back at her as she sat contentedly on Abby and then tried to guess what it could be.

She was Irish, and therefore, he assumed, Catholic. As he had been raised at the Catholic-run orphanage, he was familiar with all of the saints, and his most likely guess was that her name was Mary. Almost a third of the women in the country were named Mary, and usually the first daughter in each Catholic family was christened with that name. But she didn't look like a Mary. Jack just didn't think there was anything common about Mrs. Doyle.

He began going down a mental list of the most common names for women, concentrating on those of Irish extraction. After ten minutes, for some reason, he settled on the letter 'e'. He didn't know any of the Gaelic names, and couldn't have pronounced them anyway, so he stuck with the standard English names. He lingered for a long time over the different versions of Elizabeth, but none seemed to fit. He was almost satisfied with Emma when he looked back once more and switched to Emily. Emma was too much of a homebody name, and he'd seen the fire in those blue eyes and liked Emily better. He wouldn't ask her what her Christian name was though. Beside the fact that he didn't believe it was right for someone in his station to even ask, he didn't want her to tell him it was Gertrude or Bertha.

———

Noah spotted the first buildings of Laramie in the late afternoon, and tossed his hat into the nearby grass, roughed up his dark brown hair, then set his horse to a slow trot to prepare for his grand entrance.

———

"How are you holding up, ma'am?" Jack asked after dropping back to walk beside Abby.

"I'm doing very well. How far do you think we've gone?"

"Farther than I'd expected. I think we're a good six miles from the last camp already. We'll be stopping soon, and I don't want you to try and dismount until I'm nearby in case you fall."

"I'll wait, but I'm pretty sure I'll be all right."

Jack nodded, then removed his Winchester from Abby's scabbard and trotted ahead again. He knew there was a good campsite ahead and if he was lucky, there would be game in the grassy clearing. He pulled away from the mules and slowed down as he approached the clearing. Before he even cleared the trees, he spotted a small herd of white-tailed deer grazing about a hundred and fifty yards away. It wouldn't be long before they heard the mules, so he dropped to a shooting position, cocked the hammer to his Winchester, and aimed at an old doe that wouldn't impact the herd. His finger was on the trigger when several of their heads popped up and turned to the west. He fired, just before the herd began to run. But the doe didn't move quickly enough as the massive .50 caliber round smashed into her chest and she toppled over.

The herd was racing away as the two mules exited the trees and Jack stood, returned to Abby and slid the rifle home.

"I'll go and dress the deer, Mrs. Doyle. Can you and Joseph ride to where that stream makes that small horseshoe?" he asked as he pointed to the spot.

"What about my getting down?" she asked.

"If you don't mind walking the six hundred yards, I'll help you down right now."

"I'd prefer to walk, if that's all right. My back may not be protesting, but my anatomy below the back isn't pleased."

Jack laughed, Emily smiled, then took a firm grip on the saddle horn, swung her right leg across Abby's haunches, then slowly lowered herself to the ground.

She sighed and said, "It only hurt when my right knee had to support all of my weight, but even that wasn't so bad."

"That's good, ma'am. It bodes well for the rest of the return trip."

Emily nodded, then turned to check on Joseph who had already dropped to the ground.

"We'll be waiting for you, Mister Tyler," she said as she took Abby's reins.

"I'll unsaddle and unload the mules when I return, but I need to get something from the packs first," he replied.

ABANDONED

He turned to Billy, flipped open the right pack, pulled out his empty game bag and the sack of salt, then waved at Emily and Joseph and headed for his deer.

Dressing the animal was less desirable on the ground, but it wasn't something unfamiliar to him, and after forty minutes had filled his game bag with salted venison, then dragged the remains of the carcass a few hundred yards further north. He knew it would attract the carrion-eaters, which were just about anything with sharp teeth, including those in the air, but with almost a mile between the campsite and the carcass, he was pretty sure they'd be safe.

He picked up the heavy bag of venison and the bag of salt, then headed back to where he could see Mrs. Doyle and Joseph about a half a mile away. As he walked closer, he looked at Mrs. Doyle and wondered how she had become a nanny and what her life had been like before she took the job. She had been married and probably widowed. She didn't impress him as being a woman accustomed to luxury, but as the late afternoon sun reflected off her dark red hair, he still couldn't believe that Claude Boucher hadn't tried to assault her. She was a handsome woman.

What remained of Claude Boucher was providing much needed nourishment to the female cougar as she ripped apart what had been left by the recently departed coyotes. She ate and kept her eyes scanning for any challengers to the meat. She was really only concerned with the bears. She didn't know that the mule's carcass in the trees was the main focus of three black bears who had reluctantly agreed to share the abundance while the wolf pack still waited patiently.

Albany County Sheriff Will Higginbotham listened as Noah Gallagher recited the horrible tale of the attack by a large pack of gray wolves after the hunting party had killed a large elk in the Medicine Bow Mountains. Noah was lying on Doctor Fred Adam's treatment table having his self-inflicted wound sutured.

The sheriff really didn't care that much about something that happened out in the wilderness, and even less as it involved only one local, and if Claude Boucher was dead, then he saw it as a positive. It was just another hunting accident, so he told Noah to stop by his office when he was finished, and he'd write up his account, so he could take it back to Omaha.

Noah thanked the sheriff before the lawman stood, then left the doctor's office to return to the jail.

Everything was working even better than he'd expected. Not one person in Laramie even seemed to care that three people were dead. There would be no investigation and the sheriff was even going to write a report listing all of the deaths as he had described the horrific event. That report would speed the whole process when he returned to Omaha.

———

As the sun was setting, Noah had the sheriff's brief report in his pocket, had sent the telegram to Luke Casey notifying him that he would be returning alone in two days because of a nightmarish attack by a large pack of wolves.

He'd bought all new clothes, checked into the Metropolitan Hotel and taken a nice bath, avoiding his recent sutures, then shaved and went downstairs to the marvelous hotel restaurant and enjoyed a full supper with a nice Chablis.

———

Supper may have been served in a more rustic manner at the campsite, but the ambiance was spectacular as the sun was setting in the mountains creating an awesome display.

Jack had fried three venison steaks, sprinkling on some more salt and black pepper. He'd used some of the pemmican for grease, but the flavors of the mix added to the much-appreciated taste of the meat. Once the steaks were out of the frypan, Jack tossed in some chopped up potatoes and onions along with some salt and pepper.

ABANDONED

They had to simmer for a while to soften the potatoes, so while it cooked, they enjoyed their steaks. Jack had his three other knives, which was handy, and he gave Mrs. Doyle the only fork after cutting his and Joseph's steaks. After he cut his steaks, he dropped them onto a small piece of canvas he'd cut from his large tarp.

"Now, Joseph, we can eat like men should," Jack said as he snatched up one of his chunks of venison steak and tossed it into his mouth.

Joseph grinned, then did the same as Emily watched with a smile as she cut her steak and put the piece into her mouth with the fork.

"This is amazing, Mister Tyler," Emily said as the meat touched her tongue.

"I'm glad you enjoy it, Mrs. Doyle."

Joseph had a mouthful of venison and just nodded as he smiled, and a line of grease slipped across his chin then dripped to the ground.

Jack smiled at him, but then turned to stir his simmering potatoes and onions.

As he stirred the rest of their dinner, he began to question his decision to remain living alone. It had always seemed it was just the way it was intended. There weren't many women out here in Wyoming. It was supposedly the reason that the Wyoming Territorial legislature had given women the right to vote, but he wasn't sure it made that much of an impact. It seemed that as soon as any unattached, marriageable age woman showed up, she'd have six proposals by her second day in town. Yet, here he was sharing food with a very handsome woman, who, if she stayed in Laramie, would have probably received forty or fifty marriage proposals before she had breakfast. He'd only been in Omaha for a few days before heading west but recalled that there were quite a few handsome young ladies in the city. But that being taken into consideration, he couldn't understand why Mrs. Doyle was still just a nanny. She seemed devoted to Joseph, but in the social environment she enjoyed, he couldn't understand why some wealthy widower hadn't tried to take her away from her life as a nanny. Whatever the reason, he'd never know because in three days, she'd be on her way back to Omaha with Joseph.

He tested the potatoes, found them soft, then began to add the side dish to the half-finished steaks. Once the frypan was empty, he set the small pot of water on the grille for Mrs. Doyle's tea.

An hour later, the dinnerware all cleaned, and the venison meat pack put away for tomorrow, Jack assembled the tent and he and Joseph dragged the bedrolls inside before returning to the fire.

The air was filled with howls, barking and yips as the animals all descended on the deer carcass a mile away.

"Will they stay over there, Mister Tyler?" Emily asked.

"Yes, ma'am. I'm sure they will."

Joseph then asked, "Mister Tyler, what do you do if you see a bear or a wolf?"

"Watch him. If he sees you and starts to head your way, the last thing you ever do is run. He's probably just curious, but if you run, you set off his prey instincts and he'll chase you down in seconds. If he gets closer, try and scare him by yelling at him or throw a few rocks at him. If he doesn't leave, then it's because he's really hungry or he's crazy. That's when you shoot him."

"But I don't have a gun."

"I do, Joseph. You just make sure you don't wander off. Okay?"

"Okay."

Joseph stayed up later than he had the night before, so the conversation revolved more about Jack's adventures as a guide and

ABANDONED

some of his war stories before Joseph yawned and Emily said that she'd join him in the tent.

"Good night, Mister Tyler," she said as she stood normally, not even giving her back a second thought.

"Good night, ma'am," he replied.

After saying goodnight to Joseph, Jack watched them both disappear into the tent.

Once they were safely inside, he picked up his Winchester, added more wood to the fire, then walked to the northern edge of the camp and looked across the moonlit field. He could see shadows in the distance accompanying the almost constant chatter of the animals as they queued for their opportunity to feed.

It was close to midnight when he finally returned to the campsite and stretched out on his bedroll, with the Winchester by his side.

CHAPTER 4

Jack had a venison breakfast cooking when Mrs. Doyle exited the tent, smiled and turned to walk behind the tent. Joseph walked out just two minutes later and didn't go far before he went.

"Good morning, Joseph," Jack said as the boy approached.

"Did any of them come here last night?" he asked.

"No, sir. They all stayed up there with the deer carcass. We won't have as many visitors tonight, though because I won't need to hunt."

Mrs. Doyle walked close to the fire and sat down on a rock near the stream.

"Good morning, Mister Tyler. How far are we going to ride today?"

"That will be your decision, ma'am. We'll leave after breakfast and we'll stop when you begin to feel uncomfortable."

Emily grinned and said, "What if I don't feel poorly until we reach Laramie?"

"Then I guess my feet will give up first," he answered smiling.

"You aren't going to walk again, are you?"

"No, ma'am. I was planning on letting Joseph ride with you and I'd ride with Billy."

She glanced at the two mules and said, "Won't that be hard on the mule? Joseph's weight and mine combined aren't two hundred pounds, but you and the packs must weigh over four hundred."

ABANDONED

Jack was decidedly uncomfortable as he replied, "Yes, ma'am, I'm aware of that, but I believe you'd be more comfortable with the arrangements."

"Nonsense, Mister Tyler. I'm not some prissy, well-mannered lady or a frightened young schoolgirl. I won't be in the least bit uncomfortable sharing the mule with you to keep the loads balanced."

"If you're sure about that, ma'am, then that's the way we'll do it when we leave."

"I'm sure, Mister Tyler," Emily said decisively, ending the discussion.

Emily glanced over at Joseph hoping he hadn't noticed her frank response, realizing that for the first time in years, Emily Ann Ward had snuck out of her closet and made an appearance. It had been a long time since that had happened.

Noah boarded the eastbound Union Pacific train at 8:20 and took his seat in the first-class coach, smiling at his fellow well-to-do passengers as he passed down the aisle. He was much more comfortable using this method of conveyance than he'd had to endure the past few days. When he returned to Omaha, he'd have the Brennan carriage available for his use, too.

He settled into his seat in the third row and looked out at Laramie and snickered. *What a bunch of buffoons!*

The train's whistle sounded, then the car lurched twice before it began to roll smoothly out of the station. Noah Gallagher was on his way to fortune.

Luke Casey stared at the telegram he'd found on his office desk when he'd arrived that morning.

He had held out hope that Noah wouldn't go through with his hideous plan, and now he was holding proof that he had actually done it. Ever since Noah had confronted him with his overbilling evidence, he'd felt as if he were Gallagher's marionette, dancing to the strings he tugged and released at his whim. Now, he knew it would get worse as Noah would be the owner of Brennan Furnace and Coal and what was remaining in the family fortune left by Joseph Charles Brennan, Junior.

He already had the papers in his desk declaring Joseph Charles Brennan III legally dead and awarding the family's assets to Noah Gallagher. Noah would be in his office early on Monday morning, the 30th of August and by the end of the day would be his boss. He suspected that Noah would sell the company soon enough, although he hadn't said anything to that effect. Luke just didn't see a man like Noah taking the time to run a company. Joseph Brennan built it and worked sixteen hours a day to expand it and make it into what it was today. His son, Junior, had just let the president, vice presidents and managers run the firm, putting in less than half the hours his father had while he enjoyed the benefits of his father's dedication. When Junior became a widower, he rarely even went to the company offices and lived lavishly. His sudden death had stunned everyone, and when Noah appointed the vice president of finance, Thomas White as president, everyone, including Thomas White, had been nothing less than shocked. What left him and everyone else stupefied was when Noah had left White in his finance officer position as well, which was a fiscally treacherous situation.

In all of his worries about the future of the firm and the pending return of Noah Gallagher, Luke Casey didn't spare thirty seconds of thought about the eight-year-old boy that Noah had left to die out in the wilderness, and none at all about his nanny.

He tossed aside the telegram, then removed the file with the legal paperwork which would enable Noah Gallagher to inherit the Brennan estate and the company. He opened the folder and reviewed it once again to make sure he didn't make any errors. He didn't want to get on Noah's bad side any more than he already was, but he wasn't about to spread the word of the boy's death until his murderer returned to Omaha.

———

Joseph was already atop Billy and watching as Mrs. Doyle mounted Abby first. If he hadn't been concerned about her back and knee, Jack would have been in the saddle and swung her around to his back, but he wanted her in the saddle seat, while he'd park his keister behind the seat on the bedroll.

Emily had the reins in her hands as she pulled her left foot free of the stirrup, let Jack put his boot in place, then push up and settle in behind her. She let him take the reins and leaned forward slightly, gripping the saddle horn when Abby began to walk. But her back was still pressed against Jack's chest and the constant contact was in the forefront of both of their minds.

Despite Emily's earlier denial that being close to Jack Tyler wouldn't bother her, she knew even as she said it that although it might be true from a moral viewpoint, it wasn't close to the truth for her emotional reaction. Having him so close was affecting her greatly and as much as she wished she could rein in her physical desires, the more she wanted to revel in them.

Jack was just as bad as he held Abby's reins and his arms touched Mrs. Doyle. Unlike Emily, though, he not only knew how difficult it would be, but how dangerous as well. It was dangerous on many levels, not the least of which was the distraction it was already causing. Distraction out here could be deadly, and he had two relatively helpless human beings to protect. He had to stay focused, despite having what he considered the most impressive woman he'd ever met pressed close against him.

Once they were underway, Jack asked, "Mrs. Doyle, who can help you when you get back to Omaha?"

It was one of the questions that had been weighing heavily on her since she realized that she and Joseph weren't going to die.

"I'm not sure if anyone can. Who would believe me and an eight-year-old? His uncle would probably have a convincing story already and if we suddenly arrived, he'd just act surprised and welcome us back as if it was a miracle, and the law would probably back him because of his position."

"How about your family?"

She gnawed on her lower lip for a few seconds before replying, "My father is a manager for the company and is the one who arranged for my interview for the nanny position. He wasn't very happy with me at the time and after I took the job, he made it clear that it was the last thing he would ever do for me."

"You're kidding?" Jack asked in disbelief, "Your own father would take the side of that bastard who left his daughter and a boy out in the wilderness to die?"

"I know it sounds terrible, but you have to understand that my father supported a very large family and never thought he'd be anything more than a day laborer, shoveling coal. He's very proud of his position at the company and would do anything to protect it."

"What kind of men do they grow in Omaha?" he asked in exasperation, before saying, "Well, ma'am, I was somewhat reticent to make the offer because it's not where I'd be comfortable, but I've changed my mind. If you'd like, I'll come with you to Omaha and back your story."

Emily was thrilled with his sudden offer and said, "I'd be ever so grateful if you did, but how can you help in Omaha? Noah will have all of the legal power behind him already by the time we get there. It will be very difficult to beat him."

"You're forgetting that what he did when he abandoned you and Joseph happened in Albany County, Wyoming, not Douglas County in Nebraska. I'll see Sheriff Higginbotham when we get back to Laramie and let him know what happened and that I'm escorting you back to Omaha. The crime was in his jurisdiction, so I'll get them to file charges for attempted murder and get them to issue a warrant."

ABANDONED

"Will that work?" she asked, her hopes rising.

"Yes, ma'am. It will work. Then, we get to Omaha and let them arrest the bastard. Then you and Joseph can return to your normal lives. This is all assuming that Mister Gallagher made it to Omaha and isn't already dead. If we arrive in Laramie and find Claude alive, he'll be arrested for murder and you'll be able to return by yourselves. You can just tell them what happened."

Emily nodded, but felt somehow that Noah was still alive and well. She was about to ask what he'd do after she and Joseph were back in the house but held her tongue. It wasn't her place to ask. But the specter of having to return with no protection and no one to trust was gone and she felt immensely relieved.

She finally just said, "Thank you, Mister Tyler."

"You're welcome, Mrs. Doyle."

After a stop to rest the mules, they shared some of the pemmican and trail mix for lunch before remounting and continuing the ride eastward.

Jack was very pleased with their progress and was happy with his decision to help. Unlike Emily, though, he expected to find Claude alive and Mister Gallagher dead. However, if he was wrong, he wanted to see Mister Noah Gallagher suffer and he wished he could be the one to administer the justice.

He hadn't asked Mrs. Doyle about her life at all and didn't even know how old she was. Looking at her, he estimated her age at around thirty, but she said she'd been a nanny for six years, and obviously married before that, so she might be a couple of years older, but not much more than that. Even if she was thirty, though, she looked younger.

After another forty minutes of riding, Jack looked back at Joseph, who was beginning to nod off and startled Mrs. Doyle when he suddenly broke out into song with his deep bass voice.

"What shall we do with a drunken sailor…"

After Emily's initial surprise, she laughed and joined in with her pleasant alto, "What shall we do with a drunken sailor…"

Joseph snapped out of his drifting and caught up with the adults, singing, "Early in the mornin'…"

So, in midafternoon on Saturday, August 28th, in the foothills of the Medicine Bow Mountains, hundreds of creatures in the trees, in their dens, grazing in the grass and those that were stalking them, were suddenly entertained by a chanty being sung by three human beings as they rode two mules out of their domain.

When the song ended, there was a brief pause before Emily lifted her voice and began to sing an Irish ballad in Gaelic that neither Jack nor Joseph understood at all, but it didn't mean they couldn't appreciate the beauty of her voice as she sang. The eight hoofbeats of the two mules added a soft rhythm as she softly sang of the love of a man for a lovely, but unreachable fairy. She loves him so much that she finally gives up her immortality to be with him but must watch him die soon after they are wed. She is so heartbroken that she simply lays down beside him and wills herself to join him in death. Yet, when she does, she discovers herself returned to the land of fairies, and finds her husband waiting for her.

It was a long tale told in song, and when she finished, neither Jack nor Joseph uttered a sound. To Emily, it was the greatest compliment she could have received.

They pulled up to stop for the night just twelve miles from where Noah and Claude had set up their last camp.

After Jack helped Emily from the saddle he asked, "How do you feel, ma'am?"

"Physically, just a little sore as you'd expect after a long ride, but mentally much better after your offer to come to Omaha."

"Good."

ABANDONED

Forty minutes later, with the horses stripped and the tent set up, Jack began making the fire for the last of their venison. He had thought about adding another day's worth of meat, but knew that if they kept up this pace, they'd be camping less than a day's ride from Laramie tomorrow night. He'd catch some steelhead trout for their supper to celebrate the occasion.

When he began to cook, Emily came and sat down on the log he'd moved over near the fire while Joseph sat nearby admiring his knife.

Jack didn't turn as he cooked the steaks, but said, "Mrs. Doyle, you have the most remarkable voice I've ever heard, but don't let it go to your head because I'm not a regular theater goer."

Emily laughed, then said, "No, I understand, but thank you for the compliment."

"That was a very touching song even if I didn't understand the words, but I don't want to know them, either. I feel as if it would lessen the beauty and mystery that I've created in my mind."

"Why, Mister Tyler, that's incredibly poetic and meaningful."

"I'm just saying what I believe, ma'am."

"Then I'll keep the lyrics to myself," she said before asking a prosaic question, "Mister Tyler, how much longer do we have?"

"Altogether, less than forty miles or so. We'll be able to reach Laramie the day after tomorrow, probably around noon or so."

"Are we going to ride directly to Laramie then, or are we going to go to Saunders as you suggested?"

He flipped the steaks, then looked at Emily and replied, "That's a good question. Before, when I expected to just drop you off in Laramie, I was concerned about your safety if Claude or Gallagher was still there, but if I'm with you, we can go straight to Laramie, so I can meet with Sheriff Higginbotham. Is that okay?"

"I think that might be better. It would give me and Joseph time to recover and rest before the return trip."

"Then we'll do that. We'll ride into Laramie, I'll get a hotel room for you and Joseph, then meet with the sheriff while you rest. I want to see if which of the two returned to Laramie, then I'll pick up some clothes for you both when I'm finished and take you to the hotel restaurant and let you both eat to your hearts' content."

"I doubt if we'd eat much better than what you've given us, Mister Tyler."

"Now that is a big fib, Mrs. Doyle. Even I like what I can get at a good restaurant better than what I can cook. I'll admit to being better than most men when it comes to cooking, especially on the trail, but a good prime rib is always welcome."

Emily laughed and admitted, "I beg your pardon for the obviously excessive compliment, but I meant well."

"And, I appreciate it, Mrs. Doyle," he said as he removed the steaks from the pan and handed the tin plate and prospecting tin to Emily and Joseph respectively.

He then dumped in the last of his cubed potatoes, onions and peppers into the pan and let them simmer while he cut his steak and ate it with the knife.

After they'd finished, and the cleanup was done, Emily was sipping her second cup of tea while Jack added wood to the fire. The temperature was falling rapidly, and Jack suspected that they'd wake in the morning to a blanket of snow.

Emily and Joseph were getting so accustomed to being in camp that they almost didn't notice the cries and howls that surrounded them, but none were close tonight.

After adding the wood to the fire, Jack poked it all into place with a branch, then sat on the log beside Emily leaving a proper three-foot gap, which was almost comical considering they'd been riding all day in physical contact.

Joseph was staring at the fire as he asked, "Mister Tyler, are you going to stay in Omaha with us?"

Emily turned to hear his response.

Jack knew it was another danger area, and replied, "No, Joseph. You need to return to your world and I need to come back here. You have to go back to school in a few days, don't you?"

"Yes, sir," he replied sadly.

"Think of all the stories you'll have to tell your friends. You faced up to a grizzly bear all by yourself, Joseph. How many other boys in the school have ever even seen a grizzly bear?"

Joseph cheered up instantly as he replied excitedly, "No one has except for me!"

"And you were really brave to do it, too. That bear probably weighed more than a thousand pounds."

Then he asked, "But I thought you told me he was a brown bear."

"He is, but grizzly bears are just big brown bears, and that giant boy had definitely earned the title."

Joseph grinned when he understood that he'd faced down a grizzly bear after all.

"And then, you can show them that knife and tell them I gave it to you because you were so brave. You can tell them it was used to kill a coyote and was carved by an Arapaho warrior. Don't call him an Indian because it's kind of an insult. It sounds like you know what you're talking about when you say it was an Arapaho who carved the wolf's head."

"I will, Mister Tyler."

Jack smiled at Joseph, pleased that he'd deflected the questions about his returning to Wyoming. He knew it was the only thing he could do, but he surely would miss the boy. Yet he felt that he would do more than miss Mrs. Doyle. He began to believe he was losing what may be his only opportunity to be truly happy. But he knew she was dedicated to Joseph and would have to stay with him in Omaha, at least until he was eighteen, and after that, she'd probably just stay as his matron to run his household.

The idea made him a bit queasy.

As they sat around the campfire, Noah Gallagher's train rolled into the massive Union Pacific station in Omaha, passing other trains as they moved on different tracks preparing to head east, south, north and west along the ever-expanding web of tracks owned by the U.P.

He stepped onto the main platform with a travel bag he'd bought in Laramie and walked to the entrance of the station, hailed a cab, gave the cabbie his apartment's address on Cuming Street and stepped inside.

When Noah had first been appointed Joseph's guardian, he'd been prepared to move into the big house on Chicago Street, but realized he'd have to behave himself all the time if he was there. He had to build a bond of trust and likability with the boy, and that would be impossible if he wanted to enjoy himself. Besides, that damned nanny watched over him like she was his mother and not a paid employee. She never had trusted him, so he'd spent just enough time to get the boy to like him. It had finally paid off and he'd gotten rid of the tiresome nanny, too.

After the cab lurched away from the station, he leaned back in the leather cushion and smiled. Tomorrow was Sunday, so he'd just relax and recover from the exhausting trip, then he'd move into his new home and give the staff the news. But on Monday, he'd begin the last stage of his plan to claim the Brennan inheritance and the company. Well, at least for three months, he reminded himself as he snickered. Then, once divested of that millstone, he'd be off to St. Louis as a wealthy man.

———

Joseph was already in the tent, and Jack was letting the fire die as Emily still sat on the log to his left.

When Joseph had asked his question about whether Mister Tyler would be staying in Omaha, she wasn't surprised by his reply. She had misread the reason for his answer, believing that he simply wished to return to the solitary life that he seemed to enjoy. She would have been astounded had she known the actual reason.

"Are you going to have to make another trip to Cheyenne to drop off your gold, Mister Tyler?" she asked.

"Yes, ma'am. If I knew it didn't take them so long to assay and weigh the gold, I'd take care of it on the way to Omaha, but I might bring it along and do it on the return trip."

"That's a lot of gold to be taking on the train."

"Not really. I've taken heavier bags. I don't ride first class and I don't appear to be anyone worthy of robbing, either."

"I'd be more inclined to believe that they'd be frightened of you."

"I admit that I'm a bit scary-looking, mostly to young children."

"No, that's not what I meant, and you probably knew that just to get a compliment. You're just a very strong-looking man who wouldn't hesitate to stop anyone who tried to take what wasn't theirs. As far as your looks are concerned, I'll be perfectly honest when I tell you that I find you quite handsome."

Jack looked at her and blushed, grateful it was so dark, then replied, "Coming from you, ma'am, I'll take the compliment but recommend you get your eyes checked back in Omaha. As to the other part, I'll admit to being angered when I see someone being treated unjustly. Although, in all my years, I've never seen anything close to how horribly you and Joseph have been treated. One of the reasons I decided to accompany you all the way home was to meet Mister Gallagher and render some sort of justice myself, but I suppose that would get me in trouble with the law and might get him off, too."

"Yes, I believe you're right. I'm just very happy you're coming with us."

"So, am I, ma'am, and I won't leave until I'm sure that you and Joseph are safe."

"I know you wouldn't, Mister Tyler. I've come to believe that you're Joseph's guardian angel."

"He's a fine boy, Mrs. Doyle and after a few more years under your guidance, I'm sure he'll become a good man."

Emily sighed and said, "I hope I can deal with him in a few years. Right now, I'm all he has, but soon, he'll be meeting others who may try and take advantage of him."

"You'll be able to handle it, ma'am. You've got more sand than most men I know."

Emily smiled and said, "Thank you, Mister Tyler."

It was getting late and as much as she would have preferred to stay awake and talk, she knew that they had two more days of riding before a day and a half of train travel. She needed her rest.

"I believe I'll turn in now. Good night, Mister Tyler."

"Good night, Mrs. Doyle," Jack said as he rose.

Emily stood, smiled and then headed for the tent and disappeared inside.

Jack exhaled, then sat back on the log and looked at the embers. His way of life was being tossed around more than a brig in a tempest. Just a few days ago, he'd begun a routine return to his cabin and now, he might be going to Omaha and try and stop lawyers and well-dressed businessmen from trying to take a young boy's inheritance, or even try to kill him again. Life was a lot simpler when he could just shoot the problem.

He hoped that Claude had killed the bastard, so his life would be simpler, but then admitted to himself that he wished Gallagher was still alive, too.

But no matter what problems he met if he had to go to Omaha, nothing would bother him more than leaving the city to come back to his cabin, yet he knew that he must. He simply didn't belong there.

After pulling off his boots, Jack lay on his bedroll, pulled up the tarp and spent some time watching the moon and the stars. He began counting shooting stars that streaked across the sky to keep his mind from drifting to the redheaded woman sleeping in the tent so close by. He reached twenty-two before he slipped into sleep.

Jack was up early as usual and was preparing a breakfast of oatmeal again when Joseph popped out of the tent and trotted around behind the tent for a minute, before appearing on the other side and jogging over to the fire.

"Good morning, Joseph," Jack said.

"Good morning, Mister Tyler," he replied, then took his tin plate and spoon before sitting down next to him.

"Hungry, sir?"

"I think I'm always hungry," Joseph replied.

"Well, we'll get that stomach of yours all filled up when we get into Laramie tomorrow."

"Tomorrow? We're going to be there tomorrow?"

"Yes, sir. Unless we get eaten by bears or something."

Joseph laughed as Emily approached the fire and picked up the prospector's pan and the fork.

"Mrs. Doyle, Mister Tyler said we'll be getting to Laramie tomorrow!" Joseph exclaimed.

"I know, dear. He told me last night."

Joseph was still grinning as Jack began spooning oatmeal onto his plate, then adding some to Emily's.

He poured the hot water into her tin cup and let her add her own sugar while he ate.

Tomorrow, he thought. Tomorrow their time alone would be over, and things would begin to change. There were really only three possibilities when they arrived in Laramie involving the two men, but no matter what happened when they arrived, it would still be their last day alone. He didn't believe either Joseph or Mrs. Doyle would treat him any differently, but he would feel different. She and Joseph would be moving out of his world and back into theirs.

It would start tomorrow when they reached Laramie.

But today was another day of travel and he wanted to get at least thirty miles behind them which would only leave a short ride for tomorrow. It would mean pushing it a bit, but Mrs. Doyle seemed to be holding up very well.

Forty minutes later, Jack was riding behind Mrs. Doyle as they had Abby moving at a medium trot heading into a big forest.

It had been long two days that the wolf pack had been denied access to the mule's carcass. First, it had been the lone black bear, then he was joined by two others. Just after they'd finally gone, leaving less than half of the meat, the wolves had viciously descended on the carrion and had managed less than two minutes of feeding when a massive brown bear arrived and sent them all scurrying back into the woods. They'd gone off hunting for other prey and found nothing nearby.

Now, they'd returned to the mule carcass to find another black bear sitting astride the dwindling food supply. Their patience was nearing its end as they were all hungry. The pack leader finally decided it was worth the risk and the gray wolves began to close in on the black bear. When they were within fifty feet, the leader initiated the threat with a deep growl and exposed fangs.

The bear knew they were there long before the threat but ignored them for the time being. She was feeding heavily and wasn't about to give up her find.

The wolf pack leader's mate then added her growling warning to the black bear, which was followed by those of her three daughters and their son. It was a sound that would have struck fear into the hearts of any other creature in the forest, but not the bear.

But, knowing the wolves were closing in, she knew that she had to let them know she wasn't about to be intimidated.

They were thirty feet away when the bear suddenly rose to her hind legs, stretched out her arms and long claws, tilted her massive head back and roared her own threat. She may not have been as big as a brown bear, but for a female black bear, she was large enough to impress the wolves.

The leader then stopped his growl and backed away a few feet to reevaluate his decision while the bear remained standing, just watching them.

He'd just decided to renew the attack when a second black bear, attracted by the sound, came trotting in from the trees and ignoring the confrontation, just ran to the carcass and buried his nose in the carcass. The first black bear dropped back down to her four legs and renewed her feeding, allowing the second bear to share. She might not be happy about it, but it was better than giving it up to the wolves.

Admitting defeat again, the wolf leader led his pack away from the mule's remains, and when they were a couple of hundred yards away, settled down so they could watch the bears and await their departure.

When they stopped at their first break, Jack walked to the hoofprints left by Boucher and Gallagher and dropped to his heels to study them in detail.

Jack had been following the trail of the two men ever since they'd left the original camp where he'd found Mrs. Doyle and Joseph. He'd found their two campsites, which meant Claude was probably in a saloon or whore house by now and Gallagher was already back in Omaha. That was assuming that they were both still alive, which he doubted. He was convinced that one was already dead, and as much as he detested Claude Boucher, he hoped that the guide would be the only one returning to Laramie.

The odds were in Claude's favor. He was a ruthless, but cautious man who trusted no one. Men like that always suspect the worst in others and if Gallagher was planning on killing him, he'd never be able to get the drop on Claude. But if Claude wanted to dispose of the city-dweller, he could do it whenever it suited him. But in examining the hoofprints, he knew that both men were still alive. There had been no sudden drop in the weights that were being carried by the animals. The absence of vultures didn't mean much because if Claude had done the killing, he would have taken time to bury the body, so it wouldn't attract attention.

Mrs. Doyle stepped up behind him and asked, "What are you looking for, Mister Tyler?"

"I'm checking to see if either one has killed the other yet, ma'am, and it appears that they're still both alive. Honestly, I'd prefer that

ABANDONED

Claude Boucher was drinking whiskey in Laramie and Mister Gallagher was dead. I'd have Claude arrested and hanged, but your problem would be solved."

"Do you think that's possible?"

"It's more than likely, Mrs. Doyle. I can't imagine how Mister Gallagher could ever surprise Claude, but I don't know him well enough. What do you think?"

"That's just it. I don't know him well enough, either. I know he presents a polished exterior, but he may be just as ruthless as Mister Boucher."

Jack stood and turned to face Emily as he said, "But there's still that lingering question that I'm sure you had about his plan to eliminate Joseph. It was overly complex and left a slight chance for you and Joseph to survive. I just don't understand it."

"Neither do I. We'll probably never know, will we?"

"No, ma'am," he replied, then noticed that Joseph was already aboard Billy, and added, "I guess Joseph wants us to get moving again."

Emily turned, saw Joseph looking at them and said, "I think so," before they both headed for Abby, remounted and continued to ride east.

In Omaha, Noah was exulting in his first full day's return to civilization. He'd slept late before he bathed and shaved, then had a big breakfast at his favorite restaurant, P. Madison's.

When he returned to his apartment, he sat at his desk to write down his tasks for tomorrow. He'd see Luke Casey early, then he'd call an emergency meeting of the board of directors to give them the horrible news, and then he and Casey would go meet with Judge Lawrence D. Carstairs and have him issue the orders officially declaring Joseph Charles Brennan III deceased and naming him the legal heir to the Brennan estate. Maybe he'd treat Luke Casey to lunch or dinner, depending on how long it took.

He'd already packed his bags, which emptied all of his personal effects from the apartment and would move them to the big house when he finished writing.

He smiled at the thought as he picked up the pen.

Jack was still trying to keep his focus on his surroundings and away from Mrs. Doyle as he had Abby at a slow trot. He'd thought that after the first few hours, he'd get used to having her there and his distress would lessen, but just the opposite was true. The longer she was there, the more he became acutely aware of her femininity.

But it wasn't his eyes that suddenly snapped him out of his distraction, it was his sense of smell when he picked up the putrid scent of rotting flesh as they passed through the forest. A large animal had died nearby and that meant that predators would be near.

Emily scrunched her nose and asked, "Did something die?"

"Yes, ma'am. It was big, so it was probably a bear or maybe an elk. That means that there are probably more bears and wolves around, so keep your eyes open," he answered loudly so Joseph could hear.

Joseph heard his reply and began to search the surrounding trees but didn't see anything.

The reason that none of them could spot any threats was that they'd already passed the waiting wolves, who were just quietly studying the mule carcass and its two black bear feeders.

When they passed, though, the youngest female turned her head and picked up the same mule scent of the dead carcass and immediately yipped her discovery to the leader, who had just identified the scent as well.

The wolf pack leader stood and then led his family away from the carcass to follow the live mules.

The forest suddenly gave way to a wide open area with a large creek and Jack immediately spotted the signs of Noah and Claude's last camp.

"There's their campsite, ma'am," he said as he pointed past Emily.

"Are we going to stop?" she asked.

"Yes, ma'am."

Then, she spied something to her left, pointed and exclaimed, "I think that's my travel bag!"

Jack turned at the outcrop of boulders and saw the top half of a yellow and red flowered fabric and immediately turned Abby in that direction, towing Billy and Joseph behind.

When they were closer, Jack noticed more supplies and said, "Well, Mrs. Doyle, it looks as if only one of them left the campsite or all that gear wouldn't be there."

"One of them was killed here?" she asked, suddenly scanning the open ground.

Jack had already done so and spotted several large dark patches and wondered why there was so much blood.

"Yes, ma'am. I believe so, and I'm sure that it's Claude that's dead. If he'd eliminated Mister Gallagher, he would have kept everything," he replied, but kept Abby heading for the cache of supplies.

They reached the boulders, and Jack slid down before helping Emily to the ground. Joseph dropped from Billy and raced to follow Mrs. Doyle as she walked quickly around the boulders to her travel bag.

Jack let them go as he walked away from the two mules to study the ground around the campsite.

As Emily pulled her travel bag from the stack and Joseph began rummaging through the packs, Jack walked among the massive amounts of dried blood and knew that it wouldn't have come from one man because of the wide disbursement. He was initially puzzled, but then as he walked further, he spotted the signs of animal chaos and the wide path left by a large animal being dragged into the trees. That was the carcass he'd smelled.

He was about to return to the mules when he spotted something he hadn't expected to see. Vultures were circling about eight hundred yards south of the camp. They were right above the creek, so Jack knew that was where he'd find Claude's body.

Jack knew that somehow Noah Gallagher had caught Claude Boucher by surprise and shot him. Maybe it was when he was on his horse and had shot the horse first, which would account for the blood and the dragged animal.

But it also meant that down the creek, below the vultures, he'd be able to retrieve evidence of Boucher's murder and the ruthless guide would finally have done some good when Jack would be able to get a murder warrant for Noah Gallagher.

He turned and walked quickly toward the mules where he could see Mrs. Doyle and Joseph happily rediscovering their possessions.

They both looked at him with grins as Emily held her hairbrush in her hand.

"Mrs. Doyle, I'm pretty sure that Mister Gallagher killed Boucher and his body is down by the creek a half a mile or so. I'm going to go down there and see if I can collect some evidence to prove it to the sheriff. Having Gallagher charged with murder is much better than attempted murder."

"Okay. How long will you be gone?"

"Only a few minutes, but do you see all the saddles there? That means he must have let the horses go, too. They'll probably be close by, and all bunched together, too. I'll look for them on the way."

"Okay. We're not going anywhere."

Jack was untying the trail rope to Billy, as he replied, "No, ma'am, I reckon not," then mounted Abby and turned her south to the buzzards, glancing at the nearby trees for any signs of movement, but not seeing anything.

The reason he hadn't seen any movement was because the wolf pack leader was studying the situation in the clearing from fifty yards beyond the tree line. He watched one mule ride away with a man on top, and then turned his attention to the other mule just standing there by himself. There were two humans nearby, but they were fifty feet away.

The mule had formidable defenses with those hooves, but the wolves were all hungry and the recent taste of mule meat had whetted their appetites. He decided to launch a coordinated attack on the mule.

Jack had Abby moving at a medium trot and quickly ate up the distance to where he expected to find Claude's remains. When he arrived, he wasn't shocked to find almost nothing left of the guide after that much time with the carrion eaters. But he didn't care about the mostly skeletonized remains. He needed evidence.

Jack dismounted, then pulled his Bowie knife as he approached the body. He used the toe of his boot to flip the center of the corpse, saw the bullet hole, then, holding his breath, bent over and cut out most of the back of the shirt, grateful that Claude had been wearing a Union suit. He stepped back with the rag in his hand, blinked his eyes before looking down at the boots and knew that Claude's distinctive, rattlesnake hide boots would be conclusive evidence of his identity. He took another deep breath, stepped closer, dropped to his heels and quickly cut the right boot down the side and yanked it free, bringing most of Claude's right foot and ankle with it.

He stepped quickly away, gagging as he did. Once he was a good fifteen feet away, he used his knife to cut away the rest of the boot to the toe, then pried it apart and dumped the hideous tissue and bones from the boot.

He then turned and trotted back to Abby, leaned against the saddle and took several deep breaths. He had seen a good number of deaths in his life, especially during the war, but nothing had affected him as this had.

As he was trying to regain his composure, the wolf pack left the protection of the trees to begin its attack on the mule. They fanned out and slowly approached the animal, blocking all avenues of escape as the boulders hemmed it in from the front. They were upwind of the mule, so it wasn't aware of their approach and neither were the two humans.

The two humans were busy opening the supply pack and discovering more items that were suddenly much more precious than they'd been when they started the trip. Neither of them knew that just eighty yards away, six gray wolves were closing in for the kill.

Jack finally took the sliced boot and walked to the edge of the creek and rinsed it as best he could. He was turning around and heading back to Abby when he glanced north and saw the wolves.

He kept the boot in his hand and sprinted to Abby, tossed the boot into his saddlebag, hopped into the saddle and sent her quickly north at a fast trot as he pulled his Winchester and cocked the hammer.

Emily had her clean riding dress in her hands and smiling when she heard the unnerving sound of a deep growl and froze for a

ABANDONED

second, before dropping the dress and jumping to her feet. Joseph was still rummaging when the growl reached his ears and his head jerked up and he saw the wolves.

Billy whipped around at the sound and his head began to rock back and forth as he tried to find a way past the wolves. Instinctively, he knew that if he tried to run past them, they'd bring him down, so he turned quickly to prepare to blast out with his hind hooves at any that came close.

Emily's eyes were transfixed on the wolves, not understanding that she and Joseph were relatively safe, and that Billy was the wolves' target.

She didn't know where Jack was but saw the stock of the single-barrel shotgun sticking up from Billy's scabbard and quickly ran to the mule and pulled the scattergun while Joseph ran behind her, pulling his pocket knife and extending the blade. Neither realized that by getting closer to Billy, they had just placed themselves in great danger.

As she stared at the closing pack of wolves, their sharp teeth bared and growls rumbling from their chests, she cocked the shotgun and finally screamed, "Jack!"

Jack was still two hundred yards away when he heard her scream his name and egged Abby to a faster speed to close the gap.

The wolves were startled by Emily's scream, but it had the opposite reaction when the leader felt a sudden sense of urgency and launched himself at the mule. Emily pulled the trigger and the shotgun pounded against her shoulder, releasing a large cloud of gunsmoke and hundreds of tiny pellets of birdshot.

Two of the she-wolves felt the sting of the pellets, but the roar of the shotgun stunned them more than the small projectiles.

Billy kicked out at the leaping male pack leader but missed as the big wolf slammed into the mule's haunches, grabbing with his claws and sinking his teeth into the mule's exposed muscle near the packs.

In her panicked terror, Emily pulled back the hammer again and pulled the trigger before realizing her mistake. Joseph then pushed in front of Mrs. Doyle and brandished his knife at the animals who had recovered from the shock of the shotgun blast.

He began to shout at them as Emily reached for him and tried to pull him behind her.

Billy was still trying to fight off the big wolf who was joined by two others while the last three suddenly focused on the defenseless humans just thirty feet away.

The leader's mate had her teeth bared and her haunches tight as she prepared to spring at the big human who was hiding her cub behind her, just as she would protect her young.

Jack was less than a hundred yards out when he knew he had no time to waste and pulled Abby to a fast halt to have a steady firing platform. He'd shot from her back before and hoped she wouldn't suddenly get skittish in the presence of the wolves.

He brought his sights to bear on the animal closest to Mrs. Doyle, and once the wolf was centered, squeezed the trigger. The powerful Winchester .50-95 Express cartridge was ignited when the hammer fell, and the firing pin struck the center cap. The large caliber bullet spun down the thirty-six inches of rifled steel adding critical spin to the aerodynamic chunk of lead.

The bullet exploded out of the muzzle at over twelve hundred feet per second, and despite the air's resistance, covered the distance between Jack and the she-wolf in a little over a fifth of a second.

Emily's eyes were glued to the yellow eyes of the approaching wolf and could see the large wolf's muscles tensing for a killing leap and hoped that Jack would return in time to save Joseph when the wolf suddenly exploded before her eyes and was quickly followed by a loud roar.

ABANDONED

She whipped her head to the left, saw Jack on Abby and began to shudder in relief, despite the other wolves nearby.

The rest of the pack, even the three that had been ripping at Billy, all stopped and turned at the sound, not even noticing the destruction of the matriarch of the pack.

Jack wasn't finished by a long shot. He hadn't waited after hitting the first wolf, but quickly levered in his second round and while the other wolves were still watching, fired his second round at one of the other wolves in front of Mrs. Doyle and Joseph.

The only other male wolf in the pack felt the impact of the bullet as it smashed through his chest and threw him two feet to his left. He didn't move after hitting the ground.

Now, the wolves had to decide to confront the attacker or run.

When the third wolf in front of Mrs. Doyle was Jack's third victim, the decision was immediate and the remaining three dropped from Billy, who was beginning to wobble from the wounds he'd received, and as soon as the pack leader had yelped his decision, they were racing toward the trees, a hundred yards away.

Normally, Jack would have let them go, but not this time. He knew the leader was in the front of the escaping wolves and led him before squeezing his trigger, his fourth shot almost decapitating the leader of the pack as the massive round punched through his neck.

The other two kept running, but Jack picked off the fifth before she reached the trees, and the last escaped into the pines. Jack knew she wouldn't return.

He then nudged Abby to a fast trot to reach Mrs. Doyle and Joseph. He didn't think that they'd been hurt, but it had been close, and he knew they both must have been terrified.

After seeing the nearest wolf blasted away just a few feet in front of her as it was preparing to spring, Emily hadn't noticed the other wolves' deaths, but stared down at the big female that lay just three feet in front of her.

Joseph had watched as he peered from behind Mrs. Doyle's skirts, and was amazed at Mister Tyler's shooting skills as he picked off one wolf after the other.

Now, he watched as Mister Tyler trotted close on Abby, slid his rifle back into its scabbard, then quickly dismounted.

Jack rapidly approached the obviously shaken Emily Doyle, and asked, "Ma'am? Are you all right, Mrs. Doyle?"

Joseph stepped out from behind her and replied, "That big one was getting ready to attack us, Mister Tyler, and I think Mrs. Doyle was very afraid. She pushed me behind her to save me."

"I saw that, Joseph. She's a very brave lady. But even brave people can be afraid."

Emily blinked, then pulled her eyes slowly from the wolf saw Jack standing in front of her then put her hands over her face and began to cry, shaking violently.

Jack put his arms around her and felt her shuddering as she wrapped her arms around him and let the terror that had just taken over her mind drain through her tears.

As she shook, she stammered, "It…it was going to kill us, Jack. Those teeth…those eyes…"

"It's all right now, Mrs. Doyle. That last one won't return. It will have to go and see if another pack will take it in. You're safe now. I'm here and I shouldn't have left you and Joseph alone, not for a minute."

She was still shuddering and crying as Jack held her then began to sing the one song of which he knew every word of every verse from having heard it so often.

"Mine eyes have seen the glory of the coming of the Lord…"

Emily could feel the deep vibrations in his chest as his deep bass voice filled the air around her. It was a battle hymn meant to inspire the Union forces, but to her, now, it was much more. She listened to each word and let them flow through her.

Jack sang all five verses of the song, and finished the last stanza with a powerful, "Glory, glory, hallelujah! While God…is…marching…on!"

Emily just stayed and listened to his pounding heart for another fifteen seconds. Her fear was gone and all she felt was an immense peace and security she wouldn't have imagined possible just a short time ago.

She finally released her arms, and Jack immediately did the same as she stepped back, exhaled and wiped her face with her hands.

She swallowed, then said, "Thank you, Mister Tyler. I apologize for being so upset."

Before Jack could reply, Billy emitted a loud bray to let everyone know he was in pain. Jack turned to his mule and saw the deep gouges and scratches that the wolves had inflicted on him and didn't know if he'd be able to go on.

He stepped over to Billy, then began stripping him as he bucked and jumped when the heavy packs and leather crossed the tears in his hide.

Jack just dropped them all in place and grimaced as he examined Billy's wounds.

"How bad are they?" Emily asked as she walked to Jack's side.

"They're not fatal, but they'll keep him from carrying anything. I'll take some of the fat from those wolf carcasses and spread it on his wounds, which will be all I can do for him."

"Is it safe to stay here?" she asked.

"It will be when I get rid of the carcasses. I'll just toss them in the creek over there and let them go downstream."

Joseph asked, "How will we get home, Mister Tyler?"

"I'll look for the horses that Mister Gallagher cut loose, but if I can't find them, we'll take what we need, and you and Mrs. Doyle can ride Abby and I'll walk alongside. We won't get back as soon as we had planned, but we'll get there by tomorrow night, I think."

Joseph glanced at the nearby water and said, "That's a big creek, Mister Tyler. How can you get across?"

"It's not a problem. I'll just walk across and not even get my feet wet, Joseph."

Joseph giggled and looked at Mrs. Doyle who was just smiling. Their almost pleasant day may have been turned into chaos by the arrival of the wolf pack, but she and Joseph were untouched and for that, she was grateful. She was much more thankful for Jack Tyler.

Jack picked up the shotgun, then walked back to his pack, pulled out a box of twelve gauge #4 buckshot shells, replaced the used shell with the new one, then gave it back to Mrs. Doyle.

"This is loaded with buckshot now. It'll kill anything close short of a bear and if you hit him in the face, he's not going to stick around."

She accepted the scattergun and said, "Thank you, Mister Tyler."

"You're welcome, ma'am," he answered, neither of them acknowledging her use of his Christian name when she was in danger.

As he returned to Abby to search for the horses, he glanced back at Mrs. Doyle who was walking hand-in-hand with Joseph back to the recovered supplies and confirmed his belief that her first name was Emily. He almost hoped he never found out her real name, but knew it was just a matter of time before he was disappointed. He climbed back into Abby's saddle thinking, "Harriet Doyle?"

He rode to the creek, expecting that if the horses were in the area, they'd stay near water and was rewarded when he looked to the north and spotted three animals about a mile and a half away. He wasn't sure they were horses, though. They could be elk or deer, although he doubted it.

―――

Noah stood before Anna Thornton, Mary Flaherty and the stork-like Wilbur Moore with his two travel bags on the floor behind him.

"I don't know if you've heard yet, but there was a horrible incident on the hunting trip. Our camp was attacked by a large pack of wolves and everyone was killed. I escaped with just a large gash to my side. I'm sure that you're all as upset as I am by this tragic event, but life must go on. I'll be moving into the large bedroom and expect you to continue your duties as before."

They all nodded, and only the cook, Anna, seemed to be shaken by the announcement of the deaths of the boy and Emily. She considered Emily a friend as well as a fellow employee.

"You're all dismissed. Mister Moore, take my bags into my room."

Wilbur Moore bristled and replied, "Sir, Miss Flaherty should do that. I am the steward of this household."

Noah raised his eyebrows.

"Mister Moore, your job is what I say it is. Now, move my bags," he snapped, then smiled at Mary Flaherty and said, "Besides, Miss Flaherty is much too pretty to be doing such strenuous work."

Mary Flaherty smiled coyly at Noah while Wilbur Moore grudgingly walked past his new boss, picked up the two heavy bags, and carried them to the big bedroom in the second floor.

Noah had his eyes on Mary Flaherty for some time now and thought she'd be entertaining until he left for St. Louis. It wouldn't matter what her condition would be when he departed. If the new owner of the house didn't mind having a pregnant maid, she might even keep her job.

Jack set Abby to a trot so they wouldn't be gone too long and soon was gratified to see three horses all staring at him and they were on this side of the wide, deep creek that would have been called a river in many parts of the country.

The horses watched him approach, and unlike the wild creatures that called the area home, were happy to see a man. None had been born mustangs and preferred the comforts of a barn and the regular supply of oats that men provided.

Jack reached the horses, then made a loose trail rope looping it around each horse's neck more as a guide than anything else, mounted Abby and headed back at a walk as the horses readily followed.

When Emily heard the multiple hoofbeats, she looked up from her things and saw Jack walking the three horses around the boulders and smiled.

Joseph saw them at the same time and exclaimed, "Mister Tyler found the horses!"

Jack waved as he saw them walking out from behind the boulders, then dismounted from Abby when he reached them.

"They were just over a mile north of here near the creek. Now, you'll each have your own horse to ride back tomorrow and we're back on schedule."

"Wonderful!" Emily exclaimed, but not feeling wonderful at all.

ABANDONED

After the recovery of the horses, Jack began to move the wolf carcasses to the creek for disposal. He hadn't had to use any of their fat for Billy when Emily gave him a can of processed pork fat that they had used for cooking. It was probably better for Billy, and Jack was happier not to have to carve up the wolves, feeling a bit guilty for having to kill off almost the entire pack.

He dragged them two at a time to the creek and once there, took each one by the paws and once off the ground, whirled around twice and hurled them into midstream to ensure that they were carried a decent distance away. Once all five were in the water, he set about cleaning up the large amount of blood on the ground by just burying it under dirt. It wasn't perfect, but with the other carrion available in the area, he knew it was enough.

With everything settled in the campsite, Jack decided that as late as it was, they'd be better off here than anywhere else and would make a good fire near the boulders, and now that they had more plates and flatware, he'd be able to cook a better dinner.

They finished off the pemmican and trail mix as they set up camp. There were now two tents, so Jack only built the larger of them for Joseph and Mrs. Doyle. He set it up with four bedrolls inside, so they'd be more comfortable.

Emily and Joseph were decidedly quiet as they organized what they would take with them tomorrow when they returned to Laramie, and Jack was so busy he hadn't noticed.

But he cheered them both up when, after everything was set up for the night, he said, "Well, folks, let's go and catch our supper."

Joseph asked, "Catch our supper?"

"Sure," he said as he opened his own pack and pulled out two fishing lines with hooks already attached and a small tobacco tin.

"What will we use for bait?" asked Emily.

He showed her the tin and answered, "Bugs."

Jack knew that the trout preferred the morning hours for feeding, but out here, the competition for food was high and the abundance of steelhead and cutthroat trout made it fierce.

Thirty minutes later, an excited Joseph was bouncing alongside Jack with his first catch, a three and a half pound steelhead trout while Jack carried three more. Emily has just served as a spectator watching her men fish. She didn't think of Jack as anything else now but knew that it was only a dream. He'd be returning to his cabin after she and Joseph were safe in Omaha and Mister Casey found a new guardian for Joseph.

As she listened to Joseph chatter excitedly about his catch, she wondered if he wouldn't be better served by living here rather than in the business world that was his legacy. She was certain that he liked and admired Jack Tyler, maybe even as much as she did. But again, she knew it wasn't her decision to make. It would belong to whomever was appointed as his guardian after the reprehensible Noah Gallagher was returned to Laramie to face trial for murder.

It was that thought that inspired her to ask, "Mister Tyler, did you find the body?"

"Oh, I'm sorry. I forgot to tell you in all the excitement. But, yes, I found Claude Boucher's body and I had to remove evidence from the remains to give to Sheriff Higginbotham."

"May I ask what you took to return, or is it too abhorrent to discuss?"

"I'll admit that it was about as bad as it gets, but I cut out the back of his shirt where there was a bullet hole, and I took one of his boots because he was the only one who I knew wore rattlesnake skin boots."

"I won't ask for any more details, but do you believe it will be enough for a conviction?"

"Yes, ma'am, and I'm pretty sure that my word would have been enough. The folks in Laramie won't appreciate some Eastern city boy coming out here and killing one of their own, even if he was one of the most despised men in town."

Emily smiled and said, "I never considered Omaha to be in the East. We always think of it as New York, Philadelphia and Boston."

"It's just that he'd be looked as an outsider, I guess. But suffice it to say that the shirt and boot will ensure his conviction."

They reached the camp and Joseph plopped down and watched as Jack showed him how to clean the fish, and then let him clean his own catch under careful supervision while Emily sat on a nearby rock and watched her men.

Supper was decidedly more expansive with all of the added cookware and even a second, much larger cooking grate which prompted Jack to build a second firepit nearby. It allowed him to heat Emily's tea water at the same time as well.

The trout was excellent and after the full meal, Emily helped Jack with the cleanup as they walked to the nearby creek to clean the pots, frypans, and plates. Joseph remained behind to befriend his horse again.

As they washed, Jack noticed she was sitting on her heels as he was and asked, "Is your knee completely better now, ma'am?"

Emily smiled and said, "Mostly. It's still sore if I touch the front of the kneecap, but it doesn't hurt when I move anymore."

"That's good," he said as he scrubbed out a frypan.

The sun was setting behind them, turning the whole clearing red, and Emily knew that this would be the last night that they'd be alone in the great outdoors. She wasn't sure that she'd have another chance to talk privately to him again and wanted it to be a more significant discussion. More importantly, she wanted him to know more about her. He'd told her about most of his life, yet he hadn't even asked her what her Christian name was. He was treating her with deference and respect, and she was fed up with that type of treatment. She felt she should let Emily Ann Ward free again, only this time voluntarily.

She put down the plate she was washing, then looked over at Jack and asked, "Jack, why haven't you asked about my life at all?"

He couldn't ignore her use of his Christian name this time, and looked into her blue eyes and replied, "I just didn't believe it was my business. If you wanted to talk about it, then you would, but if you didn't then I'd respect your decision. I can understand it, too."

Emily Ann Ward stared at him and asked pointedly, "Why would you understand my not wanting to discuss my life? That makes no sense at all."

Jack was a bit befuddled by Mrs. Doyle's sudden direct manner and felt his discomfort level take a few more steps up the ladder as he replied, "Well, Mrs. Doyle, it's just that, well, you see, you and Joseph are, well, um, more socially acceptable than I am. Look at me. I live alone in a cabin with a wolf for a companion when he's around. You and Joseph live in a big house in a city with a maid, a cook and probably a coachman. It would be rude for me to inquire about your background."

Emily glared at him and growled, "Jack Tyler, that is the most cowardly utterance I've heard from you since you shouted at that bear. How dare you even think something like that?"

A chagrined and flummoxed Jack Tyler replied, "You may think that, ma'am, but it's true and you know it. Joseph is a well-mannered, thoughtful lad who has surprised me at every turn, and I know it was because of your guidance that he is that way. But when you return to Omaha, he'll be going back to school with his friends as he should, you'll return to your room in the big house and I'll return to my cabin. We live in two different worlds, Emily, and mine is just not allowed to mix with yours."

Emily was surprised by his use of her Christian name because she hadn't recalled giving it to him, but Jack was startled after it had slipped out because he suspected he'd just made a fool of himself for using his imagined name.

He waited for her to chastise him for calling her 'Emily', but she didn't.

Instead she said quietly, "That's just your perception, Jack. You know nothing of my background at all. If you did, you might see me as nothing like the woman of your imagination."

When she didn't say anything about his use of a name of his own creation, he initially thought she might not have noticed, but still said, "I apologize for calling you 'Emily', Mrs. Doyle. It was a foolish thing to do."

A confused Emily asked, "Why was it foolish? If anyone has earned the right to use my Christian name, it's you, Jack. I just don't recall telling you what it was."

"But I called you 'Emily'. Is that your Christian name?" he asked in surprise.

"Yes, but you're acting as if you didn't know that. Did I tell you my name and forget that I had?"

"No, ma'am."

"Did Joseph give it to you?" she asked.

"Um, no, ma'am, it's just that, well, you see, I was wondering what your name might be and I spent some time going through names and settled on Emily. It just seemed to suit you."

Emily sat back down and smiled at him before she said, "Well, thank you for that. My full name is Emily Ann Ward Doyle. My father is Dennis Patrick Ward and my mother was Mary Margaret before she passed away when I was nine. I have four brothers and four sisters and I'm number five in the line. So, now you should have an idea that I'm far from being a member of the upper crust."

"But you must admit that even at that, your current position as a nanny to a boy who'll soon run a large company is much different than mine."

"I'll admit no such thing. You made it sound as if only finishing your ninth year in school was some sort of failure, but I've met few men with your extensive knowledge and the ability to express it, even among those who think of themselves as every other man's better. I only finished my tenth year before I was married, Jack."

Jack felt the barriers drop away as he asked, "What was that like, Emily? Is that why you believe I might think less of you?"

"It's partly because of my marriage. What made it such a bad marriage was all my fault. My husband, Brian Doyle, was a decent man, and a baker by trade. In the traditional way, he asked my father for my hand when I was seventeen, and he readily agreed because Brian had his own bakery and was doing well. I had no say in the matter and married him after two months' courtship. He treated me with respect and deference, never even raising his voice. I should have been happy in the marriage, but I went into the marriage with a simmering layer of anger about having no control over who I married, and I detested his almost subservient behavior. Most women I know would have been ecstatic to have what I had. I had a husband who worshipped me and provided me with anything I asked if he could afford it. But his sycophantic behavior made me cringe, and I was incredibly guilty for feeling that way. Even when I told him about it, he smiled, patted me on the knee and said it was all his fault and he'd change. If he changed, it was to become even more submissive and accommodating. I wanted him to talk to me, to let me be part of the marriage, but he thought for some reason that I was too delicate."

That in itself was unbelievable because he was shorter than me by almost three inches and I was physically stronger than he was. I began to wonder if he was actually afraid of me for a while because my father probably had told him of my stubbornness and rather direct manner, but it wasn't that either. He was just a mild man who wanted to please not only me, but everyone. I was just the closest and received the most attention."

ABANDONED

When I was nineteen, we had a little girl, Mary Jean, and my husband began to look at me in awe as if I was a mythic mother, and I grew even angrier as he insisted on taking care of more of the chores when he could, including caring for our new daughter. When we had our second child, a son named Michael James, two years later, he hired a cook and cleaning woman to help me. To anyone who was welcomed into our home, we appeared to be a happy, complete family. And, as far as Brian and our children were concerned, it was. My children were the center of my life, but I felt immensely guilty for not fully appreciating my husband. I knew he deserved better, but he just never treated me as anything more than a delicate china doll. There was simply no excuse for my treatment of my husband."

Then, everything changed in February of '72, when a terrible flu raced through Omaha, infecting entire families. Most of them pulled through, but the disease hit our home hard. I was sick for three weeks and when I finally came out of my stupor, I was told that my two precious children had died, and then, just two days later, Brian died, and my guilt over how I had treated Brian, coupled with the loss of my babies turned me into a morose, almost catatonic statue. I moved back in with my father and the two sisters and one brother that were still at home and stayed there for more than a year."

Emily took a deep breath, then continued.

"As you might expect, I was visited by many suitors who sought my hand, but I rejected each of them because of the guilt I still felt over my treatment of Brian. Many of them were well off and my father was frustrated and angry with my constant refusals of marriage. It was my father, who had risen to the position of manager for the Brennan Furnace and Coal Company, that arranged for me to apply for the position of nanny after Joseph's father lost his wife in childbirth six years ago. I knew that my father hoped that once I was employed, Mister Brennan would be smitten, and it would lead to my marrying the widower, but that didn't happen."

Jack finally interrupted and asked, "Why wouldn't he be?"

Emily smiled at the subtle compliment and replied, "Would you believe it was for exactly the same reason that you just gave me? He wouldn't lower himself to even dabble with his inferiors. Joseph's father wasn't interested in me in the least as a prospective mate or even a bed partner. In fact, he wasn't looking for a mate at all but enjoyed the soirees and balls and the young socialites that attended them. He'd been denied his chance to sow his wild oats when his father was alive and then married an uninspiring woman that his father had deemed acceptable. When she'd died, Junior saw it as his chance to regain those lost wild years that his father had stolen."

After Joseph Charles Brennan, Junior, interviewed me, he referred me to Wilbur Moore, the steward, as a likely candidate for the position of nanny. Now, because I knew why my father wanted me to take the position, I originally thought I'd just be able to do the interview then walk away, but that all changed when I met Joseph and fell in love with the little boy. I suddenly wanted the position at any cost."

Then, she paused in her narrative. As shameful as her treatment of her husband had been, it was the next event in her life that haunted her even more and had never even been told to the parish priest in confession. But she felt almost obligated to bare her soul to Jack Tyler. She would risk his disappointment and disgust by telling him, but she had to take that risk.

She looked into his eyes, still blue in the red light of the setting sun, then swallowed.

"This is very difficult for me, Jack. I've never told it to anyone, not even Father Ryan. But you need to understand that I'm not what you apparently believe me to be."

Jack just looked into those blue eyes and nodded, before Emily took in a deep breath and began her confession.

"As I said, after I met Joseph, I wanted to be his nanny more than anything else in the world, but even if his father wasn't interested in me, Mister Wilbur Moore, the steward was. He didn't even couch his terms for letting me have the position but told me bluntly that my duties would include satisfying him at his convenience."

She took another deep breath, then said, "I didn't even balk. I accepted the job and it wasn't long before I had to meet his conditions of employment. I was so ashamed of myself, much more than I had been because of the way I treated Brian. But I was with Joseph, and my only fear was becoming pregnant again, which would result in losing everything. It remained that way for almost two years, but Mister Moore had a similar arrangement with Anna Thornton the cook, so it wasn't that often. Then, the maid, Mary Connor, quit and was replaced with a much younger Mary named Mary Flaherty. Wilbur Moore then shifted all of his attention to the younger woman. None of us became pregnant, and we all believed it was because of the steward's lack of masculinity. He was a tall, thin man reminiscent of the character Ichabod Crane, with, to put it politely, less manhood than a much shorter man, or a boy, for that matter. As Joseph grew older, we became so close that I was able to reject any further advances by Mister Moore. Even he knew that he'd be fired before Joseph would let me go."

Then she sighed, looked at Jack and said, "So, Mister Tyler, what do you think of me now? Do you still see yourself as some social inferior?"

Jack smiled at her and said, "Emily, you are still the most remarkable woman I've ever met, but again, let me remind you that there weren't many in my life."

Emily sighed in relief, then smiled slightly and said, "I'll gladly accept that."

"Now, Mrs. Doyle, I've been meaning to ask you for one favor that I was hesitant to ask as we were riding, even though it won't be an annoyance any longer."

"An annoyance, Jack?" she asked with raised eyebrows.

"Yes, Emily, an annoyance. As we rode, I simply couldn't see past your piled up hair. But I'll also admit that I wondered how it would look just hanging loosely across your back."

Emily laughed lightly, then reached up and began pulling out hairpins and tossing them away as her long hair started tumbling across her back. By the time the last pin had been removed and she tossed her head to settle it down, Jack was mesmerized.

"Is that acceptable, sir?" Emily asked.

Jack didn't reply for fifteen seconds before she asked, "Jack? Are you okay?"

He finally blinked several times and said, "Yes, I think so. It's just that…well, your hair is so…so, well, amazing."

Emily was going to laugh until she saw the glazed look in his eyes and she settled into a more serious mood.

The moon began to peek over the eastern horizon as they both understood the incredibly massive shift that had just taken place.

Jack finally whispered, "We should go back now. Joseph is probably getting worried."

Emily nodded slowly and replied quietly, "Yes. We should."

Despite the agreement, there was another thirty seconds before Jack finally stood slowly and then once he was on his feet, put his hand out and Emily took his hand then rose until she stood just eight inches before him.

She looked up at him and said softly, "You held me when I was afraid. I felt your chest vibrating against me when you sang and then I listened to your heartbeat."

Jack just replied, "Yes."

"Can you hold me again, Jack?" she asked quietly.

ABANDONED

He just reached around her, pulled her gently close to him and felt her arms around him. He could feel her thick hair under his hands as she rested her head on his left shoulder.

Neither spoke as they stood under the darkening sky while they were serenaded by coyotes, wolves, owls and insects, all underscored by the rushing water of the nearby creek.

Once she was comfortable in his arms, Emily knew that there were many obstacles before them but somehow, nothing else mattered anymore. But she felt something else, too. She felt free again. She could be Emily Ann Ward when she was with Jack, even though she'd still have to be Mrs. Doyle when she was around Joseph and when they were back in Omaha.

Jack just drank in all that was Emily, unsure of their future, but reveling in the present. He wanted to kiss her but knew that it would make things much more difficult, especially with Joseph just a hundred feet away.

"I suppose we have to go back now," Jack finally said.

He felt her head nod, so he released Emily, then smiled at her before bending down to collect the cleaned pots pans and plates.

Emily waited and when he had them all, they began to walk slowly back to the horses. Joseph had left his horse and was busy whittling a piece of driftwood with his new knife.

When the adults returned, he didn't notice any change except for Mrs. Doyle's hair, but thought she might be getting ready to wash it, then grinned at Jack and showed him the shaved driftwood.

"What did you make there, Joseph?" he asked.

"It's a spear, in case any of those wolves come back," he explained.

"It seems a bit short. Maybe if we have time tomorrow, I'll show you how to make a good one."

"That would be great!" he exclaimed but went back to whittling.

Emily smiled broadly at Jack, who returned her smile, but didn't understand the reason for the smile. She was thanking him for liking Emily Ann Ward as much as Mrs. Doyle.

After Joseph was in his bedroll, Jack and Emily lay side by side on two bedrolls, her hair splayed out like a giant carpet beneath her. She'd brushed it earlier, and knew she'd have to brush it again when she returned to the tent, but she wanted to please Jack.

They looked at the stars over their heads and Emily said, "I've never seen the stars so bright before."

"Unless it's cloudy, they're always like this. In the winter, when it's really cold and the wind is calm, they take your breath away. The moon is more of an intruder than a desired participant."

Then Emily Ann Ward asked, "Have you been with many women, Jack?"

Jack turned his head, believing that he could no longer be stunned by her questions, and replied, "Not as many as you might expect. Remember, I've lived most of my life with nothing but male companions. From the orphanage, where we weren't allowed to even talk to the girls, then the army, then the railroad labor camps. We had camp followers in the army and with the railroad that I used from time to time, but that ended when there was an outbreak of venereal disease in the winter camp at North Platte in '67."

"So, you haven't been with a woman since then?" she asked as she still stared at the stars.

"No, I haven't," Jack answered honestly, thinking it would end the flow of the conversation.

"I haven't been with a man since '76, and I'm not sure I've ever been with a real man," Emily said matter-of-factly.

ABANDONED

Jack admitted to himself that she had thrown him off kilter and asked, "Emily, what has happened to you? Are you usually this blunt?"

She looked at him and asked, "Are you afraid or angry?"

"No, not at all. If you must know, I like you better this way. I hated not knowing if what I said would hurt your feelings or make you angry inside. I've been holding back a bit myself just to spare you any possible discomfort. But now, if I know you'll tell me what you think, it makes things much better."

Emily looked at him momentarily, smiled at his answer, then turned back to look at the stars to answer his question.

"I was always this way before I was married. It was why I couldn't understand my husband's treatment of me like a delicate flower. I had never been a quiet girl. Then, after I was married, I behaved myself for a while, and that was part of the reason I was so angry inside. I couldn't say what was on my mind and I resented it. Then, when I returned to being myself, I thought it would make my husband angry, which is what I wanted, but it didn't. No matter what I did short of hitting him, which I never did, he continued to believe I was some sweet girl he'd just met at the church, so I went back into a shell because it didn't matter how I behaved. Then, when I began work at the Brennan household, I had no choice. I had to behave, or I would lose Joseph. I feel as if I can never let him see me as I really am, either. But tonight, after telling you about my life, all of it, warts and all, I don't feel shackled any longer. I can't tell you how invigorating it feels to be able to express myself freely again. It's as if I can breathe again, and I'll never be able to thank you enough."

"So, this is the real Emily?"

"Yes. It's the real me, but tomorrow, when Joseph is with us, you won't see her again. Not unless we're alone in private. I just wanted you to understand. It's not that I'm crazy or anything, it's just that I don't want to risk losing Joseph."

"Even if you were crazy, Emily, I wasn't about to run away."

"Oh?"

"No, ma'am. You're much too interesting. You may have discovered yourself, but I'm still in the process of investigating all that you are."

"I'm intrigued, Mister Tyler," Emily said.

"So, why bring up our seventeen years of combined abstinence?"

"It was on my mind, I guess. After you held me, I wanted you to kiss me, but you didn't, and I wasn't sure why."

Jack rolled up on his right elbow and looked at Emily, who turned to face him. He almost didn't know how to answer the question but remembering how she wasn't happy with her worshipful husband made him decide to answer her honestly.

"Joseph was why, Emily. I knew if I kissed you, I wouldn't be able to stop after that, and Joseph was just a hundred feet away."

"That's the only good reason, I imagine. What excuse do you have now?"

"I don't need an excuse, Mrs. Doyle. When I want to kiss you, or make love to you, I'll let you know."

Emily laughed softly, then said, "Now that's an answer I can live with, as long as you don't wait too long."

Jack smiled at her, then dropped back down to his back, satisfied that she was happier that he hadn't behaved like her husband and hadn't acted too surprised by her new, blunt behavior.

He was about to say something about Ursa Major when Emily's newly revealed blunt behavior did surprise him when she suddenly rolled on top of him and kissed him, and not softly.

Jack's reaction was instantaneous as he pulled her close to him and felt her hair flow all about them both.

ABANDONED

Emily ended the kiss, pulled her head back slightly and asked, "Is that blunt enough for you, Mister Tyler?"

"We could have a bear sneak in behind us, you know. I can't see through your hair."

"Well, that's your fault, sir, and it's going to stay this way now, so get used to it."

"My! My! Blunt and feisty! Is this the same woman that I held quietly in my arms just a short while ago?"

Emily answered quietly, "Yes, Jack. It's the same woman. The same woman that wept in your arms when you returned after stopping those wolves. Just because I can be blunt and feisty, doesn't mean I can't be afraid or tender. I can be all of those things, Jack. But you're the only man that has seen them all. You inspire me, Jack Tyler, and you let me be me without boundaries. And I love you for that, and for who you are."

Jack slipped his right hand under her hair and touched her cheek.

"I suppose I should tell you that I love you, Emily, but I don't want it to be a reciprocal, almost required declaration. I want you to be overwhelmed or at the least, surprised. Is that okay?"

Emily kissed him lightly then said, "You have no idea how much better your answer was than I could have hoped to hear. Now, how much further do we take this tonight?"

"As much as I want you, Emily, we have Joseph just a few feet away and as much noise as I think we'll be making, I think we should hold back until we can have full rein to do whatever comes to mind."

Emily sighed and said, "Again, you surprise me. I know how much you would like to ravish me. It's not exactly a secret, you know. And trust me when I tell you that I want you just as much, if not more. I've never had a real man before and I can tell that you are all that and more. It's probably just as difficult for me to postpone the inevitable, but I agree that it's probably better. But at least grant me some level of satisfaction. Please?"

Jack really didn't need to be asked but began to kiss Emily and before he slid his lips to her neck, felt her hands wandering over him.

She began to emit a low, growling moan as he kissed her neck and began to feel her.

The heavy petting and kissing went on for almost ten minutes before a painful Jack Tyler whispered, "Emily, we've got to stop. I'm not going to be able to ride for a week."

She didn't reply, but kissed him once more, slid her hips slowly back and forth twice, then slipped off to her bedroll, her long hair sliding across Jack's face.

When she was flat on her back again, she gasped then said, "My lord, Jack! How were you able to stop?"

Jack groaned and replied, "Don't ask. I'd rather fight a grizzly bear with one of your hairpins than go through that again."

"I'm never going to use one of those damned things again. And don't get me started on corsets, either."

"You wear corsets?" he asked in surprise.

"Of course, I wear them. It would be the height of poor fashion to be seen without one in the crowd that frequents 1710 Chicago Street in Omaha. Of course, that didn't apply to Mary Flaherty, the young maid. She could get by with just a camisole because she wore her maid outfit and was less bosomy."

"And that definitely doesn't apply to you, now does it, Emily Ann Ward? Although, the idea of seeing you in a maid's outfit sans corset would be quite pleasant."

ABANDONED

Emily laughed and said, "Now who's being blunt and feisty?"

"You just bring it out in me, ma'am. As much as I would like to talking to Emily Ann Ward, I think you need to join Joseph in the tent. Tomorrow is going to be a busy day for all of us."

Emily sat up, turned to Jack and said, "You're right, Jack. It's going to be busy and important, but I can't tell you how important tonight was for me."

Jack sat up, looked at Emily, then kissed her softly and said, "I love you, Emily."

Emily felt a warm flush flow through her as she smiled and said, "I'm overwhelmed, Jack."

She kissed him again, then stood, picked up her bedroll, smiled once more before entering the larger tent quietly and disappearing.

Jack watched her go and laid back down and as he looked at the Milky Way, a long shooting star flashed across the sky lasting almost three seconds. He smiled and knew that a much brighter star had entered his life and he'd have to do all he could to keep her there.

But even as the thought was fresh in his mind, he could already see the formidable obstacles in the way, and the biggest was the love that Emily had for Joseph. He could never do anything to separate her from the boy and couldn't imagine what would happen when they arrived in Omaha.

In Omaha, Noah Gallagher looked over at Mary Flaherty as she lay naked beside him sleeping. After he'd enjoyed her pleasures, she told him about Wilbur Moore's behavior with her, Anna Thornton and Emily Doyle. He'd been disgusted that a man like that would have bedded the pretty Mary Flaherty, but quietly amused that he'd had his way with that Amazon nanny.

Tomorrow, when he returned from taking care of all of the legalities, he'd send Mister Moore packing. He didn't need a damned steward. Besides, it would give him a lot more freedom with Mary. He might give Anna Thornton a whirl, too. She wasn't as pretty as Mary, but different was good. He'd have a two or three month long personal Saturnalia while he resided at 1710 Chicago Street.

But before the fun could begin, tomorrow morning, he'd visit Luke Casey and handle the legalities necessary to inherit the Brennan estate.

CHAPTER 5

Jack had the big fire going again, and wished he had eggs, but there was bacon this time and some canned beans. He added some spices to the beans and had water boiling by the time Joseph popped out of the tent.

"Good morning, Joseph. Are you ready to get back to Laramie today?"

"Yes, sir. Will I be riding my horse again?"

"Of course. Is he your horse, or did they rent him for you?"

"I'm just borrowing him from the stable."

"Well, Mister Brennan, how about if I buy the horse and saddle for you and keep him out at my cabin in case you come and visit me again?"

Joseph gaped and then exclaimed, "*I can come and visit?*"

"Anytime you can get away from school. It's only a day and a half train ride and I'm sure Mrs. Doyle will be happy to bring you along, too."

"Wow! That's great! Do I get to meet Loopy, too?"

"Maybe. He comes and goes as he pleases, but he's usually around when I'm not there or when it gets really cold."

"He's not like those wolves we saw yesterday, is he?"

"I'm afraid so. The only difference is that he'll never hurt you even if he's hungry. He'll just beg for food, although it's not the same kind of begging you'd see in a normal dog. It's more like demanding."

Joseph laughed as he stepped up to the fire and sat on his heels.

"You're coming with us to Omaha?" he asked.

"Yes, sir. I'll be bringing an arrest warrant for your uncle, too. Then, I'll have to come back here with him to face trial for murdering that guide who led you here. I'll talk to Mrs. Doyle about the charges for what he did to you and her when she comes out. We might want to hold off on those until we're sure he's convicted, then it won't matter. If he gets off somehow, I'll have them charge him with attempted murder."

"I don't understand all that, Mister Tyler. I just want him to get hurt for what he did to Mrs. Doyle."

"So, do I, Joseph."

Emily stepped out of the tent a minute later, then disappeared behind the boulders for a few minutes before walking to the fire and sitting on a rock near Jack.

"Sleep well, Mrs. Doyle?" he asked innocently.

"Very well. Thank you, Mister Tyler," she replied.

"When will be starting back?" she asked.

"In about an hour, I believe. We should get there a little after noon, because we'll pick up the road in a few more miles and can ride more quickly."

"Which horse will I be riding?"

"Any of them. Only Billy is going to be unencumbered for our last leg."

She surprised him when she asked, "Could I ride Abby?"

"Yes, ma'am. She does have a good disposition and a smooth ride."

"Yes, she does. Imagine that. A mule with a pleasant disposition. I didn't know there were Irish mules."

Jack just grinned as he flipped the bacon and glanced at Emily who winked at him when Joseph wasn't looking.

They finished breakfast quickly, then Jack spent over an hour packing everything, even though little of it was necessary any longer. He moved his gold to the saddlebags on the horse he'd be riding along with his Winchester's scabbard. He'd cleaned the rifle last night, but it would get a more thorough cleaning when he got it back to the cabin.

After everyone was mounted, the last major obstacle on their return was the wide creek that had spooked Emily on the way out. But having Jack so close to her and with the calm Abby beneath her, the crossing was easy and soon, the three horses and two mules stepped onto the eastern bank of the creek and began the trot back to Laramie.

―――

Just five minutes after Jack, Emily and Joseph began riding, Noah Gallagher stepped into the outer office of the Brennan family attorney, Luke Casey. He didn't even acknowledge his clerk who had just risen from his desk, but walked through the inner door without knocking, and closed the door behind him.

Luke was expecting him and the manner of his entrance. It was just further evidence of the man's arrogance.

"Are we ready to go and visit Judge Carstairs, Luke?" he asked, not even bothering to remove his hat.

Luke Casey stood, turned and removed the file from the cabinet, then picked up his own hat and said, "We are."

They left the office, Luke waving his clerk back down to his seat as they passed, left the building and boarded the buggy Noah had already borrowed from the Brennan barn.

"Do you have the statement from the sheriff in Laramie?" Luke asked as Noah drove along Capitol Avenue.

"Yes, I have it. It's very simple, just like the man who wrote it. It just states that Mrs. Emily Ann Doyle, age thirty-two, Master Joseph Charles Brennan III, age eight, were both killed by wild animals while on a hunting trip in the Medicine Bow Mountains in southern Albany County. It doesn't even mention that damned guide."

Luke hesitated to ask, knowing he could face criminal charges, but knew he was already complicit in a crime, so it didn't matter.

"What happened to the guide?"

"What do you think happened to him? I surely couldn't let him return to Laramie. That bastard would have been blackmailing me for years."

Luke was about to ask a more direct question but dropped the idea. He was already sick at the thought of the boy being left out there to die. He didn't give Emily a thought. She just didn't matter.

Noah pulled up to the Douglas County Courthouse building, rolled the buggy to a stop, then he and Luke Casey exited the buggy. Noah tied off the reins, then he and the attorney climbed the steps to the expansive new building and without bothering to read the directory, headed for the chambers of Judge Lawrence D. Carstairs.

Five minutes later, they had been ushered into his chambers by his clerk and were sitting before him as he perused the documents given to him by Luke Casey.

Judge Carstairs wasn't crooked or even shady, but he enjoyed the company of the well-to-do for many reasons, not the least of which was for his reelection campaigns. He had hobnobbed with Joseph Charles Brennan Junior at the club often, and when Luke Casey had told him of the documented demise of his son, he'd been genuinely saddened to hear of the loss.

ABANDONED

Yet, all of the paperwork that was being shown to him was legal and above board. The sheriff's statement and the proof that Noah Gallagher was not only the guardian of the boy, but the closest living relative to Joseph Charles Brennan, allowed him to sign the orders naming Noah the legal heir to the estate without hesitation.

The entire process lasted less than twenty minutes, and handshakes were shared before Noah Gallagher, now the owner of Brennan Furnace and Coal Company and legal resident of 1710 Chicago Street happily danced down the steps from the county courthouse.

He drove Luke Casey back to his office without a word being exchanged on the drive, then turned down Tenth Street to ride to the company headquarters and let them know who was now in complete control of the company. He wouldn't change the name because of the costs involved and he'd let the new owners take care of that when he sold it in a couple of months.

He turned into the company buildings and pulled the buggy to a stop before the administration buildings. He stepped out and looked up at the tall, smoke-spewing smokestacks that represented money for him and smiled.

Noah took a deep breath of the sooty air, then walked into the building.

"Where is your cabin from here, Mister Tyler?" Emily asked as they rode east, now just eight miles from the roadway, which they would pick up just six miles south of Laramie.

"It's just about twelve miles that way," he answered as he pointed southeast.

"Is it pretty there?"

"I think so. I've got a full section of land with two streams and a bigger creek running through it. Except for my vegetable garden behind the cabin, I don't do anything with the land itself. I like it the way it is."

"How big is the cabin?"

"It started out as a regular cabin when I first built it, but then, after I found the gold, I began adding onto it. It looks a bit odd, but it suits my purpose. The original cabin is now the main room, then I added two bedrooms, one on each side before adding a kitchen in back and a library on one side and a big bathroom on the other. It almost looks like a sideways, squat capital 'H' if you look at it from the tall rocks in the front of my land. I even built a walkway to the privy, so I didn't have to freeze my behind off in the winter, when it's really cold. Both the front and rear entrances have mud rooms, too, so the cold air doesn't sneak in when the door opens. It's pretty cozy, even in the nasty weather."

"Where do Abby and Billy stay?"

"In the barn. They're too stinky to let into the house."

Emily and Joseph laughed, and Jack smiled back at them both. The last leg of the trip was becoming almost as pleasant as a family Sunday jaunt. Even though it was Monday and they weren't a family.

"Do you think Mister Gallagher is already working to replace Joseph?" she asked.

"I don't know how that works, ma'am. I don't even know the laws in Wyoming Territory, much less in Nebraska. I'd imagine he'd have to produce a body or a witness, but if he didn't, I'd think there would have to be a long wait before he could, um, declare things."

"Will I have to send a telegram to Omaha to find out?"

"No, I think the last thing you should do is send a telegram. Once he knows you and Joseph are alive, he might try something else. I'll talk to Sheriff Higginbotham, let him know everything, and see if we can get a warrant, and we'll deliver it personally to the law in Omaha."

She nodded and said, "I'm glad you're with us, Mister Tyler. Very, very glad."

He glanced over at Emily and replied, "I'll do anything you ask, ma'am."

"I'm sure you'll do it happily as well," she said, smiling.

They turned onto the northbound road, if one could call it that, later than Jack had expected, not reaching the road until an hour after noon. But from here, the ride was less than an hour and they picked up the pace slightly.

Jack turned to Emily and said, "Mrs. Doyle, I know that you're not happy with your appearance, even though you look fine to me, but if you don't mind, I'd like to have you and Joseph join me when I meet the sheriff, so you can back up the story. Pretty women have a way of convincing even the gruffest lawman, and Sheriff Higginbotham is far from gruff."

"I don't mind at all, Mister Tyler, and thank you for your generous compliment."

"Just being honest, ma'am," he replied.

They'd been together for the better part of a week now, and Joseph finally asked a question that Jack was a bit surprised neither had asked the first day.

"Mister Tyler, don't you ever wear a hat?"

"Not unless it's cold, Joseph. I have two hats in my pack. A woolen knit cap and a heavier fur cap with ear flaps. Both are designed to keep my head warm. I just don't see the need to stick something on my head. The good Lord already put a bunch of hair up there, so until he starts taking it away, I'll just let it do the job of a hat."

"I don't wear a hat except for that one they make me wear at Saint Ignatius, and I think it looks silly. Don't you, Mrs. Doyle?"

She did think it was hideous, but replied, "It's just what they require at the school, Joseph."

Jack looked back at Joseph and said, "Maybe if you show it to me when we get to Omaha, I'll have an accident with my Bowie knife and, oops! There goes your hat."

Joseph giggled and looked at a smiling Emily and hoped that Mister Tyler really did it.

It was around half past one o'clock when they entered the outskirts of Laramie, and Jack led them to the office of Albany County Sheriff Will Higginbotham.

Jack's horse had the injured Billy attached and the packhorse that the party had used when they departed Laramie, so when he dismounted, he tied off Claude's horse, then helped Emily down from Abby, even though she didn't need the assistance. Joseph dropped to the ground and tied off the small black gelding while Jack went to his saddlebags and pulled out the shirt with the bullet hole and Claude's sliced rattlesnake skin boot.

He stepped onto the boardwalk, opened the door and let Emily and Joseph enter before following them inside. Emily may have been a bit disheveled in her appearance, but Jack still thought she looked magnificent with her dark red hair streaming down her back and her confident manner.

The deputy looked up, saw Jack but didn't recognize Joseph or Emily.

ABANDONED

"Good afternoon, George," Jack said as he stepped forward, then pulled out the lone chair before the desk and let Emily take a seat.

"Howdy, Jack. What do you need?"

"I need you to ask Sheriff Higginbotham to come out, so I can tell you both the most incredible story you're going to hear all year, if not the decade."

Deputy George Pruitt stood, then headed down a short hallway. He couldn't imagine how good the story Jack Tyler would tell them if he claimed it was incredible.

Sheriff Will Higginbotham walked out a few seconds later behind his deputy, spotted Emily and automatically tugged at his long moustache.

"What is going on, Jack. George tells me that you've got an incredible story to tell me."

"Will, I'd like you to meet Mrs. Emily Doyle and her charge, Joseph Charles Brennan III."

Jack wasn't sure if Noah Gallagher had even notified the sheriff of their supposed deaths out in the Medicine Bow Mountains, but once he watched the sheriff's mouth drop open and his eyes almost explode, he knew. Deputy George Pruitt's expression wasn't much different, either.

"But...but his uncle said that they'd been mauled by wolves and he barely made it out of there alive. He even had a big slice on his chest and had to be sewn up by the doc."

"Will, he not only lied about the wolf attack, but he abandoned Mrs. Doyle and Joseph out in the mountains about seventy miles away. He even threw blood on their tent just before he and Claude Boucher snuck away."

The sheriff's eyes narrowed, and his jaw tightened. It was bad enough that he'd been lied to and been played for a fool, but he'd abandoned a pretty woman and a boy to die? He was beyond furious.

He snapped, "That bas..., excuse me, ma'am," then asked, "Where is Boucher? I'm going to arrest that no-account and make him wish he'd never been born."

Jack set the boot and the cloth on the desk and said, "No need, Sheriff. I found Claude's body about a day's ride from here. He'd been shot in the back and dumped in a large creek. I brought the back of his shirt and one of his boots back for evidence."

George Pruitt picked up the back of the shirt and held it out. The sheriff didn't really need the evidence, Jack's testimony would have been enough, but the shirt and boot would guarantee that bastard would hang.

"I'll go and see the prosecutor in a little while and get a warrant issued for that man. Where is he now?"

"We're pretty sure he's in Omaha, trying to take the family fortune that Joseph is rightfully supposed to inherit when he's of age."

"I'll wire the warrant and have them pick him up and extradite him back here, then we'll try him and hang him."

"Sheriff, if it's all right with you, after you obtain the warrant, I'll hand deliver it to the law in Omaha. I don't want the uncle to get wind that Joseph and Mrs. Doyle are still alive."

The sheriff nodded and said, "Okay. That's a good idea. Then, Jack, if you don't mind, I'll deputize you, so you can bring him back. You gotta be here for the trial anyway."

"That'll work for me, Will."

"Okay, when are you planning on going back?"

"Well, that depends on Mrs. Doyle and Joseph. They've had a rough time of it and were even attacked by a pack of wolves yesterday. So, I'll take them to the hotel, let them rest and get comfortable, then tomorrow, we'll stop by. We may leave tomorrow or the day after, but more than anything, we need to keep their survival quiet."

"I'll make sure of that. When you check them into the hotel, just log them in under another name so nobody will know they're here."

He nodded, then turned to Emily and asked, "Which hotel did you stay in when you arrived?"

"The Intercontinental."

"Okay, I'll take you to the Metropolitan. You and Joseph relax for a while, then I'll take you both to dinner at the hotel restaurant."

Emily smiled, then stood and took Joseph's hand.

"We'll see you in the morning, Will," Jack said before he turned, opened the door and escorted them both onto the boardwalk.

After he'd closed the door, he asked, "Mrs. Doyle, did you need to buy anything before we get to the hotel?"

"No. Now that I have my travel bag again, I'll be fine, although I might want to buy some things before taking the train back."

"We can do that," he replied as he helped her mount Abby, then mounted the horse, waited for Joseph then turned north toward the Metropolitan Hotel, which he thought was better than the Intercontinental anyway.

When they dismounted outside of the hotel, Jack gave Emily twenty dollars, so she could get her room. He took her travel bag from the pack horse and the saddlebags with Joseph's things then escorted them into the hotel. He didn't know the desk clerk, which wasn't unusual, given his infrequent trips into Laramie and his far less visits to either hotel. He set down the bags, and Emily registered as Ann Ward and her son Charles, paid the four dollars for the suite, then accepted the key.

"Well, ma'am, I'm glad I could help you," he said.

Emily smiled and said, "Thank you for your assistance, sir. You've been most gracious."

He glanced at the clock behind the desk and said, "If you don't mind, ma'am, I'd be honored to take you and your son to dinner, say at six o'clock?"

Emily smiled and replied, "We'd be delighted. We'll meet you in the lobby."

"I'll see you both then, ma'am," Jack said, then bowed slightly, turned and left the hotel.

Emily picked up her travel bags and a snickering Joseph hoisted his saddlebags, then they both walked to the room. She'd selected the suite because the clerk had told her that it had an attached bath with hot and cold running water. She would have paid the entire twenty dollars for just the bath.

Once he returned to the boardwalk, Jack attached Abby, the pack horse and the small horse to Claude's horse, mounted and headed south out of Laramie. He had a little over three hours to head back to his cabin, get cleaned up and changed, then ride back. He didn't have any time to waste.

He had the animals, even poor Billy moving at a medium trot before he even left the town limits.

"Well, gentlemen," Noah said as he stood before the assembled board members and officers of the Brennan Furnace and Coal Company, "as the new owner of the company, I don't expect to be making any changes anytime soon. So, just continue as you have been, and if you have any questions, I can be found at 1710 Chicago Street. Does anyone have any question for me now?"

ABANDONED

They all had questions and lots of them, but none of them raised a finger.

"Okay, then, this meeting is adjourned," he pronounced with finality before turning and leaving the large conference room.

Once he was gone and they heard the outer door open and close, the murmuring began. *Young Joseph had died with his nanny out in the wilds of Wyoming, yet he only had survived?* Not one single man in the room doubted for a moment what Noah Gallagher had done, but as disgusted as they were, each of them knew there wasn't a thing they could do about it. The man was now legally the owner of the company and their boss.

Soon, the rumors had reached the factory floor and one of the foreman approached Dennis Ward as he was inspecting one of the heavy presses that was leaving a noticeable crease in the stampings.

"Mister Ward!" he shouted over the din as steel was being worked into furnace parts.

Dennis turned, saw the foreman, then said something to the operator of the press, before walking to meet Ben Porter.

"What do you need, Ben?" he asked loudly.

"I just heard that Gallagher is the new owner of the company."

"How did that happen?" he asked in disbelief.

"He says that when he took the Brennan boy out to Wyoming they were attacked by wolves and the whole party was killed except for him."

Dennis Ward didn't reply but stood frozen as the cacophony of manufacturing continued to echo loudly across the expansive factory floor.

"Mister Ward?" Ben asked.

Dennis slowly asked, "Was his nanny with him, or did she stay here?"

"I don't know. You'll have to ask somebody who was in the meeting."

Dennis nodded slowly but didn't reply as he walked across the floor heading for the company's offices across the yard, already feeling sick at the possibility that Emily might have died because of him.

"But you can't terminate me! I'm the steward! I've been with the family for nine years!" sputtered Wilbur Moore.

"In my estimation, that's nine years too long. I want you out of this house in thirty minutes. I know what you've been doing, Mister Moore, and you should be grateful that I don't turn you over to the authorities. You will not be getting a letter of recommendation. Now, get out!"

Wilbur's nose rose as he said, "My salary is due for August, sir, and I shan't leave the residence without what is owed me."

Noah reached into his pocket, pulled out twenty-eight dollars in crumpled bills and shoved them into Wilbur's hand.

"That's all you're going to get, now leave before I lose my temper."

Moore snorted in derision, stuffed the money in his pocket, then snapped, "You'll regret this, Mister Gallagher. We all know what happened out there was no accident!", then pivoted on his heels and walked quickly away.

Mary Flaherty and Anna Thornton were stunned, not by the house manager's sudden dismissal, but by what he had said. Anna had suspected it, but Mary had actually believed Noah's story. When Noah hadn't even responded angrily to Moore's indictment, both immediately realized that what he had accused Noah Gallagher of doing was true.

Once Wilbur Moore was out of sight, Noah turned to the two women, smiled and said, "Now, don't you both feel safer?"

They both smiled and nodded, but neither did. What made Anna feel even worse was when Noah followed his question with an obvious inspection of her figure. It made her skin crawl. They were living with a murderer.

Jack reached his cabin in good time and quickly brought Abby and Billy to the barn, unsaddled Abby and checked Billy's wounds. He didn't have time to brush them down and apologized, but they didn't seem to mind as their faces where shoved deeply into their feed bags.

He was leading the three horses into the corral when he spotted Loopy trotting across the yard.

"Howdy, Loopy!" he shouted as he closed the gate and began to unsaddle the pack horse.

Loopy barked then slinked under the corral's lower fence rail, spooking the three horses.

Jack calmed them down, then said, "Loopy, go!", unsure if the wolf would leave, but he must have wanted to because he soon crawled back out and trotted to the back of the huge cabin.

With the horses now calm again, Jack finished unsaddling the pack horse and then Joseph's small horse. He left Claude's horse saddled, but took off the gold-filled saddlebags, hung them over his shoulder and left the corral as the three horses, still glancing back at the wolf near the back of the cabin, headed for the trough and big pile of hay in the corner.

Jack reached the back of the cabin, ignoring Loopy, opened the first door and went inside, leaving it open for the wolf should he desire to enter, then entered the kitchen door.

He dropped the saddlebags to the floor, walked down into the large cold room, grabbed a large piece of smoked venison, then climbed back out, closed the cold room door and tossed it to Loopy who had decided he may as well see if the human was going to feed him. He caught the meat, then plopped to the floor and began ripping it apart.

Jack trotted to his big bedroom, and hastily stripped off his clothes, and dropped them all in a large basket by the window.

Once he was naked, he walked across to the bathroom, put the stopper in the bathtub and began pumping water. It was going to be cold, but he didn't have time to heat enough water to make it any warmer. He grabbed a bar of white soap, hopped into the not-so-frigid water, then quickly began scrubbing away the dirt from the long ride. He left the tub five minutes later, then pulled the plug and as the water spiraled away, pumped a basin half full, walked to the sink, set it down and prepared to shave. This normally would be horrific, but he had something that made it much safer. He took his set of beard trimmers that he'd ordered from a catalog and began removing most of the heavy stubble. Once most of the hair was gone, he lathered up his face, picked up his straight razor and much more carefully than usual began scraping his face. When he finished, he was pleased to only have created a single nick. He brushed his teeth, using more tooth powder than usual, then ran his tongue across his teeth, satisfied they were as clean as he could get them.

He emptied the basin into the tub, then returned to his bedroom, opened his dresser drawer and pulled out a new shirt, underwear, socks and a pair of britches. He used his newest belt and buckle to hold them up, then pulled on his less-used pair of boots. He finally brushed his hair, and pocketed his comb, knowing his hair would be mussed on the ride back to Laramie.

ABANDONED

He imagined this was how boys felt when they were going to escort some pretty young girl to his first social event. He was almost giddy with the thought of seeing Emily again and not with any fear of wolves or bears lurking about.

Finally, he slipped his wallet into his pocket, then wrapped his gunbelt around his waist and tightened it in place. He then walked back out through the kitchen, noting that Loopy was already gone, closed the kitchen door, then the outer door and trotted back to the corral to get Claude's horse.

―――

Emily was in heaven as she lounged in the almost hot bathwater. She'd used her own lavender soap but had used the hotel-provided rose-scented shampoo and now just soaked in the luxury of the hot water.

She'd set her last clean dress on the bed while Joseph had taken his bath. It was the first time she hadn't had to almost push him into the tub. He seemed to be almost as anxious as she had been to get rid of the dirt from the last week.

When she finally left the bathroom, she felt new again and was suddenly embarrassed when Joseph looked at her while she was wearing her camisole. He didn't seem to notice, and Emily was a bit surprised by her reaction. Maybe it was because after she'd seen him behave so admirably during the dangerous times that she was looking at him more as a young man. Whatever the reason, she quickly dressed and then sat at the dressing table and began to brush her long locks. They were tangled something fierce and it took a lot of work before she was finally able to slide the brush through her dark red tresses. She knew that they needed to be trimmed, but she wanted Jack to see her with her hair clean and still long the way he liked it.

Just as Jack was, she found herself titillated as she prepared for dinner. She'd never had the feeling before and hoped it wouldn't change. She thought of herself as a mature, if not bordering on middle-aged woman, yet she felt like a teenager as she continued to use the hairbrush.

Jack pulled up to the front of the hotel as the sunset was just starting, so he knew he was on time. He really should get a pocket watch, he thought, as he tied off the horse and stepped onto the boardwalk. Then he stopped, pulled his comb from his pocket, then ran it once through his hair quickly before sliding it back. He was almost embarrassed to be seen primping, because that was what he was doing.

He took a deep breath, entered the hotel lobby and stopped. Emily was sitting in a chair with Joseph standing next to her as some man he'd never seen before towered before her, smiling and saying something that must have made Joseph angry.

Jack's anger was smoldering as he walked slowly across the floor, and Joseph turned at his footsteps, then smiled and looked back at the man, expecting Jack to shoot him.

Jack didn't pull his pistol, or even his knife, but when he was close, he said, "Excuse me, Emily, is this gentleman bothering you?"

The man turned to Jack and asked, "Who the hell are you?"

Jack smiled at Emily, who smiled back, then rose to his full height and looked the man in the eyes and with his rumbling bass voice, replied, "The same man who will geld you in the next three seconds unless you turn around and leave."

The man's hostility vanished, then without a word, just turned and walked quickly past Jack and out the door.

Jack then looked down at Emily and said, "Mrs. Doyle, may I have the privilege of escorting you and Master Joseph to dinner?"

Emily stood, took his arm and replied, "We'd be honored, Mister Tyler."

ABANDONED

Jack smiled, then turned and took Joseph's hand and they crossed the lobby and entered the restaurant. The desk clerk hadn't paid any attention. It wasn't his job to get involved in fights.

After they'd been seated, Jack asked, "Who was that annoying creature that was bothering you?"

"I have no idea. He just approached me and asked where my husband was. I politely replied that I was a widow, and he said he could remedy that and suggested we could have a trial run of our wedding night. I responded brusquely, then Joseph stepped forward to defend me when you arrived."

Jack smiled and asked, "And how brusquely was your response?"

She smiled back and replied, "Not as brusque as yours."

Jack laughed, then said, "At least I could understand his attraction, Mrs. Doyle. You would turn the pope's eye."

"Thank you, Mister Tyler, and might I say that I find myself quite taken by your appearance as well."

"Thank you, Mrs. Doyle. Now, what shall we order?"

"Someone recommended that prime rib would be a good choice upon our return, so perhaps that should be our selection."

"An outstanding choice, Mrs. Doyle," he said before turning to Joseph and asking, "And what is your preference Master Joseph?"

He looked at Jack, then at Emily and asked, "Why are you both talking so funny?"

They were both laughing as the waitress arrived and took their order for three prime ribs, one a smaller portion.

Emily sipped her tea with sugar and cream, as Jack explained his rushed return to his cabin and how Loopy had greeted him, accepted his reward for guarding the cabin in his absence, then disappeared again. She was mesmerized by how he looked clean-shaven with his hair combed. He was even more handsome yet had lost not one iota of his masculinity.

Joseph watched and listened attentively to Jack and was surprisingly saddened. He really liked Mister Tyler and saw him as his hero. Mrs. Doyle seemed to really like him, too. They smiled at each other all the time now that the danger was gone. Joseph wished that Mrs. Doyle would marry Mister Tyler and then they could move to his cabin that he'd never seen, and that was the reason for his sadness. He thought that nannies were like nuns and couldn't get married, and besides, he'd been told for as long as he could remember that he'd have to take over his father's company. So, despite his growing fantasies about living with Mister Tyler and Mrs. Doyle in the cabin with the almost friendly wolf, he knew in a short while, he'd be returning to Saint Ignatius School for Boys, living in his big house with a new guardian, and even though he'd still have Mrs. Doyle, he knew she'd be sad because Mister Tyler wouldn't be with them.

The waitress brought their prime rib with the expected baked potato and the unexpected and unwanted green peas.

Joseph may have been sad, but it didn't affect his appetite. Mrs. Doyle dug in with a vengeance, which pleased Jack knowing that Emily Ann Ward was eating, not Mrs. Doyle.

Between bites, Emily asked, "Where are you sleeping tonight, Mister Tyler?"

Jack swallowed his mostly-chewed piece of prime rib, then replied, "I was going to return to my cabin. I still have some things to do, including packing for our journey. Now, there are two eastbound passenger trains that come through each day. The 8:20, which arrives in Omaha in the wee hours of the morning the following day, and the 6:10, which arrives in early afternoon. I'd prefer to arrive during the day, so I'd recommend the later train, which would also give you a chance to do some shopping before we leave."

ABANDONED

Emily was somewhat disappointed, yet knew it was unlikely he'd be staying in the hotel when she had asked, but said, "I think the evening train would be better as well. Will you be returning in the morning to escort us about Laramie?"

"Yes, ma'am. I'll be knocking on your door at eight o'clock to escort you and Joseph to breakfast and then to Farley's Mercantile, so you'll be able to buy what you need."

"We'll be looking forward to it, Mister Tyler."

They finished their dinner, and Jack ordered some apple pie for each of them, as well as some hot chocolate for Joseph while he and Emily had more tea.

It was already past eight o'clock when they finished their desserts and Jack paid the check. He escorted Emily and Joseph out of the restaurant and into the lobby.

"I'd like to stay and talk for a while, Mrs. Doyle, but I need to get back to the cabin and pack, so I can return early in the morning."

"I understand, Mister Tyler," Emily replied.

He turned to Joseph and said, "I'll see you in the morning, sir," then surprised him by offering him his hand.

Joseph smiled and shook his hand, saying, "I'll see you then, too, sir."

Jack then stood, caught Emily's eye, winked, and watched a smile spread across her lips.

"Good night, Mister Tyler, and thank you for a wonderful, yet perhaps frustrating evening."

"You're welcome, Mrs. Doyle. I'll try to mount and ride my horse to return to my cabin but will undoubtably be uncomfortable in the endeavor. Good night to you and to you, Joseph."

"Good night, Mister Tyler," Joseph replied as he took Emily's hand.

She was stifling a bad case of the giggles as she turned and walked with Joseph back to their room.

Jack watched them leave and once they were inside the door, knew they would be safe for the night, then turned and walked out into the already chilly Wyoming evening.

He crossed the boardwalk, untied Claude's horse, mounted and wheeled him to the south heading out of town.

Across the street, Clark Gibbons watched him leave. He'd suspected that the bastard who'd threatened him in front of that redhead would be spending the night in her room, but with that kid, it was an even chance he'd be leaving. After they'd gone to the restaurant, Clark had spent almost an hour in the saloon, drinking beer and then whiskey as he'd let his resentment grow, fueled by the alcohol.

He finally slammed down his empty whiskey glass, pulled on his hat, then left the saloon and led his horse to the hitchrail at Everly's Tonsorial Parlor across the street from the hotel. He'd been sitting on the bench just stewing in his fury watching people enter and exit the hotel to use the restaurant, and none had been that pompous bastard.

Then, he caught sight of him talking to that extraordinary redheaded widow in the lobby and when she turned to go back to her room, and he'd walked out of the hotel, Clark knew he'd have his chance for revenge.

Clark didn't know who he was or where he called home despite his being a resident of Laramie for almost a year now. But the fact that he'd never seen the man, meant he probably lived out of town, which was perfect.

After the man rode off and headed south, Clark mounted his tall white gelding and set him at a walk in slow pursuit. The almost full moon gave him plenty of light and if he kept the right distance, he doubted if the man would even see him.

He left town and barely caught sight of the man almost a mile ahead, so he nudged Bronco to a slightly faster pace to match the rider and keep him within his vision. He didn't want to let him make a turn and disappear.

Jack had no idea he was being followed. Why should he? His mind was still filled with images of Emily. He hadn't exaggerated about the discomfort of the return ride, either. She was that inspiring. The other reason he didn't even bother checking his backtrail was that he'd never been followed before by anyone. Even when he was traveling through what they referred to as 'Injun territory' back East, he was never concerned. The Arapaho, Utes, and the occasional Cheyenne he'd met either ignored him or traded with him. A single man either hunting or prospecting wasn't a threat.

So, he road along the poor excuse for a roadway without any concerns at all, simply reveling in his memories of Emily.

Clark had nudged Bronco into a medium trot to close the distance. The cold night air was driving away his whiskey-induced fog and he felt exhilarated in the chase. He was just eight hundred yards behind Jack and could see him clearly in the moonlight now. He knew he was gaining and wondered where the man was going. He didn't know there were any ranches down this far south.

He didn't know that the road, such as it was, had been created by the wagons of supplies and materials that Jack had brought to his cabin over the years and his cabin and barn were the only human-built structures in sixty square miles.

Jack had Claude's horse moving at a slow trot, his hooves masking any sounds that Clark Gibbons' gelding was making. If he'd turned around, Jack would have had no problem spotting the white horse of his pursuer in the bright moonlight, but he simply never bothered.

The unusual chase continued until Jack finally turned east, leaving the roadway.

Jack had purposefully removed any evidence of wagon tracks that pointed to his cabin, making the half-road, half-trail just seeming to end in the middle of nowhere, which really wasn't unusual. Most of the roads to ranches and farms that were created by wagons ended that way, but three miles south of Laramie, there were no more ranches or farms.

So, when he suddenly turned left, leaving the roadway, Clark sped up again, wondering where he was going. He pulled his Winchester from his scabbard, unsure if the man had seen him and was setting up an ambush. He suddenly wished his gelding wasn't so white.

He reached the east turnoff just thirty seconds later and picked up Jack again as he was riding away. The cabin, as large as it was, wasn't visible in the moonlight because of the trees, so Clark sped up slightly to get even closer.

Jack made the final, curving turn around a large outcrop of rock, spotted his cabin and headed for the corral on his right, reaching it a minute later and stepping down.

He swung the gate open, walked Claude's horse inside and quickly began unsaddling him. He was humming softly as he worked and didn't hear the approach of Clark's white gelding which he'd slowed to a walk.

Clark thought this was going to be easy as he brought Bronco to a stop and raised his Winchester.

He was preparing to cock the hammer when a low, rumbling growl came from his right and he froze as the hairs on the back of his neck stood to attention and a deep chill raced through his spine. He slowly turned, bringing his Winchester's sights with him to see what was causing his instinctive terror.

ABANDONED

His horse's eyes were white as he looked at the fearsome predator just ten feet away and began to dance to his left as Loopy matched the gelding's moves by slowly advancing.

Jack heard Loopy's growl, then turned his head, shocked to see a white horse just fifty yards away with a rider pointing his Winchester at the wolf.

"Mister!" he shouted, "Lower your Winchester right now or he'll take your arm off before he eats you alive!"

He immediately dropped the horse blanket in his hand and began walking quickly to the man-wolf standoff, passing through the still-open corral gate.

Clark Gibbons was still in abject terror as he looked at the green-glowing eyes of the wolf as it continued to growl with its massive teeth bared. He'd heard Jack's warning but knew if he lowered his repeater, that wolf would leap.

He made the mistake of cocking the hammer even as Jack was quickly nearing them.

Jack knew he couldn't tell Loopy to stop, not because the wolf wouldn't back off, but because if he did, then more than likely the man on the horse would shoot Loopy. If the rider didn't obey his shouted warning, he'd have to suffer the consequences. And he soon did exactly that.

As soon as he heard the Winchester's hammer click, Loopy, whose hind legs were already coiled, leapt with his jaw wide.

Clark was so panicked in fear that he didn't even think of pulling the trigger, even though his finger was already pressed against it.

Loopy's eighty pounds of muscle smashed into Clark, his jaw grabbing the human's right arm as his momentum carried him through the man, twisting him from the saddle.

Clark's Winchester flew away as his right foot snagged in his stirrup, hanging him upside down on the right side of his panicked horse, who began to try and get away from the wolf.

Clark was screaming as his horse bucked and twisted, and Loopy refused to let his arm go.

Jack raced to the chaotic scene and yelled, "Loopy! No!", unsure if the wolf would release his grip.

Loopy surprised him when he let the man's arm loose, then turned and trotted away to the back of the house and disappeared onto the back porch.

Jack then had to calm the white horse and began to sing *The Yellow Rose of Texas*, even though he was unsure of the lyrics after the first few lines.

The horse continued to panic for a few more seconds as the scent of the wolf still filled its nostrils, but even with Clark's screaming, the horse could hear the calming, deep voice and began to settle down.

It was another twenty seconds before it finally remained with all four hooves on the ground as Jack reached out and rubbed his nose before turning to help the upside-down Clark Gibbons, whose screams had finally subsided into a combination of sobbing and groans.

"Stay still, mister," Jack snarled as he pulled his knife and was about to slice the right stirrup, then decided not to ruin a good piece of leather, slipped the knife back into its sheath and grabbed the stirrup, lifted the man's boot slightly, then yanked it free, dumping him to the ground.

Clark screamed again when he hit the hard earth, but then resumed his sobbing as Jack removed his left foot from the stirrup. It was only then that he recognized the man who had been harassing Emily in the hotel.

ABANDONED

"Did you come here to shoot me in the back, you cowardly bastard?" he growled as he looked down at the man.

"You...you humiliated me," Clark whined as his only excuse.

Jack really wanted to kick him while he was down, but the man seemed nothing short of pathetic and wasn't worthy of the anger he should have felt, so he reached down, grabbed him behind his collar and lifted him to his feet.

Before he did anything else, he yanked off the man's hammer loop then pulled his Colt from his holster and slid it in his waist under his new belt.

"Alright, let's go inside and I'll fix up that bite wound," he said as he began to walk away.

Clark thought about climbing on Bronco and heading back to Laramie to see the doc, but his arm was bleeding so badly, he didn't want to risk it, so he followed Jack as he headed for the back of his large cabin.

Even though he was injured, he was surprised to see such a large building in the middle of nowhere. He didn't see or hear any cattle and wondered what the man did for a living.

When he followed Jack near the back of the cabin, he saw the wolf sitting there staring at him and stopped in his tracks.

Jack expected him to either stop, run back to his horse, or just pee his pants, and in the moonlight, wasn't sure he hadn't wet himself, but still beckoned him to continue.

"He won't hurt you if you're with me," Jack said as he waited on the back porch.

Clark nervously began to walk and when he passed Loopy, he hurried to where Jack waited by the open back door to the mud room and scurried inside.

Jack followed, leaving both outer and inner doors open for Loopy, knowing he'd expect some meaty reward for saving his life, even though Jack was sure the wolf enjoyed every second of what he'd done.

"Have a seat at the table," Jack ordered as he opened the door and stepped down into the pitch black cold room.

He didn't need any light to find the shelf of dried meats, and grabbed a large piece of smoked venison, then climbed back out, closed the door and tossed it to the wolf, who caught it in the dim light, then trotted away so he could eat in peace, away from the stranger.

Jack then struck a match and lit one of the two kitchen lamps, picked it up and carried it to the table, set it down and took a seat next to the man, then removed his Colt and set it near the lamp.

"Let's see your right arm," he said.

Clark held out the bloody mess that had been a perfectly functioning arm just a few minutes earlier.

Jack peeled back the sleeve and said, "That's not too bad. There are only a few puncture wounds that won't even need sutures. Loopy didn't want to do anything more than pull you off your horse. If I hadn't stopped him, he would have ripped that arm off."

Clark shivered and asked, "Loopy? Is he mad?"

"No, it's short for Lupus, which is Latin for wolf. He's not rabid, so you're not going to die, either. You won't be able to use that arm for a while, though. I'll wrap it up and you can head back to Laramie."

Clark blinked in confusion and asked, "Aren't you even mad?"

"Not really, but you really ruined what was a good night. That lady you insulted in the lobby is Mrs. Emily Doyle. She's the boy's nanny and their bastard uncle left them out in the Medicine Bow Mountains to die so he could inherit the boy's fortune. I found them when the boy was fending off a grizzly bear with stones to protect her. They've been through a lot and I'll be escorting them back to Omaha tomorrow to confront that no-good uncle of his and have him arrested for murdering Claude Boucher."

"He killed Claude?"

Jack looked at him as he absent-mindedly reached behind him and pulled a towel off a shelf to wrap his arm.

"How do you know Claude? I've never met you before, and I'm a guide."

"I hired him a little over a year ago as a guide for our hunting party. After we returned to Chicago, I decided to come back here and buy a ranch. I own the C-G Connected a mile northwest of Laramie."

"I don't get into town that often, so that's probably why I don't know you. Why did you bother Mrs. Doyle? She said you made an offensive suggestion to her."

"I should have married before I left Chicago. There just aren't many women here. When I saw her sitting there and she told me she was a widow, I'll admit to being rather forward, but she did put me in my place."

"Why would you even think of saying anything like that?"

"It worked in Chicago, but I guess it's not acceptable out here."

"I don't think it's acceptable in Chicago, either. You must have been looking for a wife in the wrong places."

Jack was wrapping his arm when Clark asked, "Um, do you mind if I ask if you have any intentions regarding Mrs. Doyle?"

Instead of getting angry, Jack almost laughed as he answered, "I have every intention regarding Mrs. Doyle, and that includes doing what I told you I'd do in the hotel lobby to any man who even thinks of approaching her."

"Sorry. I'm just asking. Maybe I'll head back to Chicago to find a woman."

"That might be a wise idea, but don't try asking a woman the same question you asked Mrs. Doyle. If she agrees to your proposition in Chicago, she wouldn't be much of a wife."

"Have you been married before, then?" he asked as Jack tied off the bandage.

"Nope, but I'm getting better at understanding women now that I've talked to Mrs. Doyle for a while."

Clark rolled down his sleeve and asked, "Can I have my pistol back?"

"Go ahead. Just to let you know, Loopy wouldn't be happy if you tried to shoot me, and I'd probably get my big sticker into you first anyway."

"No, I won't try anything again. It must have been the whiskey that pushed me to even try."

"That's one of the reasons I don't touch the stuff," Jack said as he stood, then added, "the other is that it tastes terrible."

Jack walked him out the back door, didn't see Loopy anywhere, which wasn't unusual, then escorted him to his horse.

Clark picked up his Winchester, slid it into his scabbard, mounted and took his white gelding's reins.

Neither said a word as Clark wheeled his horse around and trotted away. As he rode off into the moonlit terrain, Jack caught Loopy's shadow trailing and hoped the man wouldn't be as stupid as to turn around.

He then returned to the corral and finished unsaddling Claude's horse. All of the animals were wide awake now, the horses in the corral still twitchy after Loopy's attack, but Abby and Billy were already on their way back to sleep.

After moving the tack to the barn, Jack headed back to his house to prepare for tomorrow's trip to Omaha and another day with Emily.

He closed the inner door against the night's chill, but left the outer door open for Loopy in case he wanted to use the mud room.

He picked up his gold-laden saddlebags and carried them to the library/office across from the bathroom. He set the saddlebags down, then lit another lamp before picking up the saddlebags and setting them on his desk. He pulled out the three heavy jars of gold, set them on the desk, pulled out his ledger, set it aside and then picked up one of the two jars of gold dust, which were heavier than the jar of nuggets. Alongside his far wall was what looked like a souvenir shelf with a family of six brass wolves placed on its surface. There was a large male, a slightly smaller female, then four brass cubs of decreasing sizes. He then placed the jar on the left side of the shelf, removed two of the smaller wolves from the shelf, then a slightly larger one. He then removed one peg from under each side of the shelf, leaving the larger center support in place and the shelf tilted to the left. Jack then carefully placed the second smallest wolf on the shelf in its marked position, watched the shelf close to level, then added the smallest bronze casting and the shelf titled slightly again.

After reinserting the pegs, he removed the jar of gold, set it on the desk and entered six pounds twelve ounces in his ledger. He did that with the other two jars and when he finished, he replaced the wolves in their decorative positions and added the total. Nineteen pounds and ten ounces of gold. There was just seven thousand dollars in gold on his desk. Before, it was nothing more than interesting because he had nothing he really wanted. Now, it might be useful. How, he didn't know, but that nineteen pounds and ten ounces, plus the eighteen pounds and eight ounces he had in his safe area amounted to quite a haul for only about a month's worth of labor.

It was time to put it into his safe. He knew that it was highly unlikely anyone would visit the cabin in his absence, not with Loopy patrolling the area, but he still preferred to keep it in a safe place.

There were two walls of books that would have been the most obvious choice, but that was the point. It was too obvious.

Jack pulled his heavy straight-backed chair to the eastern wall, then stood on the chair, reached on top of the bookshelf and picked up a screwdriver. Above the bookshelf were the angled boards hiding the roof. Most were secured by wooden pegs, but one was grooved, although it really appeared to be nothing more than an imperfection. He inserted the wide flathead screwdriver's tip and began to rotate it counterclockwise, unscrewing the heavy dowel. The long spiraled dowel finally released the board and he stepped down, picked up two of the jars, then returned to the chair and slid the two jars into a wide gap to the right, next to the other jars that were already there. After putting the last jar in place, he pulled a leather sack out of the left side, opened it and withdrew three hundred dollars in cash for the trip to Omaha. He normally didn't travel first-class, but this time, he wasn't going to be taking any gold to Cheyenne and he wanted Emily and Joseph to travel as comfortably as possible.

He pushed the board back into place, screwed the dowel until it was tight and flush with the board's flat surface then hopped back down to the floor.

Now that the money part of his preparation was done, he could so his normal packing, which shouldn't take long.

Northwest of Laramie, Clark Gibbons was packing as well. After having returned to his ranch, he decided he didn't want to risk running afoul of Jack Tyler or that damned wolf again, so he decided just after he'd turned his gelding back north that he'd head back to Chicago and see if Henrietta Williams would marry him. He wasn't sure if he'd return and told his foreman of his plans.

ABANDONED

Emily and Joseph were both changed and ready for sleep and had slipped under the covers of the large bed.

Joseph didn't need any songs or anything else to let him slip into dreamland, and soon was breathing deeply.

Emily looked at his angelic face and wondered what would happen when they returned to Omaha. There were so many possibilities and all she could hope was that when everything was settled, that she could still be with Joseph. She wanted to see him grow, having been deprived of being able to see her own children become teenagers and then adults. She'd made some mistakes in her life and had many regrets, but Joseph could balance them all.

The other part of that equation, of course, was Jack. She didn't want to be put into the position where she had to choose between her two men, and even now, had no idea which way she would go. She had never felt so alive as she had been with Jack, and actually shivered when she imagined what it would be like to be with him. *But would it be selfish for her to give up her devotion to Joseph for the joy she knew that Jack would give her? Would she be willing to give up the freedom of being Emily Ann Ward?* She knew that as long as she was with Joseph, she'd be Mrs. Doyle, just as she was now.

Emily barely touched her fingertips to Joseph's peaceful face, sighed, and prayed that she never had to make that decision.

In Omaha, Noah Gallagher was already sleeping, having exhausted himself. Anna Thornton lay awake next to him. After the pathetic advances of Wilbur Moore, Noah's exuberant lovemaking had been quite thrilling, but now, as she lay staring at the ceiling, she felt as if she'd sinned much worse in enjoying being bedded by a murderer.

CHAPTER 6

Jack was up earlier than usual, and began his morning ritual in rushed fashion, knowing he didn't have to cook breakfast. He was still careful when he shaved, though.

Once he'd finished shaving and brushing his teeth, he packed his toiletry items in his travel bag and headed for the kitchen. He glanced over at the table and swore when he realized he hadn't cleaned up the blood from that night visit from the ranch owner. He never did ask his name, either.

The blood hadn't soaked into the wood because of the varnish on the table's surface, one of the improvements he'd made when he acknowledged how often he spilled things. He cleaned the blood using another towel, then washed the towel and hung it to dry near the sink.

Satisfied he was ready, he walked to the corral and saddled Claude's horse again rather than Abby. He thought Billy would appreciate her companionship while he healed from his injuries.

As he saddled the horse, he reminded himself to stop at the livery where they'd rented Joseph's horse and talk to the liveryman about buying the animal. He saddled the pack horse and hooked on the empty panniers, having moved the contents into the barn for sorting later. He dropped his travel bag into one of the panniers before mounting Claude's horse, which was now his horse.

When he led the pack horse onto the roadway, the Remington and the big knife were his only weapons. He'd be on the train in a few hours and wouldn't need a rifle.

As he rode to Laramie as the sun rose, he thought about how odd it would be to return to a real city again. He imagined that Omaha had grown considerably over the last fifteen years, what

ABANDONED

with the Union Pacific drawing all of that traffic heading west. He'd have to depend on Emily's knowledge of the city to get around and was curious if he'd look out of place with his gunbelt. If he did, well, that was too bad. He wanted the pistol with him when he confronted Noah Gallagher.

―――

Clark Gibbons had already left his ranch before Jack reached the road and arrived in Laramie. After buying his ticket to Chicago, he left his horse and tack at Robinson's Livery for boarding until his return, if he decided to come back, then walked to the restaurant in the Railway Hotel for breakfast.

―――

At 1710 Chicago Street, Noah Gallagher rolled over in the big bed and smiled, expecting to find the soft skin of Anna Thornton still asleep beside him. He opened his eyes, saw the empty sheets and sat up quickly. He scanned the room, then threw back the quilts and stormed out the door, slamming it open.

He looked down both hallways, and despite his own nakedness, knowing there were only two women in the house, began hunting for Anna to let her know that her duties included staying in his bed until she was dismissed.

He trotted down the big stairway and headed for the kitchen where she should be preparing his breakfast. He strode down the long hallway and pushed open the swinging door to the kitchen to deliver his tongue-lashing and found it empty. *Where was that woman?*

He turned and pushed through the swinging door again and then swung open the door to her room and found it empty as well. Then he realized that he hadn't seen Mary Flaherty either.

He left Anna Thornton's room and went next door to the maid's room and discovered it to be empty as well. Then, he walked to the dresser and began opening drawers, finding not a stitch of clothing.

He whirled and threw open the closet door. Nothing.

Noah left the maid's room, reentered Anna's room and searched the drawers and closet quickly. The two women were gone.

Noah was furious. He walked slowly into the parlor, quivering in his rage as he walked toward the big brightly lit picture window that faced Chicago Street, and was prepared to voice his rage with a loud scream when it suddenly dawned on him that he was exposing himself to the pedestrians on Chicago Street two hundred feet away.

He didn't know if they'd seen him or not, but he quickly turned and raced up the stairs. That's all he'd need now is to have someone file a complaint against him. He could always say it was Wilbur Moore and he'd fired the steward for his perversion. Hopefully, no one had noticed.

But his anger was still there as he used the water closet then finally began to dress.

―――――

Emily had bathed again, although Joseph came to his boyish senses and declined the honor. He was already dressed and sitting on the bed when Emily emerged from the bathroom fully clothed, not wanting to revisit the awkward embarrassment she'd felt when Joseph had seen her in her camisole.

"Are we going to go to the restaurant now, Mrs. Doyle?"

"No, Joseph. We're going to wait for Mister Tyler to arrive. He said he'd be here at eight o'clock to take us to breakfast. Remember?"

"Oh. That's right," he answered as he sat on the edge of the bed and began swinging his legs while Emily brushed her hair again.

―――――

ABANDONED

Jack had reached Laramie just after seven o'clock and stopped at Cook's Livery, which was stamped on the panniers. He walked Claude's horse into the barn, stepped down, and removed his travel bag from the pannier.

"Mornin'. What can I do for ya?" asked Jacob Cook as he walked from his combination office and living quarters where he'd just finished breakfast.

"Recognize the pack horse?" Jack asked.

"Yup. His name is Pinky. Where'd you find him? I rented him out to Claude Boucher a couple of weeks ago."

"Then you must recognize Claude's horse right behind him."

Jacob had to move to get out of the morning sun to look and said, "Yup. That's him. Where's Claude?"

"What's left of Claude is on the western bank of a creek about a day's ride west of here. I found his horse and the other horses wandering nearby. Claude been shot in the back. I've already told Sheriff Higginbotham and I'll need to see him shortly about an arrest warrant for his murderer."

Jacob's eyes went wide as he asked, "Was it that feller from Omaha who done him in?"

"It was, and I'll tell you, I was a bit surprised. I didn't think anybody could get the drop on Claude. That bastard never trusted anybody."

"That's the truth of it. You say you got all of the horses? What about the mule?"

"I think the man who shot Claude shot him in front of the mule and then emptied his pistol into the animal. I found where he'd dragged a large carcass out of the clearing into some nearby woods and could smell it when we passed. But I did find the small black horse that you rented to him and I'd like to make you a deal to buy him and the saddle."

"What kind of deal are we lookin' at?"

"I'll give you back Pinky and the pack saddle because they're yours. Now Claude's horse is rightfully mine because he was abandoned. I'll trade him for the black horse and saddle, and when I return from Omaha after chasing down the lowlife son of a bitch that shot your mule, I'll buy the two best horses you can find. I'll need two nice saddles, too."

Jacob asked, "What kinda horses do you want?"

"I'd like a fairly young gelding, preferably black like that small horse and a young mare or even a filly. Her coloring isn't important, but I want her to be pretty because she'll be for a very pretty lady."

Jacob could sense some serious profit and asked, "How much would you be willin' to spend?"

Jack knew full well that he was going to make the liveryman's day and replied, "You find the right horses and you'll be happy with the deal."

Jacob grinned and said, "That's a deal. How long do you figure you'll be gone? I'll have to ride out to Humphrey's Horse Farm to do some searching."

"I should be back in a week or so. Is that enough time?"

"You bet. I didn't get your name, though."

"Oh, sorry. I'm Jack Tyler."

Jacob shook his hand and said, "I've heard the name, but never met ya. Glad to know you, Mister Tyler. When you get to Omaha and find that cuss, give him a kick in the middle for what he did to Bessie. She was a good mule."

ABANDONED

"I'll do that, Mister Cook," Jack replied.

He picked up his travel bag and trotted across the street, stepped onto the boardwalk and headed for the Metropolitan Hotel.

As Jack was walking to the hotel, the 8:20 eastbound Union Pacific train was slowing as it pulled into the station. Laramie was one of its coaling and watering stops, so it would be there for almost thirty minutes.

Clark Gibbons pulled out his pocket watch as he sat at his table, having just finished his large breakfast. He had plenty of time, so he poured himself another cup of coffee.

Jack turned into the lobby of the Metropolitan Hotel and passed by the desk and walked to Emily's room. His heart was thumping as he stood before the door and knocked twice. The door flew open not four seconds later and he stared into Emily's blue eyes and smiled.

"Good morning, Mrs. Doyle."

"Good morning, Mister Tyler."

After ten seconds of staring, Jack finally pried his eyes loose and looked down at Joseph who was already grinning.

"Good morning, Master Joseph."

"Hello. Are we going to have breakfast now? I'm hungry."

"Yes, sir, but first, if I may, I'd like to store my travel bag in your room."

Emily stepped aside to let Jack enter, then after dropping his travel bag, he quickly turned back around, took her arm and Joseph's hand and left the room, closing the door behind them.

As they walked to the restaurant, Jack said, "I had an unusual visitor last night, Mrs. Doyle."

They were turning in the lobby as she asked, "A visitor? To your cabin?"

"Yes, ma'am. He was an unexpected and unwelcome visitor and received an unexpected unwelcoming."

She laughed lightly as they entered the restaurant and were shown to a table.

Once they were all seated and placed their orders, Emily asked, "Who was this unwelcome visitor?"

"The same gentleman who insulted you in the lobby. He was apparently angry about being emasculated in public, went to the saloon and imbibed in too much liquor and decided to follow me out of town and shoot me in the back."

Emily was aghast and asked, "What happened?"

"He met Loopy," Jack said, then before she or Joseph could ask any questions, told them of the bizarre confrontation.

When he finished, Emily asked, "How could he have followed you without you even noticing?"

"I was daydreaming at night, Mrs. Doyle. I had visions of a Ward on my mind."

"Oh," Emily replied.

The waitress arrived with their breakfasts and Joseph began peppering Jack with questions about the event, even though Jack had already answered most of them.

Just a half a mile away, the locomotive blew its whistle announcing the departure of the 8:20 train.

ABANDONED

As they left the restaurant, Emily asked, "Are we going shopping now?"

"No, ma'am. We need to stop by the sheriff's office and see if he has the warrant for Noah Gallagher's arrest for murder."

"Then, we'll do some shopping?"

"Yes, ma'am."

Emily smiled as she took his arm and they left the hotel, turned right and after reaching the intersection, crossed the street, stepped onto the next boardwalk, then turned right again until they reached the sheriff's office.

Jack held the door open, let Emily and Joseph enter, then stepped in behind them.

"Morning, ma'am, Mister Tyler," Deputy Pruitt said as he stood.

"Good morning, Deputy. Is the sheriff in?"

"Yes, sir. Just head on back," he replied before returning to his seat.

Jack ushered Emily and Joseph down the short hallway and entered the only open door finding Sheriff Higginbotham at his desk.

"Well, good morning, folks. Have a seat, Mrs. Doyle," he said as he stood.

Emily sat down, and the sheriff said, "I've got your warrant, Jack. Our prosecutor, Mister Johnson, was really spitting nails over this one. Granted, nobody really liked Claude anyway, but to have some feller come out to our county and do something as despicable as to leave such a pretty lady and a handsome lad out there alone and then shoot a man in the back was too much. I've gotta admit that I felt pretty bad about it, too."

Jack asked, "Why would you feel bad about it, Will?"

The sheriff squirmed in his chair and replied, "Well, I wrote him a statement saying that Mrs. Doyle and the boy had been killed in a hunting accident. I feel like such an idiot!"

Jack said, "Don't worry about it, Will. I'll bring his shackled butt back here and you can toss him in your jail for a while before you hang him."

The sheriff was mollified, but still unhappy having been made a fool. He took a folded paper from the box on his desk along with a badge and held them out to Jack.

"Here's that warrant for you, and a badge making you a deputy sheriff of Albany County. I'll sort of swear you in, but it doesn't pay anything."

"I'm fine with that, Sheriff," Jack said as he accepted the warrant and badge.

The sheriff narrated a very informal swearing in, then shook Jack's hand and wished him luck. After saying goodbye to Emily and Joseph, the sheriff took his seat.

Jack followed Emily and Joseph out past Deputy Pruitt who also wished him good luck, then they left the sheriff's office and began walking to Farley's Mercantile, two blocks away.

As they walked, Jack said, "I bet that statement the sheriff gave to Mister Gallagher would be enough to satisfy all of the legal niceties to let Gallagher take everything that was being held for Joseph."

"I know. That's what I thought when he told us."

Joseph looked up and asked excitedly, "Does that mean I don't have to go back to Omaha at all?"

Jack answered, "Only if you want him to get away with all the bad things he's done, Joseph."

"Oh. Then I guess we have to go back. Will you arrest him now that you're a deputy?"

Jack smiled and replied, "No, Joseph. I'm just a deputy so I can legally bring him back to Laramie to face trial. When we get to Omaha, we meet with the Douglas County Sheriff and they'll arrest him and then I bring him back here."

"Are we coming back with you?"

"You'll be going back to school pretty soon, won't you?"

"Yes, but don't I have to be here to tell them what happened?"

"No, Joseph. You and Mrs. Doyle will stay in Omaha while I take him back here."

"But you'll come back right away, won't you?"

Jack looked at Emily, who was already waiting for his answer, then replied, "Yes, Joseph. I'll be coming right back."

Emily broke into a wide smile and began to breathe rapidly but didn't say anything. It wasn't necessary.

Joseph did answer, saying, "Good. I need you to cut my ugly hat."

Jack and Emily both laughed as they crossed the street.

Even after having said it, Jack wasn't really sure it would be possible depending on all those confusing legalities of guardians and wills.

———

At the Brennan Furnace and Coal Company offices, the universal concern by the managers and officers of the company over the sudden change in ownership had an added infusion of worry when that Tuesday morning, the president of the company, Thomas White, hadn't arrived. He was a fastidious, punctual man, traits which served him well as an accountant and later vice president of finance. As long as anyone had known, Mister White had never been even a minute late for an appointment or when he was due to begin his workday.

Yet, here it was ten-thirty, and no one had seen the company's president. Papers needing his signature were already stacking up, and to make matters worse, his office secretary, Arthur Hicks was also gone.

With the new company owner unavailable, the company president and his secretary both missing, the waves of nervousness and dread began to filter from the company offices down to the employees on the floor. The lightning-fast gossip of the manner of the accidental deaths of Joseph Charles Brennan III and his nanny had given rise to many rumors of conspiracies and murder that were much closer to the truth than the official story. Brennan Furnace and Coal almost stopped operating as even foremen and supervisors stopped to pass their own theories of what had happened to the boy and his nanny.

After dressing, Noah had taken the buggy and driven to Willoughby's Domestics to hire a new maid, cook and butler/coachman. He decided the maid and cook, while not hideous, would not be attractive enough to even consider as bed partners. From now on, he'd limit his frolicking to the higher end bordellos where the women knew how to please a man of substance.

As Clark Gibbons sat in his first-class seat on the train, he mesmerized his fellow passengers with the story of how a man from Omaha had left his nephew out in the wilderness to die so he could inherit the family company, but the boy and his nanny had been saved from a bear and wolves by a woodsman. At each of the stops as the train made its way along the rails, new passengers would arrive, and the tale began to take on mythic proportions.

When the train arrived in Julesburg, a gentleman boarded the first-class passenger coach with his wife. They took their seats and the train departed ten minutes later.

They were sitting two rows behind Clark, who had just finished telling the story for his sixth time and neither paid any attention until the man's wife heard him say 'Omaha', and her interest was piqued. When the man said 'nanny', she tried to listen more closely, but had missed most of it.

So, when when he finished, she nudged her husband and whispered, "John, could you ask the gentleman in the seat two rows ahead if he could tell us the story he has just told the other gentleman?"

He looked at his wife, smiled, and replied, "As you wish, my dear."

John stood took three steps and asked Clark if he would be so kind as to return with him and tell the interesting story that seemed to attract the interest of his wife.

Clark was only too happy to oblige, then left his seat, walked two rows back and sat on the edge of the seat across the aisle from the couple. His now, much improved story still kept the basic facts intact, but were now embellished with wild Indians with war paint and war bonnets, cougars and even a bison stampede.

When he finished, the couple thanked him, and Clark returned to his seat, pleased with his newest version.

Mary sat in her seat as John talked about Clark's dramatic narrative, not hearing a word he said. Despite all of the embellishments, she had latched onto the tale's foundation about the rescue of the nanny and the boy. The nanny had to be Emily.

She hadn't heard from her sister in years, but when the storyteller had described the nanny as a tall woman of about thirty years of age with long, dark red hair and a full figure, she knew it had to be Emily. There just weren't that many women in Omaha that matched Emily's description and she doubted if any of them were nannies. That meant that the boy must have been Joseph Brennan, the boy who was supposed to inherit the company where her father worked as a manager. When they returned to Omaha for the wedding of her youngest sister, Molly, she'd ask her father if he'd heard anything about Emily.

The story the man had just narrated had also included the vital detail that despite all of the terrors that Emily had undergone, she and the boy were now safe and would be returning soon to Omaha. She thanked God for her sister's deliverance and would talk to her husband when she could do so privately.

Emily's shopping was decidedly less shopping and more talking. After Jack's reply to Joseph about returning to Omaha after the trial, Emily had been so relieved she had barely looked at anything in the store. She hadn't even considered the legal issues that were already plaguing Jack's thoughts.

Joseph had been bouncing around the toys and had been searching for something that wasn't too young for him now that he'd stood face-to-face with a grizzly bear and a huge, snarling wolf.

Jack and Emily walked up behind Joseph as he was examining a bow and arrow set that looked too childish for him, when Jack walked two steps to his right and slid a large wooden box from the shelf and then after keeping it, walked further down and picked up two decks of cards.

When he returned, Joseph and Emily were both looking at him.

He held up the heavy box and they could see the checkerboard on top.

ABANDONED

"Checkers?" asked Joseph.

"Yes, sir. There are checkers inside the box and a chess set, too. We'll be able to play both on the train," he answered, then held up the cards and said, "and I'll teach you how to play poker, too."

Joseph glanced up at his nanny for approval, having heard nothing good about playing cards.

"It's perfectly acceptable, Joseph," she said as she smiled down at him.

"Okay. I don't need anything anyway. These are all for little kids and I have my knife, too."

Jack said, "Then I'll go and pay for these and we can play some checkers in the hotel before lunch and talk, too."

"What will we be talking about, Mister Tyler?" Emily asked as they began walking to the counter.

"All sorts of things, Mrs. Doyle," he replied.

By noon, the absence of the company president had resulted in the vice president of operations, James Burke, taking a buggy ride to Mister White's home on Sixteenth Street. It was a decidedly modest home, but when Vera White answered the door, she was surprised to learn her husband of sixteen years wasn't at work. He'd dressed, kissed her goodbye on her cheek as he always did, then walked down the walkway, smiling at her as he waved goodbye. There had been nothing different about his behavior at all and she was shocked to hear the news of the death of the Brennan boy and the takeover of the company by Noah Gallagher. Thomas hadn't said a word about it.

The vice president was flummoxed by the disappearance and began to suspect foul play, which would be rare, but still possible. As he boarded the buggy to return to his office and let the other upper management know that the president was still missing, he focused on the president's secretary's absence as well. That negated the foul play aspect because they both lived in different parts of the city.

He turned the buggy toward the apartments where Mister White's secretary, Arthur Hicks, lived. He didn't know the apartment number itself, but he knew the building and expected that the manager would be able to direct him to the correct apartment.

When he arrived, he entered the building and didn't have to ask anyone when he found the mailboxes near the doorway and found that apartment 1-C belonged to Arthur Hicks. He stepped down the hallway and knocked loudly on the door. No one responded, so he looked both ways down the hallway, and turned the knob. The door opened, and he quickly stepped inside, half expecting to see bodies lying on the floor in a pool of blood.

But the apartment was not only unoccupied, it was devoid of any sign of human habitation. He checked everywhere and found no clothes or any other artifacts that someone had lived there. The bed was neatly made, and the place could have been a hotel room by its sterile appearance.

He left the apartment, closing the door behind him. If he'd been concerned before, he was totally lost for an explanation now.

He left the building, climbed into the buggy and headed back to the company.

"You beat me again, Joseph!" Jack exclaimed as Joseph leaned back grinning.

"Are you sure you never played checkers before?" Jack asked.

"No, sir. Really. This is my first time," Joseph replied seriously.

ABANDONED

Emily sat next to Joseph on the couch before the low table in the hotel lobby, impressed how cleverly Jack had hidden his obviously bad moves.

"I think you should play Mrs. Doyle now. She's pretty smart, so she might put an end to your winning streak."

Emily stood, exchanged seats with Jack and watched as Joseph quickly set up the board again. She caught Jack's eye and winked.

They'd moved their travel bags out to the lobby to avoid paying for another night, already had lunch and would have dinner before walking to the train station and getting their tickets on the 6:10 eastbound train.

But now, they were just relaxing and having fun, knowing that they had a long train ride ahead of them and who knew what was waiting for them when they arrived in Omaha. It was going to be an exciting day on the first day of September.

The morning train was rolling across the plains of Nebraska, and Mary had finally been able to talk to her husband about what they'd heard from the now sleeping Clark Gibbons.

"You think that tale was true?" he asked incredulously.

"Not all of it, but if you toss aside all of the window dressings, how likely would it be for him to make up a story about a nanny who sounded remarkably like Emily and her charge, a boy who was going to inherit his family fortune in Omaha, being left to die in the wilderness by the boy's uncle? When we get into Omaha, I'll ask my father about it. If it's nonsense, then Emily and the boy will be home asleep. But if the uncle returned and has announced that his nephew and nanny both died in the wilds of Wyoming, then we'll know. I just hope that the second part of the story, about her being rescued is true as well."

"That's even less likely, my dear. If they had been abandoned out there, it was for a reason. There just is no one there except wild Indians who would kill them as quickly as the bears and wolves in his story. I'm sure it's all just a tall tale that will soon be published in one of those dime novels. I can even see the drawing on the cover. It'll have the tall, redheaded woman, her long hair flowing in the wind as she throws her hands in the air while the boy stands before a huge bear as it comes at them with his claws in the air. Then our hero leaps at the bear from behind with his huge knife plunging into the ferocious beast, saving them both and then wooing the enchanting woman."

Mary laughed but said, "I hope you're right, John."

He laughed and kissed her on the forehead before saying, "Of course, I am, dear."

The offices were closing at Brennan Furnace and Coal, and no sign of the president or his secretary had been found.

Mrs. White was distraught when he hadn't returned by 5:01 because he was never late. *Where was her husband?* She finally returned to the kitchen, served herself a double helping of dinner and carried it into the dining room. She sat at the big table all alone for the first time in decades. She had no one if something bad had happened to Thomas. He'd married her when he was still a bachelor at age forty-two, but already a well-established accountant with the company. When he'd been promoted to company president, she'd been as surprised as everyone else, and she knew he'd reached the pinnacle of his career. He was such a good man, such a sweet man.

Vera began spooning the oxtail soup as she looked at the empty chair at the opposite end of the long table. Somehow, she knew Thomas wouldn't return, but she didn't cry at all. She always had a feeling deep down inside there was a chance he'd leave her sooner or later. Even if she no longer had Thomas, she had her books and her embroidery. She had Millie, her parrot to keep her company, too. There was plenty of money in the bank, so she knew she would be able to live comfortably.

She finally filled her soup spoon with the deep red soup, held it before her eyes and said, "Farewell, Thomas, wherever you are," then slurped her soup, ignoring society's restrictions on such rude behavior.

Vera White was alone now and no one except the parrot would care what she did.

———

Jack, Emily and Joseph boarded the train at six o'clock, found their seats and set their travel bags in the rack above their heads. They had a table in back when they wished to enjoy some checkers or the poker games that Joseph was anxious to learn, but as the train began rolling east, they watched Laramie slide away in the dying light. It was Joseph who was the saddest to see it disappear.

———

Noah Gallagher had arranged to interview his applicants for the new positions in the morning, so he'd had his dinner at his favorite restaurant before returning to the empty house. But he had no sooner entered the mausoleum-like atmosphere when he wheeled about and left the house to head for the billiard club and some much-needed socializing.

———

The eastbound train leaving Kansas City for St. Louis was rolling out of the large station at the same time that Noah Gallagher was entering his billiard club. Brennan Furnace and Coal Company president Thomas White was in a first class seat and sitting next to him was his secretary, Arthur Hicks.

CHAPTER 7

The morning's eastbound train rolled into the Union Pacific's massive station in Omaha at 2:40 in the morning. As it slowly rolled to a stop at the platform, there were still several waiting relatives for the train, including Molly Ward and her fiancé, Andrew Donovan. Molly was watching anxiously to see her oldest sister, Mary step from the train. She'd only seen her sister twice since she'd married John Fitzpatrick and he'd taken the job in Julesburg, Colorado.

John stepped onto the platform first carrying two travel bags, then assisted Mary onto the wooden platform. She spotted Molly and grinned as they walked quickly to each other and embraced as John shook his future brother-in-law's hand.

Mary asked, "Molly, where's papa?"

"He's at home, finally sleeping. He hasn't been getting much rest since Emily was lost when she went on that blasted hunting trip to Wyoming. He's blaming himself for what happened because he was the one who got her the position."

John turned quickly as Mary said excitedly, "Molly, but that's not true. I don't believe Emily died. When we were returning, another passenger on the train who lives in Laramie told a story about a redheaded nanny and a boy who were rescued after they'd been abandoned by the boy's uncle, so he could steal the boy's inheritance in Omaha."

Molly's eye's widened as she turned to her fiancé and exclaimed, "We've got to tell papa!"

Mary was already smiling when she turned to her stunned husband and grinned before the men grabbed bags and they all scurried across the platform.

ABANDONED

The first sunrise in September reflected off the swirling waters of the Missouri River as it flowed south where it would eventually join the Mississippi River at St. Louis. It was a gorgeous late summer morning and showed no indications of the turmoil that would erupt before the sun completed its transit and settled in the west.

Even though he'd stayed up listening to Mary until almost four o'clock, Dennis Patrick Ward reached his office earlier than usual, arriving at 6:40 that morning after leaving instructions with Mary that someone must be at the station to meet each arriving train from the West that had connections to Laramie, Wyoming.

After Mary had convinced him that Emily and the boy were alive and were returning to Omaha, he was relieved and exultant, and now he needed to let someone in the company know. But the president was gone, so after he arrived in his own small office on factory floor, he quickly began walking to the main offices across the large yard. Even though he was now a manager, he still felt awkward entering the offices where all the bigwigs patrolled the corridors.

Dennis entered the large building and walked up the stairs to the offices of the vice presidents, unable to find anyone. He pulled out his pocket watch. It was after seven o'clock, so someone should have been here by now. He didn't know who was second in charge after the president, and he wasn't about to tell Noah Gallagher, *so who should get the news*?

He was walking back down the stairs and saw the vice president of operations, Mister Burke, entering the building and walked quickly to meet him.

"Mister Burke!" he said loudly as he hurriedly approached him.

James Burke sighed. *What now?*

"What is it, Mister Ward?" he asked in a detached voice.

"Mister Burke, last night my daughter arrived from Colorado on the train. She told me that a man from Laramie had been telling everyone that a nanny and her son had been left to die in the wilderness but had been rescued and would soon return to Omaha."

Burke shook his head slightly and said, "*What?* Why would she tell you this?"

"Because the nanny is my daughter, Emily."

"*Are you sure?*" he asked, picking up on the excitement of the news.

"I wasn't at first, but after listening to my oldest daughter describe the nanny who had been saved and the young boy with her, I'm convinced that she's right."

James Burke paused, snapped his fingers as he thought, then said, "Follow me, Mister Ward," and walked quickly across the outer room and climbed the stairs as Dennis Ward followed.

Neither man had paid any attention to the receptionist sitting at the desk fifteen feet away. The rumors of the boy's rescue would soon enter the company's grapevine with a vengeance.

―――

Noah rolled out of bed just past eight o'clock, leaving it unmade for the new maid he'd be hiring later. He shaved and dressed then left the house for breakfast. He ate quickly at the restaurant because he had to stop at the bank to withdraw some cash to pay the fees to the firm that found the domestics. He wanted to have more for his other expenses over the next few weeks and thought a thousand dollars was a nice round figure.

So, after breakfast, he drove the buggy to the First National Bank where the Brennan Furnace and Coal Company had their accounts. Even though he had the papers naming him the heir to the Brennan estate, he hadn't brought them with him, so he'd draw the money from the company accounts as the chairman of the board. Before, he'd have to concern himself with the approval of any withdrawals by the board, but not any longer. He was the owner now.

He pulled the buggy to a stop in front of the large bank, stepped outside and tied the reins on one of the long row of steel hitching posts with rings on top. It was what successful institutions do, he thought as he climbed the granite steps to the enter the double doors.

He stepped quickly to one of the eight teller windows, wrote out a draft for a thousand dollars and signed it with a flourish. He blew on the paper, then slid it across to the cashier.

"I'd like that all in twenty-dollar bills, please," Noah said as the clerk looked at the amount with raised eyebrows.

"Yes, sir," the man said, then turned and walked to a row of ledgers, selected one, then opened the green book and began flipping pages.

He stopped, looked at the sheet, then called over another cashier, who called over the head cashier as Noah watched, wondering what these idiots didn't understand.

The head cashier pointed at the page, then said something about initials and called over a third cashier who said something to the head cashier in a low voice. The head cashier listened, then asked him a question, which was answered before he nodded, and the cashier meeting ended as the head cashier joined the one that was supposed to be giving Noah his stack of twenty dollar bills.

"Mister Gallagher?" the head cashier asked, "I'm afraid we can't cash your draft. That account has an insufficient balance to cover that amount. The current balance is listed as $238.45."

Noah's mouth dropped open before he recovered and blustered, "That's not possible! You, inept people have made a mistake! That is the company account for Brennan Furnace and Coal of which I am the owner and chairman of the board."

To his credit, the head cashier didn't react to Noah's insult but calmly stated, "That may well be, Mister Gallagher, but I assure you that I was quite correct in the balance I quoted. Is not Mister Thomas White the company president and also the finance officer for your firm?"

"He is. So, what?" Noah snapped.

"Yesterday morning, Mister White withdrew a sum of fifteen thousand dollars from the account."

Noah exploded, shouting, "*You let him take that much money?*"

Again, the clerk calmly replied, "He is authorized to do so, Mister Gallagher. In fact, as Mister Smith just showed me, it was you who appointed him as president, yet also left him as finance officer. By allowing him to retain both positions, you granted him the authority to withdraw any amount from the company account without oversight. So, you see, Mister Gallagher, the small balance was far from being an error of our institution."

Other customers and staff watched Noah as he turned beet red as he blustered and wanted to scream or shoot someone, but all he did was stand at the cashier's window shaking.

The two cashiers waited for some form of response, hopefully a heart attack, but finally Noah Gallagher whipped around and stomped across the granite floor and blew out the left door.

The head cashier walked back to his desk while Mister Smith smiled at the next customer and asked, "How may I help you, sir?"

Noah reached the buggy and jumped inside, then realized the reins were still tied through that damned steel ring. He crawled back out, untied the reins, returned to the buggy and quickly made a U-turn in the cobbled street, almost hitting a couple who were crossing.

He headed for Brennan Furnace and Coal to get some answers.

ABANDONED

The train carrying Jack, Emily and Joseph back to Omaha had just departed Kearney as Noah was racing toward Tenth Street.

They'd managed a quick breakfast at the Railway Hotel's restaurant which catered to the passengers on its trains and was always ready for the sudden rush of customers.

The night had been a restless one for Emily and Jack, but Joseph was able to sleep normally as he stretched out on a leather cushioned seat. While he slept, Jack had held Emily close but because of the other passengers could do little else. It was just as well anyway. But Emily had been able to enjoy a brief release of Emily Ann Ward while Joseph slept.

But, now that they were all awake again, they were at one of the four tables in the back of the car and Jack was playing poker with Emily and Joseph. They were using checkers for their bets. Red was a nickel and black was a dime.

Joseph was studying his hand and glanced at Jack trying to read his face. Emily had already folded.

"I'll see your nickel and raise you a dime," Joseph said as he tossed a red and a black checker into the pot.

Jack narrowed his eyes and stared at Joseph, "You think you can buy this pot, mister? Well, you're wrong. I'll call," he said as he tossed his last black checker into the pot.

Joseph grinned and flopped his hand down, saying, "Three jacks."

Jack tossed his hand onto the table and said, "Well, now isn't that embarrassing. I just lost a game of poker to an almost-nine-year-old and he was holding three of me."

Joseph laughed and said, "You owe me fifty cents, Mister Tyler."

Jack reached into his pocket, pulled out a fifty cent piece and handed it to Joseph, saying, "You're a hard man, Mister Brennan."

Joseph snatched the coin and held it tightly in his hand as he asked, "Are we almost there now?"

"We're in Nebraska, but we've still got almost two hundred miles to go. We'll get there in about six hours."

"What are we going to do when we get there?" he asked as he slipped his winnings into his pocket.

"We'll take a cab to the Douglas County Sheriff's office and see if we can pry a deputy loose to arrest your uncle."

"Are we coming, too?" he asked.

Jack looked at Emily and said, "I'd feel better if you and Mrs. Doyle were in a hotel. Is that okay with you, ma'am?"

"I'd rather do that myself. I don't want to see the man again if I can avoid it."

He turned back to Joseph and said, "So, Mister Brennan, that's settled. I'll take you and Mrs. Doyle to the Carson House Hotel and I'll go and visit the sheriff."

"Okay."

———

Noah stormed into the main offices of the Brennan Furnace and Coal Company much as he'd left the First National Bank.

He didn't even glance at the receptionist as he shot past her and raced up the stairs to find Thomas White and demand to know why he'd made the withdrawal.

He barely made it to the second floor when he heard raised voices coming from the company's meeting room on his right. Five seconds later, he burst into the room and eight sets of eyes turned to look at him.

Noah scanned the room, expecting to see Thomas White, but when he didn't, he shouted, "Where the hell is that sissy, I appointed president?"

James Burke was standing at the opposite end of the long table and asked, "Mister White hasn't been seen since the night before last, Mister Gallagher, and we have some questions for you regarding the story you told about the attack on your hunting party that resulted in the death of Joseph Brennan the third."

"What about it? It doesn't matter. I have the legal authority to fire each one of you. I just want to find that bastard White. Why did he drain the company account?"

Despite Noah's question that had a potentially devastating impact on the company, Mister Burke continued, saying, "It matters, sir, because we have just received reliable information that the boy and his nanny were rescued and are enroute to Omaha as I speak. I've already sent Mister Ward to notify the sheriff's office. As a gentleman, I'd expect you to wait here for a deputy to arrive, so this matter can be rectified."

Noah's concern about the bank balance evaporated as he stared at James Burke.

Finally, he exclaimed, "That's not possible! He was attacked by that bear! I saw him being ripped apart!"

Mister Burke glared at Noah and said, "I believe you claimed it was wolves in your first account, Mister Gallagher. Your words confirm your guilt in this matter. Now, sit down and wait for the deputy to arrive!"

Noah quickly looked at the accusing eyes and shouted, "I will not sit by and be accused by you little men! You are all fired!"

He then wheeled and dashed from the room.

Mister Burke was the only man on his feet as the others all remained seated after Noah had gone.

He then looked at Alfred Baldwin, the vice president of sales and asked, "What did he say about the company's account being emptied?"

Mister Baldwin replied, "I'll go and talk to the chief clerk in finance. We may have a problem."

———

As Noah scampered across the foyer of the company to reach his buggy, Dennis Ward was sitting in the office of Douglas County Sheriff Mike Lafferty.

"Are you sure, Mister Ward? Judge Carstairs mentioned the case yesterday and he said the sheriff in Albany County had written a statement confirming the deaths of the boy and his nanny."

Dennis hadn't heard about the statement or the judge's orders and was taken aback. Maybe the story Mary had told him was just some mixed up tale after all.

"He did? Can you send a telegram to the sheriff in Laramie and ask him?"

"I can have someone do that for you, Mister Ward, but it would be faster if you sent it yourself. Just tell him that I need to know."

"Alright, Sheriff. I'll do that. I have someone in the family waiting at the station, so if she arrives, should I send her here right away?"

"Absolutely. Now, the crimes were committed in Wyoming, so we don't have jurisdiction. But we can sure arrest him under suspicion and hold him until we get confirmation from Laramie."

"Thank you, Sheriff," Dennis said as he stood and shook his hand, then quickly turned and left the large office.

ABANDONED

After he'd gone, Sheriff Lafferty followed him down the long hallway and approached Deputy Jimmy Pleasant.

"Jimmy, we may have a real problem brewing here. I want you to hang around the office while I go and talk to Judge Carstairs."

"Okay, boss," Jimmy said as the sheriff walked to the hat rack, pulled his official hat onto his head and left the large jail to cross Capitol Street to the county offices.

Noah was driving the buggy quickly down Chicago Street, almost not paying attention to the mid-day traffic. *What had happened? How had that kid been rescued? It wasn't possible!* He had left him and the nanny in a tent in the middle of the night with carnivore-attracting blood splashed all around it. There wasn't another soul within miles, not even Indians, or so Claude had told him.

Then, as he drove, he began to believe it was just a trick to get him to react exactly as he had. They'd taken the money from the bank to draw him to the company offices where they'd all set him up, telling him that the kid and the nanny were safe and coming back to Omaha. *That must be it!* And they almost had him, too. He'd made that blunder about saying it was a bear and not wolves, but it meant nothing. He had the legal papers making him the heir and owner and they didn't have a shred of proof.

Noah smiled and slowed the buggy down as he began to think of some way to turn the tables on them. That nonsense about telling the sheriff was nothing but balderdash. But as he turned the buggy into the long drive at 1710 Chicago Street, he thought it might be wise to take precautions just in the wild chance that they were telling the truth.

The train carrying the truth in the form of Joseph Charles Brennan III and Emily Ann Ward Doyle had departed Columbus, Nebraska's station thirty minutes earlier, and was now just sixty-two miles from the station in Omaha when a telegram marked urgent was delivered to Albany County Sheriff Will Higginbotham.

"Looks like there's gonna be fireworks in Omaha, George," he said to Deputy Pruitt, who'd already read the telegram.

"I'll run your reply over to the telegraph office, boss."

"Just tell them that Mrs. Doyle and Joseph Brennan departed Laramie on yesterday's train."

"Yes, sir," George said before he snatched his hat from a peg and left the office.

As he watched Deputy Pruitt walk away, Sheriff Higginbotham said aloud, "Yes, sir, there sure will be fireworks."

———

In the meeting room at the Brennan Furnace and Coal Company, chief clerk Hank Wood stood before the assembled executives with a ledger book in his hands.

"Now, Mister Wood," James Burke said, "First, I would like to know the current balance of the company account."

Wood swallowed, looked at the ledger and said, "Fifteen thousand, two hundred and thirty-eight dollars and forty-five cents."

The executives all displayed various levels of shock and disbelief at the figure.

"That's impossible!" Burke exclaimed, "It should be four times that amount!"

"Yes, sir. I agree, but that's actually the highest it's been in two years."

ABANDONED

There was suddenly a hubbub of chatter among the executives until James Burke shouted, "Quiet! All of you!", then looked back at the chief clerk.

"Can you explain how it dropped to such dangerous levels and was kept secret from the board?"

"Well, sir, you see, well, I and the other clerks weren't allowed to see any of the main books, only Mister White had that authority, so we just processed payments and paid the bills. When he was made president by Mister Gallagher, he was retained as finance officer, so I and the others were still limited in our access. It was only yesterday, when he was found to be gone that I examined the books."

"And what did you find, Mister Wood?"

"Well, sir, it appears that after Joseph Charles Brennan Junior took over control of the company, he lived somewhat extravagantly, especially after the death of his wife. He was spending more than the company was earning in profits and must have told Mister White that no one would be allowed to see the books. If this were a publicly held company, that would have been impossible, of course. But as he was the owner and the only one who would suffer the loss of his capital investment, then he wasn't obligated to share that information with anyone, not even members of the board."

James Burke closed his eyes, exhaled, then said, "Mister Gallagher just said that the company operating account has been emptied, probably by Mister White. Is that even possible? Aren't there any safeguards?"

"Normally, there would be, sir. Any withdrawal or disbursement over five hundred dollars requires the approval of the president and the finance officer, but Mister Gallagher, when he appointed Mister White president, insisted that he maintain his position as finance officer. He was warned of the danger by Mister White himself, but for some reason I never understood, made the appointments."

"So, Mister White could just walk into the First National Bank and empty the company's coffers?"

"Yes, sir. I'm afraid so."

He slowly opened his eyes and just as slowly took his seat.

"Assuming that Mister Gallagher didn't lie about the bank account, gentlemen, I believe we have a crisis on our hands."

Hank Wood stood silently watching the long faces of the executives waiting to be dismissed, but they'd all forgotten he was even there as each of them contemplated his bleak future.

Dennis Ward had remained at Western Union, sitting on a bench in the back of the large, six-operator office. He pulled his pocket watch and realized he'd missed lunch. It was almost two o'clock, and he'd been sitting there for almost an hour now.

When he'd first received the news of Emily's death, it had rocked him more than he had imagined. Of all of his nine children, it had been Emily who had created the most frustration, yet at the same time, the greatest amount of pride. All of his progeny were lively, but Emily had always spoken exactly what she thought, yet managed to avoid being rude, which was an amazing talent. She would disagree with him, and then make her point, which would infuriate him because his pride would keep him from giving in. When he'd arranged the marriage with Brian Doyle, it had been because he knew the man and thought his quiet, calm demeanor would tolerate her strong will. Brian, as many young men, were awed by Emily and was more than happy with the arrangement. Then, when she'd returned after her children and husband's deaths, and refused all of the other men, he'd seen the sudden widowing of the company owner as a godsend. After she'd gone to the big house, it was as if she had moved to Australia. For six years, he had only seen her by chance, and then he received the news of her death and had plummeted into a gloomy existence.

Then, in the dark of the night, Mary had returned and given him hope. Now, he was anxiously waiting for official confirmation that it was true.

Five minutes of added anxiety were ended when the telegrapher on the far right turned, caught his eye and waved a sheet of paper in the air.

Dennis bounced up from the bench and continued bouncing across the floor and snatched the yellow paper from his hand, read the short message, put his hand against the wall, bowed his head and began to weep. Emily was coming home.

He raced from the Western Union office and didn't slow down as he headed for the nearby Union Pacific station. He knew that Mary and her husband should be already waiting for the 2:20 arrival, but he wanted to be there to see Emily step from the train.

He'd totally forgotten about passing the information on to the sheriff or the company in his haste to see his estranged daughter.

The train was slowing as it entered the last mile before the station and Emily looked anxiously at Jack as Joseph sat on the opposite bench watching the familiar buildings go by.

"As much as I hate to admit it, Jack, I'm a bit afraid."

"Of Gallagher?" he asked.

"No, of what might happen after he's arrested. I know you'll be returning after the trial, but what happens after that? There are just so many unknowns."

"There are always a lot of unknowns, Mrs. Doyle. That's what makes life interesting. I feel bad for the man or woman that knows exactly what will be happening tomorrow, the next week and even the next year. We've had an extraordinary week, Emily. I think it will only get better now."

"You're right again, aren't you? I wish Joseph wasn't here and I'd be able to just be myself again."

"He's going to have to see Emily Ann Ward sooner or later, won't he?"

She glanced over at Joseph and replied, "I hope it's much later when he can understand better. I couldn't bear the thought of him thinking I was a mean person."

"You're not a mean person, even when Emily Ann Ward is at her worst. You're a forceful but very interesting person."

"You haven't seen me at my worst, Jack. It's what made my father marry me off to Brian Doyle and then sent me to work at the Brennans."

"Oh, I think I can deal with it, ma'am. I've taken on grizzly bears and wolves."

"They're not even close when I get my temper, Mister Tyler," Emily said with a smile.

The train was banging to a stop, so Jack never had a chance to reply.

Emily's head turned to Joseph, who was already standing and waiting for his nanny and Mister Tyler.

Emily stood, stepped out into the aisle and Jack followed. He pulled their travel bags from the overhead racks and then they stood in the queue to exit the car. Emily hadn't seen her sister Mary or her father on the platform because she and Jack were on the outside seat.

Dennis had found Mary and John just before the train's locomotive made its appearance from the north as it rounded the turn bordering the Missouri River. He let them read the confirming telegram from Sheriff Higginbotham, which added to the excitement of Emily's imminent return now that they were sure that she'd be on the train that was just arriving.

Jack had both travel bags as he stepped out onto the platform with Joseph behind him and Emily trailing. He quickly dropped them to the wooden surface, then turned to assist Joseph and then Emily, not noticing her family just eight feet behind him craning their necks to see the passengers as they disembarked.

He'd just taken hold of Joseph to lift him across the short gap when he heard a loud, high-pitched shout just behind him.

"Emily!" squealed Mary as she rushed around Jack to greet her sister.

Emily had her right foot on the lower step of the car's steel platform when she spotted Mary pushing past Jack with her arms extended and a broad smile on her face. She'd barely recovered from that shock when she caught sight of her father just past Jack's left shoulder.

She stepped down and was smothered by her shorter sister and hugged her in return.

Jack was surprised to find anyone, much less Emily's family waiting for their arrival. *How did they know they were coming?* And if they did, that meant that Noah Gallagher must know. Suddenly everything shifted from his position of surprising Gallagher to possibly being surprised by him, and Joseph would be in the greater danger.

Mary was already engulfing her sister with questions as Emily tried to answer and still look to Jack for guidance. She was just as confused as he had been but hadn't had the instant realization of the significance that her family's presence represented. She was still overwhelmed with the mere sight of her sister and her father.

Jack suddenly scooped up Joseph, turned to the man beside the woman bombarding Emily with questions, who Jack assumed was her sister, and said, "Are you Emily's brother-in-law?"

John turned to him and said, "Yes. Who are you?"

"My name's Jack Tyler. I found Emily and Joseph in the mountains. Does Gallagher know about our arrival?"

John had to take a few seconds to digest the information before answering, "I don't know. We only found out because some man on the train was telling everyone about the rescue."

Dennis overheard the conversation, then turned to Jack and said, "I'm Emily's father, but I'm not sure if Gallagher knows either. Is this Joseph?"

"Yes. We need to keep him safe. I'll go and talk to the sheriff, but I'm worried about him. Can you take Emily and Joseph to your home? I need someone to show me where the sheriff's office is, though."

John said, "I don't know where it is."

Dennis said, "It's too far to walk. You'll have to take a cab."

Jack nodded, then set Joseph down, "Joseph, I'm going to go to the sheriff's office. You stay with Mrs. Doyle."

"Yes, sir," Joseph said.

"We'll keep him safe, Mister Tyler," Dennis said as he took Joseph's hand.

"Where can I find you?" he asked quickly.

"My house is 24 Thirteenth Street."

Jack nodded again, then glanced at Emily who was opening her mouth to ask him a question, and shouted, "I've got to go!"

She then realized that Noah Gallagher must know they had returned and suddenly felt defenseless, even though she was surrounded by family.

ABANDONED

Joseph walked close to her, even though he was still attached to Dennis Ward, took her hand and said, "Mister Tyler said to stay with you, Mrs. Doyle. I think he's going to go and get Mister Gallagher."

She watched as Jack approached a waiting cabby, shouted and then climbed into the carriage and rolled away, sure that Joseph was right.

John took the travel bags and Emily picked up the bag with the checkerboard and chess set and they crossed the platform to take their own cab back to the Ward home.

———

Noah was rummaging through the office at 1710 Chicago Street, looking for cash. He wasn't in any hurry, still believing that the executives at the company were bluffing. He didn't find any money but realized that even if the company's bank account was dry, there was still the family account. He'd withdraw most of that and then come back to the house.

He left the office and was about to leave the house when he suddenly turned and walked up the stairs to the big bedroom. Three minutes later, he was walking back down the stairs wearing the same Colt he'd worn in Wyoming. He had it on under his jacket, so only the tip of the holster was visible.

He may have been seen as a gentleman because of his dress, but he considered himself quite proficient with Samuel Colt's revolvers. It was one of his more socially acceptable hobbies and had been a long-standing member of the St. Louis Gun Club.

Noah exited the house and instead of harnessing the buggy, saddled the horse. Wearing the gunbelt around his waist made use of the buggy seem too civilized, and he wanted those smirking cashiers to see him as less civilized as he withdrew a larger amount than the paltry thousand dollars that he'd try to take from the company account.

He finished saddling the gelding, then mounted and rode out of the house's large barn, forgetting to take the court orders making him the heir to the Brennan estate.

———

"They're back now?" Deputy Pleasant asked.

"Yes, sir. I just left Mrs. Doyle and Joseph with her father for safekeeping at his house. I didn't expect that the news would get here before we did, and I'm concerned that Noah Gallagher might try and kill them because they could get him hanged. He doesn't know about me, though. I have an arrest warrant for his murder of a man named Claude Boucher. He was the guide that he'd hired to bring Mrs. Doyle and Joseph out into the mountains. Do you know where I can find Gallagher?"

"Are you a lawman?" he asked.

Jack pulled the badge from his pocket and didn't elaborate on its temporary status.

Deputy Pleasant stood, then said, "I don't know where the sheriff is. He was going to meet with Judge Carstairs but should have been back by now. Do you need a ride?"

"Yes. I just arrived on the train."

Jimmy nodded, turned to another deputy and said, "Joe, can you tell the sheriff everything you heard when he gets back? Deputy Tyler and I will be heading out to the Brennan Furnace company to see if we can find Mister Gallagher."

"Okay, Jimmy," Deputy Adams said as he stayed at his small desk.

Jimmy Pleasant walked around the main desk, then snatched his hat from a peg and said, "Let's get out there."

ABANDONED

Jack pinned his badge on his jacket, followed the deputy out of the office, then turned right, walked to the edge of the building, walked down the side, then when they reached the back, they entered a good-sized barn with a corral nearby. There were six horses in the corral, but inside the barn were four more and they were all saddled with Winchesters in their scabbards.

As Jimmy Pleasant mounted, Jack looked for one with the longest stirrups, found they were all pretty much the same, then selected a tan gelding and mounted.

He followed Deputy Pleasant onto the street and they headed for Tenth Street and the most likely place to find Noah Gallagher in the middle of the day, the Brennan Furnace and Coal Company.

―――

Noah had reached the First National Bank's fancy hitching poles again, stepped down and tied the gelding's reins to the steel ring. He tugged his gunbelt up without removing his jacket and strode confidently up the steps.

He pushed through the door, then headed for the desk of the nearest clerk.

As he approached, the clerk instantly recognized him as the man who had created the scene earlier but had only received snippets of what was the cause of the dispute.

Noah stood at the desk and said, "I'd like to close my account at this sorry excuse for a bank."

The clerk said, "Please have a seat, sir, and I'll we can start the paperwork. We'll be sorry to be losing your business, of course."

Noah sat down and replied, "Maybe your snotty cashiers should have been more respectful earlier."

The clerk didn't comment, but pulled out the necessary forms for closing an account, then asked, "And your name, sir?"

"My name is Noah Gallagher, but the account is under the name Joseph Charles Brennan, Junior."

The clerk had his pen in hand as he looked up and said, "Do you have power of attorney to control the account, sir?"

"It's my account now. I have a judge's order to that effect."

As soon as the words passed his lips, Noah realized that the orders were in his other jacket pocket, and embarrassingly said, "I just recalled that I left the orders back at the house, so I'll have to return to get them. I'll be back shortly."

The clerk laid down the pen, smiled, and said, "Very good, sir."

Noah stood, gritted his teeth, then turned to leave the bank, swearing under his breath at his error.

Jack and Deputy Pleasant's visit to the company never got past the receptionist when they were informed that Mister Gallagher had left the premises and probably returned to his home. After getting the address, they returned to their horses and rode quickly out of the company yard. They rode three blocks north on Tenth Street, then turned left on Chicago.

Emily and Joseph were sitting in the parlor of her father's home as Emily answered a Gatling gun series of questions about the harrowing experience. As she answered them, she realized the adventure hadn't been nearly as terrifying as they all seemed to believe. Yes, the initial fear of being abandoned to die was horrible, as were the confrontations with the bear and then the wolves, but aside from that, she realized just how much she already missed being in the wilderness with Jack.

Joseph had long since come to that conclusion and had his ivory-handled knife in his hand as he stared at the wolf's head.

ABANDONED

Noah reached the house, tied the gelding to the front fence, then walked quickly down the paved walk, trotted up the stairs, opened the door and went inside, leaving the heavy door open behind him.

He climbed the stairway, went into the bedroom, opened the closet door and pulled the papers from his other jacket's inner pocket.

He smiled, turned and headed back down the stairs at a trot as he slid the papers into his jacket pocket, then headed for the door, exited the house, closed the door and crossed the porch.

Noah jogged down the four steps from the porch and was still smiling as he walked down the walkway. He was halfway to the horse when he saw two badged riders trot down the street. One pointed at his horse, and then the other saw him, and the sudden, crushing realization that the executives hadn't been bluffing slammed into his mind.

Noah quickly turned and raced back to the house, leaping the stairs and sliding to the door, which he threw open, slammed closed and quickly locked before running to the back of the house to lock the back door.

Jack and Jimmy Pleasant quickly dismounted and tied their horses to the fence.

"This is your call, Deputy," Jack said, "What do you want to do?"

"Was he armed?" he asked.

"I didn't see a pistol, but I wouldn't bet against it."

"Alright. I'll tell you what. I'll go to the front door and knock loudly, but step aside. If he's armed, he might shoot through the door. If he opens the door, which isn't likely, I'll just arrest him."

"What do you want me to do?"

"Cover the back in case he tries to run out of there. If I don't get any response at all, I'll go in through a window."

"Okay," Jack said as he turned and jogged away, following the wide wraparound porch as he walked rapidly across the grass.

Jimmy wasn't all that pleased about the situation and thought it might be wiser to wait. Gallagher wasn't going anywhere, but he'd made his decision and he'd go with it. He glanced at both windows, didn't see any movement and began to step along the walkway.

Inside the house, Noah, after locking the back door, had climbed the long stairway and once he was on the top landing, laid prone, slid to the edge and stuck his pistol out from under the railing. He had a view of the front door and of the hallway to the kitchen. Neither of them could enter the parlor without being in his line of fire. Once they were both dead, or at least wounded enough, he'd quickly return to the bank, get his money and make his escape. He'd have to disappear like Thomas White had done.

Jimmy Pleasant quietly stepped onto the porch, then put his back to the wall near the heavy front door and used his left fist to knock loudly. He yanked it back, expecting .44s to blast through the door, but it remained quiet. After another thirty seconds, he knocked again, then waited.

Jack had reached the back door, and after trying the door to see if it was locked, he thought that if Gallagher was anywhere, he'd be up front, so he gambled and peered through one of the back windows, not seeing anyone in the large kitchen.

But rather than stay there and wait, Jack thought, just like a trapped puma, Noah Gallagher would just be lying in wait. He was now the hunted, not the hunter. So, Jack pulled his Remington and began to walk around the porch, taking time to peer into each window. Not wearing a hat was a real advantage as he cast a less noticeable shadow when he first peeked into each room.

He'd passed the halfway point when Jimmy Pleasant decided to go in through the window.

ABANDONED

Noah had heard the knocks and shifted his Colt's sights and his concentration to the doorway. Now, he spotted Jimmy's shadow as he was trying to open a window. Noah could have taken the shot right then but wanted to be sure and he didn't know where the other deputy was.

Jimmy tried to lift the window, and thought it might be locked, but it was just stubborn and when he gave it a harder pull, it suddenly slid open and he relaxed, not realizing he had a Colt's muzzle staring at him just thirty-five feet away.

He pushed the window to the top, then pulled his Colt from his holster, lifted his left leg through the window, placed his foot firmly on the parlor floor, then bent at the waist to slip through the wide opening.

Jack was just at the parlor's window and his head was just poking above the sill when Noah fired.

The loud report echoed through the house as Jimmy felt the slug slam into his left upper thigh that was still bent beside his torso. He screamed in pain and fell as blood began to pool on the polished oak floor.

Jack's eyes had barely reached the glass when they caught the muzzle flash. He didn't mess with raising the window but rammed the muzzle of his pistol through the glass as he pulled back the hammer, aimed at the muzzle flash and fired.

Noah had seen the deputy fall, but was still alive, so he cocked his hammer for a second shot when he heard the shattering glass, then immediately shifted his aim to the source of the sound, and spotted Jack's shadow just in time to see the Remington's muzzle explode in smoke and flame.

Jack's bullet didn't hit Noah but blasted into the rail just inches to his right, blowing apart the heavy maple into splinters and shards. Dozens of the wooden missiles punched into Noah's exposed right hand, face and neck, and one quarter-inch sliver jabbed into his right eye.

He screamed in pain, jumped up and ran down the hallway, his Colt still in his hand.

Jack watched him run, and having already shattered one pane, he simply dove through the window and somersaulted into the room that was already foggy from gunsmoke. He quickly focused on the upper landing where he'd fired as he ran to assist Deputy Pleasant.

"How bad is it, Deputy?" he asked quickly while still staring at the upper landing and hallway.

"It's bad, but not too bad. I need to wrap it though."

Jack glanced to his left, then yanked down a curtain, dropping the heavy curtain rod on both of them.

Jimmy didn't complain as Jack quickly set down his Remington, pulled out his Bowie knife and sliced the curtain. He handed it to Deputy Pleasant, sheathed his knife, then picked up his Remington.

"I'm going to go and get that bastard. Can you hold on for a little while?"

"Make it quick," Jimmy replied.

"But I'm not going to be stupid about it, either," Jack said as he headed for the bottom of the staircase.

Jack's eyes were glued on the upstairs hallway as he stepped quietly up the polished stairs. This was all new to him, but it wasn't that different than finding that wounded animal in a cave. It's just that the critter wouldn't have been able to shoot him.

Noah knew that the second deputy would be coming for him. He'd reached the big bedroom and dropped behind the bed onto the floor and watched the open door through the space under the bed. He had brushed the sliver of oak from his eye first, but he had to keep his eye closed as it watered. Now, he was hurriedly pulling the painful splinters from his face and hand even as he held the Colt cocked and ready to fire. He still had the pistol in his right hand, even though he was lying on his left side.

Jack reached the top floor and glanced at the destroyed railing. He saw a blood trail going into the open bedroom door, but it wasn't enough for a gunshot wound. He knew then that Noah Gallagher was still able to pull the trigger and was waiting for him in the first bedroom on the left. If it hadn't been for a wounded Deputy Pleasant downstairs, he would have just waited Gallagher out, but he had to act quickly. He couldn't count on anyone arriving in time to help the deputy.

He dropped to the floor and began crawling toward the door. He tried to picture the bedroom and found it hard to imagine. He'd never been in such a well-furnished house. He needed to know where Gallagher was hiding.

So, when he was close to the open door, he shouted, "I know you're in there, Gallagher."

Noah didn't answer. He wasn't that stupid.

Jack then said, "You shouldn't have killed Claude. He may have been a real bastard but shooting him in the back made you a bigger bastard than he was."

Noah was shocked to hear about Claude. No one should know about the guide. *Who was this guy?*

"How do you know about Claude?" he shouted.

Jack closed his eyes and concentrated on the sound as he shouted back, "Because I'm the man who found Mrs. Doyle and Joseph. Then I found Claude's body by that creek where you dumped it."

Noah laughed and yelled, "So, you're the big hero, are you? Did you diddle Mrs. Doyle all the way back to Omaha? You know that Wilbur Moore, that skinny weasel of a steward had been taking her to his bed for years?"

Jack slid a little closer to the door then said in a loud voice, "I know you didn't because you don't like real women, or any women at all. She told me about you, Noah."

Noah snapped back, "She's a lying whore! She doesn't know me at all! I've had plenty of women, including the two that worked here."

It was enough for Jack. It wasn't perfect, but he had a good idea that Noah was in the far corner of the room and was behind something because his voice was muffled. Jack was betting his life, and probably Deputy Pleasant's when he made his decision.

Jack cocked his hammer, then lunged forward sliding into the doorway on his right side, his Remington's barrel just two inches off the floor.

Noah was watching the doorway, expecting a shouted response from the man, and had been pulling a splinter from his face with his left and when Jack suddenly slid into view and he yanked his trigger, firing through the eight inch space under the bed.

Jack was surprised to see the muzzle flare from under the bed but didn't need to take more than a fraction of a second to adjust his sights and fire, his pistol's report almost immediately following Noah's shot making it sound like one extended loud blast.

Noah's bullet slammed into the oak floor just two feet on the other side of the bed and made a long groove in the wood before it punched into the door jamb above Jack's head. But his .44 drilled into Noah's gut, just below his ribcage. The bullet had maintained its two-inch gap from the floor and ripped into his abdomen, pulverizing his stomach before quickly exiting his back and passing through the wall and leaving the house entirely.

Noah screamed, dropped his pistol, and clutched his wound as blood began to spill onto the bedroom floor.

Jack leapt to his feet and raced into the bedroom with his Remington cocked in case Noah was still armed. He reached the edge of the bed and looked down at the man who had tried to kill

Emily and Joseph, then bent over and picked up the pistol he had dropped, then tossed it onto the bed.

He knew that it wasn't a fatal wound and Noah Gallagher could survive to face trial if it was treated quickly.

Noah looked up at him with a grimace as he tried to staunch the flow of blood with his hands and snarled, "You bastard! You killed me."

"Not yet. You can live if I get you to a doctor, but I'm not going to do that right now. I'm going to help Deputy Pleasant downstairs and I'll be back," then he turned and began to walk away, before adding, "Maybe."

Noah began screaming as Jack headed for the door, "You can't abandon me here to die!"

Jack didn't believe any response was necessary or even possible as he trotted down the steps to help Jimmy Pleasant as Noah Gallagher's screaming demands for help continued to echo through the house.

Jack reached Deputy Pleasant and found that he'd passed out. He checked the wound, then tightly rewrapped the curtain bandage, stood and unlocked the door, then lifted the deputy and carried him onto the porch. He saw a crowd gathering in the street, so he quickly carried Jimmy Pleasant down the walkway.

When he reached the gaggle of onlookers, he said, "I'm new here. This man needs help."

"Use my buggy!" shouted a man from the back.

Jack swiftly walked through the parting crowd and laid Jimmy on the buggy's seat.

"I'll take him to St. Joseph's Hospital, it's just two blocks away," the stranger said.

"I'll follow," Jack said as he trotted to his horse.

As he was mounting, another man asked, "What about the wounded man screaming inside?"

"He'll live. He's the one who shot the deputy. I'll be back."

Jack started his horse after the buggy and mumbled, "Maybe."

They reached the hospital and once Jack was sure that Deputy Pleasant was in good hands, returned to his horse and headed back to the house. It had been more than twenty minutes since he'd shot Noah Gallagher and wasn't sure if he was still alive.

He reached the house, which was still surrounded by curious citizens, stepped down and after tying off the horse, wound his way through the crowd, climbed the steps to the porch and walked through the still-open door. He was surprised that no one had entered the house at all, but it was quiet inside as he climbed the stairs.

He reached the big bedroom, and as soon as he reached the other side of the bed, he found that it was too late to save Noah Gallagher. Jack reached the body, grabbed hold of his jacket and slid him out of the bedroom into the hallway. He closed his staring eyes, straightened the body to make it easy to bury, then walked back down the stairs, out the door and closed it behind him.

He walked to the crowd and said, "No one is to go into the house."

Nobody questioned the Albany County Deputy Sheriff badge on his chest as he mounted his horse and took the reins of Deputy Pleasant's horse and headed back to Capitol Street to the sheriff's office.

———

Vice president James Burke had sent Hank Wood to the First National Bank to verify the accuracy of Noah Gallagher's claim that the company effectively had no operating cash at all, and he had just returned with the bad news.

The executive officers were now encamped in the meeting room with Mister Wood and the other clerks going over expected income and expenses over the next few weeks and it wasn't a rosy picture at all. The timing couldn't have been worse for the company. A large coal shipment was due in eight days to fill the company's bins for the upcoming cold weather. Even if they collected all of their notes that were due, they couldn't cover the cost of the coal. The bill from Union Pacific wouldn't be due until the end of September, but there simply wouldn't be enough income during the month to pay it. The only positive was that payroll for August had just been met. But they were about to receive more bad news when there was a knock on the door.

Hank Wood was still standing by the door to answer the executives' questions, he opened it slightly, and saw the anxious eyes of Dennis Ward, who had finally remembered that he had to tell Mister Burke that Joseph Brennan III was safe and back in Omaha, but now had even more news.

"Yes, Mister Ward?" Hank Wood asked through the narrow opening.

"I have news for Mister Burke," he replied.

Hank turned to James Burke and said, "Mister Ward says that he has news for you, Mister Burke."

"Yes, yes. Send him in."

Hank opened the door and Dennis entered the room, looking at the men who ran the company and uncomfortably wrung his hat as the clerk closed the door behind him.

"Well, Mister Ward, was it true? Did Joseph return on the train with your daughter?" he asked.

"Yes, sir. They're staying at my house right now. But I thought you should know that the man who rescued them also escorted them from Wyoming and has a warrant for Mister Gallagher for murder."

"*Murder?*" he exclaimed.

"Yes, sir. After Gallagher abandoned my daughter and the boy out in the mountains to die, he shot the guide in the back. Emily, that's my daughter, told me that the man who returned with her had been deputized to take him back to Wyoming to face trial."

The consequences to the company's future weren't obvious until the chief clerk cleared his throat to get Mister Burke's attention.

"Sir, this presents us with an additional problem. Mister Gallagher was the chairman of the board, and the guardian of Master Brennan with power of attorney to act on his behalf. If he is arrested for murder, not to mention for the attempted murder of his ward, then he would be unable to appoint a replacement for either the president or the chief finance officer for the company. We simply have no one who can access the family account, the capital account or appoint another president and finance officer. Until a new guardian is appointed for the boy, we are hamstrung in our ability to secure a loan as well. After Mister White emptied the operating account for the company, the firm will be unable to function."

James Burke leaned back in his thickly cushioned leather chair and closed his eyes, trying to conjure a way out of the maze that seemed to have no exit at all.

Dennis Ward hadn't heard about the Mister White absconding with the company's funds and the enormity of problems that the chief clerk had just outlined left him stunned.

———

Jack dismounted in the barn behind the sheriff's office, tied off the two horses and jogged back through the small alley between the buildings, then after two left turns, entered the sheriff's office.

ABANDONED

Deputy Adams was at the desk and asked, "Where's Jimmy?"

"I left him at the hospital. He took a .44 in the left thigh, but the doctor said he'd be all right."

He stood, held up a finger and said, "Wait a minute," then trotted quickly down the hallway.

Seconds later Sheriff Lafferty strode quickly into the front office trailing Deputy Adams.

"What happened?"

Jack quickly recounted the events that had unfolded at 1710 Chicago Street and when he'd finished, he could tell that the sheriff wasn't pleased with Deputy Pleasant's decision to enter the house without letting him know, but he didn't say anything.

"The body is still in the house, and the house is unlocked?" he asked.

"Yes, sir. It's in the hallway on the second floor. I left his pistol on the bedroom where he'd taken the shot. You can see the path his bullet took when he fired."

He turned to Deputy Adams and said, "Joe, go notify Doc Fairfield and take him over there."

"Yes, sir," he replied, then hastily exited the office, grabbing his hat as he left.

After he'd gone, the sheriff turned to Jack and said, "I'm going to go and check on Jimmy. Is he at St. Joseph's Hospital or the Municipal Hospital?"

"St. Joseph's."

"Can you stay here until one of my other deputies returns? Deputy John Applewhite should be back soon. He was just serving some papers on the other side of the county."

"I can do that."

"I should be back in forty minutes even if none of the other deputies returns," he said before turning back to get his hat from his office.

As Jack was taking a seat behind the desk, the sheriff rushed past and left the offices.

Jack sat in the chair and finally had an opportunity to reflect on the consequences of what had just happened. He wasn't concerned one bit that he had done nothing to prevent Noah Gallagher's slide to Perdition, but that meant he wouldn't have to return to Laramie for a trial. He'd just have to send a telegram to Sheriff Higginbotham letting him know of Gallagher's death in a shootout. He'd promised Emily that he'd return to Omaha after the trial, but now, with no trial did that mean he would stay here?

He couldn't imagine living in a city, even one the size of Laramie. But he knew that Emily would never leave Joseph, and he both understood and accepted that. But with Gallagher's sudden death, the court would have to appoint a new guardian for Joseph. *Was there another Gallagher or Brennan out there who would step in? Would he be just as greedy as Noah?*

For all of his brave talk to Emily, he suddenly realized that he may have to return to Laramie alone. When the court found the next closest male relative to Joseph and appointed him guardian, Emily would stay with Joseph as his nanny, and the new guardian would move into the big house. Although there were no laws about nannies being prohibited from marrying, it was both impractical and frowned upon. The situation may force Emily to choose between him and Joseph, and that was something that he couldn't allow to happen. Besides, he was awfully fond of the boy, too.

He had a pencil in his hand and was tapping it on the desk trying to conceive of some kind of solution to the problem when the door opened, and a badge-wearing young man entered.

"Who are you?" he asked as he removed his hat.

ABANDONED

Jack stood quickly and said, "My name's Jack Tyler. The sheriff went to St. Joseph's Hospital to visit Deputy Pleasant who'd been shot in the thigh when he went in through the window after a suspected murderer. He'll be all right. Tell the sheriff I'll be back in the morning to write a full report. He should be back in thirty minutes or so."

"*What? Jimmy was shot? Who was the murderer?*" the new deputy exclaimed.

Jack walked past the flabbergasted deputy and said, "The sheriff will tell you. I'll be back in the morning and tell him that I borrowed one of your horses," then quickly left the office and headed back to their barn.

Dennis Ward returned to the house after the meeting dissolved with no solutions discussed or seemingly even possible. The Brennan Furnace and Coal Company was paralyzed.

Emily and Joseph were resting after the train ride in the parlor as Mary and Molly prepared dinner when her father entered.

She could tell that her father was unhappy as he removed his jacket and hat.

After the initial frenzied questions, she'd spent a few minutes alone with her father and while not erasing all of the barriers between them, had reached an armistice.

"What's wrong, Father?" she asked as he hung them on the coat rack near the door.

"The company is in a bind. Mister White has disappeared and made off with the company's money. They can't do anything until the court appoints a new guardian for the boy and grants him power of attorney. From what they were saying, that might take some time, too, because of his having to go to Wyoming and face trial before the court can start the process."

"The company president stole the money and ran away? When did that happen?"

"Monday. No one had seen him all day Tuesday, and it wasn't until Mister Gallagher arrived at the offices this morning and told them that the money was gone that they realized what had happened. Mister Tyler hasn't returned yet, obviously, so we don't know if he found Mister Gallagher."

"No, he hasn't," Emily said in a monotone as she tried to come to grips with what her father had just told her.

Joseph asked, "Can't you be my guardian, Mrs. Doyle?"

Emily smiled at Joseph, replying, "No, dear. Only men can be appointed guardians, and it's usually a member of the family."

"Why?" he asked.

Emily shrugged and answered, "I don't know, Joseph. It might be a law or just because they've always done it that way."

"I think it's stupid."

John Fitzpatrick, who'd listened to the conversation, said, "I don't believe it's a law, Emily. But your father is right about the challenge that the president's theft and disappearance has created. Maybe the courts will allow Mister Gallagher to at least sign some authorizations before he's extradited to Wyoming."

Emily shook her head and replied, "He wouldn't give them the satisfaction unless they somehow agreed not to send him back to Wyoming to face trial, and I wouldn't stand for that, and neither would Jack."

"Mister Tyler has no legal standing in this issue, Emily. Even with that warrant, if they don't allow extradition, all he can do is go back to Wyoming empty-handed," John said.

"I don't care if he has legal standing or not. Jack Tyler will not let Noah Gallagher avoid justice just to save Joseph's company."

John shrugged and said, "Nonetheless, if…"

He was interrupted by a loud knock, and Dennis, who had never moved more than four feet into the room, just turned and opened the door.

"Come in, Mister Tyler," Dennis said, "Your name was just being bandied about."

Jack walked into the room, saw Emily smiling at him and smiled back as Dennis closed the door.

"What happened, Jack?" Emily asked.

"Noah Gallagher is dead. We exchanged gunfire in the house on Chicago Street."

His simple, blunt statement caused an outbreak of silence in the room as eight eyes looked at him for more information.

Jack removed his jacket, then took off his gunbelt and hung both on the coat rack.

Emily saw blood on his shirt and quickly asked, "Were you shot?"

"No, ma'am. This is Deputy Pleasant's blood. Mister Gallagher shot him as he was climbing through a window. I'm fine."

"Could you sit down and tell us what happened?" she asked.

"Yes, ma'am."

John stood and said, "Can you wait for me to get Mary, Molly and her fiancé?"

"Sure. I'll wait."

Joseph asked, "Was it scary, Mister Tyler?"

"It was very scary. I'd rather be facing a mad wolf than some man hiding behind a bed with a Colt in his hand."

"Is that what happened?" Joseph asked in awe.

"Yes, sir."

John, Mary, Molly and Andrew Donovan all appeared from the kitchen and managed to find seating positions. Joseph gave up his chair to squeeze in beside Emily on the crowded couch across from Jack.

He spent ten minutes describing what had happened from the time he arrived in the sheriff's office, and then another ten minutes answering questions.

Once the question and answering period was done, they all adjourned to the large dining room for dinner.

As they ate, Dennis explained the mess that the company was facing because of Mister White's theft and disappearance and the unusual set of circumstances which now paralyzed the company, unwittingly made worse by the death of Noah Gallagher.

"You mean there's nobody in the company who can pay the bills?" Jack asked.

Dennis replied, "No one, and it's worse than that. Because there's no guardian, no one can access the Brennan family accounts either. According to the chief clerk at the company, the guardian only had limited access and that had to be approved by the family attorney. At least the court won't have to delay in assigning a new guardian for Joseph with Mister Gallagher's death."

"But won't they still have to find some relative somewhere?"

"I suppose so, and that could take some time. Time the company can't afford."

ABANDONED

Jack nodded and glanced at a very worried Emily across the table. He could almost read her mind because it was probably filled with the same conclusions he'd reached back at the sheriff's office as he waited for a replacement deputy. She'd have to wait until they found a new guardian who may be just as bad as Noah, and then she'd have to stay in Omaha with Joseph while Jack returned to Laramie. It was a real mess and a solution wasn't near at hand.

The conversations fell into more routine discussions of the past week's events that Jack was able to answer without much thought as he tried to come up with something.

After dinner, Jack rode Dennis Ward's horse and led the sheriff's horse back to its barn. The gas streetlights were all burning as he walked the horses across the cobbled streets.

By the time he reached the barn, dismounted and led the sheriff's gelding inside, he finally thought he might have a way out of the dilemma, but he just wasn't sure about the legal sides of the issue and he had to talk to a lawyer. He didn't know any in Omaha, or in Laramie either for that matter, but there was that family lawyer that Emily had mentioned. The one who had accompanied Noah Gallagher on his previous hunting trip.

As he rode back to the house, he needed to talk to Emily about the attorney. The man may have been Noah's fellow conspirator or Noah simply had a hold over the man, but either way, Jack knew he'd be able to get legal advice once he let the lawyer know how tenuous his situation was, and not just his future as the Brennan family attorney.

Emily was sitting in the parlor on the couch with Joseph as the rest of the extended family chatted about the day's events. She had him protectively under her arm as she tried to avoid dwelling on her personal dilemma that was looming before her like the jaws of that gray wolf. And just as she had been then, she was just as terrified now.

Jack unsaddled the horse, left him in the barn, then crossed to the back door and knocked. He wasn't family, after all.

Molly opened the door a few seconds later and smiled.

"Come in, Mister Tyler."

"Thank you, ma'am. Is Mrs. Doyle in the parlor?"

"Everyone is. Would you like some coffee?"

"No, thank you, ma'am. I need to talk to Mrs. Doyle for a few minutes, if I may."

"I don't believe you need permission, Mister Tyler," Molly said as she grinned, then headed down the hallway to return to the parlor.

Jack followed and once in the parlor, caught Emily's eyes, and asked, "Could I speak to you in the kitchen for a few minutes, Mrs. Doyle?"

"Me, too?" asked Joseph.

"Not this time, Master Brennan, but I'll probably need to speak to you privately later."

"Okay."

Emily stood and quickly crossed the parlor then passed Jack who followed her into the kitchen.

Once they'd both taken seats at the table, she asked, "What do you need, Jack?"

"Emily, I might have a way out of everything, but I need legal advice. Tell me about the family lawyer."

Emily exhaled sharply and replied, "His name is Luke Casey. His office is at 1272 Harney Street. I don't know why you'd want to see him, Jack. He was Noah's friend and went on that hunting trip with him. I don't trust him at all."

"I know, and that's why I want to see him. He doesn't know that Noah's dead and might not know that you and Joseph are back yet, either. I'll go over there early in the morning and catch him unaware. He was the family attorney, so he'd know all of the dirt. I need to know a lot more about the family. I'd imagine that he knows even more than you do."

"I'm sure he does. I was just a nanny."

Jack smiled and said, "I know better than that, Mrs. Doyle. How is Emily Ann Ward doing?"

"She's chomping at the bit to run, but I'm not sure she'll ever make it out of the gates, Jack. I'm just so frustrated, and I'll admit to being scared, too. I can't give up Joseph and I don't want to lose you, either. I can't have both and it's a frightening thing to contemplate."

"Let me worry about that, Emily. I'm not sure if my goofy idea will work, but it's all I have, and a lot will depend on that lawyer at 1272 Harney Street."

"Can you tell me what it is?"

"Not yet, because it's not likely to work anyway."

She smiled at him and took his rough hands in hers before she said softly, "I trust you, Jack. If anyone can get this disaster remedied, it's you."

"I have an incredible incentive, Emily Ann Ward."

She nodded and wanted to much more but just as it had been since she'd been with Jack, it wasn't the time or the place.

The both rose and returned to the parlor, then joined the ongoing conversations.

The sleeping arrangements were a bit different. Emily shared a bedroom with Molly, John and Mary had their own bedroom, Dennis slept alone while Jack and Joseph shared the last room. It was an ideal time for Jack to have a long, private talk with Joseph that didn't involve the normal man-boy type of conversation.

Jack was sitting on the edge of Joseph's bed as he lay under the covers.

"Joseph, I need to tell you some things that are important."

"Alright."

"You love Mrs. Doyle very much. Don't you?"

"More than anyone. She's like a mother to me."

"I know she is. But did you know that Mrs. Doyle is really like two different ladies?"

Joseph's eyebrows furrowed as he asked, "How?"

"Well, when she's around you, she has to be so very nice and sweet to make sure that she can always be with you because she loves you so much."

"And she's really not nice at all?" he asked in surprise.

"Oh, no. She's very nice and the best person I've ever met, but she's also the most honest person I've ever met and likes to say what she thinks. That can make people mad, and she thinks that if you or anyone else around you saw her that way, she wouldn't be able to be your nanny anymore."

"That's silly."

"I think so, but she doesn't, and that's what's important. I think she's still afraid that if you saw her as the lady who is very frank and honest, you won't like her as much, and that would break her heart."

"But I will always love Mrs. Doyle."

"I know that, but I believe she doesn't understand that. Now, tomorrow I'm going to see what I can do to help her, and at the same time, help you. But even if it doesn't work, I want you to understand about Mrs. Doyle. And, even if I have to go back to Laramie, I want you to let her know that it's all right for her to be the other lady."

"How do I do that?"

"Just tell her you want to meet Emily Ann Ward. That was her name when she was a girl and was the honest and direct person that I just described to you. Can you remember that name?"

"Yes, sir. Emily Ann Ward. But you aren't going back to Wyoming without us, are you?"

"I don't know, Joseph," he replied, "I honestly don't know."

CHAPTER 8

Luke Casey walked to his offices that morning a little later than usual, still unaware of the massive changes that had occurred the previous day. He was expecting another visit from Noah Gallagher, probably to fire him now that his usefulness was over. He and Noah had at best a stressful relationship once he'd shown him the evidence of the overbilling, and all he could hope for was if that bastard let him leave town with his law license still intact. He could move his practice to the state capital in Lincoln. There was a lot more legal work there anyway.

But when he opened the outer door to his office, he spotted a stranger sitting in his waiting room with his clerk.

"Mister Casey, this is Mister Jack Tyler. He needs to speak to you about the Brennan estate."

Luke hung his hat on the coat rack, then said, "Mister Tyler? What exactly do you need to discuss about the Brennan estate?"

Jack stood and replied, "Perhaps it might be better if we talked in private, Mister Casey."

Luke looked at the man who had the appearance of a rancher or farmer rather than a city dweller, but still hadn't made the connection to Wyoming.

"Very well. Come into my office," he said as he opened the door to the inner office.

Jack entered and took a seat in front of the desk while Mister Casey closed the door, walked behind the desk and sat down.

"Well, Mister Tyler, you have my attention."

ABANDONED

"Mister Casey, you are the family attorney for the Brennans, and Noah Gallagher was the guardian of the heir to the estate, Joseph Charles Brennan the third. Is that right?"

Luke began, "Yes, but...", then asked suddenly, *"Did you say 'was' the guardian?"*

"Yes, sir. I shot the bastard yesterday in the Brennan family home. He was going to be arrested for the murder of a man named Claude Boucher in Albany County, Wyoming. I'm sure that you're familiar with both the name and location."

Luke was stunned as he sat back and stared at Jack. He was enormously relieved to be free Noah, but Mister Tyler seemed to know too much about his own complicity in the murder of Joseph and his nanny. He sensed more blackmail in the offing.

"What do you want, Mister Tyler?" he finally asked hoarsely.

"I need legal advice and your cooperation, Mister Casey. It all revolves around Mrs. Emily Doyle, the boy, and the Brennan Furnace and Coal Company."

Luke swallowed. This had the potential of being much worse than the problems posed by Noah Gallagher.

"What exactly do you need?"

If Luke Casey had been stunned by Jack's announcement about shooting Noah Gallagher, he was about to receive a second wave.

"Last week, I was returning from doing some prospecting in the Medicine Bow Mountains and found a boy facing a brown bear. I rescued the boy and his nanny who had been abandoned by Mister Gallagher and Claude Boucher. They're in Omaha with her family now."

Luke grabbed the arms of his chair and asked, *"What did you say? They're here?"*

"Yes, Mister Casey, they're here. Now, you have a problem, do you not?"

"I won't agree to your statement, but there may be an unresolved issue pertinent to their return."

Jack snapped, "Cut the lawyer crap talk, Mister Casey. Talk to me like a man."

"Alright. I have a problem, and obviously you are going to propose a solution. What is it?"

"That's better. Now, you probably aren't aware that the president of the company absconded with almost all of the company's funds on Monday and disappeared. With the loss of the president, who was also the finance officer and now the chairman of the board, the company is hamstrung."

"*Thomas White stole the company's money?*" he exclaimed.

Jack answered, "Almost every dime. Now, Joseph needs a new guardian, and the company needs that done quickly, wouldn't you imagine?"

"Of course, but that usually takes time. I know how long it took to find Noah Gallagher, and I'm sorry to admit that it turned out the way it did."

"Who recommends the new guardian?"

Luke Casey suddenly realized that he was suddenly in a much better bargaining position, and Jack knew the answer to his question when he saw the fear disappear from the lawyer's eyes.

"That's my responsibility as executor of the estate, but in this case, the will requires that it also has to have the support of the board of directors."

Jack nodded and said, "Okay, I understand that. Now, does the guardian have to be a relative?"

"No, it doesn't, but there would have to be a strong case for the appointment otherwise."

"That's fine. Now, I would like to have his nanny, Emily Doyle, appointed as the boy's guardian, with all of the same authority that Mister Gallagher had been given."

"A woman?" he asked rhetorically before adding, "I've never heard of it before, but there aren't any legal prohibitions against it."

"That's my price for forgetting about your involvement in the plot to have Joseph killed, Mister Casey. I know lawyers like written contracts for such things, but in this case, I'm sure you'll agree that the less that is put on paper, the safer it will be for you. I'll give you my word and that's better than any piece of paper. Will you recommend Mrs. Doyle be appointed Joseph's guardian?"

Luke Casey made a quick evaluation of Jack Tyler, then said, "I have no problem with it, Mister Tyler, but you'd have to convince the board of directors, and I don't see how that is possible, not even in their current situation."

"I'll go and meet with them shortly, Mister Casey. If I can get their approval, how long would it take to get the legal paperwork done?"

"Not more than three days. Once I petition the court and have the approval of the board, I think we can have it done by Tuesday."

Jack nodded and said, "Alright. I'll be back later today and let you know if this works out."

Luke Casey asked, "Do you mind staying for a little while and tell me what happened? As long as I'm not in my lawyer guise, I'll be honest with you and tell you that Noah Gallagher had caught me overbilling the family and threatened to have me disbarred, and then it kept progressing until that trip. I was sickened when I knew what he had done, and you have no idea how relieved I am to know that the boy is alive and well."

"I'll tell it to you quickly, Mister Casey, but I have a lot of things to do."

Jack then launched into a hurried narrative of the events that had led to the visit.

When he finally finished, he shook the attorney's hand, then quickly left the office. Now, all he had to do was to convince a bunch of stuffy executives to agree to let Emily be Joseph's new guardian, but he had to make a stop on the way.

He had walked from Dennis Ward's house to the lawyer's office, and now had an even longer walk to visit the sheriff. As he walked, he rehearsed what he'd say to the board of directors to convince them to support Emily's appointment to be Joseph's guardian.

Jack entered the sheriff's office almost twenty minutes later and found yet another deputy at the desk.

"Is Sheriff Lafferty in?" he asked, "I need to write a statement about yesterday's shooting."

"You must be that deputy from Wyoming," he said.

"Sort of. I'm only a temporary deputy."

"The sheriff's office is the last door on the left. He's expecting you."

Jack nodded and headed down the hallway, saw the sheriff's door open and swung inside.

Sheriff Lafferty had heard his voice and as soon as Jack entered, said, "Have a seat, Mister Tyler."

"Thanks."

After he'd parked in the straight-backed chair, the sheriff said, "I talked to Jimmy about what had happened, and he said he'd screwed up and you bailed him out and saved his life in the process.

ABANDONED

I appreciate what you did for him. Now, can you tell me the whole story?"

"Of the gunfight or everything else?"

"As much as you can tell me."

"I need to get to the Brennan company as soon as possible, so I'll give you the basics. I just stopped by to let you know that I'd be in town for a few days, so you didn't think I'd skipped town without writing the long statement."

"I understand. Just tell me what you can."

Jack presented a brief version of events but spent a bit more time on the shootout.

"Do you think he would have lived if you'd gotten him to the hospital?" the sheriff asked.

"Maybe, but I had to worry about Deputy Pleasant and frankly, I couldn't have cared less about that bastard."

"I agree with you, and I'm sure Jimmy does, too."

"Well, I'll be back when I can, Sheriff. I've got to head over to the furnace company now. Could I borrow one of your horses?"

"Sure. You can keep him while you're here if you'd like. We have spares."

"I appreciate it," Jack said as he stood, shook the sheriff's hand, then quickly left the sheriff's office to get to the barn and borrow one of the saddled horses.

He turned the horse into the company's yard, spotted the offices, trotted to the hitching rail, dismounted, and tied the horse off. He was still wearing his gunbelt, but it was under his jacket, so it wasn't too noticeable.

He entered the foyer, saw the receptionist desk and after reaching it, asked, "Can you direct me to the office of Dennis Ward, please?"

The receptionist gave him instructions to the factory floor across the yard and Mr. Ward's office.

It took him a while to find Mister Ward as he walked slowly past the heavy stamping equipment and assembly areas, marveling at the size of the massive machines.

When he found the hut-like office, he entered, and Dennis looked up in surprise.

"Mister Tyler, I'm surprised to see you here. I thought you were going to see the sheriff."

"I did, but I need to meet with the executives of the company. Could you arrange that?"

Dennis wasn't sure he could, but said, "Let's go and see Mister Burke. He's my boss and in charge of operations. He can do it."

The two men left the factory floor and were soon climbing the stairs to the executive offices.

They entered the outer office of James Burke and Dennis said to his secretary, "This is Mister Tyler, the man who rescued my daughter and Joseph Brennan. We need to see Mister Burke."

"I'm sure he'll be glad to meet you, Mister Tyler," the secretary said as he stood, and walked to the inner door and tapped.

Jack wondered if he would still be glad to see him when Mister Burke found out why he was there.

They were ushered into the office a few seconds later and the secretary closed the door as he returned to his outer desk.

James Burke wasn't startled by Jack's appearance, but he was mildly disconcerted when he did spot the gunbelt and holster.

But he rose, and offered his hand to Jack, saying, "Thank you for saving young Master Brennan."

Jack shook his hand then said, "He's a remarkable boy."

"Have a seat, Mister Tyler. You too, Mister Ward."

Both men sat down as James Burke returned to his chair.

"Now, what do you need, Mister Tyler?"

"Mister Burke, I just left the office of the sheriff to give him the details of the shootout at the Brennan house late yesterday with Noah Gallagher."

"Yes, we heard about it."

"Before I visited the sheriff, I had a discussion with Mister Luke Casey, the Brennan family attorney. I believe you know him well."

"I do. Why did you see him?"

"I asked him if it was possible for him to appoint Mrs. Doyle as Joseph's guardian."

Dennis and Mister Burke both stared at him before James Burke said, "Mister Tyler, I recognize that the boy is probably very fond of his nanny, but I don't even see how that is possible."

"I've already received his approval in the matter. He told me there were no legal prohibitions against it and he said it was now subject to the board of directors' approval."

"I still see that there would be a problem. She is after all a woman and would assume much more responsibilities than just caring for the boy."

"Personally, I don't believe anything should outweigh the needs of Joseph for affection, but that being said, I also believe that Mrs. Doyle is more than capable of meeting any responsibility necessary for the position. Then there are two strong motivations for the board to support her appointment. Once appointed, the long delay in finding a replacement guardian will be avoided, then there is one other added incentive for the company."

"Which is?" he asked.

"Mister Burke, I've heard that Brennan Furnace and Coal is in a bit of a financial bind after your president absconded with your company's money, and you're also limited in your ability to resolve the issue because there is essentially no one authorized to acquire the necessary funding to continue operating."

"Yes. I'll admit to that but appointing her as the boy's guardian wouldn't solve those issues. The money is simply gone. We'd have to secure a loan and with a woman in the position our bank and any other would be hesitant to take the risk."

"But the problem could be resolved, Mister Burke," Jack said.

James Burke leaned forward, put his hands on his desktop and asked, "How?"

"I'll create an account at the First National Bank in the name of Mister Dennis Ward and give him unlimited access to the account. He'll be able to meet any obligations until everything is stable again. You wouldn't have to apply for any loans at all."

"But that would take an enormous amount of money, Mister Tyler."

"I was expecting to deposit twenty thousand dollars. Is that enough?"

James Burke blinked and asked in a subdued voice, "How much?"

ABANDONED

"Twenty thousand dollars. Now, for that, I would only have a say in who is appointed in the position of the president of the company. Once the new president is in place, he will make all decisions about the company's operation and I will have no part in it at all. My only concern is for the happiness and welfare of Joseph."

James stared at Jack trying to get a measure of the man. It didn't take long, either. He believed that Mister Tyler would do exactly as he said he would and that he really did care about the boy.

"Let's get the other executive officers together and discuss your offer, Mister Tyler," he said as he stood.

Jack and Dennis both stood, then followed Mister Burke out of the office.

The meeting didn't take long, as each man was relieved to hear of the sudden influx of cash from the most unlikely of sources. During the meeting, they all recommended that James Burke be named president, which Jack confirmed after a short consultation with Dennis Ward. Dennis was then shocked to be named the vice president of operations to replace Mister Burke.

The chief clerk, Hank Wood was appointed chief finance officer and then Mister Burke had a paper drawn up for Luke Casey supporting Mister Tyler's petition for Emily Doyle to be named Joseph's guardian.

As they left the meeting room, Jack walked with Dennis Ward and said, "It's too late today, but Monday, we need to go to the bank and open that account."

Dennis asked, "You really have that much money?"

"That's about half of it. I prospect for gold but never knew what I'd do with it. I have over thirty thousand in a bank account in Cheyenne, a smaller account in Laramie, and about seventeen pounds of gold at my cabin."

As they walked down the stairs, Dennis almost missed one as he was distracted by the very thought of having that much gold and seemingly not to care about it.

"I can't believe they made me a vice president. I was shoveling coal on that factory floor twelve years ago," Dennis said as they crossed the foyer to the door.

"Then you probably know more about how the place works than most of them," Jack said as he unhitched the horse and Dennis continued to his old office, knowing he'd be moving into the grander office on the second floor soon. That meant he'd have to buy some new suits, too.

Jack mounted the sheriff's horse and headed out of the yard for Luke Casey's office. He wanted to get the paperwork done and ready for the judicial approval, then he'd return to the Ward home and have a long talk with Emily and Joseph.

Once she was appointed guardian, there were still many questions to be answered, but he knew her biggest worry about losing Joseph would be gone.

Luke Casey was slowly shaking his head as he stared at the sheet of paper in his hand.

"How on earth did you get them to approve this? They know that they'll be making Mrs. Doyle the chairman of the board for the company, don't they?"

"They do. But on Monday, the Brennan Furnace and Coal Company will be operating normally. As the family attorney, can you hire the Pinkertons to find Mister White and get the company's funds returned?"

"I'll go to their office shortly. I'll have them return as much of the cash as they can recover, but it would be too embarrassing to try the man for theft."

"That's fine. So, what do we do next?"

"I'll go and file the papers with Judge Carstairs' office this afternoon and if you come back later, around four o'clock I'll let you know when the hearing will be. It will be a formality, anyway, but Mrs. Doyle and Joseph will both have to be present."

"Okay. I'll see you at four o'clock, then," Jack said as he stood and shook the attorney's hand.

Luke Casey was feeling like a normal lawyer again rather than the chained shyster controlled by Noah Gallagher.

Jack mounted the horse and headed back to Thirteenth Street with a sense of accomplishment and a serious case of uncertainty. He may have solved the biggest problems facing Emily and Joseph, but he knew he'd created more complex issues when Casey mentioned that Emily would be chairman of the board for the company. He didn't even know what the job entailed, but it sounded as if it required her to remain in Omaha.

Jack may not want to live in the city, but maybe if they bought a house out of town in the open country it would be almost the same. He knew it wouldn't be, but he couldn't leave Emily.

Five minutes later, he dismounted, then led the horse into the small barn. He was going to unsaddle the gelding but decided he should talk to Emily and Joseph first.

He left the barn and hadn't taken two steps past the door when Emily and Joseph both exited the back door onto the porch and as Emily smiled, Joseph shot across the porch, barely touched the back steps and raced across the yard.

"What's the matter, Joseph?" he asked as the boys skidded to a stop before him.

"Mrs. Doyle told me that you were going to try and fix everything. Did you do it?"

"Maybe. I need to talk to you both," he replied as he waited for Emily to reach them.

"Maybe?" she asked before she stopped.

"Emily," he began, using her Christian name in front of Joseph for the first time, "I just finished talking to Mister Casey about the guardian issue, and have already talked to the executives at the company as well. Can we sit and talk somewhere? Privately?"

"Privately meaning two or three of us?" she asked.

"All three of us. I need Joseph's thoughts as well."

"Why don't we go back to the barn?" she asked.

Jack nodded and waited for Emily and Joseph to begin walking before he turned to walk beside her. He was pleased that she still wore her hair straight and hadn't restored that huge bundle of hair on the top of her head.

Once inside, Joseph hopped onto a stack of two hay bales while Emily sat on a single bale beside him.

Jack remained standing and said, "As I just mentioned, I talked to Mister Casey about the new guardian. He told me that he would be the one appointing the new guardian and that it had to be approved by the board of directors of the company. Well, I convinced him that you, Emily, should be the new guardian."

Emily's eyes flew wide as she put her hands to her chest and exclaimed, "*Me?*"

"Yes, Emily. You. Then, I went to the company and had them agree to support your appointment to the position. I just dropped off the paper with Mister Casey and he's going to see the judge about it this afternoon. He said you and Joseph had to see the judge to make it official, but it was just a formality."

Emily was still flabbergasted and asked again, "Me?"

ABANDONED

"Yes, ma'am."

She opened and closed her mouth twice before asking, "How is that even possible? I'm a woman and I'm not even a relative. How did you do it?"

"With Mister Casey, it was fairly simple. I essentially blackmailed him by telling him that I would forget about his involvement with Mister Gallagher. The board of directors was more of a challenge, but their precarious financial situation that had been created by the unexpected withdrawal of the company's cash gave me an opportunity to make them an offer that they couldn't refuse."

Emily stared at Jack and said, "You bribed them?"

"Not exactly. I told them I'd create an account in the First National Bank that your father would manage, so the company would be able to meet their financial obligations until everything settled down. I'm going to move twenty thousand dollars into the account later today."

"You're giving them twenty thousand dollars?" she asked in astonishment.

"No. I'm letting them use the money, but frankly, I don't care if they spend it all, either. What was important that they agree to make you Joseph's guardian, and they did."

Joseph then asked, "Mrs. Doyle is my guardian now?"

Jack smiled at the boy and said, "Almost. You'll have to see the judge on Monday or Tuesday and he'll sign some papers to make it official, but I'm almost sure that by Wednesday, Mrs. Doyle will be your guardian."

Joseph grinned, looked at Emily, then his grin faded as he asked, "Does it mean you won't be my nanny anymore?"

Emily smiled, touched his cheek and replied, "No, Joseph, I won't be your nanny anymore. You won't have a nanny. You'll just have me."

Then, he glanced at Jack, before asking, "Will you be Emily Ann Ward now?"

Emily was startled by the question before replying, "I'm guessing that Mister Tyler told you about that?"

"Yes, ma'am. Is it true that you want to be the other lady but didn't want to scare me?"

"It wasn't so much that I didn't want to scare you, Joseph. It was that I had to be as nice as I could be or Mister Gallagher or before that, Mister Moore or your father could fire me, and I'd lose you."

"But they can't fire you anymore. No one can. So, can you be the other lady now?"

"I can, but you might not notice the difference for a while."

"Mister Tyler said that you were still a nice person, but different when you were Emily Ann Ward."

"That's a good way to describe it, Joseph," she said, then turned to Jack and asked, "What happens now, Jack?"

"That's the question I can't answer, Emily. Mister Casey told me that you were going to be the chairman of the board for the company once you were named Joseph's guardian, and I don't know what effect that will have on what we want to do."

Emily was aghast as she asked, "I have to be the chairman of the board?"

"That's what Mister Casey told me."

Emily was shaken as she sat on the bale of hay. When Jack had told her that he'd somehow magically convinced the attorney and the board of directors to name her his guardian, she had been ecstatic with the news, but now, a huge obstacle had been tossed into their way.

"How can I do this, Jack? I don't know anything about business?"

"I don't either, Emily. I've been trying to come up with some solution, but it may take lawyers to figure something out."

Joseph then offered his own, simple solution when he asked, "Mrs. Doyle, if you aren't going to be my nanny anymore, does that mean you can get married?"

Emily had to pry her mind from the vexing chairman of the board issue, then turned to Joseph and said, "Being a nanny doesn't mean you can't be married, Joseph."

"It doesn't? Then you can marry Mister Tyler?"

Jack looked down at Joseph and then slowly brought his blue eyes back to Emily, who had just had the same initial revelation that had begun to blossom in his mind.

"Emily, I don't know what it says in the will that controls all of this but come with me this afternoon when I'm supposed to meet with Mister Casey and we can ask some very important questions."

Emily nodded and said, "Yes. Of course, I'll come."

Joseph asked, "May I come, too?"

Jack replied, "You will be the most important person in the room, Joseph."

Joseph grinned as Jack finally dropped down onto the hay bale beside Emily.

"Emily, if this all can be worked out legally, would you marry me and return to Laramie?"

Emily kissed him and then answered, "Even if we had to ride on mules."

"I'm coming, too, aren't I?" asked Joseph.

Jack looked past Emily and said, "If you do, Master Brennan, it will be as Joseph Charles Tyler and you'll have Emily Ann Ward Tyler as your mother, not your guardian or your nanny."

Joseph looked at Emily, his face threatening to split in half as he said, "You've always been my mother, Mrs. Doyle," then dropped to the barn floor, and hugged her.

Emily was in tears as she held Joseph and looked at Jack's smiling face, hoping that this would all work. There were still so many things that could derail their desire to stay together, but she trusted Jack to take care of the big things and would let Emily Ann Ward handle the rest.

―――

Jack had escorted Emily and Joseph to lunch at a nearby restaurant and during the long conversation, told her of her father's promotion to vice president of operations, which tickled her, knowing that he'd have to work behind a desk in a fancy suit now.

They didn't return to the Ward house until almost two o'clock and told the rest of the family except for Dennis, who was still at work, of their plans. The news caused an immense amount of conversation, not the least of which involved the subject of the marriage and where and when it would be held.

Jack had to drive the buggy to the company to take his prospective father-in-law from his office to the First National Bank to open the account. It was a startling ride for Dennis Ward, who was barely adjusting to have Emily in his life again, but after the initial shock had subsided, was overjoyed that his strong-minded daughter had found her match in Mister Tyler.

They opened the account which Jack did with a small amount of cash, but then gave the clerk a draft for twenty thousand dollars on his Cheyenne account, which raised eyebrows. He told them that the transfer probably would be completed on Monday morning, which posed no difficulties for the company.

ABANDONED

After their brief stop at the bank, Jack drove Emily's father back to the company where he could tell them about the new account and let them breathe a sigh of relief while he drove back to the house to pick up Emily and Joseph to see the family lawyer.

Just before four o'clock, Jack, Emily and Joseph pulled up in the buggy before Luke Casey's office.

When they entered, his clerk was momentarily thrown off kilter when he saw Joseph but waved them into Luke's office. He may have known that Joseph was alive and back in Omaha but seeing him was still a bit unnerving.

Luke Casey was more than unnerved as he caught sight of the two people whom he had known Noah was taking to their deaths just two weeks earlier. He couldn't look at their faces as Jack held out a chair for Emily and then pulled a third chair to the front of the desk for himself.

The family attorney concentrated on Jack as he said, "I talked to Judge Carstairs and he set the hearing for two o'clock on Tuesday afternoon. He was a bit surprised with the choice of guardians, but after I clarified everything, I'm sure he'll approve it. Oh, and I also contracted with the Pinkertons to find Mister White."

"Mister Casey, when I talked to you this morning, you mentioned that if Mrs. Doyle became Joseph's guardian, she would be the chairman of the board. Is that a requirement of the will?"

"Indirectly, as Joseph would be the owner and chairman of the board if he were an adult, the guardian assumes the chairmanship along with powers of attorney that are granted the position. But in a practical matter, the chairman of the board is more of an administrative position and the board itself is more advisory in nature than in a publicly held company."

"I have no idea what that all means, but the reason I brought Mrs. Doyle and Joseph along is that we may want to change things a bit."

"Change things?" he asked.

"Yes. Mrs. Doyle and I wish to get married and then adopt Joseph. He'd still be the heir to the Brennan estate and it could be held in trust for him when he achieves adulthood."

Luke Casey was staggered by the suggestion. It took him almost a minute to understand the ramifications of what Jack Tyler had just proposed.

He finally asked, "Mister Tyler, why would you consider this? I thought you were satisfied with the appointment as we had discussed."

"I was until I realized that it may keep Mrs. Doyle here. I want to marry her for the only reason a man should ever marry a woman, and we want to adopt Joseph for the only reason a couple should adopt a child. I love her and we both love Joseph."

Luke Casey was still flabbergasted and wrestling with the idea as he sat staring at Jack.

Jack held Emily's left hand as she held Joseph's with her right as they watched the lawyer mentally grapple with the issue.

After another minute, he asked, "When are you going to be married?"

Jack looked at Emily, then replied, "We haven't gotten that far yet. It all depended on what you told us."

Mister Casey looked at Joseph, who was obviously very happy with the idea, then asked, "Can you be married on Monday? If you come to the hearing as a married couple, I think we might be able to convince Judge Carstairs to modify the guardianship order to approve an adoption. It's not better than a fifty-fifty chance, but at least I'm sure he'll approve the appointment of Mrs. Doyle as guardian. After that, you'd have time to take care of the rest if he decided not to approve the adoption at that hearing."

Jack nodded, squeezed Emily's hand and said, "Okay. We'll see what we can do. We'll talk to you again on Monday."

"That's fine, but please don't tell me you've changed your minds again."

"That, Mister Casey, will never happen," Jack said as they all rose.

As the buggy rolled down the cobbled streets of Omaha, Emily asked, "Jack, I know you said that you were raised at a Catholic orphanage, but are you a Catholic? It doesn't matter to me, but it will make things faster."

"I was baptized and confirmed a Catholic, Emily, although I'll admit to not having gone to Mass once since leaving the orphanage. If I had to go to confession now, I'd probably be in there for a month and a half and then another three months saying my penance."

Emily sighed and said, "I'm not much better. After what I did to keep my job, I haven't been able to receive communion because I never could go to confession and tell them what I had done."

"So, Emily Ann Ward, what do you want to do? We could be married in the courthouse on Monday, but I have a feeling that you want to be married by a priest."

She looked at him and said, "I know it's asking a lot, Jack, but I just feel this would be my chance to live my life as I always wanted to live it. I don't want to start it under a cloud."

Jack smiled at her and asked, "Who can you talk to who can handle all of this so quickly?"

Emily kissed him, then smiled as she said, "Father James Duffy at Saint Mary Magdalene's. It's just two blocks from the house on Chicago Street."

"Do you want to go there now and talk to him?"

"Would you mind?"

"No, ma'am. Just point me in the right direction."

Emily guided him to the church with a mixture of nervousness and hope. She had known Father Duffy for years, and he'd asked her often why she only came to Mass but failed to take the sacraments. Even though she'd give him vague answers, he hadn't pressed the issue. Now, she hoped that he'd be understanding rather than judgmental.

Jack was doing this for Emily but thought it might be an opportunity to unburden himself of some of the things that he'd done that weren't exactly Christian in his way of thinking. Most recently, it involved letting a man die who might have lived if he'd hurried back.

They pulled to a stop at the rectory of St. Mary Magdalene parish and Joseph bounded out on the left side as Emily stepped out on the right. Jack climbed out of the buggy, tied the reins to the hitching rail and they walked up the steps of the building.

Jack knocked on the door and after twenty seconds, it opened, and Jack was surprised to see a priest answering the door rather than the housekeeper.

He spotted Emily, broke into a big smile and said, "Emily, this is a pleasant surprise. Please come in."

"Thank you, Father Duffy," she said and entered the rectory.

Joseph followed, and Jack took up the rear as the priest closed the door behind them.

"I heard the horrible stories of what happened out West and just recently was told that you'd returned unharmed along with young Joseph."

"Yes, Father. This is Mister Jack Tyler, the man who rescued us from certain death and brought us back to Omaha."

Father Duffy turned to Jack and shook his hand as he said, "I won't diminish your accomplishments by telling you that you were an instrument of God, Mister Tyler, but I can't tell you how overjoyed I was when I heard of Emily and Joseph's salvation."

"I'd like to believe that I was that instrument, Father."

"So, if you'll all have a seat, you can tell me what brought you here this afternoon. I'm sure that there are many things that need to happen to correct what Joseph's uncle had done."

"Most have already been corrected, Father," Emily said, "Mister Tyler went with a deputy to arrest Mister Gallagher for murder and they had a gunfight in the house on Chicago Street. Mister Gallagher is dead."

Father Duffy sat back in his chair and asked, "Is that why you've come? To arrange for a funeral mass?"

"No, Father," she replied, "It's to see if it would be possible for Mister Tyler and I to be married in the church on Monday. I know this is a very unusual request, but it is what we desperately wish, and it would solve many different problems."

To his credit, Father Duffy didn't deny the request out of hand, but said, "There are many things that would prevent that from happening so quickly, Emily. There would be the bans and the necessary instructions being the two most time-consuming."

Then he turned to Jack and asked, "Are you a Catholic, Mister Tyler?"

"Yes, Father, although I'll admit that I haven't been to Mass in eighteen years."

His eyebrows rose as he sighed then asked, "Your extended absence has made it more difficult, but not as impossible as if you'd been of a different faith."

Then he turned to Emily and said, "Before we go any further in this discussion, perhaps you both need to tell me why it is so urgent."

Emily nodded, glanced at Jack, then back to Father Duffy.

She started telling the story, beginning with the departure from Omaha on August 16th, and when she reached the point of Jack's arrival, she alternated telling the story with Jack and sometimes Joseph.

Father Duffy didn't ask a single question as he sat in his chair with his hands folded and his index fingers peaked in front of his lips, digesting the incredible tale.

Jack took over the narrative once it reached their arrival in Omaha and told him about the meetings with Luke Casey and the board of directors. He left nothing out, including his offer to keep the company functioning with his own money.

He finished by saying, "It was when Joseph asked if Emily could be married now that she would no longer be his nanny that triggered the idea that if we were married and adopted Joseph, then we could live our lives as a normal family. Joseph would still inherit the family fortune, of course, but he'd still be with Mrs. Doyle and I would be his father and help Emily guide him to being a good man."

Father Duffy then said slowly, "I'd have to get permission from the bishop, and you'd both have to return to the good graces of the Church, but I believe I can make arrange for a wedding on Monday."

Emily sighed, then said, "Father, it would mean so much to us. I've wanted to confess my deepest sin for so long but was afraid. I confessed it to Jack when we were in the mountains and I felt free. Now, I'm ready to confess it to you and to God and ask for His forgiveness."

Father Duffy smiled gently at Emily and said, "We can do that when you're ready, Emily," then turned to Jack.

Jack answered his unasked question, "I'll follow Emily, Father, but it will take some time."

He smiled more broadly and said, "Why am I not surprised?"

ABANDONED

Then Joseph said, "I haven't been to confession in three weeks now, Father."

"And I'm sure you've committed grievous offenses during that time, Joseph. Do you want to go first?"

"Out here?" he asked, looking at Emily.

"Yes. Out here. It's not any different than the confessional. Would you rather do it in private?"

"No, I suppose it's okay," Joseph said before he stood and walked to where Father Duffy was sitting.

He dropped to his knees and then lowered his head and began his confession, which was close to being a typical young boy's release of his wrongdoings, but with the added twist of admitting he wanted to hurl a rock at his uncle's head if he showed up after he'd left them alone.

After Joseph returned to his chair to say his penance, he was surprised when Mrs. Doyle began her confession while he was there and could hear her sins.

Emily began with her more acceptable sins, if there was such a thing, including missing mass, her almost rejection of her family and her horrible treatment of her husband. But after she'd spent five minutes with sins she would have readily confessed, she finally reached the admission of fornication with Mister Moore simply to get the job of nanny and to keep it.

Father Duffy was surprised because Emily was so distraught as he'd heard other women confess to doing the same thing for much less honorable things than to be allowed to love a child. He was also surprised at what he didn't hear. He had expected her to confess to having sinned with Mister Tyler, but she hadn't. He was sure that she was giving an honest confession, and to him, it cemented his determination to argue on their behalf when he went to see the bishop.

When she finished, he gave her a surprisingly light penance, then she stood, smiled and sat back down feeling lighter than she'd ever felt before.

Jack was next and knew where he'd start his own admission of guilt. He told Father Duffy about how he'd almost beat Ian Collins, the director of the orphanage, to death when he was just fifteen. The priest asked him why he'd done it and after Jack explained, he just nodded and let Jack continue.

Jack didn't confess missing church all those years because he had already done so but talked about some of the things that he'd done during the war that he wasn't proud of, including pilfering from dead Confederates. He breezed through his years working the railroad and then finally reached the gunfight, and to him, his second biggest sin, allowing Noah Gallagher to die. His confession was bookended by Ian Collins and Noah Gallagher. Two despicable men who deserved the punishment administered by Jack, yet he didn't see it that way. To Father Duffy, it told him more about the man confessing his sins than anything else. Most men would have been proudly bragging about both events, but Jack Tyler thought it was he who had done something wrong.

It hadn't taken a month and a half, but Jack's confession still lasted almost twenty minutes. To Emily and Joseph, it reinforced their own faith in Jack and increased their determination to stay with him no matter where it was.

When he finished, Father Duffy absolved him of his sins then, shocking Jack, gave him a single Our Father as penance. He stood, returned to his chair and silently prayed, wondering why Father Duffy had been so lenient.

Father Duffy stood, smiled at them and said, "Now, on Sunday, I expect to see you all at Mass and at the communion rail. I'll see the bishop tomorrow morning and let you know after Mass."

They rose, and Jack said, "Thank you, Father."

"You're welcome. Now go home and get some dinner. I'm starving."

They laughed and after shaking his hand, Jack, Emily and Joseph left the rectory in good spirits.

Once they were back in the buggy and on the street again, Emily took his right hand and said, "Jack, I didn't believe I could love you any more than I did, but I do."

He turned and kissed her quickly, then smiled at her and Joseph before saying, "I hope the bishop allows this to happen, Emily. I didn't think it was possible before, but now I do."

"So, do I," she said.

Joseph then chimed in, saying, "Me, too!"

Dinner that night at the Ward residence was a happy, excited tempest of conversation as John and Mary, Molly and her fiancé, Andrew, and Dennis all asked questions about the almost endless changes that seemed to be exploding almost by the minute.

"So, what are you going to do tomorrow?" Mary asked.

Jack said, "I've got to go and see the sheriff again. I never had a chance to write out my statement. I forgot to send a telegram to Sheriff Higginbotham, too."

Joseph then asked, "Are we going to go back to the big house now?"

Jack paused, looked at Emily, then said, "I've got to do that, too, Joseph. I need to get it cleaned and repaired before anyone goes back there and probably need the sheriff's permission, too."

"Oh, that's right. I forgot about that," Joseph said.

Jack had forgotten about it as well and had to get to the house before Joseph or Emily saw the blood that he'd left in the bedroom and Deputy Pleasant had left in the parlor. He'd have to get the window fixed, too.

That night, Jack and Joseph played poker with John and Dennis in the kitchen while the ladies were in the parlor discussing Emily's wedding on Monday.

All of the problems that had caused Emily so much worry since they'd left Laramie were gone. She was going to marry Jack in three days and then be Joseph's mother and not his nanny. Maybe she'd even give him a brother or sister. She couldn't remember ever being this happy.

But even as they relaxed and planned for the marriage and then the hearing on Tuesday, Jack's complex repair of the Joseph guardian situation was beginning to unravel with a simple misread by the telegraph operator in Omaha who mistook a '4' for a '9' in the account number provided on the First National's Bank transfer request to the First National Bank in Cheyenne. The request wasn't received until after the bank closed for the day and the weekend, so it wouldn't be handled until Monday morning.

The next morning, Jack took Emily and Joseph shopping at the large department stores for more clothes, including more for himself as he was staying longer than he had anticipated and had nothing close to approaching wedding or marrying clothes. They also wanted to pick out their wedding bands.

As they were shopping, Father Duffy was visiting the bishop with his petition to waive almost all of the requirements that the church required for coupled preparing to marry.

It was at the bishop's residence that the second thread holding Jack's plan together snapped when the bishop refused to grant Father Duffy's request. He rarely gave dispensation for anything and this one wasn't even close to meeting his strict criteria. Father Duffy hadn't expected the response, but he hadn't spent much time with the bishop before today, either.

He returned to his parish disappointed and somewhat embarrassed. He'd have to break the news to the couple tomorrow. If they wanted to be married in the church, it would take two months.

Even as the priest returned to his rectory and then his church to hear the normal Saturday confessions, the third, and least likely problem occurred when a tall thin man sat being interviewed with a domestic service employment agency on Fourteenth Street.

"Mister Moore, you said you've managed a household for nine years, but don't specify which household on your form. Was it in another city, perhaps?" asked Anthony Darby.

"No, sir, but I parted on less than friendly terms and it was entirely due to the crass and belligerent attitude of the new owner of the home."

"And may I enquire as to the name of the employer?"

"I was employed by Joseph Charles Brennan, Junior nine years ago and he had no complaints during the time he owned the home. It was only after his passing and an obnoxious nephew named Noah Gallagher took over as the guardian of the man's son that issues arose."

Mister Darby asked, "You haven't heard about Mister Gallagher's recent demise in a shootout in that very house, then, Mister Moore?"

Wilbur Moore stared at the man and replied, "Excuse me. Did you say demise in a shootout? In the house? How did that happen?"

Mister Darby began, "I'm surprised you haven't heard about it. It's all over town. It seems that…"

The ex-steward listened intently as the gossip unfolded. *The boy was back and so was Mrs. Doyle?* Then, the interviewer even added on the news that the company's account had been raided by the ex-president, and the rumor was that Mrs. Doyle was going to be named as the boy's new guardian, which the man presented as a bit of a scandal, as the woman had spent more than a week with the man who had returned with her and the boy to Omaha. He implied that the man had threatened everyone with his pistol to get them to agree to the terms.

Before he even finished, Wilbur Moore began to think of how he could profit from the news. There had to be something that he could do. After all, he knew something about Mrs. Doyle that no one else knew.

He withdrew his application to be represented by the agency, then left the offices to talk to his circle of fellow butlers and heads of households that could provide him with more information.

One of them was the butler that worked in Judge Carstairs' home.

Early in the afternoon, while Emily and her sisters were preparing for a wedding that wasn't going to happen, Jack returned to 1710 Chicago Street. He wasn't going to be able to do anything about the broken window or the bullet hole he'd put through the back wall until next week, but he needed to clean the blood and pick up one of Joseph's three school uniforms. If he was going to church tomorrow, he'd have to wear his uniform from St. Ignatius school for some reason. Jack figured it would be the last day he'd wear it before they left for Laramie, so maybe he'd get to fulfill his promise to Joseph and slice the hat with his Bowie knife.

When he entered the house, he glanced to the left where Deputy Pleasant had been shot by the window and, except for the missing curtain and a bullet hole in the wall, there was no evidence of the shooting. The sheriff must have had someone come in and clean up the blood when they'd had Gallagher's body removed.

He walked up the stairs and checked on the main bedroom and found it clean except for his hole in the wall and groove in the floor and the shattered door jamb where Gallagher's shot had hit. The splinters had even been removed.

Jack had to find Joseph's room and when he did, he saw the three school hats lined up on pegs along the wall and snickered. He felt sorry for Joseph having to wear the things. They were just flat dark blue hats, which wasn't bad, but the lighter blue ribbon that encircled the crown didn't just wrap around the outside. Part of it hung over the back edge and ended in a golden tassel.

Jack plucked one from the wall, tossed it onto the bed, then opened his dresser drawers until he found the uniforms that completed the ensemble. It took three drawers to find it, and when he pulled one free, his snicker returned. It had short pants and a normal shirt and a hideous gold and blue plaid sweater that would probably enrage any Scotsman.

He found the fairly normal dark blue stockings that went with the outfit and packed it all in a satchel that Joseph must have taken to school with him.

After a quick tour of the large house, he took one more look at the large bedroom and thought it might not be a bad place to have his and Emily's wedding night. As he had told her on the trail, he expected that it wouldn't be a very quiet rendezvous, and the house was big enough that Joseph could be downstairs and, if he slept deeply enough, might not notice.

His last thoughts as he left the house were of Emily, and not all of them were of the wedding night. He closed the door behind him wondering what they would do with the house. It was a well-built structure and maybe they should rent it out until Joseph reached eighteen and he could either sell it or move back to Omaha.

As he rode back on the sheriff's horse, he began to think about the future. Now that everything seemed to be resolved, the only question seemed to be when he and his bride would return to Laramie with their adopted son.

Jack was smiling as he trotted down Chicago Street to 24 Thirteenth Street. Why shouldn't he? He was getting married in two days to Emily Ann Ward.

CHAPTER 9

Sunday morning, September the sixth, began as a chilly, cloudy day as a hint of what would be coming in a couple of months. It was more like late October than late summer. But the weather had no impact on the joy in the Ward home as they all prepared to attend Mass.

Jack, Emily and Joseph would borrow the buggy to drive to St. Mary Magdalene and meet Father Duffy while the rest of the family walked to their usual parish church.

There was no breakfast, of course, but there would be a large brunch when they all returned around nine-thirty.

So, at seven-thirty, the Wards, John and Mary Fitzpatrick, accompanied by Molly's fiancé, Andrew Donovan walked out of the house as Jack, Emily and Joseph rolled west along Davenport heading for St. Mary Magdalene Church.

Joseph sat on Jack's right in his goofy hat and short pants and wasn't happy. He thought he'd be able to wear the clothes that he'd worn on the hunting trip, but Emily had reminded him that he was still a student at St. Ignatius and had to follow the rules – at least until Tuesday.

After parking the buggy, Jack took Emily's arm and Joseph walked alongside Emily still out of sorts about his wardrobe as they climbed the steps to the church.

Once inside, they chose a pew and waited for the Father Duffy to begin the Mass. He entered the altar five minutes later and began the practiced ritual. Jack found that the often-heard and repeated Latin phrases came easy to him, which really wasn't any great surprise. For the first decade of his life, he had heard them daily at the orphanage, and he didn't expect them to change anytime soon.

The only English part of the Mass was the reading from the Gospels and the sermon. Father Duffy didn't seem as energetic as he had yesterday, and Jack wondered if he was just tired.

After the Mass ended and the congregation rushed out of the church to go home and have something to eat, Jack, Emily and Joseph waited to talk to Father Duffy. Jack and Emily were holding hands as they anticipated being told that Father Duffy would be able to perform the ceremony later that day or tomorrow morning.

It was ten minutes after the Mass ended that Father Duffy finally walked down the side aisle and asked them to follow him to the sacristy. Jack could tell that something had gone wrong just by the expression on his face, and he was sure that Emily had noticed as well.

Once inside, Father Duffy didn't mince words as he said, "The bishop refused my request for dispensations. I'm sorry, but I won't be able to marry you until the normal requirements are met."

Emily asked, "Why would he do that, Father?"

"The bishop is new to the West, having just been appointed from his position as monsignor at St. John's parish in Philadelphia. I explained to him that because of the very practical situations that we face with Catholics marrying non-Catholics, non-Christians and even Indians, we have to be more flexible than in the heavily populated cities of the East. He pointed out how St. Louis had changed and expected Omaha to do the same. I'm sorry, Emily. Maybe I just didn't state your case well enough."

Emily looked at Jack in distress and asked, "What will we do, Jack?"

Jack replied, "We'll tell Luke Casey to return to the original plan. After you become Joseph's guardian, we can take our time. We'll get there, Emily."

She smiled and nodded before saying, "You're right. There's no reason to panic."

ABANDONED

"No, ma'am."

Joseph was following the conversation and understood that Mrs. Doyle and Mister Tyler weren't going to get married soon, but things were still all right. Now, he just wanted to change clothes.

Jack and Emily both assured Father Duffy that the bishop's refusal was just a bump in the road and that they'd continue along the path to marriage and adoption.

Father Duffy was relieved and heartened to hear them and blessed all three of them before they left the sacristy and then the church.

Once in the buggy, Joseph removed his hat and asked, "Are you all right, Mrs. Doyle?"

Emily smiled at him and replied, "Yes, dear. I'm fine. On Tuesday, the judge will appoint me your guardian and then we'll move back into the house and decide what to do next."

Jack glanced over at Emily after listening to what she had just told Joseph and when she had said they would be moving into the big house, it dawned on him just how important being married to her really was. If they lived in the big house, he couldn't. She would be Joseph's guardian and there could be no hint of scandal. The same problem that had been there when he had just asked Luke Casey to make Emily the guardian had returned in spades.

Emily hadn't realized it yet, or just hadn't said anything by the time they returned to the Ward house. Jack had to unharness the buggy's horse while Emily and Joseph went inside. Everyone else was already there and the brunch had been set on the dining room table.

He took his time thinking about what he would do after Tuesday's court decision as a misty rain began to fall. He knew that Emily would agree to a civil marriage but agreeing to it and wanting it were two different things. He didn't want to start a life with Emily that way.

But maybe there was a solution to the housing dilemma. It wouldn't be ideal, but it would satisfy society's moralistic view.

Inside the house, Emily had told everyone about the bishop's decision, and that she and Jack would follow the normal process and be married in two months.

It was Mary who asked, "Are you and Joseph going to live in the big house, then?"

"Yes," Emily replied.

"Where will Jack live?" asked her father.

Emily opened her mouth to reply, then froze. *Where would Jack live?* She realized that even if he rented a nearby apartment and visited the house, scandal would surround them within hours and she'd risk losing everything if someone filed a complaint with the judge about her immoral behavior. They would be limited to strolls in the park and church attendance. It was ironic that Joseph's recently deceased guardian had visited brothels and had numerous women to his apartment with no repercussions whatsoever, but if the man she loved visited her even if it was to spend time with Joseph, it would be an outrage that would offend the sensibilities of the women in the neighborhood.

She finally answered, "I don't know. We haven't discussed it yet."

"Well, I'm sure that Jack will understand," her father said.

When Jack entered the house ten minutes later, his hair was matted down from the light rain and he looked like a sad dog as he removed his jacket and hung his gunbelt in the kitchen.

Emily heard him enter, stood, then walked quickly into the kitchen with Joseph trailing. The moment she saw him, she knew that he'd already realized the situation. She picked up a towel and handed it to him.

Jack smiled at her sadly, accepted the towel and began drying his face and hair.

"Jack, I just realized that moving into the big house might be a problem."

"I know, Emily. But I already thought of something to handle that."

"You have?" she asked.

"It's not great, but don't you have a maid and a cook?"

Emily blinked and slowly said, "We did, but you didn't see them when you had the shootout, did you?"

"No, there was no one in the house other than Gallagher."

"Not even Mister Moore, that hideous steward?"

"No, ma'am. It was empty then and it was empty when I returned yesterday afternoon."

"That's odd."

"Well, tomorrow, you need to find the maid and the cook. They'll be like chaperones, so at least I'll be able to visit you and Joseph at the house without concern of a scandal."

"You're going to live here?"

"Not immediately. I'll return to my cabin to set things up for an extended absence. I'll bring Abby and Billy to the livery and bring my gold to Cheyenne and deposit it before returning. I'll rent a place here and we'll go through the church's hoops until we're married, then we can adopt Joseph and return to Laramie. Is that all right?"

In response, Emily smiled, then quickly hugged Jack and kissed him.

"Thank you, Jack. I was very worried about how we could still be together, and I wouldn't be in danger of losing Joseph."

Jack looked down at Joseph and asked, "Can you suffer wearing that ugly hat for two months, Joseph?"

Joseph grinned and replied, "I guess so, but you're still going to cut it in half with your big knife, aren't you?"

"You bet."

With the last remaining problem behind them, Jack took Emily's arm and they returned to the dining room and a filling brunch.

―――

"He's going to approve that redhead as the boy's guardian?" Wilbur Moore asked as he held the cup of coffee in both hands.

Ralph Smith nodded and replied, "He's going to hear the case on Tuesday afternoon and was saying that despite the unusual nature of the request, there was no legal prohibition against a woman being named as guardian, even though she was a non-relative. He didn't know how the company's board of directors had been convinced to agree to the appointment, but it all seemed in order."

Wilbur snickered and said, "I wonder what the judge would do if he heard that the woman had behaved as a common trollop."

Ralph asked in a low voice, "Do you mean with that cowboy who returned with her from the wilds of Wyoming? Most of us believe he'd had his way with her."

Mister Moore smiled slightly and replied, "Maybe so, but I wonder if he noticed she had a large freckle on her right buttock."

Mister Smith's eyes went wide as he asked, "You? You had her?"

ABANDONED

"Many times. I've had all of the women that worked in the house at one time or another. Are you telling me that you've never enjoyed the company of Miss Arden?"

Smith snickered and replied, "You've got me there, Wilbur. But that redhead must have been a wildcat in bed."

"No, she was quite tiresome, really. Now, the new maid, Miss Flaherty, she was much better."

Ralph Smith leaned forward and said, "Tell me about her, Wilbur."

Wilbur was only too happy to describe her in detail, as he already was thinking about how to use Mrs. Doyle's anticipated appointment to guardian to his advantage.

For the Wards and their guests, the rest of Sunday was spent mostly indoors as the gray, almost-drizzle continued to fall outside.

Emily tried to imagine why the staff had left the house and where Anna Thornton or Mary Flaherty had gone. She was sure that it had something to do with Noah Gallagher, but also knew were she was most likely to find Anna Thornton, because Anna still had family in Omaha. She had no intention of looking for Mister Moore and hoped he'd taken a plunge from the bridge over the Missouri River.

After breakfast Monday morning, Dennis Ward left the house in one of his new suits heading for his new office and position as vice president of operations.

Emily would take the buggy to find Anna Thornton. She was anxious to find Anna, and not just because she needed a chaperone in the house. She wanted to know what had happened while she was away in Wyoming. She couldn't imagine that Mister Moore had left the two women alone but didn't expect that Noah Gallagher would have bothered either of them, knowing how much he disliked her.

Joseph rode with her in his school uniform. It was the first day of class at St. Ignatius School for Boys and Emily wanted him to return to his routine. His original protests after having been told that he was going were diminished when Jack reminded him that he'd have his ivory-handled knife with the wolf's head to show the other boys and the stories that went with it.

Jack was going to return the horse to the sheriff's office where he would finally write his long statement for the sheriff and send the telegram to Sheriff Higginbotham in Laramie.

He'd sent the telegram first because it was fast, and he didn't want to forget to send it again. That job done, he rode to the sheriff's office and finally returned the horse to the small barn behind the jail.

When he entered the front office, he spotted the sheriff and two deputies in the main office. He recognized Deputy Adams but didn't know the name of the second one, the man who'd returned after the shooting.

Sheriff Lafferty looked up as he entered and said, "There you are. We were just talking about you."

"How's Deputy Pleasant?" Jack asked.

"He's doing a lot better than the docs expected. He should be able to pull desk duty in another week or so."

"Thanks for having the blood in the house cleaned up. I went by there to take care of it and it was already done."

"Just cleaning up a crime scene. Are you going to write that report for me?"

"That's it."

ABANDONED

Sheriff Lafferty said, "John, show Mister Tyler where he can write his report."

"Yes, sir," replied Deputy John.

Jack followed the unknown lawman, who turned out to be Deputy John Applewhite, into a small room where he took a seat, then removed some blank sheets of paper from the drawer and dipped the pen into the inkwell.

Writing the report of the gunfight took more than a half an hour, but when he finally finished and gave it to Sheriff Lafferty, the extended telling of the full tale took more than an hour and then longer once the questions began.

After he finished, he left the sheriff's office to make the ride to see Luke Casey and to tell him that they'd have to revert back to their original plan. It would make his job easier, anyway.

That meeting only took ten minutes because, as Jack had suspected, he really wasn't eager to try Judge Carstairs' patience with the adoption request.

By the time he finally headed back to the Ward house, it was past lunchtime.

Emily arrived at the Thornton house on Jackson Street after dropping off Joseph at school. She pulled the buggy to a stop, stepped out and tied the reins to a hitching post.

When she knocked on the door, she wasn't surprised when Anna herself opened the door just thirty seconds later.

Emily smiled, but Anna just stood there gaping at her with her eyes wide open. It was as if she was seeing a ghost. The astounding news of her and Joseph's return hadn't reached the Thornton home yet because they moved in different social circles.

Finally, Anna asked quietly, "Emily?"

"Are you all right, Anna?" Emily asked in concern.

"You're alive?"

"I am. May I come in?"

Anna realized that they were still at the doorway and replied, "Oh. I'm sorry. Yes, please come in."

Emily entered the house as Anna closed the door behind her and still stared at Emily.

Anna said, "Emily, how are you still alive? Mister Gallagher said you and Joseph were dead and he owned everything now."

Emily took a seat in the small parlor as Anna sat down across from her.

"Noah Gallagher is dead, Anna. He was shot in the big house by the man who rescued me and Joseph after he'd abandoned us out in the mountains."

Anna just sat back as the enormous revelations hit her.

Emily then asked, "What happened while we were gone, Anna?"

Anna then asked, "Can you tell me what happened first, Emily?"

"I can, but let's move to the kitchen and we can share some tea. This may take some time."

The two women then walked down the hallway and Anna set the tea kettle on the stove before they sat at the kitchen table.

Emily then retold the story that she now could recite without pause.

ABANDONED

When she finished, Anna made the tea as she began to explain what had happened with Noah Gallagher and Mister Moore and how he had used both her and Mary before they decided to leave the house because they were sure that Mister Gallagher had murdered her and Joseph.

They had each finished two cups of tea when Emily told Anna how she was going to be made Joseph's guardian on Tuesday and would like to have her and Mary Flaherty return to the house without Mister Moore.

Anna was pleased with Emily's offer and readily agreed. Then, once the details were settled, Anna asked about the man who had rescued them and wanted all of the titillating details. Details that Emily wouldn't have shared with her sisters but would with Anna. They had shared much worse details before.

———

It was almost ten o'clock before Cyrus Mandell, the processing clerk at the First National Bank in Cheyenne, reached the telegram from Omaha requesting a transfer of twenty thousand dollars from Jack's account.

Everything seemed proper, so he did the paperwork, had the chief clerk verify everything and had the transfer telegrams written and placed in the outbox for delivery to Western Union.

At a little past eleven o'clock, the telegram was tapped out and arrived in Omaha forty minutes later. With such a large amount, one would believe that extra care would have been paid to the additional information on the telegram rather than just the account number listed, but it wasn't. It didn't help that the account that was credited with the deposit belonged to J. L. Taylor, either.

The simple number error in the original transmission had done its damage. At the end of the business day, the new account created by Jack for the company's use, still had its original starting balance of ten dollars, and the account of J. L. Taylor now had a balance of $20,276.11.

Emily let Anna go and tell Mary the news as she drove the buggy back to the house to tell Jack what she had learned from Anna.

Jack had finally pried himself loose from the sheriff's office, took the same tan gelding and headed back to see Emily. It seemed that in the rush of the past few days, they had little time to be alone together. He missed Emily Ann Ward.

Emily was turning the buggy onto 13th Street when she spotted Jack riding toward the house. He hadn't seen her, so she just kept the buggy rolling and watched him. She felt a flush of warmth as her eyes drank in his strength and masculinity. She remembered that night under the stars when they'd shared their only real moments of physical intimacy and wanted him to take her to the big house right now while it was empty. She wanted it so badly, she decided to ask him to ride back with her to the big house.

But, by the time she'd reached the house, the same, lingering inhibitor prevented her from even thinking about it. It wasn't a moral issue, but a practical one. She believed that as manly as Jack was, she would probably become pregnant the first time they made love and that would end all of their plans, including Joseph. It was always Joseph, and most women might have begun to resent the boy for being the obstacle to her satisfaction, but not to Emily. Joseph was simply that important to her.

So, when she pulled the buggy to the back of the house and Jack finally spotted her and smiled, she just smiled in return and forgot her lascivious thoughts.

Jack, on the other hand, and quite surprisingly, just wanted to be with Emily and talk to her without restrictions. So, when she slowed the buggy to a stop, he halted his unsaddling of the mare and walked to where Emily still sat with the reins in her hands.

"Mrs. Doyle, would you care to join me for a late lunch?"

ABANDONED

"Why, Mister Tyler, that's such a kind offer. How could any woman refuse?"

"Let me finish unsaddling the gelding, then I'll join you in the buggy."

"I'll be waiting anxiously," she replied with a smile, and let the lascivious thoughts creep back into her mind, but just for entertainment purposes.

Jack made quick work unsaddling the horse and led him into a stall in the small barn before trotting back out to the buggy, stepping inside and taking the reins from Emily who didn't move much as Jack slid in close.

He turned the buggy around and they were soon back on 13th Street and heading north.

Emily began telling him about events at the big house while she and Joseph were gone, and that she'd arranged for both Anna and Mary Flaherty to return on Saturday, when everything should be settled. Jack had already set Friday as the day for his return to Laramie to configure his cabin for an extended absence.

Lunch was a long, happy hour as the couple took their time, and then, when they left the restaurant, drove the buggy to a park near the Missouri River and Jack was able to enjoy a full uninterrupted hour with Emily Ann Ward.

Emily's lusty mindset had dissipated as she just reveled in being herself and sharing the time with Jack. Despite the upcoming separation, each was committed to doing what was necessary to following the rules of the government, church and society, written and unwritten, before they finally would leave Omaha and return to Laramie.

The buggy arrived at St. Ignatius School for Boys just before classes ended for the day.

"How can you find Joseph among all the others?" asked Jack as he watched the front door of the school.

"You'll see," Emily said with a smile as she held Jack's hand.

They were now sitting a more respectable eighteen inches apart as the doors flew open and the various sized boys in identical uniforms poured through the doors like a swarm of blue locusts.

Jack didn't see Joseph until suddenly, he spotted a bare head among the flying tasseled blue ribbons and smiled.

Emily glanced at Jack and asked, "Find him yet?"

"Yes, ma'am," he replied as Joseph spotted Emily's long red hair and raced toward the buggy.

He was grinning widely as he hopped inside beside his nanny and said, "All of the boys really liked my knife and even Mister Horner asked me to tell them what happened in the mountains. It was great!"

Jack had the buggy moving back onto the roadway when Emily asked, "Did you tell them how you faced a grizzly bear and a pack of fearsome, growling wolves?"

His head bobbed up and down as he replied, "Yes, ma'am. At first, some of them thought I was making it up, but when Bobby Sheets asked me if I was afraid, and I told him I was scared to death, I guess they finally figured out that I wasn't fibbing at all."

Jack looked quickly at Joseph and said, "I'd be more than happy to tell them just how brave you were, Joseph."

"No, it's okay, Mister Tyler. The only two that don't believe me are bullies anyway and I don't like them."

Jack smiled as Joseph continued chattering all the way back to the Ward home and was still talking as he and Emily went into the house while Jack unharnessed the horse.

ABANDONED

The day of the hearing arrived in marked contrast to Sunday's dismal weather. It was a glorious late summer day and the temperature even at eight o'clock was almost seventy degrees.

For the second day, Dennis Ward was the first out of the house in his second new suit, feeling less self-conscious after his first day in the new position when he had absent-mindedly walked to the factory floor before turning around and heading to his new offices across the yard.

Because the hearing wasn't until the afternoon, Emily wrote a note for Joseph saying that they would pick him up from the school at one o'clock. He grumbled that he should have gotten the day off before he followed Emily and Jack to the buggy.

After dropping him off at school, Emily was returning the buggy when she spotted a familiar and unwelcome apparition standing at the hitching rail. She thought about returning to the school, but instead, she took in a deep breath and strode purposefully toward Wilbur Moore who watched her approach. He'd never met Emily Ann Ward before as she'd quickly retreated into Mrs. Doyle's façade after seeing two-year-old Joseph. He was about to be introduced.

"What are you doing here?" she snapped as she reached the buggy.

Moore was momentarily taken aback, but then regained his confidence and said, "Mrs. Doyle, it would behoove you to maintain a cordial tongue."

"I'll do nothing of the sort, Mister Moore. Now, I will repeat my question. What are you doing here?"

"I've heard that you are trying to become the guardian of Joseph Charles Brennan the third. Is that right?"

"It doesn't concern you, Mister Moore. I've already talked to Anna Thornton and she told me that you'd been terminated by Mister

Gallagher before he died, so I suggest you leave and seek employment elsewhere. You will not be rehired."

He raised his eyebrows and said, "Oh? What makes you believe that I'm seeing employment? I have no need for such menial labor any longer, Mrs. Doyle. With you as the new guardian, you will have access to the family accounts. Granted, it is limited, but it is more than enough to suit my needs. I am not excessively greedy, Mrs. Doyle. I will be more than happy with, say, two hundred dollars a month?"

"Are you insane? Why would I pay you a penny after what you did to me?"

He smiled and said, "It's precisely what I did to you that is the reason for you to pay me, Emily, if I may call you by your Christian name. You came willingly to my bed whenever I summoned you. You could have left the house at any time, but you didn't. Now, Mrs. Doyle, how do you think Judge Carstairs will react to your appointment as the boy's guardian if he knew that you spread your legs at the snap of my fingers?"

Emily growled, "Listen to me, you, perverted, weak man. The man that brought me and Joseph from the mountains is here with me. You probably knew that. But did you know that we're going to be married? Jack Tyler has more man in his little finger than you have in your whole pathetic body. He shot and killed Noah Gallagher and I don't believe he'd even waste a bullet on you. He carries a massive knife that would suit his purpose much better. So, Mister Moore, get away from me. Now!"

Wilbur Moore then asked in a quiet, menacing voice, "Don't you dare insult me, you whore!"

Then, he turned and walked away, his long thing legs striding in almost a comical goosestep, except there was nothing funny about Mister Wilbur Moore.

Emily watched him leave and felt her heart pounding. She wondered if she had done the right thing in antagonizing him.

Maybe she should have made promises to him then told Jack and let him handle the former steward. But it was too late now to take anything back. Her next question was whether or not to tell Jack about his visit.

She climbed into the buggy and sat for a few minutes weighing the question. If she told Jack, she was concerned he might go and find Moore and get in trouble. To Jack, it would be nothing more than a threat that needed to be addressed, just like an attacking wolf or bear. She finally decided it wouldn't matter because she believed that Moore wouldn't do anything until after she was appointed as Joseph's guardian. Why would he? If he tried to interrupt the hearing, he might cost her the position and he'd be unable to blackmail her as the future guardian.

So, as Emily started the buggy forward, she just let the incident slide away. She should have understood Wilbur Moore's motives as much as the practical side of the issue.

Wilbur Moore, despite his somewhat clownish appearance, was a proud and vindictive man. He had expected Emily Doyle to give in easily to his demand and had been initially amused by her combative behavior. That had shifted to anger and then outrage as she continued to belittle him. *A woman dared to insult him?* Suddenly, the money was secondary to him as he decided to simply ruin the woman.

When Emily turned the buggy down the Ward home's drive, she spotted Jack as he had just finished unsaddling the tan gelding he'd borrowed from the sheriff's office. He'd received a reply from Sheriff Higginbotham and a request for more information, which he must have just sent.

He turned when he heard the buggy roll into the yard and waved at Emily, who returned his wave then brought the buggy to a stop.

"Feel like going for a ride, Mister Tyler?" she asked with a grin.

"With you, ma'am? You shouldn't have to ask," he replied, as he clambered inside and then just leaned back and looked at Emily as she waited for him to take the reins.

"Aren't you driving, Mrs. Doyle?"

Emily laughed, then turned the buggy around and headed back to the same park where they had enjoyed a very pleasurable hour yesterday afternoon. She thought it might be the last time they could be alone together for quite some time and wanted to make the most of it.

Once the horse had stopped and was cropping the grass, Jack took Emily's hand and smiled.

"Emily, in a few hours, you'll be Joseph's guardian and he'll be under your guidance until he's a man. As much as I look forward to being there and helping you, I'm much more anxious to be your husband. I know we can't do anything more than what we did back in the mountains and believe me when I tell you how incredibly difficult that is for me. But it's only a couple of months before we'll get married and that will make our first night together even more special."

"I know how you feel, Jack. I was thinking of asking you to take me to the big house yesterday and, well, take me in the big house. I want you at least as much as you want me, but I can't risk losing Joseph."

"I know that, Emily. When I return to Laramie, I'll spend an extra day or two to make our bedroom a special place for us."

She smiled and asked, "How far away will Joseph's bedroom be?"

He laughed, then replied, "Probably not far enough. Maybe if it was in Cheyenne."

Emily put her hand around his neck, pulled him close and kissed him. They were alone, so they managed another ten minutes of serious exploration before they mutually ended the tour before it reached its obvious destination.

They spent another hour mostly talking, but with an occasional slip back into their discovery mode before Jack finally turned the buggy around to return to the Ward home. They needed to prepare for the hearing at two o'clock and that meant that Emily was even going to put her hair up.

Emily had almost mentioned Wilbur Moore's visit three different times but had been distracted each time. Now, it didn't matter anymore. They'd have lunch, return to the school to pick up Joseph, and go to the courthouse.

Dennis Ward was sitting at a bank clerk's desk with Larry Wilcox, the new chief clerk at Brennan Furnace and Coal. There were three bills that needed paying and the transfer from the First National Bank was supposed to be completed yesterday, so he was prepared to write his first drafts on the new account once the balance had been verified.

The clerk returned to his desk, sat down and said, "I'm sorry, Mister Ward, but there is no change in the account you opened last week."

"But you told us that the transfer would be done by Monday morning. Was there a problem?"

The clerk lowered his head and replied in a low voice, "Mister Ward, at the risk of appearing to be distrusting, but when we made out the request, did you really believed that a man dressed like Mister Tyler would possess anywhere near that amount? I doubt if he has another hundred dollars to his name."

"But he told me he had at least another ten thousand dollars in the bank in Cheyenne and seventeen pounds of gold in his cabin in Wyoming," Dennis said quietly, but forcefully.

The clerk sighed and said, "Mister Ward, wealthy people don't even keep seventeen ounces of gold in their fancy homes. I'm sorry, but the transfer didn't go through."

"Did you receive any rejection for insufficient funds?" he asked.

"No, we didn't. But that's not unusual. If you'd like, I can have our chief clerk check for possible errors in the request, but I'd be surprised if there was one. We double check them before they're transmitted."

"Could you do that please? I'll wait here."

"Very well, but it could take some time. The chief clerk is in a meeting."

"I'll wait," Dennis said as he slumped in the chair.

The new company chief clerk, however, was convinced that the bank hadn't made a mistake and that the bank clerk was correct in his assessment of Mister Tyler's net worth.

"I'll see you back at the office, Mister Ward," Larry Wilcox said as he rose, then walked quickly across the bank's lobby to pass the bad news to Mister Burke before he left for that hearing to confirm the board's approval of the nanny as the guardian and chairman of the board.

There had been some rumbling among the executives that Mister Tyler was bluffing and playing them all for fools in their hour of desperation. He was promising them a life preserver, just so he could get Mrs. Doyle appointed the boy's guardian and then marry the woman and gain control of the company. It was like Noah Gallagher all over again.

It was just after one o'clock when Larry Wilcox raced the company buggy back to the factory.

———

ABANDONED

Wilbur Moore had walked down to Capitol Street and entered the county offices. He headed for Judge Carstairs' courtroom and pulled up a chair. He knew he was early, but he wouldn't be sitting when the hearing started. He'd be standing in the cloak room in the back of the courtroom and make a dramatic appearance shocking everyone when he exposed Emily Doyle for the harlot that she was.

Jack and Emily were waiting outside of St. Ignatius School for Boys and this time, instead of hoards of uniformed boys, only a single almost-nine-year-old exited the door, pulled off his hat and grinned at Mrs. Doyle and Mister Tyler as he trotted down the stone steps. Mister Tyler was wearing a light jacket, but Joseph could see the tip of the knife's sheath sticking out from under the jacket's hem on the left. He hoped that Jack would at least cut up this one hat before he left for Laramie.

"Are we going to the court now?" Joseph asked as he walked beside Emily.

"Yes, Joseph. Now, while we're talking to the judge, you just be quiet. If he asks you any questions, you answer them politely. Okay?"

"Yes, ma'am."

They reached the buggy and Jack helped Joseph inside, so he didn't get dirt on his school uniform as Emily carefully boarded on the other side. Jack stepped into the buggy, took the reins and turned the buggy toward Capitol Street and the county offices.

"*It wasn't there? Not any of it?*" exclaimed company president James Burke.

"No, sir. Not a penny. The clerk at the bank said he wasn't surprised. He doubted if Mister Tyler had that much money. Who does? Personally, sir, I agree with the speculation that others have offered that Mister Tyler was just hoping to benefit from the situation, so he could install Mrs. Doyle as the boy's guardian and gain control of the company."

James Burke was the only man in the company who had spent any length of time with Jack and hadn't shared that opinion, but now, with the absence of the promised funds, he had to act.

"Alright, the hearing is in less than an hour. Get the rest of the board together and have the company carriage ready. We need to get to the hearing and withdraw our support of the nanny's appointment."

"Yes, sir," Larry Wilcox said as he turned on his heels then raced from James Burke's office.

Even though Dennis Ward was the new vice president of operations, his appointment to the position and to the board hadn't been approved yet, so his absence wasn't necessary.

Dennis Ward continued to sit at the clerk' desk, his spirit crushed by the belief that Jack wasn't what he had believed him to be. In the short time he'd known Jack, he'd come to admire and like the younger man and had been overjoyed when he and Emily had announced their upcoming marriage. He'd even been more impressed when Jack had told him that he would wait to marry his daughter until the church was satisfied with their preparations. Now, it appeared the entire house of cards that had been built, from his ascendency to the new job, to Emily's being named the guardian of the boy was collapsing.

Jack pulled the buggy to a stop before the county courthouse, let Joseph out, then clambered out after him and inspected his dark blue uniform for dirt, having to brush his bottom. Emily was smiling as she rounded the buggy and watched Jack's cleaning action.

She then said, "Don't forget your hat, young man."

ABANDONED

Joseph sighed, then replied, "Yes, ma'am," before plucking the hated head topper from the buggy's seat and putting it on his head.

Jack took Joseph's left hand and Emily took his right as they walked up the steps of the courthouse and entered the building.

Just after they entered, Luke Casey arrived on his horse, dismounted, then tied him off before going to his saddlebags and taking out his satchel. He quickly trotted up the steps having just seen his clients enter the courthouse.

The carriage carrying the six remaining board members of the Brennan Furnace and Coal Company departed the company's yard and rolled quickly up Tenth Street before taking a left on Capitol Street.

Dennis was still sitting morosely at the clerk's desk when he spotted the clerk and another man walking quickly in his direction and noted the chagrined look on both of their faces.

"Mister Ward, I'm terribly sorry," the chief clerk said before they reached the desk.

He then said, "There was an unacceptable error in the transfer of the funds from the First National Bank in Cheyenne. Somehow the account number was changed, probably by a telegrapher, and the deposit was made into a different account."

Dennis may not have been a finance whiz, but asked, "Don't you even check the account holder's name?"

The chief clerk grimaced and replied, "Yes. That should have been caught as well, but the man doing the deposit failed to notice the difference in Mister Tyler's name and the wrong account holder's name, but they were close. Please accept our deepest regrets and apologies for the error. This is the most egregious mistake I can recall."

Dennis Ward suddenly looked at the clock on the wall. It was 1:54, so he said, "Quickly. Give me a new balance sheet and I need it signed. I have to get to the courtroom."

The clerk who had been so quick to judge Jack Tyler's value as a customer, dropped to his seat and began to write, then turned to the chief clerk and said, "I don't have the correct balance."

The chief clerk rolled his eyes, then trotted back to the wall of ledgers behind the cashier's window, snatched one down then scribbled the amount on a scrap of paper and hurried back.

When Dennis Ward took the receipt, it was 1:59 by the bank's clock. He was still blowing on the wet ink as he crossed the lobby and hastily exited the bank. The hearing was three blocks away.

Jack, Emily and Joseph were all at the plaintiff's desk with Luke Casey. The defendant's desk was empty. It was just a routine hearing, after all. Yet the benches in the gallery were surprisingly full as reporters and the general public who had gotten wind of the tale were there to witness its conclusion. Yet even they had no idea of the sudden twists that it would soon take.

They all rose as Judge Lawrence D. Carstairs entered his courtroom and took his seat at the elevated bench before the flags of the United States of America and the State of Nebraska. Everyone sat as the judge picked up some papers from his desk.

"I have before me the petition requesting the appointment of Mrs. Emily Ann Doyle as guardian of minor child, Joseph Charles Brennan the third. I have read the documents and have no objections to its legality nor its purpose in providing for the welfare of the boy. So…"

And that was as far as he got as the doors flew open and the members of the board of directors of the Brennan Furnace and Coal Company shot through the open doors.

ABANDONED

"Your honor," said James Burke loudly as the group approached the bench, "the board of directors of the company withdraw our support for Mrs. Doyle's appointment."

Everyone had already turned at the disturbance and the four faces at the plaintiff's table were all stunned by Mister Burke's declaration.

Judge Carstairs was already slamming his gavel loudly and calling for order before the hubbub could get out of control.

"What is the meaning of your intrusion, sir?" he asked, even though he knew James Burke quite well.

"Your honor, we agreed to Mister Tyler's request because he'd offered to provide financial assistance to the firm after we suffered a significant loss. We were just informed that Mister Tyler had neither the intention nor the ability to provide that support but was hoping that it wouldn't be discovered until after he had been able to have Mrs. Doyle installed as the boy's guardian."

Judge Carstairs thundered, "Is this so, Mister Tyler? Did you offer to financially assist the Brennan Furnace and Coal Company in exchange for making Mrs. Doyle guardian of Joseph Charles Brennan?"

Jack was past his shock and confusion for what Burke had just said, stood, looked at the judge and replied, "Yes, Your Honor, I did, but it was far from what Mister Burke claimed. The money is there, I just don't know what happened."

"But you did essentially bribe them to make Mrs. Doyle the guardian."

"No, Sir. It wasn't meant as a bribe. It's still my money. I just let them access it, so the company wouldn't fail. It belongs to Joseph, not them and not me."

The judge looked at Jack and then at James Burke before finally looking at Emily and Joseph. He believed Jack and was about to tell

James Burke that it was too late to withdraw his support when the courtroom was again disturbed as the cloakroom door slammed open and Wilbur Moore made his grand entrance.

He pointed at Emily and shouted, "My name is Wilbur Moore, and I was steward of the Brennan household for nine years. That woman is not fit to be the boy's guardian! When she first applied for the position, she said she'd do anything to get the job and implied that it included joining me in my bed. As you can see, she is quite a comely woman, and, to my shame, I agreed. I put up with her less than satisfactory performance as the boys' nanny because she constantly offered herself to me. I am humiliated to admit to giving into my lust, but her insatiable demands were overwhelming. Now, that whore has undoubtably given herself to Mister Tyler to have him support her in her desire to be the boy's guardian. Do not let this wanton slut of a woman to disgrace the family name!"

The reporters were writing furiously as the crowd of mostly men shifted their eyes to the comely yet shocked Mrs. Doyle.

Jack shook in his boundless fury as he glared at Moore, unable to speak while Emily was horrified to hear the sordid truth of what she had done being manipulated and broadcast into a much tawdrier behavior that would have embarrassed a two-dollar prostitute. But what caused her even more stress than the substance of what he had shouted, it was that he had done so in Joseph's presence.

The judge looked at the stricken Emily and asked loudly, "Mrs. Doyle, is there any truth to what that man has claimed?"

Emily turned to the judge and looked like a fish out of water, her mouth opening and closing without a word slipping out.

The judge took her lack of denial as the truth and Wilbur Moore's accusation, plus the board's removal of its support left him no choice.

He banged his gavel to silence the loudly murmuring crowd and exclaimed, "Petition denied. Case closed."

He rose from his bench to leave as Wilbur Moore cackled, when the volcano named Mount Jack Tyler finally erupted in a deep, rumbling shout.

"You lying bastard!" he screamed as he turned, shoved his way through the crowd without any difficulty as they all scrambled to avoid the danger in his fiery eyes.

Wilbur Moore turned to run, but his way was blocked as Jack's immensely strong hands grabbed him by his shoulders, yanked him back and despite their almost equal heights, slammed him against the back wall near the cloakroom and with his right hand lifted him four inches from the floor as he stared in terror at the blue eyes that told him he was about to die.

Everyone else, including the judge stood frozen in place as Jack ripped his big knife from his sheath, then snapped it before Wilbur's eyes.

"You, pathetic lying bastard! Mrs. Doyle told me what you did to her and the other women in the household. Do you want me to bring Mrs. Thornton and Miss Flaherty here, so they can tell the judge?"

"No," he choked out in a croak.

"I have half a mind to take this knife and take that tiny little man you have between your legs and make him a little girl, but I want you to apologize loudly for what you forced the women in that house to do just to keep their jobs. Tell them!"

Wilbur Moore's eyes were fixed on the hideously sharp point of the monstrous blade inches from his eyes as he said as loudly as he could muster, "I lied. I made the women do things they didn't want to do. I told them they'd be fired if they didn't come to my bed."

Jack snarled, "You forgot to apologize to Mrs. Doyle."

His eyes were still on the knife as he said, "I'm sorry, Mrs. Doyle. I really am."

Jack then growled, "I don't believe you, Moore. Now, it's time for me to deliver justice for what you did to the ladies. Say goodbye to that poor excuse for your manhood."

The crowd gasped as Jack suddenly turned the knife downward, sliced through Mister Moore's belt and as his britches fell to the floor at his feet, his eyes rolled back, and his bladder released.

Jack just let him go, kept his knife in his hand and walked back to the front of the courthouse using the same path he'd used to reach Wilbur Moore which had grown even wider.

Emily had no idea what would happen after what he'd done, and she just didn't care any longer. She just watched her man in admiration.

His next target was James Burke and the board of directors who now grew pie-eyed as they watched him stalk in their direction. They backed away slightly, not wanting to suffer the same humiliation that Wilbur Moore had just undergone.

Judge Carstairs was so mesmerized by what had just happened that he just stood with his gavel in his hand and completely forgot he was still in his own courtroom. This was theater.

Jack didn't brandish his knife at the board but used it almost as a pointer.

"Now, you gentlemen seem to believe that I'm some sort of fraud, and that I have a secret plan to take over your company. Well, gentlemen, it's not your company. It's Joseph's company. That was why I let you use the money. It was so Joseph's inheritance would still be waiting for him on December 26th, 1889 when he turns eighteen. I expect you to run his company as well as his grandfather did when he created it and gave you all a livelihood. That's all I expected from my money. Why it didn't show up in the account I have no idea, because it was in my account in Cheyenne before we arrived here."

ABANDONED

But you showed your true colors when you marched in here and tried to take Joseph away from Mrs. Doyle. Not one of you understood the reason it was so important to me for her to be named as Joseph's guardian. Emily Ann Doyle loves Joseph with every fiber of her being. He loves her as much as any child could love his mother. Yet, that wasn't important to anyone. Not to any of you. Not to Mister Casey, and not even to you, Judge Carstairs. Every day, children are abandoned by their so-called parents and left at the doors of orphanages or churches and men like you don't care. Others are left without parents and men like you don't give them a second glance because they are just children and not heirs. You all saw Joseph as an heir, a fortune-in-waiting, or a future company owner. Only Emily Doyle saw him as a young boy that needed love and guidance, and only she provided that for him. What that bastard lying in his own urine said was proof of just how much she loved him."

He paused and looked at the beatific face of Emily Ann Doyle, smiled and said, "Look at Mrs. Doyle. I doubt if any one of you men has seen a finer example of womanhood, yet she rejected countless offers of marriage that would take her away from Joseph. She endured unwanted sexual advances by the man who ran the household rather than to lose Joseph's love. She and Joseph had been abandoned to die because a greedy man had the same view of Joseph that you all share."

Just a few days ago, there was an attack by a pack of hungry, snarling gray wolves that had descended on Mrs. Doyle and Joseph. Mrs. Doyle pushed Joseph behind her to protect him as a wolf prepared to spring at them. How many of you love your own children that much?"

His eyes scanned the executives, the crowd and then the judge before he continued with his accusations.

"Just three days earlier, when I first came upon Joseph and Mrs. Doyle, I found Joseph leading a grizzly away from where his injured nanny lay unable to move. He loved her so much that he was willing to sacrifice his life for the mother he believed her to be. An eight-year-old boy! And now, Judge, you are willing to deny her the ability to stay with him to satisfy some insipid moral code or some worthless clause in a piece of paper."

Jack glared at each of them in turn before his eyes reached a smiling Emily and an awe-struck Joseph.

"Joseph, could you step over here please?"

Joseph walked to Jack, his uniform hat's tassel dragging on the floor.

When he was close, Jack held out his hand and said, "May I have your hat, Joseph?"

A smile began to blossom on Joseph's face as his arm swung up and the hated hat with it.

Jack took the blue flat headwear, then tossed it into the air just two feet above his head and as it was briefly suspended motionless in the air, his right hand flashed past, the steel blade a blur as the razor-sharp blade slashed through the felt and ribbon and the two halves dropped to the floor.

Jack sheathed his knife, held Joseph's hand then held his other hand out to Emily.

Emily, before she moved, suddenly began yanking out her hairpins, tossing them onto the plaintiff's desk, and when the last one was removed, shook her hair and walked quickly to Jack.

She took his hand and Jack said loudly, "Let's go home, Mrs. Tyler, and take our son with us where what matters is right and wrong, not what is written by governments or churches."

Emily and Joseph were both ecstatic as Jack turned to the judge and said, "Judge, you can have the sheriff try and extradite me from Laramie or send the U.S. Marshals after me. It doesn't matter. We're going home."

With that pronouncement, Jack, Emily and Joseph walked down the aisle, just as they had expected to do in a church yesterday. The crowd quickly parted as they left the courtroom in stunned silence.

As they exited, Dennis Ward came huffing into the building, saw them and asked, "Is it over?"

"Yes," Jack said, "It's over."

Dennis watched them leave, then turned to go into the courtroom to tell the executives about the discovered money. When he passed through the doorway, he thought he was entering a roomful of mannequins.

He walked up to James Burke, who looked at him and said quietly, "Your daughter is a lucky woman."

"I think so, Mister Burke," he replied, then said, "The bank made a mistake. They put the deposit into the wrong account."

That woke up the rest of the board who realized that the company was in good shape again.

It was then that the murmuring started, and Judge Carstairs suddenly gaveled the room to order again and called over Mister Burke and Luke Casey.

When they were close, he said, "I'm reversing my previous decision. Mrs. Doyle is appointed the guardian of Joseph Charles Brennan the third."

They both agreed and then the judge turned to the armed bailiff and said, "Get that stinking excuse for a man out of my courtroom and have housecleaning in here as quickly as you can."

He then cracked his gavel, shouted, "Court adjourned," and walked quickly from the bench, waving Luke Casey into his chambers to complete the always necessary paperwork.

―――――

The buggy pulled away from the courthouse and Emily was almost cutting off the circulation in Jack's right arm as she vacillated between wanting to cry or laugh. She'd been so horrified by Wilbur Moore's accusations before so many people despite its obvious falsity. She simply couldn't imagine how her reputation could survive such a verbal onslaught. Then, she'd been crushed when the judge had denied her the guardianship knowing she'd lost Joseph.

Then, Jack happened. Her Jack, with his blunt, ferocious attack on Wilbur Moore that showed him to be the cowardly manipulator of women that he was, had tempered the validity of his words, but Emily understood by submitting to Moore at all still carried weight with Judge Carstairs. Jack couldn't change that, or so she believed.

Then, he'd delivered that magnificent, thrilling speech that called them all out as heartless, self-serving men who failed to understand Joseph was just a boy. She could see it in their eyes when they realized the truth of the indictment.

But it was when they were preparing to leave that she received the greatest thrill when Jack had told them essentially to go to hell and that he had already married her, and they'd adopted Joseph. Now, they were going home, and she knew without a doubt that no one would pursue them. Not with her man by her side. The only man who loved Joseph as a boy.

Her euphoria crashed when Joseph looked at her and asked, "Mrs. Doyle, those things that Mister Moore said before Mister Tyler scared him…"

Before he finished, Emily quickly began to reply, "Joseph, what he said…"

Then she was cut off when Jack interrupted saying, "Joseph, I'll explain it all to you later, man-to-man. Okay?"

"Yes, sir," Joseph replied.

Emily looked quickly at Jack and felt relieved she hadn't had to answer the question that Joseph was about to ask. She had been ashamed enough about what she had done, but at least Joseph hadn't known, but now, the whole city would know once those reporters wrote their stories. She didn't care about what the city thought of her, but she was horrified about what Joseph may think of her when he understands what those words meant. She hoped that Jack could make him understand what had happened and why.

She had to put that behind her for now and asked, "Where are we going, Jack?"

"To the big house. I'll drop you and Joseph off there, then I'll take the buggy back to your father's house and return riding the sheriff's horse."

"No, I meant when are we leaving for Laramie?"

"Is tomorrow too soon?" he asked as he smiled at her.

"I was thinking tonight might be better."

"I don't have to go back to that school?" asked Joseph suddenly.

Jack replied, "You can't, sir. You don't have a proper uniform anymore."

Joseph laughed and almost reminded Mister Tyler about the two other hats in his room but figured that he probably knew anyway.

"Jack, are we going to get married before we leave?"

"No, ma'am. We'll get married in Laramie by Father Schneider at St. Mary's. He won't bat an eyelash about such things as dispensations. He'll just be tickled pink that I found a Catholic girl to marry and will start going to church again."

"How do you know him if you don't go to church?" she asked.

"We play poker at his rectory with Sheriff Higginbotham, the butcher, Paul Kane, and the custodian, Jim Richards, once a month when I go into town for supplies."

"You're kidding!" she exclaimed, finally releasing his arm.

"No, ma'am. He's one heck of a player, too. He rarely bluffs, but when he does, he'll maul the three of us. He doesn't talk religion at the poker table, at least not directly. He drop hints every now and then, though."

"What is going to happen to me?" asked Joseph.

"Well, sir, now that depends. Once Mrs. Doyle and I are married, I suppose we could try and adopt you, but you wouldn't want an ornery old prospector like me for your father, would you?"

Joseph stood in the buggy and turned to Jack shouting, "You can be my father?"

"Sit down, young man!" Jack ordered, then added, "See? You've got me behaving like your father already."

Joseph was giggling as he plopped back into the leather seat while Emily smiled at her men, hoping that Jack could work his magic with Joseph later when he tried to explain what Wilbur Moore had said.

———

After he'd dropped them off at the big house, Emily began tidying up and started a fire in the cook stove for dinner while Jack drove the buggy back to the Ward house.

He had no sooner pulled it to a stop when the back door opened, and Molly, her intended Andrew, Mary, John and Dennis all poured out onto the porch and quickly made their way to the buggy.

"Jack!" said Dennis loudly, "Where are Emily and Joseph?"

"I left them at the big house and I'm going to go back there with the sheriff's gelding as soon as I get him saddled."

"You can come back here now, Jack. The judge made Emily his guardian. Mister Casey has the papers and said to come by tomorrow morning with Emily, so he could tell you what she had to do."

Jack wasn't surprised by the news which made no change in their plans as he walked over to the gelding, trailing the family and began tossed the saddle blanket across his back.

"We'll go see him, Mister Ward, but it really doesn't matter. We'll be leaving for Laramie as soon as we can. We'll be married in St. Mary's in Laramie after we get there, and we'll adopt Joseph. I've had it with all of the mazes and hoops that civilized society has created to keep us from just being happy. It's no reflection on you or your family, Mister Ward, and you are all welcome to come and visit whenever you can. I'll even pay for the tickets. Just use the money in the bank here."

"About that, what do you want me to do with it?"

"Keep the company afloat until it's making money again. When you feel it's safe, let me know and I'll wire you the account number in Cheyenne, so you can send it back. I don't need it. Like I told them in the courtroom, it's just to make sure that in nine years and two-and-a-half months, Joseph will have his grandfather's legacy."

Mary asked, "Father said that the executives told him how you made them all ashamed of themselves. What did you tell them?"

He tossed the saddle over the geldings back and began to tighten the cinches as he replied, "Not much, ma'am. Just that they should have seen Joseph as a boy and not a dollar bill."

"Are you coming back tomorrow?" asked Dennis.

"Yes, sir. I'm sure Emily will want to see everyone before we go."

"Won't you stay for our wedding on Saturday, Mister Tyler?" asked Molly.

Jack looked at a smaller and younger version of Emily, smiled, then nodded and said, "Yes, ma'am, I believe we can do that. I'm sure Emily would like to be there."

Jack finished saddling the gelding then swung into the saddle, then walked the horse out of the barn.

"We'll see you tomorrow," Jack said loudly as he waved to the family.

He headed out onto the street and turned right then made the left onto Chicago Street. He didn't have a concern in the world, but he should have.

After he'd been dumped unceremoniously behind the courthouse, a humiliated and furious Wilbur Moore walked down the back alley and walked quickly to his apartment that he recently rented after being terminated by Noah Gallagher. He quickly removed his dry, but still smelly trousers, tossed them into the sink and quickly washed his lower half with a wet towel before pulling on a fresh pair of pants.

He didn't have a pistol, but he knew where there was one available, so he left his apartment, trotted down the stairs and crossed Cass Street then turned right on Chicago Street. He knew that the big house was empty because he'd been inside it twice, hoping to find Mary Flaherty or even Anna Thompson, but the house had been empty. He'd found blood on his second visit and wondered which of it belonged to Noah Gallagher.

He used the back alley to approach the house, and passed the small barn, then hopped onto the back porch and used his house key to unlock the back door.

After Jack had gone, Emily wanted to take advantage of the big house and was in the bathroom on the first floor soaking in the tub. It was the same bathroom that the hired help used when she was hired help. She didn't know that the house was now her responsibility, not that it would have made any difference.

ABANDONED

Joseph was on the second floor, going through his toys that he now looked at with the eyes of a much older young man and was separating them into those he'd take with him to Laramie and those he'd leave here for donations to younger children.

Emily was singing one of her Irish Gaelic ballads softly as she gently washed her skin with her lavender soap and didn't hear the back door open.

Wilbur heard her singing before he opened it and stopped. *What if that bastard was here with his knife?* Jack was the one he wanted to shoot, but he expected to find him at the Ward house, not here. He almost turned to leave but decided that Jack Tyler must not know he was there because he didn't hear him moving, so Wilbur thought he had the advantage. Besides, he knew the house better than anyone.

He left the door open and began to walk through the kitchen quietly. He needed to make it to the office to find the gun, but decided that until he got there, he'd be safer if he had a weapon, so he slid a twelve-inch butcher's knife from the knife drawer and the sight of the big blade reminded him of Tyler's use of his blade to humiliate him. He'd use the pistol to keep Tyler still then, cut him where he'd hurt the most. The same spot that Tyler had threatened to cut on him.

Emily was still singing as she began to shampoo her hair, then stopped to laugh lightly when she remembered pulling those hairpins out in the courtroom. She finished working the lather as her laughter ended, rinsed her hair twice quickly and slipped deeper into the warm water and enjoyed the flowery scent of the soap and shampoo.

Then, she heard a creak in the hallway and suspected that Jack might be back and was going to try to surprise her by swinging the door wide and catching her in her naked glory. She smiled and looked at the locked door and waited to see if the knob turned. But instead of a turning knob, she heard a second creak further down the hallway, and then a third. Someone was trying to be stealthy in the house and it wasn't Joseph because he was too small. It was a man and she didn't believe it was Jack.

She began singing softly again to mask her movements as she slowly stepped out of the tub and kept watching the doorknob as she hurriedly pulled on her camisole, slipped on the new robe she'd bought in preparation for their wedding night, and began to look around the room for anything she could use as a weapon but found nothing except a hand mirror. It wasn't much but it would have to do. She tied the cloth belt around her waist and approached the locked door.

Joseph had finished with his sorting, popped to his feet and, because he was eight years old, ran out of his room and when he reached the staircase, knowing that Mrs. Doyle was in the bath, hopped onto the railing stomach down and slid down the curving rail.

Wilbur had heard the footsteps before he reached the office and knew it was the kid. He forgot about the pistol, glanced at the closed door of the bathroom, then walked quickly down the rest of the hallway and just as Joseph dropped off the bottom of the bannister, rushed into the parlor.

Joseph saw the movement, thought he'd been caught by Mrs. Doyle, then began to apologize as he turned, and froze. It was Mister Moore and he had a big knife!

Joseph shouted, "You can't be here! Mister Tyler will come here and kill you just like he killed Mister Gallagher, so you'd better leave right now!"

Emily heard Joseph's warning, and quickly unlocked the door and rushed into the hallway with the mirror in her right hand and her long dark red hair dripping onto the polished floor.

"You!" she shouted as she raised the mirror above her head.

Wilbur didn't hesitate, but pointed the butcher's knife at Joseph and snarled, "Get over here, boy!"

ABANDONED

As soon as he turned his head to threaten Joseph, Emily hurled the mirror at Moore, but the only part that hit the former steward was the handle and it glanced harmlessly off his left shoulder.

By then, he'd grabbed Joseph by the arm and placed the point of the knife on the boy's back.

"I'm not going to waste any time, Mrs. Doyle. I'm going to kill this brat and then, I'm going to wait for that bastard who threatened me in the courtroom. But I want you to watch him die, Emily."

Emily was desperate and knew that if she rushed Moore, he'd just shove that knife right through Joseph. She seemingly had no options and looked at Joseph, knowing how terrified he must be. But when she looked into his eyes, she saw something she didn't expect. She saw Jack's calm strength.

Joseph felt the knife's point against his spine and knew he didn't have long, but he had to stop Mister Moore because he said he was going to kill Mister Tyler, and then he'd probably hurt Mrs. Doyle.

He looked at his beloved nanny and slipped his hand into his right pocket and slowly pulled out his pocket knife. He'd tried opening it before with one hand and hadn't quite been able to master it, but now, he had to get it done. But even then, there wasn't enough time.

Emily looked up at Wilbur Moore knowing she needed just a few seconds of distraction for Joseph, so she said quickly, "Wait!", then slowly began to untie her robe's belt.

Moore may have set his heart on killing the boy, but there was enough animal lust demanding that he see what she was going to show him. He let the boy's arm go as his eyes were transfixed on the upcoming show, expecting her to be naked under the robe.

Emily knew he was paying attention as she opened the robe, revealing her camisole-cloaked self, but even that, because of the wet skin underneath, provided a captivating, and critically distracting sight to Wilbur Moore.

Joseph felt the sharp point move away from his back. It wasn't much, but he now had his left arm free, so he could use both hands to pull the blade free from the ivory handle. But first, he needed another distraction.

Joseph suddenly slammed the heel of his left shoe onto Wilbur Moore's right small toe. Wilbur shrieked, dropped the knife and automatically jerked his right foot back from the pain.

Joseph then yanked the five-inch steel blade free, whirled and slammed it home into Wilbur Moore's right buttock. The ex-steward screeched in pain as he grabbed for the knife still sticking out of his backside. Joseph didn't take time to pull the knife free but sprinted across the parlor to Emily, who grabbed his hand and raced for the bathroom because it was the closest and had a heavy lock.

Wilbur Moore screamed, then yanked the knife free and threw it to the floor. His rage was spectacular and all he wanted now was to kill them both.

Emily and Joseph flew through the open bathroom door as Wilbur Moore took a moment to check his wound and Emily slammed it closed and quickly threw the heavy lock.

Satisfied he wasn't going to die, Wilbur Moore picked up the butcher knife, ran to the bathroom door and tried to push it open, but once he found it locked, he knew that it was too heavy to breach easily and needed another method to break into the bathroom. He then turned and raced for the office for the pistol. He'd shoot the lock to pieces, shoot that little bastard first, then that damned redheaded bitch.

Emily expected him to try and get into the bathroom, but all she could do was to pull Joseph close to her as they lay on the floor, hidden by the heavy cast iron bathtub.

———

Jack was just a hundred yards away with the gelding at a walk when he heard a scream coming from the big house through the broken glass in the parlor and set the horse to a fast trot to cover the distance. He knew that Emily and Joseph were inside, but that wasn't a woman or a boy's scream.

He spotted four passersby that were stopped before the house, and when he pulled up to a rapid halt, he dropped down from the saddle, held out the reins to one of the men and shouted, "Go and get the sheriff!"

It only took seconds before Wilbur found the Colt in the desk drawer, quickly checked it for ammunition, and found it loaded. He then limped out of the office, his pants now soaked in his blood, cocked the hammer and approached the locked bathroom door.

Jack ran down the seventy-yard walkway and had just reached the porch steps when Wilbur fired.

Emily and Joseph cringed together as the bullet smashed through the bathroom door near the doorknob and lock, then ricocheted off the far end of the bathtub, making a loud, deep clang before it slammed into the far wall.

Jack leapt onto the porch, pulled his Remington, and instead of trying to test the door, which was probably locked, he turned to his right and walked quickly to the still broken window.

Jack had just reached the window when the first report of the Colt exploded through the house followed by the ringing sound of the echo of the bullet bouncing off iron or steel. He knew he had to let his mind stay in control and not let his heart take charge if he wanted to save Emily and Joseph. That shot hadn't hit either of them because there wasn't any scream or shout. It had hit something heavy.

He was looking through the broken glass and noted the gunsmoke was in the hallway close to the parlor, so the shot had to be fired in the hall. Even though it was highly unlikely, he couldn't be sure that the shot hadn't been fired by Emily, so he couldn't shoot blindly down the hallway. She and Joseph might be standing there having just shot the intruder. He also made a quick guess that the most likely culprit was that skinny bastard in the courtroom.

Wilbur then lowered the smoking revolver and slammed his shoulder into the bathroom door, expecting it to give way easily, but it he bounced painfully off the oak door and cursed as he looked at the large hole just below the doorknob. He'd missed the crucial mechanics of the latch and lock altogether.

He stepped back to aim at the door jamb near the doorknob knowing he couldn't miss and cocked the hammer.

Jack cocked his Remington's hammer and shouted through the broken glass just as Wilbur was preparing to fire his second shot, "Moore, I'm going to come in there and make you a eunuch!"

Wilbur Moore almost jerked the trigger on his cocked Colt when he was startled by Jack's shouted threat. Instead, he whipped the pistol in the direction of the parlor, unsure of Jack's whereabouts.

In the bathroom, Emily hugged Joseph and whispered, "We're safe now, Joseph. Jack is here."

She felt Joseph nod, then closed her eyes but still worried because as much as she loathed Wilbur Moore, he still had a pistol and Jack was in real danger.

Jack knew his shout alerted Moore, or whoever was in the house, but he had to draw the man's attention away from Emily and Joseph. He'd been hoping the intruder would enter the parlor to look for him, but he hadn't been that lucky. The shooter was still in the hallway and had a clear view of the front door and the parlor.

He then stood straight, turned and walking on his tiptoes, stepped as quickly as he could along the side of the house on the porch heading for the back door. He knew that the kitchen door was off to the side and anyone in the hallway couldn't see it. The question was whether or not it was locked. He assumed that if

Moore had gotten into the house, it was still unlocked, but all he could do was hope.

Jack reached the back of the house as Wilbur still stared into the parlor, waiting for another shout at least. Jack was relieved to find the back door not only unlocked but left wide open. He wasn't going to shout a warning this time as he silently stepped through the door with his cocked pistol level.

It had only been a minute since Jack's shouted threat and Wilbur was getting nervous. *Where was that bastard?* He finally decided that maybe he had somehow gotten into the house. He didn't know about the broken window but thought that maybe Tyler had slid one open. He glanced quickly toward the kitchen, spotted no one, then turned back to the parlor where he expected Jack to be trying to open a window.

So, just as Jack was entering the back door, Wilbur had his cocked Colt ready as he slowly stepped toward the parlor, his eyes shifting from side-to-side, looking for that knife-wielding Neanderthal.

The gun-wielding Neanderthal was approaching the hallway and was certain that he'd find the shooter standing about thirty feet down the long corridor and wasn't disappointed when his eyes found Wilbur Moore's silhouette in the gunsmoke haze.

Jack growled, "I warned you, Moore."

Wilbur was stunned to hear the voice from behind, but whirled to fire, still expecting Jack to be standing there with that giant blade of his, preparing to geld him. He received his second shock of the past few seconds when he saw him standing with a cocked pistol.

Wilbur didn't have a chance to aim but jerked his trigger finger back when he spotted the threat even as he watched Jack's Remington's muzzle light up and felt the .44 slam into his chest, on the right of his sternum. He fell back, stumbling into the parlor, as the bullet passed out of his back and slammed into the heavy maple sideboard on the far wall.

After falling onto the polished hardwood, Wilbur lay gasping, writhing in pain as blood flowed from his chest and air rushed directly in and out of his right lung, bubbling as it mixed with the blood, rendering the lung unusable. Just like Noah Gallagher, Wilbur's wounds weren't fatal if they were treated quickly. He needed to have the holes in his chest blocked before doctors could sew them closed. He needed emergency first aid from the man who had put the bullet through his chest.

Jack walked quickly down the hallway, spotted the hole in the locked bathroom door, assumed that Emily and Joseph were hiding inside and shouted, "Are you all right, Emily?", without stopping.

"Yes, Jack!" she shouted back in relief when she heard his voice.

As she and Joseph began to stand, Jack continued to where Wilbur Moore lay gasping for air as blood continued to pool around him.

Jack holstered his pistol, flipped his hammer loop in place and took a knee next to the thin, hateful man.

"If you were a wounded critter out where I live, I'd put you out of your misery, but I don't have any excuses this time, I suppose," he said before he stood and pulled a leather-bound book from the nearby parlor table.

He hated to do it for someone as worthless as Moore, but he pulled his big knife and sliced off the front and back covers and then returned to Moore, dropped the two flat pieces of leather on the floor, pulled Moore's belt from his pants, then sat him up.

Emily and Joseph exited the bathroom and entered the parlor expecting to find Jack standing over a dead Wilbur Moore but found him assisting the former steward.

Jack slapped one of the leather book covers over the wound, then saw Emily and asked, "Emily, could you help me, please?"

Emily didn't reply but scurried to his side and took a knee.

ABANDONED

"I need you to loop the belt around the book cover before I lay him back down."

"Okay," she said before she picked up the belt and moved around behind Moore and pressed the belt against the book cover.

Jack lowered Moore atop the book cover and belt then placed the second book cover on the front of the wound and took the ends of the belt from Emily and tightened it against his chest before slipping the tang into the notch. It wasn't great, but Moore was already beginning to breathe better.

"Joseph, toss me a cushion from that chair," Jack ordered as he pointed.

Joseph hurried to the chair, pulled the seat cushion and brought it to Jack, who slid it under Moore's head before standing.

"That's all we can do for him. I need to get him to the hospital right away."

He looked at Emily still in her robe, then was about to leave himself when he heard a voice from outside shout, "This is Deputy Sheriff John Applewhite! Open the door!"

Jack turned and walked quickly toward the door and shouted back, "Deputy, this is Jack Tyler. I have a man with a gunshot wound that needs medical help."

Before the deputy could respond, Jack unlocked the door and swung it wide to admit the deputy.

Wilbur Moore turned his head toward the approaching two men and felt as if he was in a dream. He then closed his eyes to see what the rest of the dream was like.

Deputy Applewhite looked at Moore and said, "I've already sent someone for a doctor after they reported gunshots. What happened?"

Jack turned to Emily, who said, "He came into the house while I was in the bath and pulled a knife on Joseph and was going to kill him when Joseph stomped on his foot and then stabbed him with his pocket knife. We hid in the locked bathroom and he had just fired through the door to break in when Jack arrived."

Jack took over the narrative from where Emily had ended and before he finished, an ambulance arrived from St. Joseph's Hospital and a doctor and two corpsmen with a stretcher ran onto the porch and entered the front door.

Everyone stepped aside as the doctor took charge and after a quick examination, had the two corpsmen roll him onto the stretcher and take him out of the house.

He turned to Deputy Applewhite and said, "You did a good job on that emergency repair, Deputy," then hastily followed the stretcher bearers out of the house.

Once they were gone, Deputy Applewhite turned to Jack and said, "Why did you save this one? I read your report and you didn't do anything for Gallagher."

"I had an excuse for myself with Gallagher, Deputy. I had to take care of Deputy Pleasant. I couldn't let Moore die, even though I hated the man for what he had done to Emily and what he was trying to do to Joseph."

"I'm going to head back and tell my boss what happened. When can you stop by and make a statement?"

"In a little while."

"Okay. I'll let the sheriff know," he said before nodding to Emily, turning and heading out the door.

Jack followed him, closed the door, then on his way back to Emily and Joseph, bent over and picked up Joseph's knife.

ABANDONED

He handed it to Joseph and said, "You'll need to clean the blade before you close it again, Joseph."

The boy accepted his knife, nodded and said, "Yes, sir."

Jack then smiled at him and said, "I'm really proud of you, son."

Joseph looked up at Jack, smiled and then turned his eyes to Emily, but didn't say a word before he turned to go to the kitchen and clean his blade as his father had told him to do.

Emily glanced down at the blood scattered all over the floor and said, "I'll clean the floor."

Jack approached Emily, put his arms around her and pulled her close, her hair wetting the backs of his hands.

"After I return from the sheriff's office, we need to talk, Emily," he said as he looked into her blue eyes.

"Yes," she agreed quietly.

"Do you mind staying in this house tonight?" he asked.

"Only if you stay with us."

"I had no intention of leaving you alone, Mrs. Tyler. As far as I'm concerned, they can gossip and finger wag all they want. Oh, by the way, the judge made you Joseph's guardian after all and we have to stay here until after your sister's wedding on Saturday."

Emily smiled, then said, "You sure know how to make a girl happy, Mister Tyler."

"I've got to go and make that report, Emily. I'll be back in an hour or so."

"We'll be waiting. Will you have your talk with Joseph when you return?"

"Yes, ma'am."

Jack then turned on his heels, trotted away and then left the house. He'd have to walk to the sheriff's office, but it was just as well anyway. He needed to think about what he would tell Joseph when he returned.

Jack didn't walk the entire way to the sheriff's office, but almost halfway there, they stopped at Dempsey's Livery and Carriage Rental and rented a buggy until Sunday. It didn't cost him too much time and he arrived at the sheriff's office ten minutes later. It was better to use a buggy, anyway, as he had learned that in a city like Omaha, a man jogging down the street wearing a gunbelt was bad enough, but with that massive Bowie knife, he presented a disturbing sight. Even in Laramie only half of the residents carried a pistol these days. He guessed once there were more women in town, that percentage would drop even lower.

The statement only took him another twenty minutes as he had to narrate the story to Sheriff Lafferty and the two deputies in between sentences. He also had to spend a few minutes explaining what had happened in the courthouse that was already setting Omaha abuzz.

While he was writing the statement, a message arrived from the hospital that Wilbur Moore had died fifteen minutes after he arrived. It didn't change anything other than now, the report for justifiable homicide had to be approved by the county prosecutor. Emily and Joseph's statements would only be necessary if the prosecutor balked, but Sheriff Lafferty didn't think that was even remotely possible, especially as Jack had tried to save Moore's life after shooting him.

Jack drove back to 1710 Chicago Street as the sun was setting and the gas streetlamps were being lit.

He stepped out of the buggy outside the small barn and spent another few minutes unharnessing the gelding before settling him into a stall with a full feed bin and trough. Jack walked quickly across the back yard, hopped onto the porch, strode to the back door and was surprised to find it locked, but understood why Emily had decided to secure the house, despite the open window.

He knocked on the door, saw Joseph through the window and heard the door's lock click open before the door swung wide.

"Good evening, sir. May I enter?" he asked.

"Yes, sir. You may," Joseph replied with a straight face before walking back into the room.

He entered, closed the door and smelled something delightful cooking on the large stove and spied something even more delightful standing near the large stove.

"That smells good, Emily," he said as he unbuckled his gunbelt and hung it on the brass hook near the door, "How long before it's ready?"

She glanced at Joseph, then back at Jack and replied, "Long enough for you to have your talk with Joseph."

Joseph looked up at him expectantly, hoping Jack would finally clarify the great mystery that everyone seemed to understand but him.

Jack smiled down at him and said, "Let's let Mrs. Doyle cook, sir, but first, I need to pass along the word I received while I was at the sheriff's office. Wilbur Moore died fifteen minutes after he arrived at the hospital."

Emily looked sharply at him and said, "I suppose that will make the newspaper stories even more sensational."

"I suppose so, ma'am. Don't worry about what they write. We'll be leaving soon anyway."

"I won't, but…", she began to say, glanced down at Joseph, then looked back at Jack, hoping Jack understood that her only real concern was about who might read what they would be printing.

Jack nodded in understanding, then turned back to Joseph and said, "Let's go and talk, Joseph."

"Okay," he said as Jack began to leave the kitchen for the hallway, then trotted after him.

Emily watched her men leave, sighed, then returned to dinner preparation.

Jack reached the parlor, glanced at the newest bullet hole in the room in the maple sideboard, then after Joseph reached him, surprised the boy when instead of sitting down, headed for the long, curving stairway to the second floor.

Once they passed the landing with its bullet-damaged railing, Jack turned into the main bedroom with its own bullet holes in the door jamb and in the outside wall under the window and the gouge in the floor.

He sat on the edge of the bed and waited until Joseph hopped onto the bed, then looked at him expectantly.

Jack said, "Joseph, I'm new at this because I've never had a son before, so if you don't understand anything that I tell you, let me know and I'll try to explain it better. Alright?"

"Yes, sir."

Jack inhaled sharply, then asked, "Now, I don't know what you know about this subject yet, so I'll need to ask you if you know how a man becomes a father or a woman becomes a mother."

Joseph looked at him seriously and said, "No one knows, do they? People get married and the lady has a baby. Isn't that right?"

Jack groaned inside. He was going to have to do it all. He had learned the facts of life at the orphanage when he was thirteen, at least that was when he'd been taken aside and had the process explained to him officially. He'd already picked up a lot of information from older boys, and much of it was, to say the least, wildly exaggerated. He needed Joseph to understand it the right way.

"No, Joseph. Getting married is just a ceremony that tells everyone else that a man and a woman are now a husband and wife and that they can be a family under the law. Animals don't get married and they have babies, don't they?"

"Oh…that's right," he said as he nodded slowly.

"Well, you see, when boys start getting older…" he began, as Joseph listened intently.

Jack had explained the physical aspects of coitus after he'd described the changes that Joseph would be undergoing over the next few years as Joseph sat with a queasy look on his face.

As soon as Jack finished with the biological portion, Joseph exclaimed, "That sounds awful!"

Jack had expected his response because of his age, then said, "I know it does, Joseph. But, don't you wonder why people and animals want to do it so much?"

"Because they want to have children?"

"Sometimes. But when you start becoming a man physically, you'll start to really notice girls. By the time you're thirteen, all you'll think about is girls and you'll want to have sex with them."

"*I'll want to do that?*" he asked in disbelief.

"More than you want to shoot a Winchester. It's hard to explain, Joseph, but trust me, the things that are important to you as a young boy will fade in comparison to how important girls and women will become. Sex in itself is very enjoyable for both men and women for a reason, Joseph. In the Bible, God said to Adam and Eve, 'Go forth and multiply', but made it feel good to make them want to have children. If men didn't want to have sex with women and women didn't want them to do it, there wouldn't be any people on the earth and no other living creatures either."

Joseph scrunched up his face and asked, "Then why does everybody act like it's dirty?"

"That, sir, is one of the truly stupid things that mankind has forced upon itself. None of God's other creatures are embarrassed by it, but maybe it had to do with the original sin in the Garden of Eden where once Adam and Eve had been cast out, then first felt shame in being naked and put on clothes. I have no idea, but it has gotten to the point where women dress from their neck to their ankles and no one can even say the word 'sex' in polite society. Now, I'm not saying that we should all run around naked having sex with anyone we see. Besides, I'm glad that most of the men and women out there are clothed because seeing them naked would definitely qualify as disgusting."

Joseph giggled slightly, but then asked, "Does this have something to do with what Mister Moore said?"

"Exactly. It has everything to do with what Mister Moore said, and what I said in the courtroom afterwards. I just told you how men really want to have sex with women, and there are a lot of different terms for that. Most of them aren't said in polite society and I'll tell you about them later. But some of the more acceptable terms are taking a woman to bed and making love. When Mister Moore shouted that Mrs. Doyle had tried to take him to her bed, he was telling everyone that it was Mrs. Doyle who had wanted him to have sex with her, but she didn't. Now, even after I defended her, she knows that everyone will know that she let him do it and she's probably worried that you'll think less of her, despite his lies."

"I know he was lying, Mister Tyler, I just didn't know what it was about."

"Some men, like Mister Moore, don't worry about whether the woman wants him or not, but forces himself on her using threats. He did that to Mrs. Doyle and the cook and maid, too. He did it because he could fire them if they didn't do what he told them to do. If you remember what I told them in the courtroom, the reason Mrs. Doyle let him do it was because she loved you so much, she couldn't bear to be without you. She has sacrificed a lot to stay with you and protect you since becoming your nanny. Remember I told you about Emily Ann Ward, the much different side of Mrs. Doyle?"

"Yes, sir. You said she was very firm and direct."

"That's right. Well, that is the real Mrs. Doyle, but she had to hide it from everyone, especially you. She didn't want to be seen as a troublemaker by the others and was afraid she'd frighten you. So, for six year, she's held Emily Ann Ward, her real self, inside. Emily Ann Ward would never have allowed Mister Moore, or any other man touch her unless she allowed it, but Mrs. Doyle had to it, just for you."

Joseph looked up at him and asked, "Will she let you touch her?"

Jack smiled and said, "Joseph, let me explain the most important thing about sex that I haven't explained yet. Remember I just said that one of the politer terms for having sex was 'making love'?"

"Yes."

"Well, it shouldn't be used that way because having sex isn't always making love. Love is what two people share, just like what you and Mrs. Doyle do. She loves you very much and you love her just as much, don't you?"

"Yes, sir, more than anybody."

"That's real love, Joseph. When she hugs you, doesn't that give you a warm feeling inside?"

Joseph nodded and said, "I like to hug her back, too."

"That's because we want to be close to the people we love. When a man loves a woman and a woman loves that same man, when they kiss and then hug, those desires that God put there in His wisdom, make them want to be even closer. And making love is the combination of the emotional need to be loved combined with the physical need to have sex. It makes for an incredible sense of being together as one."

Joseph thought about it for a few seconds, then said, "I remember that my father would bring home ladies to this room and they'd make noises that would wake me up. Once, I left my bed and walked down the hall and opened the door and saw him and the lady on the bed without any clothes. He yelled at me to go away, so I did. The next morning, I asked him what it was, and he said they were playing a game and I should never come into the room again when he had a lady with him. Was that having sex and not making love?"

"Yes, Joseph. That's exactly what it was."

"Have you made love to a lady?"

"No, Joseph. When I was in the army and working for the railroad, I paid ladies to have sex with them a few times, but it wasn't making love. There are places where ladies accept money to let men have sex with them. The women who work at those places have many names from the acceptable 'prostitute' to the much more common 'whore'. Mister Moore called Mrs. Doyle that name as an insult, but Mrs. Doyle is the least whore-like woman I've ever met. She's an extraordinary lady and you can never let what anyone says about her shake your belief in her."

"Do you want to make love to Mrs. Doyle? I see you kissing her a lot."

"Very much, and she wants me to make love to her, too, but she was afraid that she might lose you if someone else found out about it. Now that we're leaving Omaha, that part doesn't matter, but she's probably still upset you might not be proud of her anymore after what Mister Moore said. She loves me, Joseph, but you are the center of her world. It's very important that you let her know that you will always love and respect her, just as I will."

"You didn't have to tell me to do that, Mister Tyler. Mrs. Doyle is more important to me than that stupid company or all the money that I'm supposed to get."

Jack smiled at the boy and said, "Okay, Joseph. I apologize for even suspecting that you might change your opinion of her. Now, Mister Joseph Charles Brennan the third, how about if we return to the kitchen and I introduce you to Emily Ann Ward?"

Joseph grinned and said, "Okay."

Jack stood and as they began to leave the room he said, "This might be a bit embarrassing to you, Joseph."

"No, it won't," he replied as they turned into the hallway.

Emily heard them coming down the stairs as she was setting the table and wondered what Jack had told Joseph that could explain how she'd offered herself to that skinny bastard and still allow him to think of her as his beloved nanny.

She had just set down the last fork when they entered the kitchen and saw smiles on both of their faces. Emily didn't ask any questions about their talk but would soon get her answer.

Joseph hopped onto his seat at the table while Jack approached Emily and then took her into his arms and said, "Joseph would like to meet Emily Ann Ward. He said that she would be a lot more interesting than the sweet, polite Mrs. Doyle he's known for the past six years."

She had her arms around Jack as she looked past his left shoulder at a grinning Joseph, paused for a few seconds then asked, "Oh? She'd be more interesting than the woman who fed and clothed him without complaint for six long years? The same woman who dressed him in that hideous uniform and told him he looked handsome? That woman?"

Joseph was still grinning as he replied, "Yes, ma'am."

She looked back at Jack and asked, "And how much Emily Ann Ward does young Master Brennan understand, Mister Tyler?"

He kissed her and let his right hand slide to her soft behind and pull her against him while Joseph giggled.

Emily Doyle would have been aghast at Jack's obvious display of carnal lust, but Emily Ann Ward had no such reservations, as she then threw her arms around Jack's neck and kissed him even more passionately as Jack's left hand slid to her other bottom cheek to mash her against him.

She finally ended the kiss and hoarsely whispered, "We need to eat, sir. This can wait."

Jack stepped back, smiled and said, "Yes, ma'am. I just wanted our son to see his mother while he had a chance to get out of the arrangement."

Emily turned to the now-snickering Joseph, wagged her finger at him and said, "You are not getting out of this arrangement, Joseph. You are stuck with us whether you like it or not!"

Joseph nodded and replied, "I like it."

Emily turned to start serving dinner but said to Jack as she did, "I have no idea what you told him, but I'm happy that you did."

"I'll tell you later tonight, ma'am," he replied as he took a seat across from Joseph.

Once he took his chair, he looked at Joseph and wiggled his eyebrows, making him giggle again.

As they ate dinner, Jack told them about the rented buggy and the visit they'd have to make to Luke Casey's office in the morning, so Emily could be told what her responsibilities would be as guardian.

ABANDONED

Emily asked, "Does it matter, Jack?"

"I have no idea. I don't even know what the guardian is supposed to do in the first place other than act on Joseph's behalf. You probably know a lot more than I do."

She nodded as she swallowed a bit of potatoes with gravy and then said, "He was supposed to be a mentor and guide for Joseph, but he wasn't. He spent as much of the family account as he could get away with on himself."

"How much is in the family account and why did the company panic when they lost most of the company's account?"

"I have no idea about that balance. I do know that Noah Gallagher was given a hundred dollars a month as a stipend to be the guardian and if he needed to spend more, he'd have to get the approval of Luke Casey, the executor. That's probably why the company was so afraid because they couldn't touch the family account, either."

Jack took a bite of roast beef, then after he hastily chewed and swallowed, asked, "I guess we'll find out more tomorrow. After dinner, I need to clean my pistol."

"Can I watch?" asked Joseph, suddenly interested in the conversation.

"Yes, sir. You need to understand how to care for your weapons as well as use them."

Joseph nodded, then pulled out his cleaned pocket knife and looked closely at the wolf's head carved into the ivory, then strangely, thought about Loopy, wondering what the wolf was doing outside the empty cabin.

―――

Hundreds of miles away in the wilderness, the she-wolf that had been left on her own after the pack's attack on Billy, was winding her way eastward. She'd tried to join four other wolf packs and had been rejected by each one, having to leave its territory. She was hungry, having to subsist on small rodents and insects, but continued to move, searching for acceptance.

She knew she was approaching human territory as she crossed some wagon tracks then after another few yards stopped and began to snoot at the ground. She was entering another pack's domain. But as the continued to sniff, she realized that it wasn't a pack, but a single wolf. He was alone, and he was young, so the she-wolf continued onto the male's domain. Maybe he needed a mate, and if he accepted her, they could start their own pack.

———

After dinner, Jack had shown Joseph how to clean a pistol, then they spent some time fixing what they could in the house to make it more livable until they left. Tomorrow, after the visit with the family lawyer, he'd hire a repairman to fix the damage. Luckily, it was still late summer, and the weather wasn't cold enough to cause a real problem tonight.

But Jack still built a good fire going in the fancy fireplace before they settled into the parlor to talk about what they would need to do before they left. Jack had Emily close to him on the couch while Joseph sat on the carpet which had remained remarkably free of blood stains somehow.

Emily said, "Jack, remember I told Anna Thornton and Mary Flaherty they could return to the house to work when I thought I'd be living here as Joseph's guardian? She's going to be here on Saturday. What do we do about that?"

Jack replied, "It's a perfect solution to what we'd do with the house while we're gone, Emily. If Mrs. Thornton and Miss Flaherty wish to stay here, they can be caretakers for the house until Joseph is old enough to be able to dispose of it or live here. She and Miss Flaherty will still be paid and if either of them or both of them, for that matter, wish to marry and stay here, they can."

ABANDONED

Emily smiled and said, "That's a wonderful idea, Jack. Their pay was taken out of the family account anyway, and they won't have to pay Mister Moore any longer."

"I wonder who had to pay to bury him?" Jack asked rhetorically.

After the fire had begun to die down, Jack excused himself to take a bath leaving Joseph and Emily a chance to talk alone for the first time in their new relationship.

As it turned out, there wasn't much of a change as Joseph discovered that Emily Ann Ward really wasn't that much different than Mrs. Doyle, except she seemed more comfortable and answered his questions more quickly.

One of his questions that she didn't answer quickly was when he startled her by asking, "Are you and Mister Tyler going to make love tonight?"

Even Emily Ann Ward was flustered by the query for a few seconds before she replied with her own question, asking, "What did he tell you in that talk, Mister Brennan?"

"He said a lot of things that I still don't understand, but he said that he wanted to make love to you and you wanted it, too."

"And what do you think about that?"

"I think you should. Mister Tyler is going to be my father and I want you both to be happy."

She smiled at her ward and said, "You are an amazing young man, Joseph."

Joseph just smiled at Emily, knowing he'd made her happy. Trying to save her from a grizzly bear was important but making her happy was much better.

When Jack emerged from the bathroom, taking a little extra time to examine the flight path of the bullet that Wilbur Moore's shot had taken through the door and off the tub into the wall, he was surprised to find Emily alone in the parlor.

"Where's Joseph?" he asked.

"He's in his room. Do you know what he asked me after you were in the bath?"

"I'm afraid to ask after our long talk."

"That must have inspired him because he asked me if you were going to make love to me tonight."

Jack laughed lightly and asked, "What did you tell him?"

"I asked him what he thought, and he said that we should."

He then looked at Emily and asked, "What do you think, Emily Ann Ward?"

She sighed before answering, "Would you understand if I would want to wait? I mean, after all this talk and teenaged kissing and groping that we've been doing, it sounds as if I've lost my mind, doesn't it?"

Jack walked to the couch, sat beside her, smiled and said, "No, it doesn't sound as if you lost your mind, Emily. It sounds like that Irish Catholic upbringing and your recent return to the good graces of Mother Church have given you pause."

"I know. I feel like such a hypocrite."

Jack laughed and said, "I'll grant you that, ma'am. But, if you'd rather we slept in different rooms, I can survive until we tie the knot in Laramie. I survived thirteen years, so I think I can wait another week."

She kissed him softly before asking, "You don't think Joseph will be disappointed, do you?"

"Maybe, but not as much as I will. I was looking forward to our night together, despite my own return to the good graces of Mother Church."

Emily almost changed her mind again, but Jack kissed her first, then stood and said, "I'll sleep downstairs and you can take the bedroom next to Joseph's. Okay?"

She nodded, stood, then kissed him again before walking quickly across the room and hustling up the stairs before she stopped at the top landing, smiled down at him, then disappeared down the hallway.

Jack let out a deep breath, then walked uncomfortably to the first bedroom on the bottom floor. Unbeknownst to him it was the same bedroom that Wilbur Moore had occupied and used to have his way with Emily, Anna Thornton, and Mary Flaherty.

CHAPTER 10

Joseph never commented about the lack of noise the night before, either during breakfast or on the ride to Luke Casey's office. He assumed that either he had slept through it or they weren't as noisy as his father had been.

At the meeting with Luke Casey, they finally learned about the many rules involved in being Joseph's guardian, which shouldn't matter much longer anyway. The family lawyer had told them about what had happened after they'd gone and what Judge Carstairs had told him in his chambers when he'd gone to pick up the paperwork.

"Suffice it to say," he concluded, "the judge wasn't happy with the theatrics, but it wasn't directed at you, Mister Tyler, but at Mister Moore and the executives of the company."

Jack mentioned the damage to the house, and Luke said he'd have the repair work done after they'd gone.

When Emily told him of their plans to let Anna Thornton and Mary Flaherty live at the house and act as caretakers, he had no problem with it at all because they were both on the payroll anyway. It was then that Mister Casey gave Emily the account book for the family bank account and she showed it to Jack who raised his eyebrows at the figure. It showed a balance of only $17, 462.27.

Emily asked, "Why is it so low, Mister Casey?"

"Most owners of operating companies don't have a lot of liquid cash on hand. Their wealth is in their company; the equipment, supplies and customer base. It was actually more than double that amount before Joseph's grandfather died. His father was more devoted to spending money than making it. It should start going back up now that things are stable again and the company is on sound financial footing. By the time Joseph inherits, it should be a sizeable amount."

"I won't be making any expenditures from the account, Mister Casey," Emily said.

Remembering that Mister Casey had admitted to double-billing the family, Jack asked, "But I assume you'll be sending Mrs. Doyle monthly lists of expenditures and the current balance?"

Luke Casey cleared his throat and replied, "Yes, of course."

Their tasks concluded at the attorney's office, they drove the buggy to the Thornton residence, and Jack and Joseph stayed in the buggy while Emily told Anna about the new arrangements. Anna was ecstatic, especially when Emily told her that she and Mary could marry and still stay as caretakers of the big house. Anna found Mary yesterday and she was very pleased with being able to return to the house without Wilbur Moore's presence.

When Emily told her about the steward's demise, Anna nodded appreciatively and said she'd tell Mary. She told her to see Mister Casey for the key on Monday rather than Saturday as they'd originally planned because Mister Tyler was still in the house with her, which caused a giggle from Anna that Emily quickly suppressed when she explained their sleeping situation, not that Anna believed her.

Jack and Joseph were talking about guns and wolves when Emily finally returned to the buggy and they set off for the Ward house.

After they entered the house, they found that none of them had heard about the second gunfight at the house and it was an enthralled group that sat in the parlor listening to the story.

Molly was pleased to know that Emily would be staying in Omaha for her wedding and once that news had been passed along, they broke into male and female groups to discuss totally different topics.

The rest of that week was filled with routine preparations for Molly's wedding and the departure of Jack, Emily and Joseph the following day.

The only really surprising news was when Dennis Ward casually mentioned that he'd be bringing a guest to the wedding – Mrs. Vera White. It appeared that he'd admired Mrs. White for some time, and once her husband deserted her, he had gone to her house in his new position as vice president of operations to offer any assistance she may need. Vera White had forgotten all about the parrot after his visit, and probably Mister Thomas White as well.

———

The day of Molly's wedding arrived and as it was to be held at nine o'clock because everyone would be fasting for the Mass, things were very hectic at the home beginning just after sunrise.

Jack had driven Emily and Joseph to the house allowing Emily to contribute to the mayhem, while the men coalesced in the kitchen just talking, unable to have their coffee because of the required fasting. Both rooms were full as the rest of the Wards and in-laws had arrived for the wedding.

The wedding itself was as most weddings were, with damp-eyed women and some men, a bride made more beautiful by the occasion, and a beaming husband-to-be waiting at the altar. The priest conducted the ceremony unerringly, and even though it was the first wedding he had ever attended, Jack simply couldn't find anything that enthused him. Maybe it was because he really didn't know either the bride or groom very well. He just stood beside Emily and unintentionally compared her to the bride and found that there was no comparison, even though Molly was her sister and shared many of the same physical characteristics. There was just something special about Emily.

Joseph stood on Emily's other side and Jack could tell he was bored in addition to being hungry. Joseph had his right hand in his pocket feeling his pocket knife's smooth handle and the carved wolf's head, trying to picture the carving as his fingers slid over the surface.

After Molly and Andrew were pronounced Mr. and Mrs. Andrew Donovan by the priest, the couple took each other's hands, then turned and walked smiling down the aisle as families and friends smiled back at them.

Then, it was back to the Ward home for food at last and congratulations for the newlyweds, who would remain in Omaha for their honeymoon.

All of Emily's extended family were there, and she met many of her nephews and nieces for the first time. Most of them lived within thirty miles of Omaha, but didn't get into town that often, and rarely as an entire group.

Jack and Joseph were introduced to the enormous clan of Irishmen and women, Jack noting that only Molly and Emily were redheads among the adults, but many of the children had various hues of red hair. The suddenly too small house was filled with laughter and conversation as they mingled.

After an hour, they returned to the big house and were able to change into more comfortable attire, Jack, Emily and Joseph lounged in the parlor to talk about the trip to Laramie tomorrow.

They would be taking the late afternoon train, which would depart the station at 4:40 and arrive in Laramie at 8:10 on Tuesday morning. Most of their things were already packed including a crate of books, as Emily, in her new position as guardian, had authorized Jack to raid the library of anything he'd like to take back to the cabin. Joseph would need something to read, after all. Surprisingly, Jack only took thirty-six volumes because he had most of the others in his cabin already.

That fact inspired Emily to ask, "Jack, just how big is your cabin? You described it to me when we were on the trail out of the mountains, but I must have misjudged how big it is."

"The original cabin that I thought was all I would ever build is thirty feet wide by twenty-four feet deep, but then, after I found the gold, I added the a large bedroom on each end of the original cabin, each about sixteen feet by twenty feet. Then I added the kitchen, bathroom, and an office/library and the two mud rooms. I also added that long corridor to the privy. So, it's pretty roomy. Now, the barn doesn't even look like the house. It's just a regular barn that I had built. It has six stalls for horses and a big loft and even a small smithy. There's a big corral on the west side, too."

"I can't wait to see it," she said excitedly.

"Me, too," Joseph said, then asked, "Will we see Loopy?"

"Maybe. It's up to him. If you see him, just stand still and call me over, so I can introduce you."

"Okay. Where will I go to school?" he asked.

"You'll be going to Laramie Public School #2. There isn't a Catholic school."

"So, there will be girls in the class?"

"Yes, sir. You're going to have to get used to having those females around for a change."

"And so, will you, Mister Tyler," Emily said sharply.

"Yes, ma'am," Jack replied as he grinned.

Their sleeping arrangements for their last night in Omaha were the same as they'd been since Emily had requested that they postpone their anxiously awaited gymnastics. Each night as Jack lay in his bed, he hoped that Emily would change her mind and sneak into his room while Emily lay awake upstairs anticipating the imminent arrival of Mister Tyler. Both would be disappointed.

They awakened that Sunday morning, each in his or her respective bedroom, made their beds, then Emily and Joseph took

ABANDONED

their turns bathing while Jack shaved in the downstairs bathroom before finishing all the packing.

They drove the buggy to church, returned ninety minutes later and then had breakfast. Jack then loaded the buggy with the things that were going to be shipped, then drove to the Union Pacific train depot, got their tickets and had the two trunks and the crate of books marked for shipment to Laramie.

On his return to the house on Chicago Street, he left the buggy with the livery and walked the two blocks, entering through the back door after cutting through the alley.

They had eaten a late Sunday brunch, so Emily was planning on an early dinner before the long train ride, which gave them a few empty hours to fill. The chess and checkerboard was already in one of the trunks, so Jack thought a few games of poker might fill the gap, but it turned out not to be necessary when there was a loud knock at the front door.

When Emily swung the door open, she broke into an enormous smile as she spied a crowd of relatives spilling across the porch onto the front yard.

Her father grinned at her and said, "Everyone wanted to say goodbye, Emily."

Emily was still smiling as the mass of Irish and a few non-Irish swirled into the house. She greeted each of them as they passed until she finally closed the door and another Ward family gathering began.

Jack and Joseph joined the mix, but this was all about Emily, so after a while, Jack wound his way to the only unoccupied spot on the first floor, climbed a few steps and took a seat on the large staircase, marveling at the sheer numbers of her family.

Jack sat watching Emily as she shared memories and excitedly talked to her relatives. He then spotted Joseph as he was showing his ivory-handled knife to a circle of awed Ward boys and admiring Ward girls and smiled. Joseph was suddenly aware of young ladies.

As a boy who had grown up in the cold surroundings of an orphanage, this was his first real introduction to what having a family really meant. The adults in the parlor and nearby hallway had grown up together and shared everything from disaster to triumph. They'd been there when one of their brothers or sisters needed them.

Jack began to wonder if he was doing the right thing by taking Emily and Joseph away from this. Joseph's family could now include all of the people he saw below him. There didn't have to be any more worries about his own greedy relatives like his Uncle Noah. Emily and her huge extended family could ensure that he was happy and safe.

He concentrated on Emily, watching her hands dance and her eyes flash as she spoke. His memory failed him when he thought she was happier than he'd ever seen her before.

He glanced at the grandfather clock in the corner. It was almost three-thirty. They'd have to leave in another forty minutes to catch the train.

As he looked back at Emily, he began to believe he wasn't being fair to her, so after five more minutes, he stood and walked down the stairs. He had to answer questions as he passed newly-introduced Wards whose names he couldn't recall as he wound his way through the packed parlor until he was close enough to Emily to catch her eye.

She was just finishing the story of the wolf pack's attack, and her blue eyes were animated when she caught Jack's face, completed the sentence and then asked, "Jack?"

"Could I see you for a moment, Emily?" he asked.

She nodded then had to squeeze between two Ward males and took his arm. He led her to the front door, opened it and then once on the porch closed it behind him.

ABANDONED

"What's wrong, Jack?" she asked.

"Emily, right now, I want you to be the most Emily Ann Ward you've ever been. Okay?"

She folded her arms and said, "Alright."

"I've been watching you while you were talking with your family and I've never seen you happier. I feel like I'll be depriving you of being with your family by taking you and Joseph back to Wyoming. I mean, you grew up here with them and you're more comfortable here in the city. I want to know if you want to stay here. I don't belong here, but more than anything, I want to make you happy."

Emily asked, "So, you're asking me if I'd like to stay in Omaha while you return to Laramie?"

"Yes. Joseph would stay with you, of course."

"Yes, of course." she replied, then after a short pause, said, "Well, I'm very happy that you noticed it in time. The thought of moving out to the wilderness away from my family has had me concerned for some time. I am very grateful for your considerate offer, Jack. Thank you. Will you have our things sent back to the house when you get to the station?"

Jack may have asked to have an Emily Ann Ward reply, but this was far beyond blunt. This was a bolt of devastation that ripped through him.

Emily smiled, said, "Goodbye, Mister Tyler," then opened the door, walked inside and closed the door behind her, leaving a frozen Jack Tyler standing on the porch.

He was motionless for more than a minute, his heart and soul deflated. *She hadn't even shed a tear!*

He was just about to turn to go down the steps when the door opened again, Emily stepped back out, then closed the door behind her as she glared at him.

"Mister Jack Tyler! Just what was that pathetic attempt to try and get rid of me? I can't believe the same voice that crushed those men in the courtroom made such an offer. Did you really believe that I would want to stay here? I'm just enjoying seeing my family that I haven't seen for a while. You never had a family, did you?"

"No, ma'am," he replied quietly.

"Families can be a pain in the ass, Mister Tyler. My family is no different. Yes, they can be wonderful at times and it's nice to see them again, but I'd much prefer to be with the man and boy that I choose to live with than the ones I was born to live with. Do you understand me, sir?"

"Yes, ma'am," he repeated even more quietly.

"Alright, then. Enough of this nonsense. Now, you will come back into the parlor, say your goodbyes to my enormous family and invite them all to come to Wyoming. They'll all say that they will, but none will ever set foot on a train. Then, Mister Tyler, you, I and Joseph will board the train to Laramie, you'll marry me as you promised to do, and that night, sir, you will make love to me until the sun comes up in the morning."

Jack looked at her still-beautiful, but angry face and said, "Could I have Mrs. Doyle back, please?"

Emily broke into a smile, kissed him and said, "It's too late. You're stuck with me."

He took her arm, as she opened the door and they entered the house to say their farewells to the extended Ward family.

After Emily's robust confirmation of her desire to accompany Jack to Laramie, the remainder of the time in Omaha passed almost instantly. He didn't have to hire a cab to get to the station but were seated in various modes of conveyance as the entire Ward entourage paraded down Jones Street to the station.

ABANDONED

The huge family took up almost half of the platform as Jack, Emily and Joseph boarded the train and once they found their seats in the first-class passenger car, waved to everyone as the train began to move north before making the turn west.

Once the train was underway, Jack sat at the window and Emily sat at the aisle. Joseph sat in the seat in front of them, then after ten minutes turned, knelt on the seat and looked at Jack.

"Mister Tyler, can we come back to visit sometimes?"

He glanced over at Emily, smiled, then replied, "How about next summer?"

Joseph nodded and then asked his guardian, "Mrs. Doyle, do you know Lauren's address?"

"I'm afraid I don't know any of their addresses, Joseph, but I'm sure we can get it for you. Are you going to write to her?"

"She asked me to, and so did two other girls, but I liked her the best."

Jack said, "You should be polite and write to all of them, Joseph. It's what you write that's important."

"Oh. Okay," he said as he smiled, then dropped back down to his seat.

Emily looked at Jack, smiled and rested her hand on his left knee. Their son was interested in girls.

On Tuesday morning, the train pulled into the Laramie station twenty minutes later than scheduled when they had to wait for a large herd of cattle to cross the tracks outside of Cheyenne.

But after they arrived, Jack arranged to have the trunks and crate brought to the cabin after giving the freight office directions. He knew Loopy didn't pay any attention to wagons and hoped he hadn't changed his habits while he was gone.

Jack was carrying the one travel bag as they left the platform and Jack said, "Emily, do you want to see Father Schneider while we're here?"

Emily may have been tired, but replied, "How far away is the church?"

"Just two blocks north. We can set up the wedding, then we can have lunch at Nellie's Café before we head to the cabin."

"That's a wonderful idea, Jack," she said as she took his arm.

They were all glad to be on their feet again, so they just walked the two blocks and turned into the small rectory adjoining St. Mary's Roman Catholic Church.

Jack knocked on the rectory door, and it was answered moments later by Father Schneider, which was not a surprise to Jack as his housekeeper was close to seventy.

Emily was surprised that he was so young, probably younger than she was.

Father Schneider looked at Jack, then Emily, smiled and said, "Now, what's a pretty lady like you doing with a heathen like Jack Tyler? Come in, please."

As he stepped aside, Jack let Emily, then Joseph enter the rectory before stepping past Father Schneider who gave him a wink and a slight smile.

Once they were all seated, Father Schneider asked, "Can I guess that you're here to ask me to marry you to this wonderful young lady, Mister Tyler? I can't think of any other reason for you to be here on a Tuesday morning. It surely isn't to let me take more of your money at the poker table."

"That, and to let you know that this wonderful young lady convinced me to return to the loving arms of the Holy Mother Church. We asked to be married in Omaha while we were there, but the bishop denied the parish priest's request for dispensation from the bans and instructions."

"Now, that's unusual. When did you wish to be married?"

"How soon can it be arranged?"

"Two hours, I think," he replied as he looked at Emily and asked, "Unless he was fibbing about being a good Catholic again. He wasn't, was he?"

Emily was taken aback by the priest's casual reply of just a two hour wait, but said, "Oh, no, Father. We went to confession again on Saturday, and Mass on Saturday and Sunday because we attended my sister's wedding on Saturday."

The priest looked back at Jack and said, "Now, that is a miracle. If you'll give me the particulars for the marriage license, I'll get the paperwork done and arrange for witnesses. If you come back in an hour or so, I'll have everything ready."

Emily was still astonished by the apparent ease of the process but nodded.

After leaving the rectory, she asked, "Jack, did that really just happen?"

"Yes, ma'am. Now, it's too early for lunch, but there is something we can do before we come back to get married."

"Where?" she asked.

"Cook's Livery. I usually used Robinson's down the street, but I had to drop off the pack horse that Noah Gallagher had rented and bought Joseph's black horse that he'd ridden on the hunting trip."

Joseph exclaimed, *"You bought him? Is he there?"*

"No, sir. He's at the cabin waiting for you. But what I did was to make a deal with the owner. I gave him Claude Boucher's horse and saddle for Joseph's horse, then, I told him I wanted two special horses and saddles for you and me, Emily. I have no idea what to expect other than the guidelines I gave him and told him I wanted the best he could find."

"Is this a wedding gift?"

"No, ma'am. I'll give you that tonight when you give me mine."

"It will be my pleasure, sir," she said with a straight face.

They reached the livery and before they even entered the barn, Jack saw their new horses in the corral. There were eight horses in the fenced area, but the two that stood out were both black with black manes and tails. The slightly shorter mare had four white stockings and a white slash that ran the length of her nose, but the gelding was completely black.

Emily noticed them as well and asked, "Is the one with the white stockings mine?"

"I'm sure she is. Let's go and see Mister Cook and settle the bill."

Jack wasn't sure who was more excited about the new horses when they entered the barn and Jacob Cook looked up at them as he was preparing to lift a horse's back hoof for shoeing.

He dropped the hoof and said, "Welcome back, Mister Tyler. I heard you got that bas..., man, who shot Bessie. I've got your horses out in the corral. Ain't they beautiful critters?"

"They are. Did you get the saddles, too?"

"Sort of. They're still over at Wilkerson's. I didn't want to get 'em dirty over here. They're really nice, too. Are you ready for the damage?"

"Sure. Let me have it."

He grimaced slightly before saying, "Well, like you said, you wanted the best, so it'll cost you four hundred and thirty two dollars for everything."

Jack didn't bat an eye and asked, "Do you want a draft, or do I have to go to the bank and get you some cash?"

Jacob Cook relaxed and said, "A draft will be fine. Do you want to hang around while I go and get those saddles for ya?"

"No, we have to do some things, but we'll be back in couple of hours. Where can I write this draft?"

"Follow me," he said as he headed for his office/living area.

Emily quickly said, "We're going to be out in the corral," then pirouetted and trotted out of the barn as Joseph ran to catch up.

She opened the gate and headed for her new horse.

When she reached the mare, she said, "Hello. My name is Emily. What's yours?"

She laughed lightly, then as she began to stroke the mare's neck, started to sing softly in Irish Gaelic as she kept her blue eyes focused on the horse's big brown eyes.

A few minutes later, Jack entered the corral and made his way past the other horses, until he was just four feet behind Emily, letting her continue to sing. He looked down at Joseph and they shared a smile.

When she finished, she turned and smiled at her men and said, "I'll call her Byan, which means lady. It's spelled like 'bean', but I won't be writing it anywhere."

"It's a beautiful name, Emily," Jack said before he turned to the taller all-black gelding and asked, "What should we name this tall boy?"

"Well, if I have a lady, he should be a gentleman, don't you think?" she asked.

"And that is?"

"It's pronounced 'fyer'."

"Do you think he'd mind if I called him Fire?"

Emily laughed as she continued to stroke Byan, and answered, "I don't think he'll object."

They left the corral and then walked to the sheriff's office, so Jack could fill in Sheriff Higginbotham about all that had happened, return his deputy's badge, and also to ask a favor.

When they entered, Sheriff Higginbotham was standing next to the desk talking to a seated Deputy Pruitt. As both men turned to look at them, Jack noticed a familiar face in the jail cell, and he was sure that Emily spotted him as well.

"Welcome back, folks!" the sheriff exclaimed.

"Good morning, Will," Jack said as he pulled out his badge and handed it to the sheriff.

"Who's your guest?" Jack asked.

Sheriff Higginbotham glanced back, then answered, "That's Mister Clark Gibbons. He shot Orville Jenkins, the stock manager over at the U.P. He's goin' to trial tomorrow."

Jack looked at the man who'd tried to shoot him before they'd returned to Omaha as he sat on the cot hanging his head.

"He shot Orville? Is he okay?"

"Yup. He only winged him."

ABANDONED

"Why did he shoot Orville? He was going to shoot me a couple of weeks ago outside my cabin, but my wolf friend surprised him."

"Why didn't you tell me? I would've arrested him."

"It doesn't matter. But why did he shoot Orville?"

The sheriff grinned and replied, "Seems he went off to Chicago to get a wife, and he musta told his foreman he was gonna sell the ranch. So, the foreman sells the entire herd, takes the money and skedaddles with the rest of the ranch hands. They boarded the westbound train the next day and disappeared. Well, when Mister Gibbon comes back on the train with his fiancée and her brother, he takes 'em out to the ranch and finds it empty, then comes back here in a huff and goes to the stockyard and confronts Orville. Now, Orville tells him that it was all perfectly legal, which it was on his end, because Mister Gibbons gave the foreman the right to sell the critters. It was what the foreman did with the money that broke the law. But Mister Gibbons there didn't see it that way, got into an argument, and when his fiancée said she and her brother were going back to Chicago, he went a bit crazy and pulled his pistol, shot Orville in the left arm, then began shooting the rest of the office. When we got there, he was still pulling his trigger like there were live cartridges in those cylinders."

"That's a strange one, Will," Jack said.

"Yup. It's not as serious as your case, but it's strange enough," he replied.

"Will, I need a favor. Emily and I are going to be married in an hour or so, and we want to adopt Joseph. Now, the folks back in Omaha made a big deal out of it, but I figure we can get it done a lot easier out here. Can you talk to Judge Anderson about it? Emily is already his legal guardian."

"I'll do that, Jack. Just write down all of the names and stuff so I can give it to the judge. And congratulations to you both," he said as he smiled at Emily.

Emily smiled back as Jack wrote down their three names and handed the sheet to Deputy Pruitt.

As they turned to leave, the sheriff said, "And you owe me the full story of what happened back east, Jack!"

Jack opened the door, turned back to the sheriff and said, "It'll take a while, Will."

After Jack closed the door behind them, they returned to St. Mary's rectory and, true to his word, Father Schneider had the paperwork ready and his two witnesses waiting. One was Mrs. Hatfield, the rectory's elderly caretaker and his cook, and the other was their poker-playing partner, the custodian, Jim Richards.

It took only five minutes to complete the paperwork before they went into the church. The wedding was as simple as imaginable but meant everything to Jack and Emily as Father Schneider read the vows in English for them to repeat. It technically wasn't a Catholic ceremony, which was why it was so informal. Father Schneider had married many non-Catholics since he'd arrived in Laramie and would formalize the marriage on Sunday. But even without asking, he knew why they wished to be married. Like most of the population in Laramie, he knew about the rescue and the trip to Omaha and had even read the papers from Omaha about the events that had taken place in Judge Carstairs' courtroom.

There were many reasons why this marriage was taking place, but he could tell by looking at the couple that the most important reason was the one that really mattered. They loved each other.

He pronounced them husband and wife, let Jack kiss his bride then he surprised Jack and Emily by kissing her himself.

They returned to the rectory and completed the forms, Jack shook the witnesses' hands and Emily gave each a kiss on the cheek. Joseph just stood and smiled at them, because he knew where they'd be going next. He was going to be adopted.

Now that they were officially and legally married, Jack looked at his wife and said, "Mrs. Tyler, I believe it's time to visit Judge Anderson."

She smiled, looked down at Joseph and asked, "Are you ready, Joseph?"

He nodded and said, "Yes, ma'am."

They said goodbye to Father Schneider, left the rectory and walked to the county courthouse. Jack had only met the judge once, but Jack was sure that the sheriff had greased the skids.

As they walked, Emily recalled how everything was supposed to be prepared in Omaha for their marriage and adoption, but that had been denied and reduced to just being named Joseph's guardian and then it all had just crumbled into chaos. She'd only believe that Joseph was their son after it happened.

They found Judge Anderson's offices less impressive than the oak-paneled rooms and courtroom of Judge Carstairs in Omaha, but on the other hand, when they entered the outer office, the judge's clerk stood with a smile on his face to greet them as if they were old friends.

"You must be Mr. and Mrs. Tyler and Joseph. We've been expecting you. Follow me."

He turned, opened an inner door and said, "They're here, Your Honor."

"Send them in," Judge Anderson said from inside the room as the clerk waved them in.

After they entered the judge's chambers, the clerk followed with some papers.

Judge Anderson wasn't wearing his judicial robes as he sat behind his desk, smiling at them.

"Have a seat, please," he said as he beckoned to the three chairs before his desk as the clerk laid the forms before him.

After they were all sitting, he said, "I read in the newspapers what had happened in Omaha and I'm embarrassed for the legal profession that's reached a stage where they've forgotten why the laws were written in the first place. Now, you are petitioning to legally adopt Joseph. Is that right?"

"Yes, Your Honor. My wife, while legally his guardian, would much prefer to be his mother and I want to raise him as my son, and not some boy living in my house."

"You understand your responsibilities in becoming his father?" he intoned.

Emily glared at the judge and said, "My husband saved our lives twice, saved my reputation and has done nothing but treat us both with respect and love," then paused and added, "Your Honor."

The judge looked at Emily, then a smile spread across his lips before he said, "I'm sorry, Mrs. Tyler. I just had to ask that question. I'm sure that Mister Tyler will be a wonderful father and you will be a perfect mother."

Emily blushed, which for a redheaded Irish woman, was nothing short of spectacular, before saying, "I'm sorry, Your Honor. It's just my Irish temper."

"No, it's alright, Mrs. Tyler. Let me just fill out these forms that my clerk gave me and, if you don't mind, Mister Tyler, can you tell me about that tempest you created in the courtroom in Omaha? The stories that were published and reached us here I'm sure were lacking in accuracy."

"I don't mind at all, Your Honor," Jack replied.

The judge just had to sign the forms, which he did with a flourish as Jack began to tell him about the confrontation. He didn't back off of what had happened to Emily because he'd read the same newspapers that had evidently made their way to Laramie and although they hadn't used the same language either he or Wilbur Moore had used, the vague implications were worse.

The judge finished signing long before Jack ended his monologue, but Jack could tell how tickled the judge was as Jack described his big-city associate's discomfort.

Just twenty minutes after entering the judge's office, Jack and Emily Tyler and their son, Joseph, exited the offices and then the courthouse. Joseph was practically dancing as they crossed the street to Nellie's Café where they had a filling steak lunch to celebrate the wedding and adoption.

They stopped at the Western Union office to send a telegram to Luke Casey to let him know of the marriage and adoption, but that it wouldn't change anything except for adding Tyler to Joseph's and Emily's last names.

Everything was done in Laramie and it was time to collect Fire and Byan and ride to the cabin that only one of the group had ever seen, and that included the two horses.

Jack was still carrying their lone travel bag as they reached Cook's Livery and as soon as they entered, saw their two black horses waiting in their exceptional leather finery. It was truly worthy of the magnificent horses that would wear it and Jacob was grinning as he held out the reins to the newest of newlyweds.

"Well, Mister Tyler, what do you think?"

"I think we got a bargain, Mister Cook," Jack replied as he took Fire's reins and they led the two horses into the afternoon sun.

He then turned to Emily and asked, "Are you ready to ride Byan home, Mrs. Tyler?"

She put her left hand on her hip and said, "No, Mister Tyler. I am riding with you. Our son can ride Byan. I wish to arrive at our new home as we rode on our first day together."

"Very well, Mrs. Tyler. I will grant your request, but just remember that I am your husband now, and may take advantage of my new position."

Emily walked toward Fire and replied, "Just remember that you, sir, are now married to Emily Ann Ward Tyler."

Jack snickered as Emily mounted, then pulled her left foot out of the stirrup to let Jack put his left boot in, then swung his long right leg around Fire's rear and slid in behind her.

Once they were all in the same riding positions that they had taken that first day, they started the two blacks down the street and then headed south after leaving Laramie. Once alone on the road, Emily and Jack became more comfortable as his right hand found better things to do than hold the reins. Emily was using her left hand to her advantage while Joseph pretended not to notice.

But five minutes later, Jack and Emily agreed that it would be wiser to keep their hands where they belonged. It was another hour and a half to the cabin and they'd never make it.

They were more than halfway there when Emily asked, "What's that ahead of us?"

"That's probably the freight wagon delivering the trunks and the crate of books. I told them to leave them on the front porch."

"Won't Loopy attack them?"

"No, ma'am, he ignores wagons, or at least he always has in the past. He's quite good at detecting real threats, and I don't have a clue how he does it."

Emily didn't reply, but leaned back a bit more, enjoying the ride.

Joseph had his pocket knife out and hoped he'd meet Loopy soon.

ABANDONED

They turned east thirty minutes later, and Joseph began trying to find Loopy in the trees and rocks but couldn't see any sign of him. But, when they turned the corner and the barn and corral came into view, he forgot about the wolf and tried to see his black horse in the barn but was thwarted by the mostly closed barn doors.

After a few seconds, he pried his eyes off the large barn and looked at his new home and his eyes began to expand. His father had always described it as a cabin, and it was made out of logs, but it was enormous. He remembered that he had said it was like a squat capital 'H', and it was, but it was a big capital 'H'.

Emily was even more surprised at the size of the log structure. It was a lot taller than she had expected it to be, too. She smiled when she saw the boarded, snakelike structure that ended at the privy. It may not be a water closet like she had in the big house in Omaha, but it was a lot better than the privy she'd had to run to in January when she was a girl.

The two freighters had just unloaded the crate and were climbing back onto the wagon when they spotted the two horses and waited for them to arrive, hoping Jack would give them a tip.

When they reached the front of the house, Jack slipped off the back of Fire and approached the wagon, pulled out two five-dollar bills and handed one to each man. It was a much larger tip then they had expected. Usually, they didn't get anything more than a 'thanks', but occasionally a quarter or even a dollar. *But five dollars? That was almost a week's pay.*

"Thanks, Mister Tyler," the driver said.

"I appreciate you boys having to drive all the way out here. Don't worry about my wolf. He won't bother you because he sees me talking to you."

"*You have a wolf?*" the driver exclaimed as his eyes quickly scanned the terrain.

"Kind of. He stays around the cabin when I'm gone and keeps folks away. He's not really a pet, though. Wolves make terrible pets."

"Well, we'll be goin' then," the driver said as he tossed a quick salute, then snapped the reins.

The wagon rolled quickly away, and Jack walked back to the horses where Emily stood holding the horses' reins with Joseph beside her watching the wagon roll away.

"Why did you tell them about Loopy if he won't bother a wagon?" she asked.

"I always tell men who come out here about Loopy. I want the word to get around in case anyone wants to visit while I'm gone."

"Oh."

They led the two horses to the barn as Joseph ran ahead to see his own horse again. When they got inside, Joseph was already petting the horse's neck and Jack glanced at Abby and Billy. They weren't locked in the stalls and had probably wandered around quite a lot judging by the relative lack of dung on the floor. The black gelding, on the other hand, hadn't left the protection of the barn very often and needed to be exercised and have his stall mucked out. But that could be handled later. Now, they needed to unsaddle the two new horses, brush them down and move their things into the cabin.

It wasn't until almost sunset that Jack had the trunk and crate in the main room as Emily and Joseph explored their new home. Emily was very pleased with the kitchen but mentioned that changes would have to be made in the décor. Jack didn't mind at all because he had his own family now and so far, neither had shown the slightest tendency to be a pain in his behind or anywhere else.

Emily fashioned a quick dinner while Jack and Joseph unpacked the trunks. Joseph asked for the south bedroom because it allowed him to look out the window at the barn and his horse. He also thought he'd have a better chance to see Loopy in that direction because that's where the trees were the closest.

The sun had long gone, and Jack had a fire crackling in the large fireplace but hadn't lit fires in either of the heat stoves. They sat in the main room pretending to talk about the next day's activities while the adults anxiously awaited Joseph's first yawn. Jack had Emily snuggled in close on the couch while Joseph sat in a thickly stuffed chair ten feet away. The surprisingly comfortable furniture had surprised Joseph and Emily as both had expected crude, handmade chairs, tables, and beds. The kitchen was completely outfitted with china, glassware, cookware and flatware, too.

Joseph asked, "Mister Tyler, now that you are my father and Mrs. Doyle is my mother, what should I call you?"

Jack glanced at Emily then replied, "If it's all right with your mother, I'd prefer Dad and Mom over the more common Mama and Papa. I guess it's because I always pictured Mama as a gray-haired older lady and that doesn't fit your new mother."

Emily laughed and said, "I'll agree with my husband, Joseph. I'll be Mom and he'll be Dad. Okay?"

Joseph grinned and answered, "I like that better, too."

"Tomorrow, we'll take care of your horse and you, sir, will help me clean out the barn. Have you named him yet?"

"I get to name him?"

"Well, we aren't going to do it. He's your horse. You'll take care of him, so you get to name him."

He thought about it for a minute, then looked at Emily and said, "If it's all right with you, Mrs. D..., I mean, Mom, I'm not going to use your Irish words. I'll call him Quin."

"No, that's fine, Joseph. How did you come up with Quin?" she asked.

"Well, Dad named Loopy because it was close to lupus, so I chose Quin because it's close to equine."

Jack nodded and said, "That's very impressive, Joseph."

Joseph smiled at his parents and then…yawned.

Emily sat up quickly and said, "Looks like someone needs to get ready for a good night's sleep."

Joseph didn't get a chance to respond as his parents both stood and herded him into his new bedroom and Emily set out his nightshirt while Jack pulled back the blankets and quilts on his new bed.

Minutes later, Joseph was tucked in, his parents had each kissed him on his forehead, then hastily left the room, closing the door behind them. Joseph was a bit confused to find himself in bed earlier than usual but closed his eyes and began to imagine his new life where he rode his horse and listened to the howls of nearby wolves.

After closing Joseph's bedroom door, Jack and Emily barely made it ten feet before their excruciatingly postponed tension was released. The initial bit of groping on the beginning of the ride to the cabin had only kindled the fires of lust and passion as they kissed and probed their way across the main room and finally reached the north bedroom.

Jack kicked the door closed with his foot because his hands were too busy, as were Emily's. This wasn't going to be any thoughtful, tender episode of expressed love. That would come later. This first time would be a chaotic display of unharnessed lust that had been building since that first ride on Abby.

Buttons flew across the room as articles of clothing were shed and tossed aside while they forgot about anything but each other.

Just fifteen minutes after quickly kissing Joseph's forehead, Emily and Jack were writhing and grabbing each other without inhibitions or proscriptions. There were no rules as Emily begged and Jack willingly complied. They made no attempt to disguise their unfettered passions and were emitting sounds that could only be made in the act of mutual attainment of ecstasy.

Joseph was still awake and wondered why he had never heard his parents when they were making love in the big house. It didn't matter, he supposed, all that mattered was that his parents loved each other and loved him. He rolled over onto his side, happier than he'd ever been before.

Joseph was the first one to awaken the next morning, and despite the chill in the cabin, needed to use the privy – now! He hopped out from under the toasty covers, opened his bedroom door, and trotted out into the main room, saw his parents' bedroom door still closed, then ran down the short hallway toward the kitchen, opened the door after the office/library and jogged down the long hallway to the privy. He could have just gone out the back doors and used the porch but didn't want to find Loopy staring at him. At least not yet, and surely not as he was peeing.

Jack heard the doors open and close, opened his eyes, and had to pull a few strands of dark red hair from his face before he looked at his contented wife just inches away. After that initial, wild coupling, they'd rested for all of twelve minutes before a second, much more sedate, but equally passionate exchange of love. It was the second act that meant so much more to each of them. The tenderness and thoughtfulness that never had a chance to blossom the first time were in abundance once their lust had been mostly released. Their combined abstinences were over and would never be repeated.

Jack kissed her softly, then watched as her blue eyes were uncovered and she smiled at him, then kissed him back and said quietly, "I have to pee."

She bolted from the bed, throwing back the quilts and Jack, despite his own bladder's demands, couldn't help but enjoy the magnificence of Emily Ann Ward Tyler. She hurriedly threw on the thick robe she'd worn in the encounter with Wilbur Moore, then yanked the door open and disappeared, heading for the privy.

Jack slid out of bed almost as quickly, pulled on his britches, left the bedroom and turned to go out the front door as Emily almost collided with Joseph who was leaving the privy entrance.

"Good morning, Mom," Joseph said as Emily gave him a short wave and scurried down the hallway.

Jack waved to Joseph before opening the front door, then passing through the large mud room and leaving the cabin to use the front yard as his temporary privy.

When he returned, he restarted the fire to warm up the cabin while Joseph was getting dressed.

An hour later, Joseph and Jack were in the barn, cleaning out the deposits left by Abby, Billy and mostly Quin, and refilling the feed bins and troughs.

"When do I have to go back to school?" Joseph asked.

"You'll have this week off, then Monday morning, we'll ride into Laramie and enroll you in your new school."

"I don't have to wear a uniform, do I, Dad?"

"No, sir. We just have to make sure you stay warm. And now that you and your mother are here, I think I'll buy a carriage, so we can get you to school when it gets cold. You don't want to make a long ride when it's twenty below zero and the wind's howling."

"It got pretty cold in Omaha."

"It gets colder sooner and longer here, Joseph, but it's not too bad once you get used to it."

ABANDONED

They saddled the three black horses and led them to the back hitching post. Joseph mounted Quin as Jack prepared to step onto the porch to let Emily know they were ready to go when the back door opened, and Mrs. Tyler popped out. She had a gold ribbon around her hair to keep it from getting so badly tangled on the ride, and it made her look younger. Jack wondered if they'd reach the point where folks began to think she was his daughter.

She smiled and explained, "I was watching through the window," before she stepped across the small back porch and untied Byan's reins.

She and Jack mounted, and the new family set out, so Jack could show them their new home.

They hadn't ridden ten seconds when Joseph pointed to a small square building and asked, "What's that, Dad?"

"That's the smokehouse. When I go hunting, I smoke the meat in there and store it in the cold room in the cabin."

"Can I go hunting with you?" he asked quickly.

"Of course, you can. But only to learn about animals and how to hunt. You won't be able to shoot a gun."

"Okay. I understand, Dad."

Jack smiled at his son before glancing at Emily who was just smiling as she scanned the ruggedly beautiful landscape.

Jack took over two hours showing Emily and Jack his land, and both were impressed with the diversity in such a relatively small space. There were the two small streams and the larger creek. Joseph was about to ask if there were fish in the creek, but Jack didn't have to answer when a large cutthroat trout leapt from the water for a fly that had ventured too close to the surface. The forested areas covered the north, east and the southeastern parts of the land and a tall, forested hill took over to the south and west.

"Jack," Emily asked, "Who owns the land surrounding yours?"

"Ours, Emily," he replied, before saying, "and as far as I know, it's still owned by the Laramie Landholding Company. When the Union Pacific showed up, they were given land grants by the Federal government, and the Laramie Landholding Company was created by some speculators back in Cheyenne and bought acreages all along the railroad's property. I could have bought some of the land grant property, but I liked this better, so I bought it from them. It was actually cheaper than what the railroad was asking anyway, for some reason."

"So, someone else could buy the land surrounding your, I mean, our land?"

Jack hadn't paid much attention to it before, so he replied slowly, "They can. Do you think we should be the ones to do it, Emily?"

"How much would it cost?" she asked.

"I paid $2.25 an acre for this property, or just under fifteen hundred dollars. If we bought the adjoining five sections, we're talking about seventy-five hundred dollars even if I could still get it at that price."

"And you gave twenty thousand dollars to Joseph's company," she said with a bit of a grimace.

Joseph quickly said, "I don't care about the company, Dad. I think you should buy the land. I don't want other people to get it."

Jack smiled at Joseph then said, "We don't need the company money, but it would cut our account in Cheyenne almost in half. But, then, what's money for?"

Emily and Joseph both smiled, then Emily asked, "When do you want to see about buying it?"

"How about Monday after we enroll our son in his new school?"

ABANDONED

"Perfect."

With the decision to expand the property, Jack extended the tour to the surrounding land before they returned to the cabin for lunch.

The next few days were all about settling in for the new family, although the nights were about Jack and Emily attempting procreation at every opportunity.

Joseph's only disappointment was that he'd never met Loopy and asked Jack where the wolf was hiding. Jack told him it was possible that Loopy sensed the arrival of more permanent residents and decided to stay away. Joseph still held out hope that he'd see the big gray wolf.

On Monday, they rode into Laramie and Joseph was enrolled and left at his new school while Quin was boarded at Cook's Livery, his original home.

Jack and Emily then went to the Laramie Landholding offices on Third Street to see about the properties adjoining theirs.

When they entered, Jack was a bit surprised when he recognized the same man who'd sold him his property twelve years earlier at the same desk. He swore the man hadn't aged a day.

"Mornin', folks," he said with a smile as he rose from his chair.

"Good morning, Mister Jackson. I don't know if you remember me, but I'm Jack Tyler and I bought a section of land down south a while ago."

"Oh, I remember you, Mister Tyler. You've been in the newspapers a lot lately, too. What can I do for you?" he asked.

"I'd like to see about buying some more properties that adjoin mine," he said.

"I can help you with that, well, at least with some of them," he said as he stood and walked to a four-foot by eight-foot map behind his desk.

"You bought down here. Is that right?" he asked as he pointed to Jack's section.

"That's our section, right where you're pointing."

"Okay. Now I can sell you the sections to the south and east of your land, but the ones to the north are part of the Union Pacific's land grant and you'd have to talk to them."

That wasn't exactly a surprise to Jack because when he'd bought the property, he'd been told by the Union Pacific's land office that the property he wanted wasn't theirs. Now, it appeared, he'd be buying some of theirs after all.

"How much for the one section east, and the two bordering them on the south?"

"I can give them to you for the same price you paid for your section, $2.25 an acre. Will that work for you?"

"I can do that. Can we do the paperwork right now? We'll go over to the Union Pacific offices and see about the other two."

"Sure, but you won't be able to buy them both, you know. One they can sell, and the other is government land."

"Oh, that's right."

So, after he wrote the draft for $4,320.00 for the three new sections and shook Mister Jackson's hand, they left the office and just walked the two blocks to the Union Pacific land offices on First Street.

Jack wasn't surprised that the one section north of his property cost him almost twice as much at four dollars an acre, so, after writing out another draft for $2560.00 for the land and getting the

ABANDONED

paperwork, they left the office and went to the county land office to register their new purchases.

When they entered the county land offices, Jack was back on familiar turf as he knew the county land clerk, Henry Dobson.

"Morning, Henry," Jack said loudly as they entered the small office.

"Howdy, Jack, ma'am," he said as he nodded at Emily, "What can I do for you?"

"We just bought four of the sections of land around my property ten miles south of town and I need to get them registered and have my wife's name added to the deed."

"Not a problem," Henry said as Jack slid the contracts across the counter.

Twenty minutes after entering the land office, Jack and Emily stepped out into the morning sunshine the owners of five square miles of Wyoming Territory, and the sixth section that completed the two by three section plot was owned by the Federal government and would probably always remain untouched. It was a lot of land to own when its only purpose would be to stay the way it was.

"Now what do we do, Mister Tyler?" Emily asked.

"We go to the bank and have your name added to the account here. We'll get it added to the Cheyenne account when we go there to deposit the gold."

As they crossed the street, Emily asked, "When will we be going to Cheyenne?"

"After we're all settled, and Joseph can miss a day of school."

They reached the opposite boardwalk and turned right before Emily said, "Jack, I'm uncomfortable with Joseph having to make that long ride into Laramie to go to school every day. What if there's a blizzard?"

"This is Wyoming, Mrs. Tyler. They understand that. We'll have his books at home and we can teach him his missing work whenever he can't make it to school. It's not unusual for them to miss two weeks or more. As long as they keep up with the work, it's fine."

They turned into the bank and after just ten minutes, completed the paperwork and Emily was shown the balance of the Laramie account. It was only $1436.10, which surprised her because Jack said it was just a small account.

They left the bank and walked to the Lindsay Carriage Works to add an enclosed carriage to their day's expenditures. Earl Lindsay didn't have what they wanted, so they worked out a modified design from one of the carriages he had in his expansive shop. It would look almost like a fancy buckboard as Jack wanted some space in back for supplies and still have room for three passengers. When they finished, Earl thought he might make more of the two-horse conveyances once people saw it. He told them he'd have it done in a week and after they picked out the team, Jack and Emily left the carriage works to get some lunch.

———

Joseph was a bit uncomfortable at first in the strange environment of his new school that was nothing like his old school, but Mister Wheeler seemed to be a kind man and a good teacher. The other students in his class already knew who he was and, with the exception of the two older boys who viewed him as some sissy boy from back East, accepted him as just another kid and not an heir. When they broke for recess that morning, he was surrounded by most of the boys, and four of the six girls who peppered him with questions about his adventure in the mountains. Naturally, that included showing them his knife and its wolf's head. The two biggest boys stood off to the side and snickered at the obvious lies the kid was telling.

ABANDONED

During lunch, Emily asked, "Jack, how much time can Joseph miss at school?"

He shrugged and replied, "I don't know if there's a limit. I know that some of the folks on the ranches and farms only send the kids to school when they can, but home school them. The school gives them tests and makes sure that they're not falling behind, but I don't know if they have to be in the school for a certain amount of time. We can always let him stay in town with another family and pay for his boarding, but I'd rather not. I believe we can teach him just as well, and I can teach him what he needs to live out here."

"I agree with you. You have a lot of books at the cabin, so, do you think we could keep him there most of the time? I always read to him and reviewed his homework while he attended St. Ignatius."

"I don't see why not. We just set up a schedule for different subjects and bring him to school when we can."

Emily nodded and took a bite of her chicken dinner, her concerns put aside.

After lunch, they walked to the sheriff's office where they spent almost an hour telling him the story of everything that had transpired in Omaha.

Clark Gibbons' trial hadn't taken much time earlier that morning. He'd been found guilty and sentenced to five years in the territorial prison. Deputy Pruitt had already taken him to his new home just outside of Laramie.

Jack and Emily then rode to Cook's, retrieved Quin and led him to Joseph's new school to wait for the end of the school day.

He was all grins as he bounced out of the school and trotted to his parents and his horse, then quickly mounted after sliding his books into the saddlebag.

"How was it?" Emily asked as they turned their horses south.

"Great! Most of the boys are really nice and wanted to see my knife. They heard about how I stabbed Mister Moore already."

"Most of the boys?" asked Jack.

"Well, two of the biggest boys made fun of me, but I didn't care."

"How about the girls?" Emily asked.

"They're okay, but none of them are as pretty as Lauren."

Emily suppressed a giggle as they continued south and told him about their decision to do most of his schooling at the cabin, but for the next few weeks, they'd still be taking him to school and would find out first-hand from the teacher about the rules regarding home schooling.

As they rode, Jack said loudly so both could hear, "After all of the land purchases, I need to get a better handle on how much we have remaining, so I'll show you where the gold and money vault is when we get back."

Emily replied with a grin, "Are you sure you can trust your sweet, innocent wife with that information, Mister Tyler?"

He glanced at her and said, "You're right. Never mind. I'll handle it myself."

Emily stared at Jack as he was looking straight ahead. She had meant it as a joke and he'd taken it seriously?

ABANDONED

After another fifteen seconds, without turning, he said, "Now we're even for you leaving me on the porch back in Omaha after telling me you were staying."

Emily snapped back, "Oh, no we're not! You deserved what I gave you, Mister Jack Tyler!"

Jack turned, grinned at his wife and said, "Can I make it up to you with a lot of gold, ma'am?"

Emily shrugged as she smiled and said, "I suppose."

As he'd promised, Jack showed them the gold vault and the cash he had on hand. Even though he still had over a thousand dollars in cash, including a Mason jar full of silver coins, it was the gold that astonished both Emily and Joseph. Two jars of nuggets and four of gold dust sat on the desk as they stared at them.

"Each jar has roughly six pounds of gold. I tried using the bigger jars after the first time, but they were too heavy, so I switched to the pint-sized, but they were too heavy, too. So, I just use the half-pint jars and only fill them halfway. I weigh them using the shelf over there. I'll show you how it works later. I have this ledger to keep track of the gold and the money in the accounts in Laramie and Cheyenne, but I'm not very good at keeping track of the interest they earn, which was why the amount in Laramie was higher than I expected. I only get the balance in Cheyenne when I deposit the gold, so I'm not sure how much it is now because I made the last trip to Cheyenne in June."

"Jack," Emily said quietly, "it's almost frightening seeing that much gold just sitting there."

"It's really just rocks and dirt that people want."

"Are you going to go prospecting again soon?"

"Not until next spring, usually in April. Did you and Joseph want to come along?"

"Will it be to the same place where you found us?"

"Almost. It's another eight miles west of there."

She looked down at Joseph who was staring up at her with hopeful eyes.

She smiled and nodded before saying, "I think we'll be coming along."

"Good. It won't be anything like our last journey."

"It wasn't all bad, Jack. I seemed to recall some aspects that were quite pleasant."

"Pleasant, but painful, ma'am," Jack replied as Emily laughed.

As he replaced the jars and cash, Jack was already thinking about next year's trip in late spring and how much nicer it would be to have Emily and Joseph along. But before they could make the trip, he'd have to make sure that each of them would be capable of self-protection. He hadn't even thought about the other possibility, that Emily might be carrying their child.

He dropped to the floor, replaced the chair and then Emily walked to the kitchen to prepare supper while Jack and Joseph walked to the barn to muck it out and brush down the horses. The barn was getting crowded now with Abby, Billy and the three blacks, and Jack knew that he'd need more space for the new carriage and the two horses that would pull it. He'd stop in at Smith's Construction tomorrow after they dropped off Joseph and arrange to have a second barn, or carriage house built to accommodate the increased horse population and the new carriage.

―――

The next morning, they escorted Joseph into school rather than just dropping him off, so they could talk to Mister Fred Wheeler, his teacher. They stayed longer than expected, because after the conversation about the amount of time Joseph could remain at home being taught by his parents, Mister Wheeler asked if Jack could talk to the class about what had happened in the mountains, as he could already sense some trouble brewing with the class bullies, Mike Lindsay and Johnny Painter.

Emily just sat by and listened as Jack gave a very factual account of the story, limiting it to events in the Medicine Bow Mountains, but emphasized Joseph's confrontation with the grizzly and the wolves. He explained that he'd given Joseph his pocket knife because of his bravery and how he'd used the same knife to kill a mad coyote. He didn't talk about the discovery of Claude Boucher's remains, but at one point, did pull his giant Bowie knife and said that he'd threatened to use it on the man who'd caused all the problems. He didn't say which man, and they all assumed it was Joseph's uncle. Jack wanted the big boys in back to see the knife because it made a bigger impression than a pistol for some reason. It may not be as much of an impression as Loopy could make but he thought it would be sufficient.

The tale took almost thirty minutes, and then he spent another thirty answering questions. But when they left the classroom, even Mister Wheeler was impressed and was sure that the chances of a bully retaliation against Joseph were gone.

The good news was Jack and Emily were told that the school promoted or demoted students to the next year by a test that was given at the end of each school year. Joseph had already been tested the day before and was placed in the fourth year, not the third as his age had dictated. His parents were surprised it wasn't the fifth or sixth year.

They boarded their horses and headed for Smith's Construction and Sawmill on the east end of town. It only took forty minutes for them to choose an existing design and sign a contract. The were told it would only take two weeks to have the new carriage house built and Jack and Emily left the office another four hundred and sixty dollars poorer.

After leaving Smith's, as they walked to their horses, Jack said, "Emily, I want to go and talk to Jacob Cook before we get some lunch."

"You want to get another horse?"

"No, ma'am, I want to see if I can find another critter," he replied as he mounted Fire.

"Do I want to know which kind?" she asked.

"A dog," he replied, surprising Emily.

They trotted along toward the livery and she asked, "Why do you want to get a dog?"

"For a couple of reasons. The most obvious is to make Joseph happy and give him a friend to have with him. You see how much he wants to see Loopy."

"Yes, but what are the other reasons?"

"This is going to sound harsh, Emily, and I apologize if I sound cruel, but I believe it's necessary."

"Okay."

"I want him to have a dog with him that is his friend. Most dogs will protect their friends, and I know that Loopy is still nearby and I don't think he'd attack you or Joseph, but he's still a wolf. Wolves and dogs don't get along very much. If Joseph has his dog with him and Loopy or some coyotes or a puma approach, the dog will protect Joseph."

"Are you saying that you're planning on sacrificing the dog to protect Joseph?"

"If it comes to that, yes."

ABANDONED

Emily understood what Jack was saying and as cruel as it may have sounded, she knew that he was making the right decision.

"I agree with you, Jack. Besides, it's only a chance that the dog will be hurt, isn't it?"

"Yes, and if we get a big dog, it's not even a good chance. Like I told you before, most animals shy away from people, and a human with a big dog are too much trouble. Now any wolves, coyotes, bears and cougars that live around our cabin are probably much more familiar with humans than the ones out in the mountains, but still, they'll avoid people if they can."

"Let's go and see if Mister Cook knows where we can find a dog, then," she said as they trotted down Second Street.

Jacob Cook directed them to, of all places, the now-vacant C-G Connected ranch. He said that one of the ranch hands had told him that they had a mutt give birth to a litter of eight pups in June. He gave them directions to the ranch and they rode northwest out of town, finding the access road just fifteen minutes later.

"Is this even legal?" asked Emily as they progressed down the access road toward the barn.

"I don't care, ma'am. Those puppies have been abandoned and we are going to rescue them."

"All of them?" she asked in surprise.

"As many as we think is possible, Mrs. Tyler," he said as they approached the barn.

They dismounted and could hear yapping from inside the barn. The door was partially open, and as Jack swung the door wide, the smells of an unclean barn assaulted their nostrils.

"There are the puppies," Jack said as they entered.

"Where's their mother?" she asked as she looked around.

Jack stopped and scanned the barn and began counting small dogs. There were only four, and they were very thin.

"I think their mama went out to get some food for them and didn't make it back. They haven't been fed in a while, Emily. Look how skinny they are."

"Where are the other four?"

"I don't know. Either they ran away to get their own food, someone took them already, or some critters came inside and took them. I don't see any bodies anywhere, though."

Emily had walked to the four skinny little dogs and began petting them as they bounced at her feet using energy they probably didn't have.

"They're so cute, Jack. We have to take all of them."

"We will, but I need to find a way to get them out of here," he replied as he began to search the barn.

He found some empty burlap oat sacks in the back of the barn and used some pigging strings that were in a wooden box to lash two of them together.

"Okay, Mrs. Tyler, let's put two into each bag and I'll just hang them over the back of my saddle and we'll go back to town and visit the butcher to get them something to eat."

Emily smiled at Jack as she picked up one of the puppies and slid him into the open burlap bag. She put two dogs in each bag, then Jack lifted the bags, which weren't heavy at all, despite the age of the puppies. They were less than half the weight they should be.

Once they were securely hung behind Jack's saddle, they mounted and left the C-G Connected, scanning the grounds for any sign of the other dogs, but not finding any.

ABANDONED

"What kind of dogs are they?" Emily asked as they rode back to town.

"They look like plain old mutts to me, but they're going to be big mutts. They're coloring is a lot like a gray wolf or a coyote, but that doesn't mean much. It's the size of their paws that tells me they're going to be good-sized dogs when they're finished growing. Our job now is to make sure that they grow."

"We'll do that. Are we going to go and get some lunch now? I'm pretty hungry."

He looked over at his new wife and asked, "You're not pregnant already, are you?"

She laughed and said, "You'd think so after all of our attempts, but no, I'm not. I'm just hungry."

"Well, let's get these starving critters something to fill their empty tummies and then we'll fill ours."

"That sounds fair."

They reached Laramie ten minutes later, stopped at the butcher and bought some steaks, then drove to Cook's Livery and asked him to keep an eye on their puppies while they had lunch.

He was surprised at the skinny dogs when Jack and Emily let them out of the sacks, and then grinned as they attacked the meat that was set before them.

"I'll watch 'em for you, but I don't think they're goin' anywhere 'til you get back."

"Thanks, Jacob," Jack said as he took Emily's hand and they left the livery, leaving their horses with Quin.

"Joseph is going to be a happy boy when he sees what we have in those sacks, but where will you keep them? You're not going to let them live in the cabin, are you?"

"No, ma'am. But unlike Loopy, they'll stay in the house most of the time. It's important that they become friends with Joseph. Four dogs will also keep them all safer. It'll be almost like having a tame wolf pack when they're older."

"What will you do with all of the puppies they'll produce? Or haven't you thought that far in advance?"

"I haven't had to think about it, ma'am, because they're all males, or didn't you notice?"

"They are? What are the odds of them being all boy dogs?"

"Maybe the females followed their mother out of the barn leaving all the boys to play. I have no idea, but I know that more puppies won't be an issue."

After lunch, they walked back to the livery and when they entered, were surprised to see all of the puppies just laying flat on the barn floor.

"What happened?" Jack asked as Jacob walked in their direction.

He glanced back and said, "They're okay. After they finished eating all that meat, they all just fell asleep."

To prove Jacob's statement, three of the four raised their heads, then dropped back down to return to sleep.

Jack saddled Quin, then all three of them slipped the lethargic puppies back into the burlap sacks and hung them on Fire's saddle. They mounted and led Quin out of the barn and headed for the school to surprise Joseph.

As they rode along, Deputy Pruitt came trotting down the road waving to get their attention. Jack and Emily pulled their horses to a stop and waited until the deputy arrived.

"Jack, you got a telegram waiting for you in the Western Union office. They weren't sure where you were, so they asked us. I told the delivery boy I just saw you, so he didn't have to make the long ride."

"Thanks, George. I'll head over there."

"What's in the bags? They're moving."

"Puppies. Emily and I stole them from the C-G Connected, just to let you know. They're really skinny, George. I don't think they'd have lasted another week."

"That's kind of a surprise. That place has only been empty for a couple of weeks."

"I guess they didn't pay any attention to them for a while before that. Anyway, I'll go and check on that telegram."

Deputy Pruitt saluted, then wheeled his horse around and headed back to the office.

"Are you going to wait for Joseph or are you coming along, ma'am?" Jack asked.

"I'm too curious to see who would be sending you a telegram."

They turned their horses toward the Union Pacific station that also housed the Western Union office and arrived just five minutes later.

Jack hopped down, entered the office and walked back out after five minutes. He handed the telegram to Emily as he mounted Fire.

"That didn't take long," she said as she folded the telegram and slid it into her pocket.

"No, ma'am. Your father said he'd be sending a letter explaining what happened. I sent him a telegram telling him that the First National Bank in Omaha has my account information, so they can return the twenty thousand dollars to my account in Cheyenne."

"I wonder how they caught up with Mister White so quickly," she said as they headed back to the school.

"Mister Casey had the Pinkertons after him just two days after he'd gone. I guess they ran him down."

"Does that mean we won't be going to Cheyenne anytime soon?"

"We'll probably still go. I need to make sure the money's there and get a more accurate balance after the latest deposit, and we have to get your name on the account, Mrs. Tyler."

Emily just nodded, still awed by the casual way that Jack talked about the money as if it were just numbers on a ledger, which, in a way, was all it was. Except for those spooky jars of gold in his ceiling.

———

When Joseph walked out of school, he was chatting with two other boys about his age, then spotted Jack and Emily and waved, not noticing the squirming bags of burlap behind his father.

It was only when he was close enough and heard a sharp yip from one of the bags that he noticed them and raced the last few feet.

"*Dad, what do you have in the bags?*" he exclaimed as he reached the horses.

"We have four skinny boy dogs that you have to make into fat boy dogs," he replied.

"*Four? There are four?*" he asked in disbelief as he approached the left side bag.

"Yes, sir. Now, put your books into your saddlebag, mount Quin and we'll head home, so we can start feeding them."

ABANDONED

"Yes, sir!" he shouted as he quickly turned, dropped his books into his saddlebag, took Quin's reins from his mother and bounced into the saddle.

As they rode back to the cabin, Jack let Emily explain why they decided to get him a dog and how they wound up with four. To his credit, Joseph wasn't upset when he was told that the dogs were there to protect him from wild predators. He'd already seen what wolves could do to a large animal like Billie, and knew he'd be little more than a snack if they were hungry enough. But he still promised himself that he'd keep his dogs as safe as he could. He wished he was old enough to have a Winchester, though.

They returned to the cabin as the sun was low in the sky and Jack said that for the first night, the dogs would stay in the barn with the horses and mules and that they'd be safe.

After Emily went into the house to start cooking, Jack and Joseph led the horses into the barn and Jack set the bags on the floor, letting Joseph handle the puppies. They were much livelier now than they'd been in the livery, and quickly besieged Joseph who sat on the floor letting them attack him with their tongues. He was laughing as Jack unsaddled the three horses, not complaining about the lack of help. A boy needed to be a boy sometimes.

Jack was surprised when Emily entered the barn just ten minutes later as he was unsaddling Quin. She had a two large bowls of chopped smoked venison and smiled at the sight of Joseph with his four new friends.

"Here's their supper, Master Joseph," she said as she set them on the floor nearby.

The puppies' attention immediately shifted to the food and they bolted from Joseph and quickly had their faces buried in the bowls in an undeclared race to the bottom.

Joseph stood and said, "They're going to be fat again really fast, I think."

"If that's any indication, they'll outweigh you in a week."

Joseph laughed and then helped Jack with the brushing after his mother returned to the house to cook for the humans.

That night, they explained to Joseph about his modified school schedule. If the weather was good, they'd take him to school, but if it wasn't, or they wanted to go somewhere, like the Medicine Bow Mountains or Cheyenne, then he'd stay with his parents. But on those days, he'd study for at least four hours and then have another hour of homework. He was ecstatic when Jack told him that part of his new curriculum would be spent with him, learning the skills of an outdoorsman.

They also told him about the new carriage and the carriage house, which were nothing compared to the arrival of the puppies. Joseph had taken the easy way out in naming the puppies, calling them Matt, Mark, Luke and John. He said he didn't think it was fair that one would have a longer name than the others. Matt might think he was better than his brothers.

Joseph went to school on Wednesday and Thursday, but they took the morning train to Cheyenne on Friday, so Jack could deposit his gold. The saddlebags containing the six jars of gold were pretty heavy, but Jack made no big deal about their value. To anyone just looking at him, they were just a pair of old saddlebags.

They arrived in Cheyenne at 10:20, and immediately went to the First National Bank. Jack walked to the desk of Mike Calder, who already stood when he spotted Jack. Like everyone else, he'd read all the stories, and when he spotted Jack with the tall redhead and the boy, all of the pieces seemed to fall into place.

Mike was the only clerk who knew what Jack had in his saddlebags, as per the agreement Jack had with the bank after the first deposit.

"Good morning, Jack," said Mister Calder.

ABANDONED

"Good morning, Mike. This is my wife, Emily and our son, Joseph. I'm sure that you've read all the stories about us and suffice it to say that most are either wildly exaggerated or inadequate. Anyway, I have another deposit and I need to have my wife added to the account."

"That won't be a problem. Let's go to the assay room and we'll start the process."

"Emily, did you and Joseph want to come along?"

"I think it would be very instructive."

Jack smiled and replied, "That's one way to look at it."

The clerk led them to a back room where Jack set the saddlebags down and began to take the jars out and set them on a desk near some scales.

The assayer then began to ascertain the gold's purity and weight but knew from experience that Jack's finds were always as pure as possible and there was no sand or any other foreign material in the dust.

Joseph was fascinated by the process and asked the assayer questions about what he was doing, which he answered quickly without any slowing in his procedures.

When he finished, he wrote down the value of the gold, gave one copy to Jack and the second to Mike Calder. There was a total of 590.4 ounces of gold in the six jars for a total of $13,284.00.

"That's the most you've ever brought, Jack. I don't suppose you'll let me know where it is, will you?" asked the assayer.

Jack quickly scanned the room and whispered, "I found it in the mountains."

The assayer and Mike laughed because it was the same question and answer they shared each time Jack made a deposit.

After they returned to the desk, Emily took a seat while the clerk walked to a room, then returned a few minutes later with some forms. He then sat at his desk, slid the forms to Emily, who signed them and then waited for them to dry as she stared at the new balance. It was $42,698.10.

She looked up at Jack who said, "Don't forget we did just buy all that land, so that accounts for the lower amount."

Emily thought he might be joking, but he wasn't. It simply didn't impress him at all.

They left the bank, did a little shopping, had lunch and caught the westbound train reaching Laramie after sunset. They decided to have supper in Laramie rather than waiting until they reached the cabin, so by the time they did get back, it was almost ten o'clock at night.

Emily tucked Joseph into bed and then joined her husband in theirs. It was the first night that they had been married that all they did was fall asleep in each other's arms. There was something about a train ride that was tiring.

―――

Over the next few weeks, the new carriage house was built, the new carriage and team were driven to the cabin and put into their new home and the puppies continued to eat and grow. Jack had built a large doghouse with a bit of ingenious engineering. The structure had two entrances that were hinged to open in the same direction. Both were then kept closed by a heavy spring. If the dogs wished to enter the house, they just pushed open one door, which closed behind them, but exited the other door. He built it in the lee of the cabin to minimize the impact of the wind. They had a hard time opening the doors at first, but soon mastered the principle, especially after they'd grown.

They received the letter from Dennis Ward explaining that the Pinkertons had found Mister Thomas White and his secretary, Arthur Hicks, in New Orleans. As per their instructions, they simply

ABANDONED

'suggested' to Mister White that he return the cash he'd stolen rather than face prosecution for grand theft. He only was able to produce $13,290 of the company's funds, and after the Pinkerton's fees were subtracted, the balance of less than thirteen thousand had been deposited in the company's account, allowing for the return of Jack's twenty thousand dollars.

The new vice president of operations also explained that he had also asked that Mister White agree to Vera White's request for a divorce, which he readily signed using an unusual claim for such a long-standing marriage. Thomas White had remained in New Orleans, legally blameless for the lost two thousand dollars, and free of his wife. After the divorce had been granted, Vera then filed for an annulment from the church because the marriage had never been consummated, the one reason for annulment which could be easily proven.

Emily's father included all of the information because there would be another Ward wedding soon, but it would be a small affair and because of the time of year, he didn't expect them to attend.

Jack had asked her if she wanted to go and Emily had demurred.

With his now almost ever-present canine companions, Joseph almost forgot about Loopy, but would sometimes look out his window to see if he could spot the gray wolf, but never did.

The weather was growing markedly colder as September gave way to October. They pickled and preserved the vegetables from the garden and Jack took Joseph on two hunts in their expanded property and had harvested three white tailed deer. He showed Joseph how to dress the animals and recover as much meat as possible and make use of every part of the animal, just as the Arapaho, Utes and Cheyenne did. They smoked almost all of the meat and stored it in the cold room for the winter, even though they still bought beef in Laramie.

Joseph was still disappointed with the absence of Loopy, and even Jack was surprised that the wolf hadn't been seen, even after they'd harvested the deer. But they'd left some of the meat a few hundred yards out and it had quickly disappeared, but Jack wasn't sure it had been taken by his wolf neighbor or other carnivores.

Emily and Joseph were adapting well to their new home even as the first snows began to fall in mid-October. He told them they were a bit late this year, which they thought was a joke at first, but he assured them he'd seen snows in late August.

Joseph had begun a letter-writing puppy love romance with Lauren Ward, and, as his father had told him, also wrote to the other two Ward girls, but with an almost encyclopedic style.

November passed quickly, with the dogs no longer eligible to be called puppies, and Joseph spending more time at home, learning from his mother, his books and his father.

On the sixteenth of November, Jack and Joseph were returning from a hunt and had their game bags full of meat when Joseph finally met Loopy.

They were wearing their heavy jackets and their fur caps with the flaps pulled down over their ears as they trudged through the eight inches of fresh snow when they passed around a large boulder.

Joseph was on Jack's right and asking if more snow was coming when he stopped and froze as the big gray wolf stood staring at him. His heart was threatening to leave his chest as it pounded inside his ribs.

"Hello, Loopy," Jack said as he smiled.

Loopy then turned and barked twice, and a she-wolf warily approached from among the boulders.

"Congratulations, Loopy," Jack said as he reached into his game bag and tossed a large chunk of meat in the direction of the she-wolf.

ABANDONED

Loopy just turned and watched his mate snatch the meat and then walk away, quickly disappearing among the boulders.

Jack looked at Loopy and said, "I left the rest of the harvest a way back, but I guess you know that, don't you?"

Jack then grabbed another chunk of meat and lobbed it to Loopy who let it drop into the snow and just kept looking at Jack. He looked at the human for another twenty seconds, then snatched the meat and followed the tracks of his mate.

"I'll bet that's where they're building their den for the winter," Jack said as he began to walk, and Joseph stepped behind him using his father's deep boot steps.

"Was that a lady wolf?" Joseph asked as he looked back where they'd gone into the rocks.

"Yes, sir, and unless I'm wrong, I've seen her before."

"She lives here?"

"She used to live out in the Medicine Bow Mountains. I'm pretty sure she's the wolf that ran into the trees after her pack attacked Billy. The one that I let escape was a she-wolf and had the same coloring and that unusual triangle shape on her left side."

They were walking as quickly as they could through the snow and Joseph asked, "Did she follow us because she was mad?"

"No, sir. She probably was rejected by other packs for some reason or other and kept walking until she found Loopy's territory. She'd know he was a lone male wolf and might accept her as his mate. It looks like she got lucky, or he did."

"Is she going to have babies now?"

"Not until spring but when she does, we'll have a new wolf pack by this time next year."

"Will they come to the cabin and hurt the dogs?"

"No, I don't think they will. I'm a bit surprised that the she-wolf even came out of her den. We'll be fine, but I don't think the deer, elk or other critters will appreciate having the wolves around. It helps that we're not ranchers or farmers. Keeping cattle or chickens or pigs is hard when there's an active wolf pack in the area."

"I'll stick to my dogs."

Jack laughed and said, "A wise decision, sir."

They reached the cabin twenty minutes later and left some of the venison in the smoke house and set the fires going before heading to the back of the cabin and going into the kitchen.

Joseph saw his mother and exploded with the news of their encounter with Loopy and his mate as he hurriedly removed his gloves, jacket and hat. Jack set the game bags in the cold room for the time being before removing his cold weather clothes and then taking his bloody gloves to the sink to wash them. He'd treat the leather later.

After that first encounter with Loopy, Jack would make an occasional trip out to their den and leave them some meat near their tracks, but never saw him or his mate. The only signs they had of the wolves were their howls in the night.

———

December arrived and aside from the letters that seemed to be arriving from Omaha regularly, mostly for Joseph and mostly from Emily's niece, Lauren, the cold days and nights were spent in teaching and learning. The four dogs were spending more time inside but had learned quickly that it wasn't permissible to use the cabin as their dog privy.

On those days that Joseph was able to go to school, Jack and Emily were able to do some shopping and the new carriage proved to be a wise purchase.

ABANDONED

On the Sunday before Christmas, as they were returning to the cabin after Mass, Emily asked, "Jack, are we going to go to Midnight Mass on Christmas or a regular daytime Mass?"

"I thought Midnight Mass would be nice. We'd ride home in the dark with the glory of the Milky Way and the half moon to light our way."

Emily pulled her husband close, kissed him and said, "You still know how to make a girl happy."

Christmas Eve's weather was moderate and allowed the drive to Laramie for the midnight Mass without any worries about being stranded. They couldn't eat dinner, but Emily packed some food in the carriage for the two-hour return trip as they rolled out onto the road for Laramie shortly before ten o'clock.

Father Schneider was surprised and delighted that they'd made the night trip to town as he welcomed them to the church along with most of the town's other Catholics.

The church was decorated with a large, locally crafted creche depicting the birth of Jesus and the atmosphere of the ceremony was decidedly joyous and celebratory, as it should be.

An hour later, as Jack drove the carriage back to the cabin, they all shared the food Emily had packed. Joseph was beginning to drift off and Emily wasn't that far behind by the time they arrived at the cabin in the wee hours of Christmas morning.

Jack steered the carriage to the lee side of the cabin, just past the unoccupied dog house and let Emily and Joseph out so they could go into the cabin and start the fires while he unharnessed the team.

Once he'd watched them enter the cabin, he drove to the carriage house, slid open the doors and drove the cabin inside. It took him almost a half an hour to remove the horses from the harness and make sure they had feed and water before leaving the carriage house, closing the heavy doors behind him and almost goose-stepping through the snow to the cabin.

He reached the cabin and went inside the back mudroom, stomped the snow off his boots and then entered the kitchen, not expecting to find Joseph awake.

But when he opened the inner door, he found both Emily and Joseph waiting for him with big smiles as the four dogs sat behind Joseph.

"Merry Christmas!" they shouted.

"Merry Christmas," he replied as he took off his gloves, jacket and his fur cap.

"I've got some milk heating for hot chocolate," Emily said as Jack approached.

"That sounds perfect," he replied.

"Can we open our presents now?" asked Joseph.

Jack smiled and answered, "It's Christmas, isn't it?"

Emily slid the milk from the stove and began to make the hot chocolate while Jack walked to the office followed by Joseph who was trailing the dogs. Once inside, he opened his large closet where he usually stored his gear for his journeys into the mountains, and began to take out the wrapped gifts, handing them to Joseph until his arms were full, then piled the rest on the floor before lifting them himself. He didn't recognize some of them and assumed Emily had just mixed hers in with the ones he had bought. Hers were all wrapped better, too.

"Let's bring this to the main room," Jack said.

"Okay," Joseph grunted under the weight before he began walking.

Jack smiled, then after he'd gone, took the long box from the closet and followed Joseph to the main room.

Joseph saw the tall box that his father was carrying along with the rest of the presents and felt his heart begin to pound. He knew that there was only one thing that could be that long. *He was getting a Winchester for Christmas!*

Emily walked into the room with a tray and three cups of steaming hot chocolate, set it on the table and they each took one before taking a seat.

Jack picked up the first wrapped gift and paused as he looked at Joseph and then Emily.

He then said quietly, "This is the first real Christmas I've ever had."

Emily leaned over on the couch and kissed him gently, but didn't say anything.

Jack smiled at her, then handed the package to Joseph, and then the second to Emily. Joseph unwrapped his gifts one by one but kept glancing the long boxed gift.

They drank their hot chocolate in between unwrapping the gifts.

Emily received some nice, fur-lined gloves with a matching hat to keep her head warm, some heavy slippers and a warm, woolen coat. Joseph's gifts were all along similar lines, although he did get a set of poker chips in a fancy box and a dartboard and dart set.

Jack received a fancy silver pocket watch and a very nice pocket knife to replace the one he'd given to Joseph. He thanked Emily after he'd read the engraved inscription inside. It was a simple: *To my beloved husband on our first Christmas together. Emily Ann Ward Tyler.*

It was when Jack reached the last of the square packages that the theme shifted. Jack handed the box to Emily, who carefully pulled apart the wrapping paper and opened the heavy box.

She glanced at Jack, then pulled out a Remington pistol like his own in a matching holster and gunbelt, but with a smaller knife in the sheath.

"While you're out here, Emily, it's always a good idea to have a gun and a knife with you. I'll show you how to use it later. You won't have any problems with the pistol."

"Is it because of my manly hands, Mister Tyler?" she asked with a smile as she removed the shining steel weapon.

"There's nothing remotely manly about you, Mrs. Tyler. But you do have good, strong hands."

"Thank you, Jack. Believe it or not, I was going to ask you to buy me a pistol."

"I'm not surprised. You need to keep me at bay sometimes," he said before he laughed and reached for the long box.

Joseph was already beginning to reach for the last gift when his father held it out to his mother, saying, "This last one is yours, too."

She set her pistol down, then accepted the long box. As soon as the first sheet of wrapping paper was removed, she recognized the Winchester logo on the end and knew what it was.

Joseph was almost in tears as he watched his mother slide the new repeater from the box.

"Jack, can I assume you'll be showing me how to use this as well?" she asked as she slid her fingers along the carbine.

"Yes, ma'am. That's the carbine version, so it only has a twenty-inch barrel, which makes it easier to handle. It fires the same cartridge as the pistol, too."

ABANDONED

Joseph wanted to at least get a chance to hold the weapon, but it was his mother's gift, not his, so he sat silently rubbing Luke's head as he watched her admire the carbine.

"Thank you, Jack. It's a beautiful gun. I'll be a real frontierswoman before you're done with me."

"I think you were one long before I met you, Emily," he said as he smiled at her.

Joseph looked at the pile of presents and suddenly realized to his horror that he hadn't gotten anything for his new mother and father. He may have been upset about not getting the Winchester, but he felt much worse when he realized how selfish he'd been.

"Dad, Mom," he began, "You gave me all of these wonderful presents and I didn't get you anything at all."

Jack reached over and picked up the almost-nine-year-old and sat him on his knee.

"Joseph Charles Brennan Tyler, whatever are you talking about?"

Joseph looked at this father with sad eyes and said, "I didn't get you anything. I'm selfish."

Jack put his arm around him and said, "Now, that's not true at all, Joseph. See that beautiful lady sitting over there smiling at us? She wouldn't be there if it wasn't for you. I wouldn't be so very happy if it wasn't for you. I'd be sitting alone in this dark, cold cabin on this Christmas morning with no one to share the joy of the day. You made all that happen, Joseph. It was your determination not to be without Mrs. Doyle that brought us together here to celebrate this Christmas. So, don't you dare to say that you haven't given us anything. You've given us everything."

Joseph looked into his father's blue eyes, then turned to look at his mother's blue eyes. There were tears sliding from hers, but she had a loving smile on her face as she gazed back at him.

He then turned back to his father and hugged him as Jack wrapped him in his arms.

"Thank you for a wonderful Christmas, Joseph," he whispered.

Joseph nodded but began to cry.

Emily stood, walked to her men and rested her hand on Joseph's back.

He sat up straight, wiped the tears from his face, smiled at her and said, "Merry Christmas, Mom."

Emily smiled back, then looked at Jack and said, "Merry Christmas to both of my men."

Joseph dropped to the floor then hugged his mother as she looked at Jack and smiled.

It took them a few minutes to put away their gifts as the wrapping paper was all tossed into the fire before they crawled into their beds and fell asleep just before the predawn began to lighten the sky.

―――

Emily prepared a full Christmas dinner, including a roast turkey, while Jack and Joseph went to check on the horses and mules with the four dogs in tow. While they were walking to the barn, a wolf's howl sounded from the southeast.

"Is that Loopy?" Joseph asked.

"Yes, sir. You'll be able to tell difference between him and his mate soon."

After they finished taking care of the horses, they returned to the warmth of the cabin and the much anticipated Christmas feast.

Two hours later, they were eating the abundant food with the four canines all waiting for their own Christmas gifts.

ABANDONED

Jack looked past the turkey at Emily and said, "After dinner, if you'd like, I can show you how to use your pistol."

"On Christmas? Are you lapsing into your heathen ways, Mister Tyler?" she asked in faux shock.

He laughed and then said, "How about tomorrow, then?"

"That's better," she replied before taking a big bite of mashed potatoes with turkey gravy.

Naturally, after an enormous meal, an equally massive cleanup was necessary, and in the spirit of the day, Emily's two men shared in the work. The rest of Christmas was in relaxed conversation with a nap mixed in as the previous early morning's activities caught up with them by early afternoon.

The 26th of December, Joseph's ninth birthday arrived with a blizzard howling outside, putting a halt to any outdoor work other than the necessary care for the horses and mules, which Jack took care of himself. The cabin remained draft-free despite the punishing winds and the two heat stoves and fireplace kept the cold at bay.

After he returned from the barn and carriage house, Joseph watched as his father hung his dartboard on his bedroom wall, not having even mentioned his birthday. After the horror of forgetting to get any Christmas gifts for his parents, he wasn't about to ask about any birthday gifts. His mother sat on his bed watching them, and she hadn't mentioned his birthday, either. Birthday presents aside, he realized how much he'd miss Mrs. Thornton's chocolate cake this year.

Jack finished the job and stepped back, admiring his handiwork.

"Well, Joseph, do you want to play a game?"

"Okay," Joseph said as he walked toward the foot of the bed, which was the furthest spot from the dartboard.

Jack turned to Emily and said, "Mrs. Tyler, could you give me the darts, please?"

Emily looked around and said, "Where do you keep them, Joseph?"

Joseph turned, pointed at the shelf beside the bed, didn't see the darts and said, "They should be right there."

Jack said, "Maybe they fell on the floor between the bed and the wall. Could you check, ma'am?"

Emily flopped onto the bed and stuck her hand down into the gap, and said, "I think I found them."

Then she pulled a long, wrapped box out and said, "I don't recall the darts being this heavy."

Joseph's mouth dropped open as Jack said, "That doesn't look like darts."

He then turned to Joseph and asked, "Why don't you see what's in the box?"

Jack didn't have to ask twice as Emily grinned and handed the heavy gift to Joseph.

He plopped onto the bed beside his mother and ripped open the paper hoping that he wouldn't be disappointed a second time. He wasn't.

Less than a minute later, he was holding his own Winchester '73 carbine just like the one his mother had been given yesterday. He then noticed that there was an engraving in the metal. It just said *Joseph Tyler*. There was no Charles, no Brennan and no Roman numerals.

He looked up at his mother and her smiling face, then quickly turned to his grinning father.

ABANDONED

"Thank you, Mom and Dad. This is the best birthday ever!"

He laid the carbine on the bed, then hugged and kissed Emily, then dropped from the bed and hugged his father and then kissed him on the cheek, too, even though he was nine now.

"I couldn't give that to an eight-year-old, Joseph," Jack said.

Joseph grinned as he scooped up his Winchester and said, "I should have guessed that, shouldn't I?"

"Not really. It was just that I had to give you something special on your birthday," Jack said, then added, "Oh, and I have a gunbelt for you in the office, too, but it only has a knife and some loops for spare cartridges for the Winchester. When you're older, we'll add a pistol."

"Will you show me how to use my Winchester when you show Mom?"

"I'll show you both after lunch," he replied.

Emily then stood and said, "I'd better get out to the kitchen and start baking that chocolate birthday cake."

Joseph couldn't wipe the grin from his face, even after Jack said, "How about a game of darts?"

The rest of Jack's birthday was filled with cake and firearms instructions as the winds continued to buffet the cabin, but neither he nor his parents minded.

As Jack had expected, Emily had no difficulties handling the pistol, and he thoroughly enjoyed showing her how to hold the Remington as he was able to let his hand slip from time to time while Joseph giggled.

The rest of the winter passed slowly as Joseph and the dogs continued to grow and Jack and Emily continued their attempts to add to the size of the family. They managed to get in some live fire shooting during the spells of warmer weather and the hours of dry-firing practice that they'd had during the bad weather paid off.

The only tragedy of the winter was when Billy suddenly died during a late January blizzard. Jack used Abby to drag his carcass out of the barn and then as close as he could get it to Loopy's den. He didn't see the wolf but could tell that he and his mate have been out hunting just by their tracks.

As the weather began moderating, they began to plan for their trip into the mountains at the end of April. Joseph was able to attend classes in the school again and found that he was actually ahead of his fourth year classmates, some of whom had also missed a lot of the winter classes.

Two days before their departure, Jack and Emily rode with Joseph to Laramie trailing Abby who was wearing a real pack saddle. Jack realized that he'd need a lot more supplies for this trip, even though he had most of Noah Gallagher's equipment, including the large tent.

After dropping Joseph off at the school, Jack and Emily filled the panniers with food and other things that they'd need that Noah had neglected, as well as an increased supply of .44 cartridges for the Winchesters and Remingtons. Emily also asked that they bring the two-barreled twelve-gauge shotgun, remembering the sickening feeling when she faced the snarling she-wolf with an empty single-barreled shotgun.

They departed the cabin on the 28th of April because it was a new moon that night and Jack wanted to have moonlight when they stayed at the prospecting site. The four dogs, while young, were all easily capable of coming along and would provide them with an added layer of protection. When they had to cross the big creeks, each hoofed animal would have a dog attached to help them cross.

ABANDONED

Emily felt comfortable in the saddle as Byan walked beside Quin with Fire on the other side of the small gelding. She had her Remington on her right hip, her big knife on her left, and her Winchester in the scabbard. She was, as Jack had suggested, very much a frontierswoman.

That first day, they passed the spot where Noah had killed Claude Boucher and they saw no evidence that anything of any significance had happened there and continued westward without stopping.

For three days they rode as the weather stayed surprisingly comfortable, but brisk. There had been no confrontations with creatures or Indians, which Jack told her was normal.

On the afternoon of the third day, they reached the clearing where Jack had found them.

Emily asked, "Jack, could we set up camp here tonight?"

Jack wasn't sure if she would want to stay here or rush through like the ground was hot lava, so he just smiled and said, "Yes, ma'am."

They brought the horses and Abby to a halt and dismounted. Jack led them to the brook to drink while Emily and Joseph strolled the familiar ground inspecting for any vestiges of their last stay here and finding no signs at all that humans had ever visited the spot. Each of them carried a Winchester this time, not wanting to take any chances.

Jack brought the horses back from the water and led them to some grass and as they began to graze, started to unload and unsaddle them, beginning with the heavy panniers that Abby carried.

Emily and Joseph returned and helped unsaddle the animals before Jack and Joseph began setting up the tent. The camp site, including the fire pit, was fully established just an hour after they'd stopped and after Jack had the fire going, they each took a seat near the rushing water of the nearby brook.

Emily took a sip of her tea and said, "There's not a sign that anything happened here, Jack. It was as if it was all just a dream."

Jack looked at his wife, and then glanced at Joseph and asked, "Did you want to climb to the shelf where I found you?"

Emily turned and looked at the shelf and said, "No, I don't think so. It's just another rock outcrop now."

Jack nodded then said, "You know, I think you're wrong that nothing is here that links this place to that day."

"Why? Do you see something?"

"No, ma'am, but I know where there is something we left here."

"Where?"

Joseph had no idea what it was either, so Jack just smiled, set down his tin cup, then stood and walked to the brook as Joseph and Emily followed him.

Jack knew roughly where it was, and after walking up the hill six feet, he spotted it under the rushing water. It was just a few strands of faded cloth, but he reached into the water and pulled up the rock and the piece of canvas came with it. He separated the shred of tent from the rock and held it out to her. She took the cloth and gazed at it.

"This was the part of the tent you cut out," she said quietly.

"It is."

As she and Jack looked at the cloth, Joseph looked at the hole that had been left in the brook's bed by the stone's removal, then

ABANDONED

dropped to his heels, reached into the water and pulled out a smaller, but much shinier rock.

"Is this gold, Dad?" he asked as he showed his father the large nugget.

Jack and Emily looked at the gold in his palm and Jack said, "It sure is, Joseph. That's a pretty good-sized nugget you found there."

"Do I put it in one of the jars?"

"No, sir. You keep that one. It's pretty special, don't you think?"

Joseph nodded, then slipped it into his pocket.

They returned to the fire, Emily with her cloth and Joseph with his gold nugget.

They stayed there for just the one night before moving another eight miles the next morning to be closer to the gold-bearing stream. Jack showed them the pool at the bottom of the rapids where he had found the biggest deposit.

For a full week, they stayed in the spot, Jack showing Emily and Jack how to pan for gold. They alternated panning and searching for nuggets, and at the end of the week, had filled three of the small jars with dust and two with nuggets. It was time to return.

That night after Joseph was in the tent happily sleeping with his Winchester beside him and his gold nugget still in his pocket, Emily and Jack sat on a log drinking some tea as their breaths made clouds before their mouths in the chilly night air.

"It really is beautiful out here, isn't it, Jack?" she said as she gazed at the splendor of the Milky Way stretched out across the sky.

"I always thought that the stars' only purpose was to put me in my place. To make me realize my own insignificance, but they really are more than that, aren't they? They let us know that we're all part of something greater than any of us. Yet for all their glory, Emily Ann

Ward, they'll never come close to inspiring me as much as you have."

Emily kissed him then said, "Let's go to bed, husband."

The next morning, they closed up their gold camp, and by eight o'clock were riding east.

Less than two hours later, they were crossing the brook where Joseph had found his nugget. Emily glanced up at the rocky shelf and found it hard to believe the miraculous changes in her life. Just a few month ago, she and Joseph were on that tiny outcrop of rock waiting to die, either from starvation or by an attack of some fanged, sharp-clawed beast, abandoned by the man that law required to protect her son.

But the man who now rode beside her, her husband and Joseph's father, had saved them and defied written and unwritten laws to do what was best for Joseph as a boy and for her as a woman. A woman named Emily Ann Ward.

EPILOGUE

June 16, 1890
Omaha, Nebraska

Jack smiled at his son as he straightened his bow tie then stepped back.

"That's as good as it's going to get, I think."

"Dad, I feel like this this is choking me," he said as he slipped his finger between his celluloid collar and his neck.

Jack laughed and said, "It's only for a few hours and then you can burn it for all I care."

"I probably will. I don't know why we have to go through this. I don't seem to recall your wedding being all that fancy."

"You understand why you had to come here and go through this flamboyant ceremony, Mister. Your mother provided the answer on the porch of this house ten years ago when she said that families can be a pain in the ass. Well, sir, today your family is being a pain in the neck. They insisted that you and Lauren get married here so the entire family could attend."

Joseph laughed and said, "That's an understatement."

Jack then said, "You know, your mother and I never expected your puppy dog romance with Lauren to last more than a month, but you surprised us both."

"There were a few times that I was tempted to stray, but Lauren was always the one."

"She's a lot like your mother, isn't she?"

"Yes, sir. Lauren Mary Ward is very much like Emily Ann Ward. It's why I love her so much and why there was never really any doubt in my mind."

"Well, we're ready to go, son. Let's get in that buggy and ride to Saint Mary Magdalene Church to let Father Duffy finally marry a Tyler and a Ward."

Joseph hugged his father, then the two men left the house at 1710 Chicago Street for the church.

That first summer, as promised, Jack and Emily returned to Omaha, so Joseph could spend some time with Emily's niece, Lauren. They needed to clear up some things anyway and expected that Joseph would lose interest in the young Ward girl after two weeks, but Joseph had become more attached to her, not less.

Over the succeeding years, the trips to the mountains began to become less frequent as family events interfered and they finally stopped in '88, as the finds had begun to decrease steadily after '85. Their Cheyenne account was so large by then it really didn't matter.

Joseph had graduated at the age of sixteen, then enrolled in the just-opened University of Wyoming in Laramie, following their motto of *'Domi Habuit Unde Disceret'*, 'He need not go away from home for instruction'. He was in his last year now, but unlike many of the colleges and universities of the day, didn't prohibit students from marrying, which wasn't surprising from the only state or territory that allowed women to vote and hold public office.

He'd kept ownership of the Brennan Furnace and Coal Company, which had recovered nicely under the direction of James Burke. The performance of the company increased the Brennan family account dramatically as well, giving Joseph a lot of flexibility in his choice of where he would live and what he would do with his life.

ABANDONED

The big house that they were using to prepare for the wedding housed Anna Thornton, now Anna Dunne and her family, and Joseph had signed the deed to the house over to the former cook yesterday.

Mary Flaherty had been Noah Gallagher's last victim when she discovered that she was pregnant by him and had been ostracized by her family. She'd moved into house with Anna but had died in childbirth along with her baby just eight days before Jack, Emily and Joseph had returned to Omaha for their first visit. At Mary's request, no one had told Emily of her plight, making it worse for Emily when she was told.

But this visit was one of joy and love with not a hint of sadness. The church was overflowing with Irishmen and women of all ages and sizes as the marriage ceremony between Joseph Charles Brennan Tyler and Lauren Mary Ward began.

Jack stood at the altar with his son as they awaited the bride, and he glanced over at his own bride standing in the first pew. Emily still took his breath away when he looked at her. Her dark red hair had streaks of gray beginning to arrive, but she still wore it long which stood out among all of the piled hair and buns in the church. Emily only wore two pieces of jewelry; her gold wedding band that Jack had made from gold they had harvested, and a simple necklace made of a gold chain with a single, large nugget. It had been a gift from her son on their second Christmas in the cabin.

Standing on Emily's left was a redheaded, blue-eyed girl; seven-year-old Margaret Ann Tyler. On her right was six-year-old John James Tyler, with sandy brown hair and blue eyes. John was trying to attract the attention of his big brother, Joseph, so he could make a face at him and get him to laugh on the altar.

Emily spotted his attempt and squelched the idea with an Emily Ann Ward glare.

A minute later, the bride was escorted down the aisle by her father, Peter Ward, and all eyes were on her as she floated down the aisle toward her waiting groom.

Just as he had done when he'd been at Molly's wedding, Jack compared the young, pretty Lauren to his now forty-two-year-old wife and smiled to himself when he believed there was no comparison. His mind was telling him that the younger Ward was probably prettier and had the glow that surrounded brides, but his heart told him that none could compare to Emily Ann Ward and never would.

Joseph had bought four sections of land just to the west of the Tyler land and had built a house for him and Lauren before the wedding. It was a frame structure, but solidly built with more amenities than his parents had in their cabin as Joseph's gesture of thoughtfulness for his bride.

Luke and Matt lived with Joseph and Lauren in their house while John and Mark stayed with the Tyler children. It really didn't matter much as there was less than a mile between the two houses and the dogs traveled between them. The four dogs had grown to be as large as a she-wolf and had never been bothered by the large pack of wolves that still claimed the land as their territory.

Loopy had been pushed out of his position as the leader of the pack by a younger male and he and his old mate had returned to the den southeast of the cabin where all of the pups had been born.

Jack and Joseph still hunted the area and left meat near the den for Loopy, but rarely saw him or his mate.

On a chilly night in early September, Jack sat beside Emily on the couch as John and Margaret played checkers on the floor before the big fire.

John had just jumped one of Margaret's men, then as she studied the board, he turned and asked, "Dad, when can I go hunting with you and Joseph?"

"Maybe next year, but you can't carry a gun until I think you're ready."

ABANDONED

"How old was Joseph when you gave him a gun?"

"He just turned nine, but he already showed me just how brave he was when he stood up to a grizzly bear to save your mother."

Margaret stopped thinking about checkers as she looked at her mother and John asked, "He did?"

Emily smiled and said, "He did. We never told you the whole story before because we didn't think you were old enough to understand some of it, but your father and I think you should hear it now."

"Is it scary?" asked Margaret.

"Sometimes," she replied as both children stood, checkers forgotten, and then plopped down in front of their parents.

Jack let Emily start the story that they knew Margaret would soon hear when she settled in for her first year in school anyway.

As their children sat mesmerized by the incredible tale of abandonment and rescue, the story was accented by the howl of a lone she-wolf in the darkness southeast of the cabin.

———

#	Title	Date
1	Rock Creek	12/26/2016
2	North of Denton	01/02/2017
3	Fort Selden	01/07/2017
4	Scotts Bluff	01/14/2017
5	South of Denver	01/22/2017
6	Miles City	01/28/2017
7	Hopewell	02/04/2017
8	Nueva Luz	02/12/2017
9	The Witch of Dakota	02/19/2017
10	Baker City	03/13/2017
11	The Gun Smith	03/21/2017
12	Gus	03/24/2017
13	Wilmore	04/06/2017
14	Mister Thor	04/20/2017
15	Nora	04/26/2017
16	Max	05/09/2017
17	Hunting Pearl	05/14/2017
18	Bessie	05/25/2017
19	The Last Four	05/29/2017
20	Zack	06/12/2017
21	Finding Bucky	06/21/2017
22	The Debt	06/30/2017
23	The Scalawags	07/11/2017
24	The Stampede	07/20/2017
25	The Wake of the Bertrand	07/31/2017
26	Cole	08/09/2017
27	Luke	09/05/2017
28	The Eclipse	09/21/2017
29	A.J. Smith	10/03/2017
30	Slow John	11/05/2017
31	The Second Star	11/15/2017
32	Tate	12/03/2017

ABANDONED

33	Virgil's Herd	12/14/2017
34	Marsh's Valley	01/01/2018
35	Alex Paine	01/18/2018
36	Ben Gray	02/05/2018
37	War Adams	03/05/2018
38	Mac's Cabin	03/21/2018
39	Will Scott	04/13/2018
40	Sheriff Joe	04/22/2018
41	Chance	05/17/2018
42	Doc Holt	06/17/2018
43	Ted Shepard	07/13/2018
44	Haven	07/30/2018
45	Sam's County	08/15/2018
46	Matt Dunne	09/10/2018
47	Conn Jackson	10/05/2018
48	Gabe Owens	10/27/2018
49	Abandoned	11/19/2018
50	Retribution	12/21/2018
51	Inevitable	02/04/2019
52	Scandal in Topeka	03/18/2019
53	Return to Hardeman County	04/10/2019

Made in the USA
Coppell, TX
19 December 2019